I SURVIVED

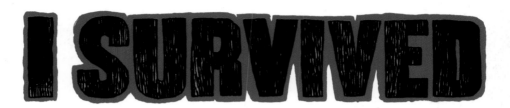

THE SHARK ATTACKS OF 1916

PHOTOS : 151 CENTER RIGHT: COURTESY THE TICHNOR BROTHERS COLLECTION/BOSTON PUBLIC LIBRARY; 151 BOTTOM LEFT: COURTESY NJ MARITIME MUSEUM; 152 BOTTOM RIGHT: COURTESY OF UNIVERSITY OF OREGON LIBRARIES; 152 TOP AND BOTTOM LEFT, 153 TOP AND CENTER LEFT: COURTESY OF JOHN ALLAN SAVOLAINE FROM "STANLEY FISHER: SHARK ATTACK HERO OF A BYGONE AGE"; 153 CENTER RIGHT: THE BRONX HOME NEWS, 1916; 153 BOTTOM: UNIVERSAL HISTORY ARCHIVE/GETTY IMAGES; 154 TOP LEFT: SEATOPS/IMAGEBROKER/SHUTTERSTOCK; 154 CENTER LEFT: SEATOPS/IMAGEBROKER/SHUTTERSTOCK; 154 BOTTOM RIGHT: ANDREA IZZOTTI/SHUTTERSTOCK; 155 LIFEGUARD: IURII RACENKOV/SHUTTERSTOCK; 155 BANDAID: TAB62/SHUTTERSTOCK; 155 NECKLACE: EYEEM/ALAMY STOCK PHOTO; 155 CENTER LEFT: VW PICS/GETTY IMAGES; 155 BOTTOM RIGHT: VLADOSKAN/GETTY IMAGES

LIBRARY OF CONGRESS CONTROL NUMBER AVAILABLE
ISBN 978-1-338-12094-3 (PAPERBACK)
ISBN 978-1-338-12095-0 (HARDCOVER)

10 9 8 7 6 5 4 3 2 1   20 21 22 23 24

PRINTED IN THE USA   113

FIRST EDITION, JUNE 2020

EDITED BY KATIE WOEHR AND RACHEL STARK
ADAPTATION BY GEORGIA BALL
ART BY HAUS STUDIO
PENCILS BY GERVASIO
INKS BY JOK AND CARLOS AÓN
COLORS BY LARA LEE
ART ASSISTANCE BY DARIO BRABO
LOGO AND FONTS BY CARLOS AÓN
LETTERING BY BETSY PETERSCHMIDT
BOOK DESIGN BY KATIE FITCH
CREATIVE DIRECTOR: HEATHER DAUGHERTY
SPECIAL THANKS TO AL SAVOLAINE

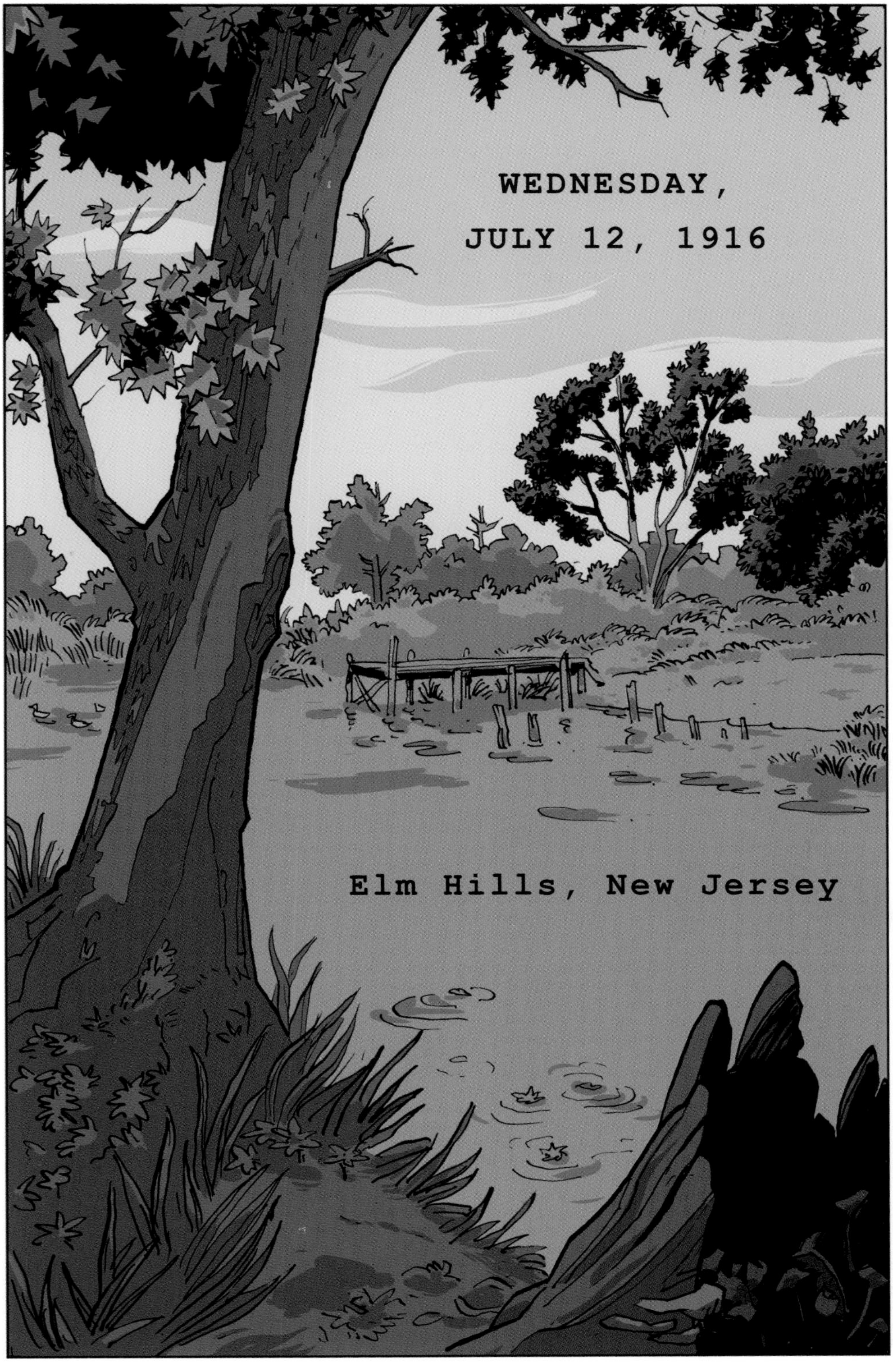
WEDNESDAY,
JULY 12, 1916
Elm Hills, New Jersey

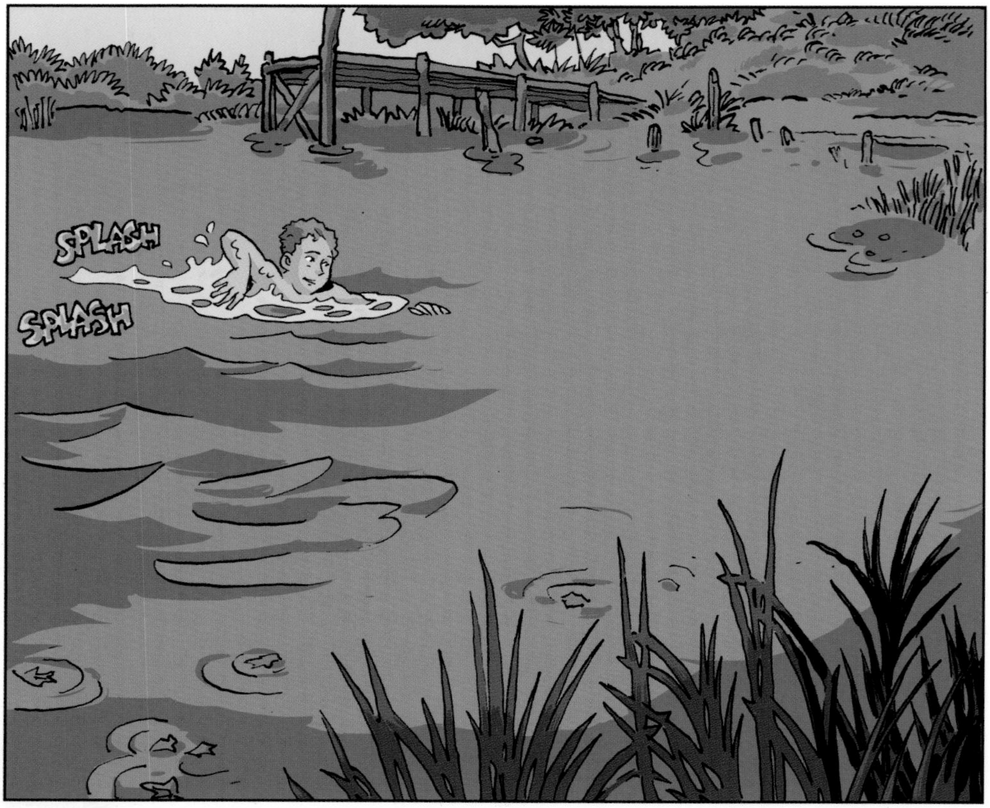
SPLASH
SPLASH

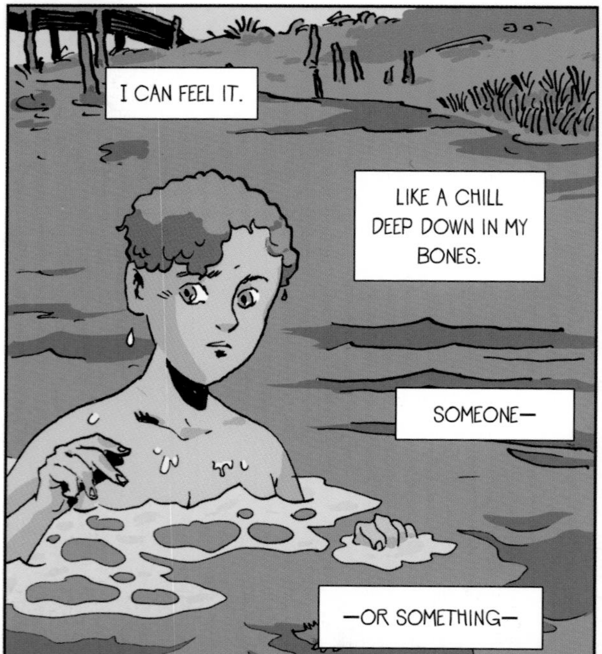
I CAN FEEL IT.
LIKE A CHILL DEEP DOWN IN MY BONES.
SOMEONE—
—OR SOMETHING—

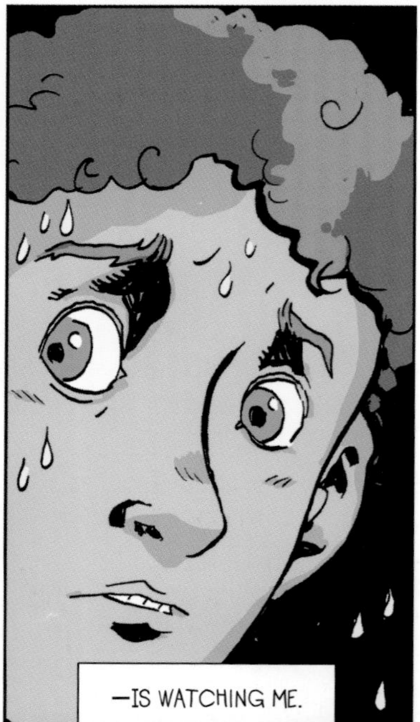
—IS WATCHING ME.

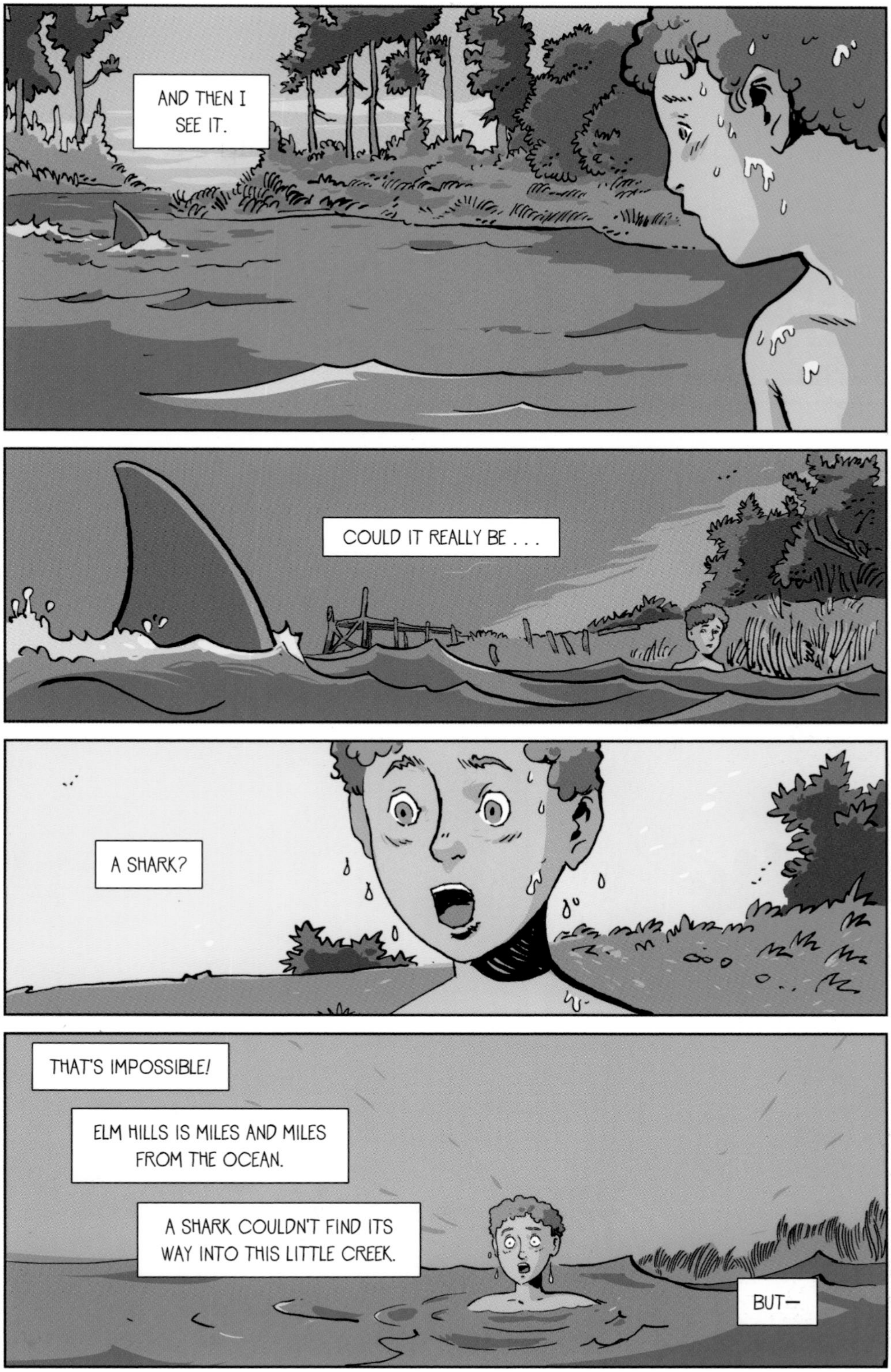
AND THEN I SEE IT.
COULD IT REALLY BE . . .
A SHARK?
THAT'S IMPOSSIBLE!
ELM HILLS IS MILES AND MILES FROM THE OCEAN.
A SHARK COULDN'T FIND ITS WAY INTO THIS LITTLE CREEK.
BUT—

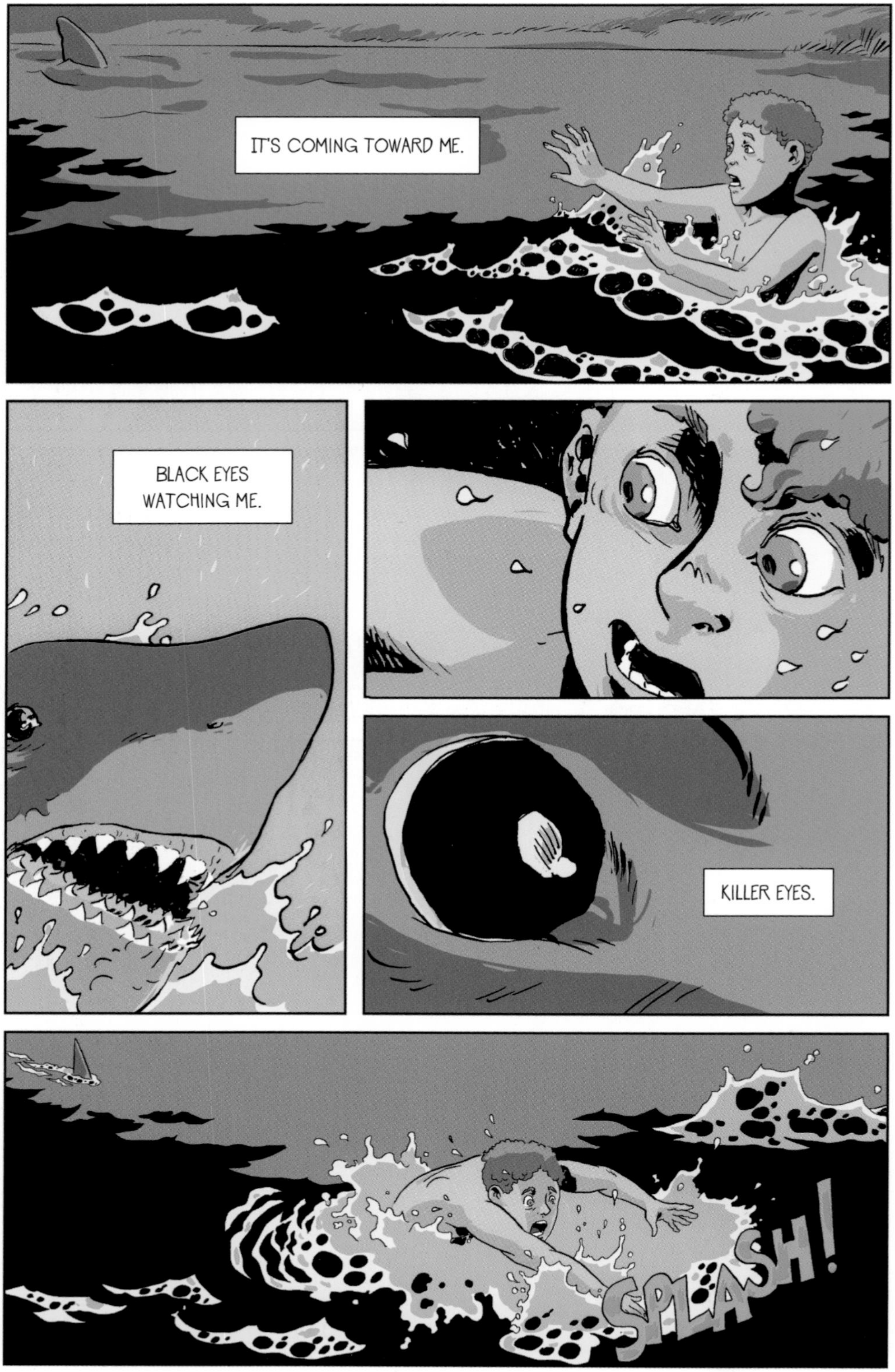
IT'S COMING TOWARD ME.
BLACK EYES WATCHING ME.
KILLER EYES.
SPLASH!

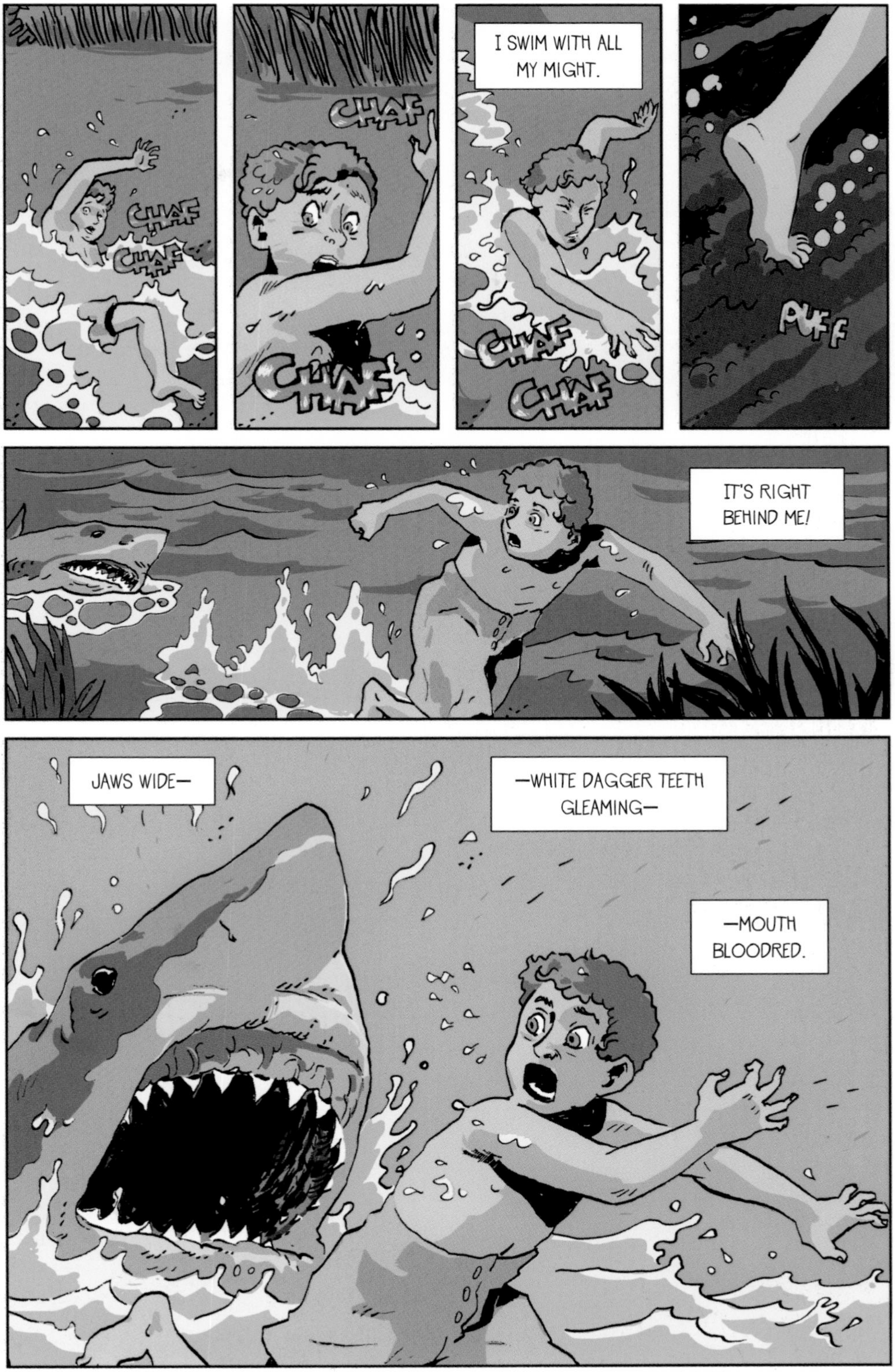
CHAF
CHAF
CHAF
CHAF
I SWIM WITH ALL MY MIGHT.
CHAF
CHAF
PUFF
IT'S RIGHT BEHIND ME!
JAWS WIDE—
—WHITE DAGGER TEETH GLEAMING—
—MOUTH BLOODRED.

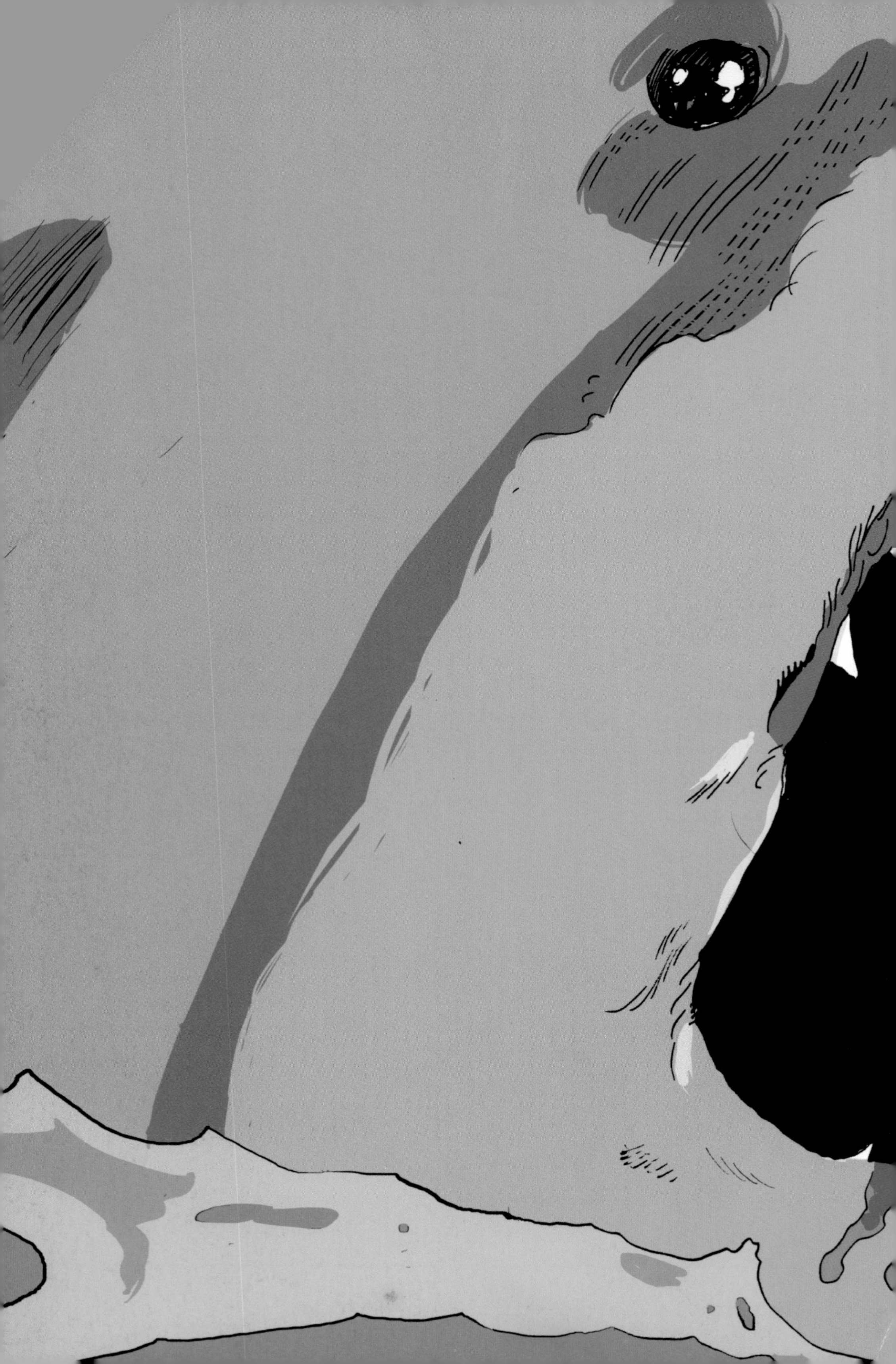

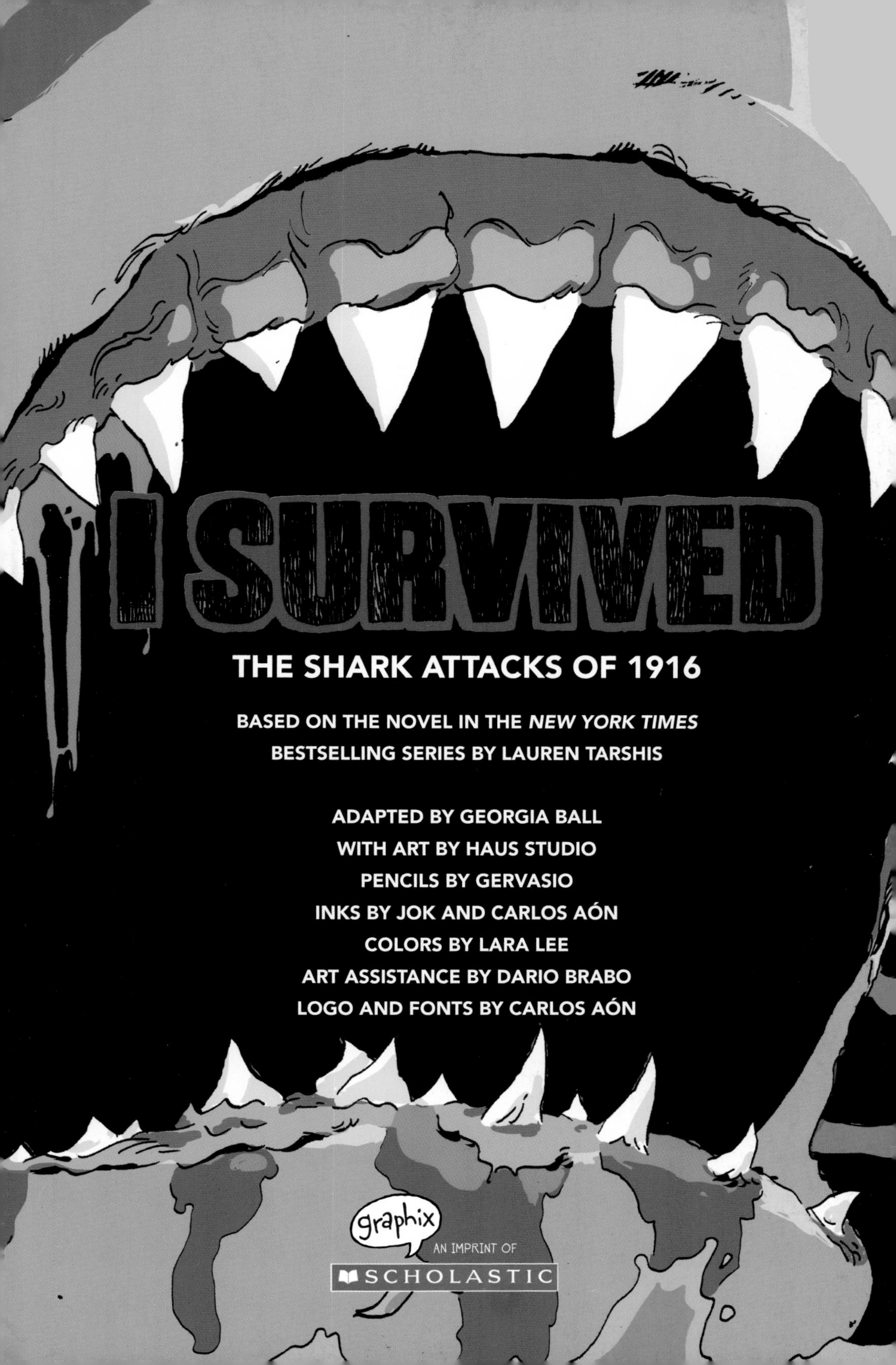

I SURVIVED

THE SHARK ATTACKS OF 1916

BASED ON THE NOVEL IN THE *NEW YORK TIMES*
BESTSELLING SERIES BY LAUREN TARSHIS

ADAPTED BY GEORGIA BALL
WITH ART BY HAUS STUDIO
PENCILS BY GERVASIO
INKS BY JOK AND CARLOS AÓN
COLORS BY LARA LEE
ART ASSISTANCE BY DARIO BRABO
LOGO AND FONTS BY CARLOS AÓN

graphix
AN IMPRINT OF
SCHOLASTIC

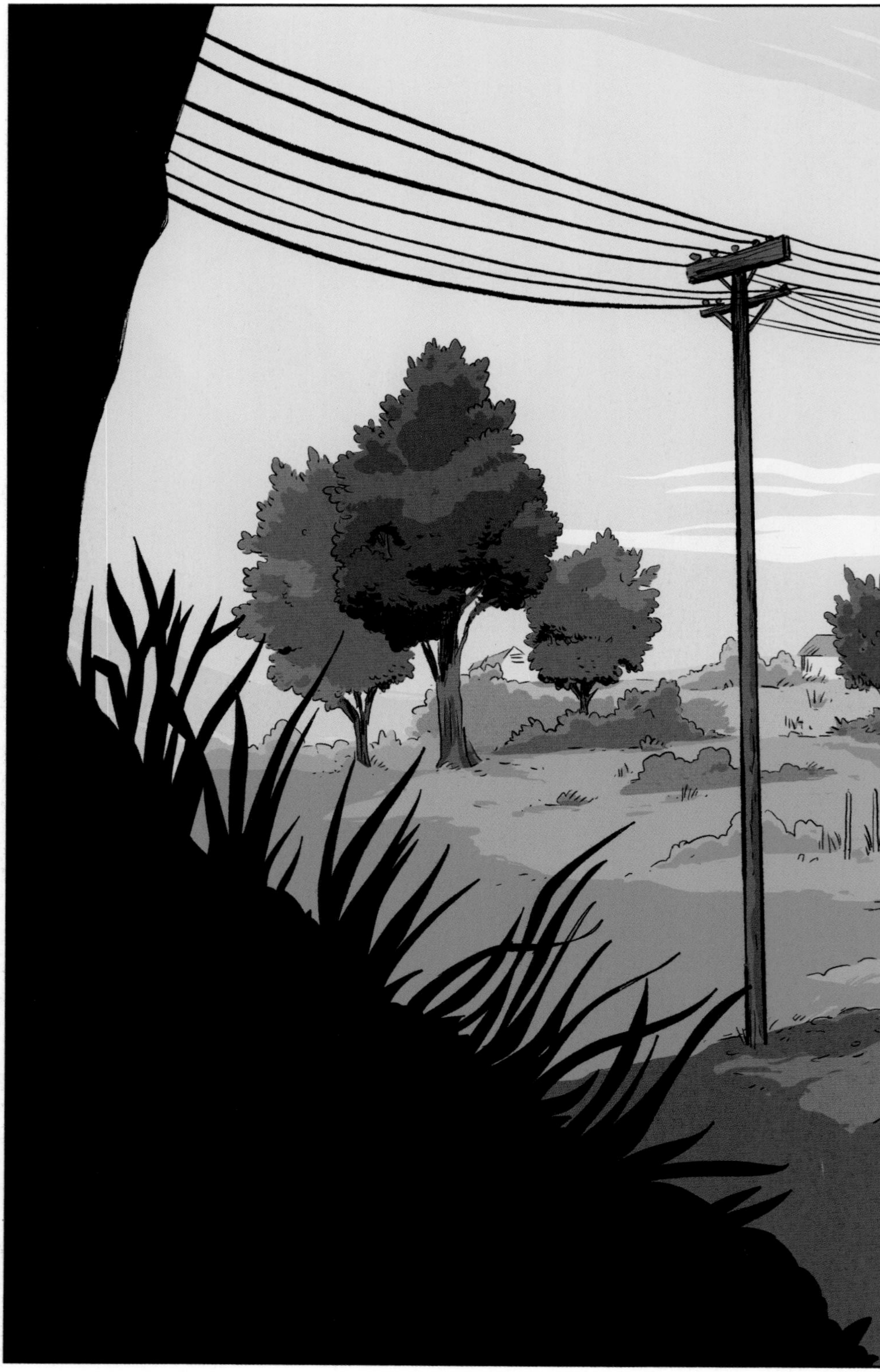

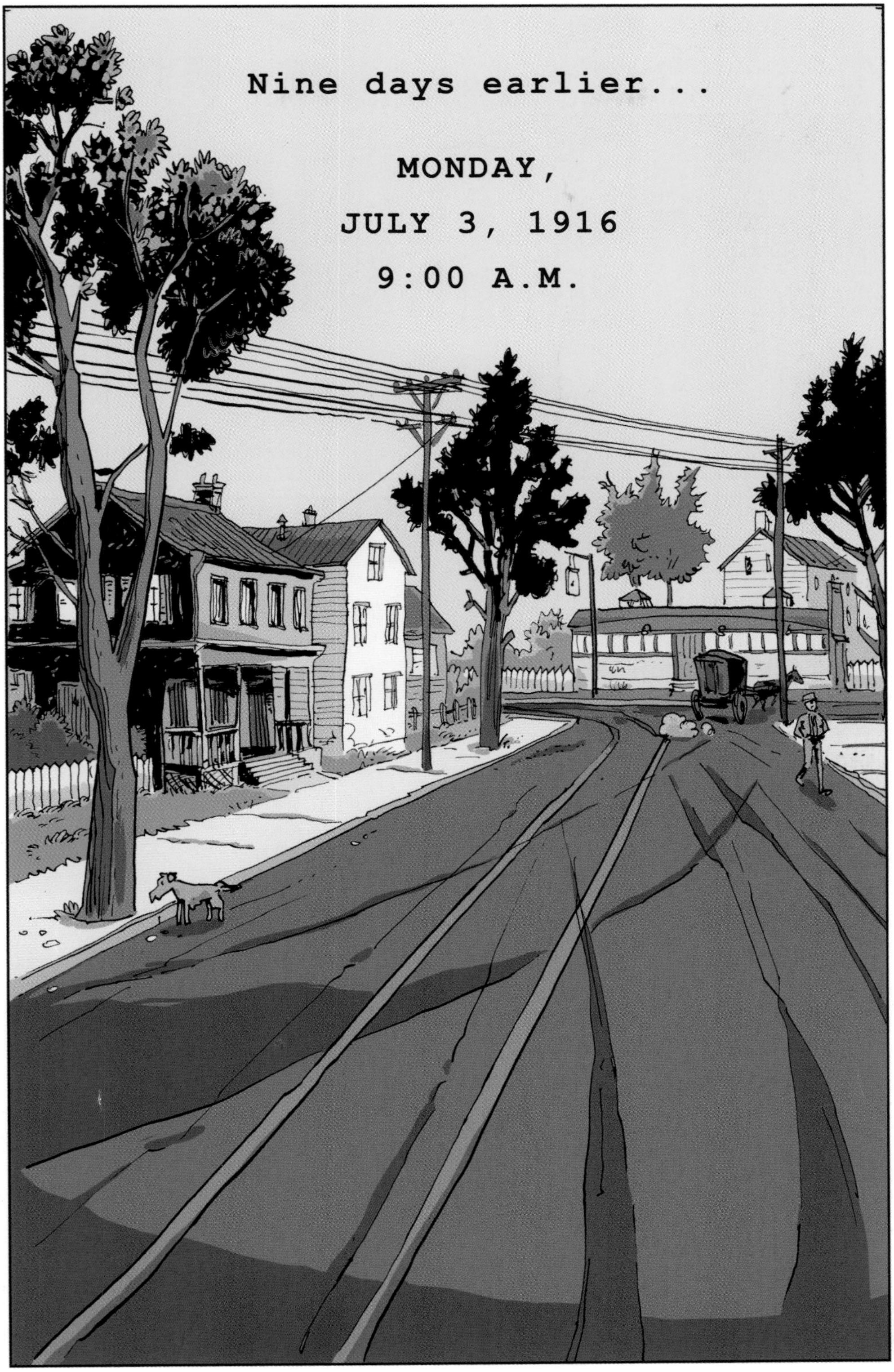
Nine days earlier...
MONDAY,
JULY 3, 1916
9:00 A.M.

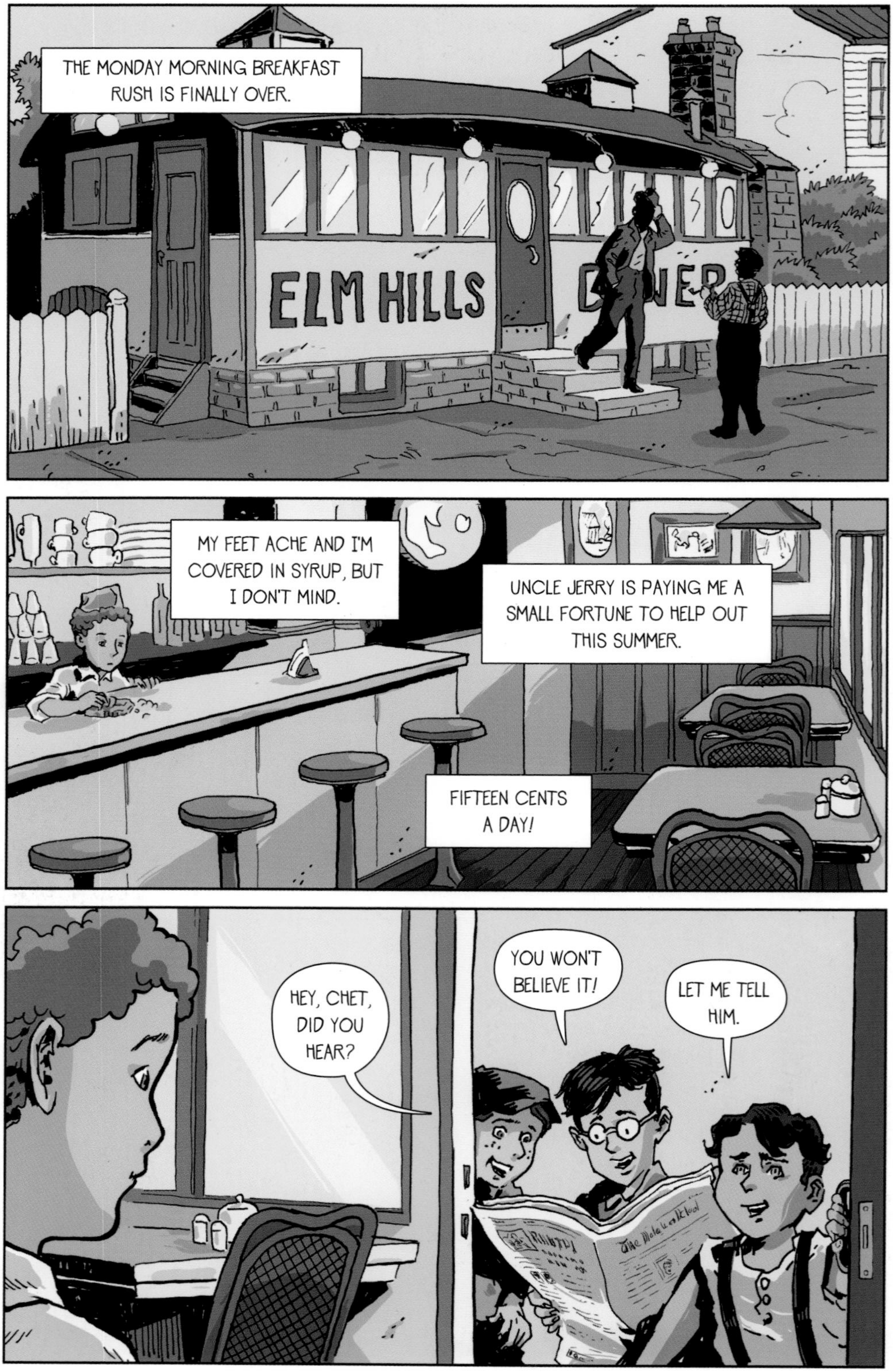
THE MONDAY MORNING BREAKFAST RUSH IS FINALLY OVER.
ELM HILLS
MY FEET ACHE AND I'M COVERED IN SYRUP, BUT I DON'T MIND.
UNCLE JERRY IS PAYING ME A SMALL FORTUNE TO HELP OUT THIS SUMMER.
FIFTEEN CENTS A DAY!
HEY, CHET, DID YOU HEAR?
YOU WON'T BELIEVE IT!
LET ME TELL HIM.

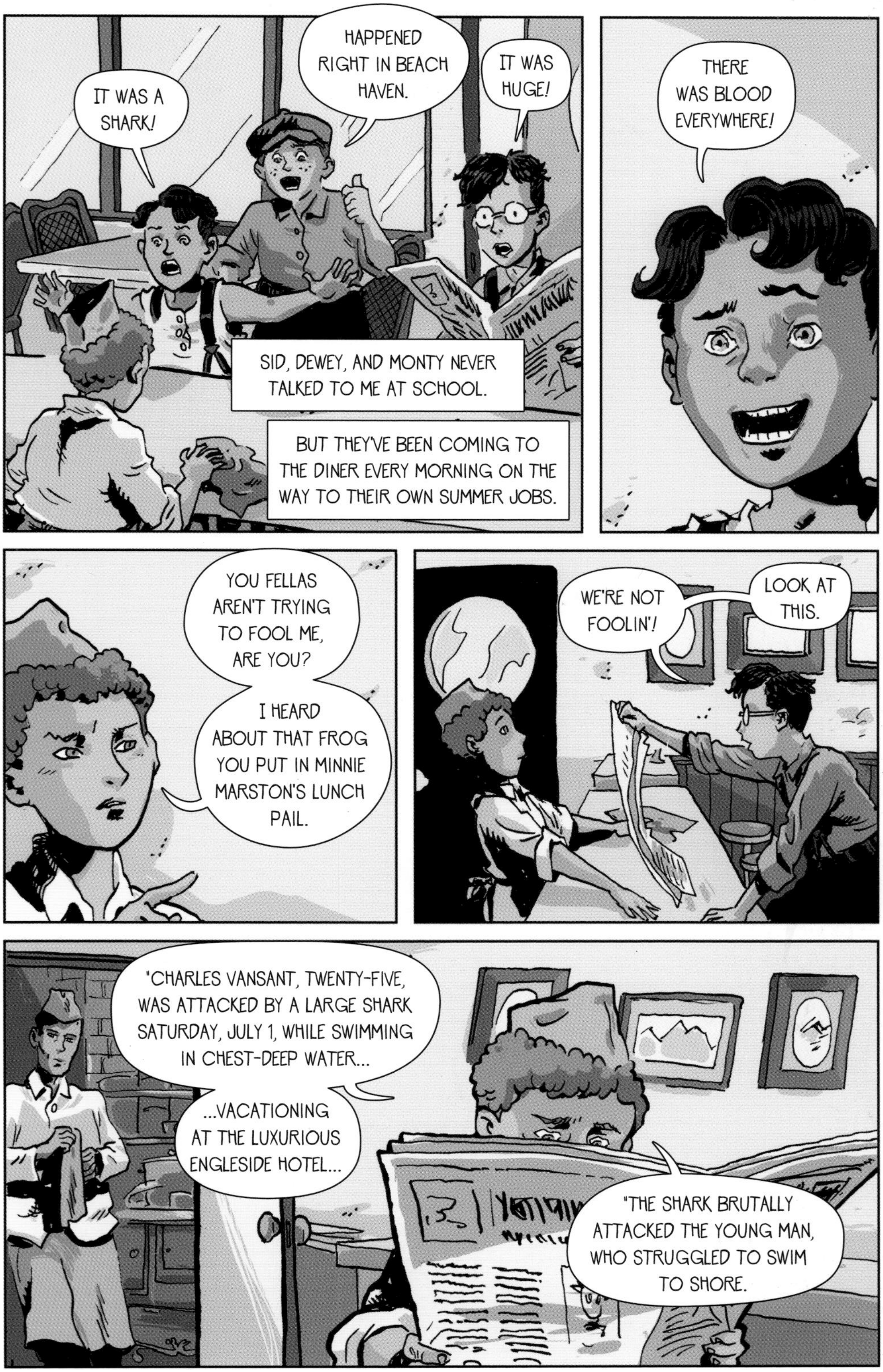
IT WAS A SHARK!
HAPPENED RIGHT IN BEACH HAVEN.
IT WAS HUGE!
SID, DEWEY, AND MONTY NEVER TALKED TO ME AT SCHOOL.
BUT THEY'VE BEEN COMING TO THE DINER EVERY MORNING ON THE WAY TO THEIR OWN SUMMER JOBS.
THERE WAS BLOOD EVERYWHERE!
YOU FELLAS AREN'T TRYING TO FOOL ME, ARE YOU?
I HEARD ABOUT THAT FROG YOU PUT IN MINNIE MARSTON'S LUNCH PAIL.
WE'RE NOT FOOLIN'!
LOOK AT THIS.
"CHARLES VANSANT, TWENTY-FIVE, WAS ATTACKED BY A LARGE SHARK SATURDAY, JULY 1, WHILE SWIMMING IN CHEST-DEEP WATER...
...VACATIONING AT THE LUXURIOUS ENGLESIDE HOTEL...
"THE SHARK BRUTALLY ATTACKED THE YOUNG MAN, WHO STRUGGLED TO SWIM TO SHORE.

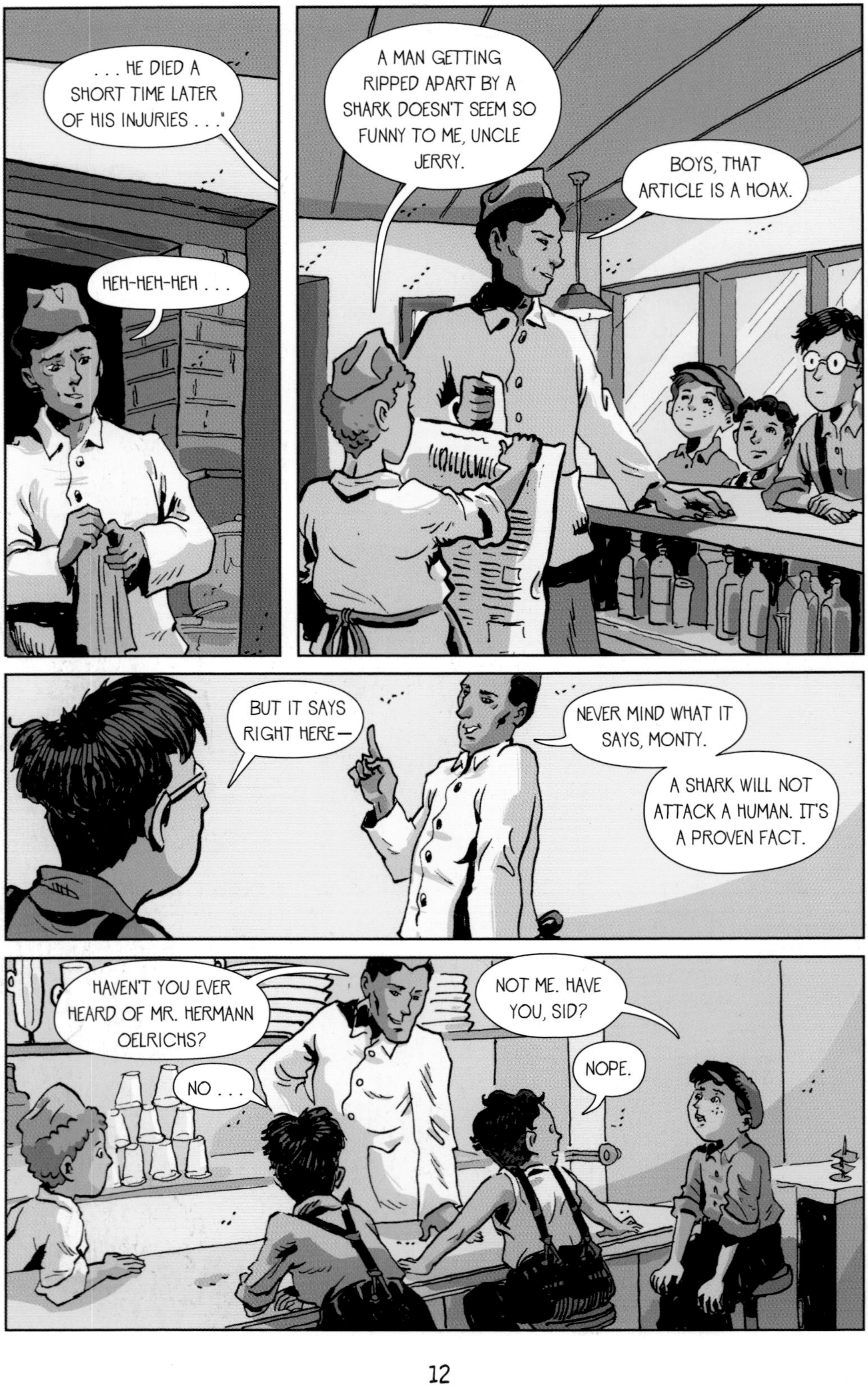
. . . HE DIED A SHORT TIME LATER OF HIS INJURIES . . ."
HEH-HEH-HEH . . .
A MAN GETTING RIPPED APART BY A SHARK DOESN'T SEEM SO FUNNY TO ME, UNCLE JERRY.
BOYS, THAT ARTICLE IS A HOAX.
BUT IT SAYS RIGHT HERE—
NEVER MIND WHAT IT SAYS, MONTY.
A SHARK WILL NOT ATTACK A HUMAN. IT'S A PROVEN FACT.
HAVEN'T YOU EVER HEARD OF MR. HERMANN OELRICHS?
NO . . .
NOT ME. HAVE YOU, SID?
NOPE.

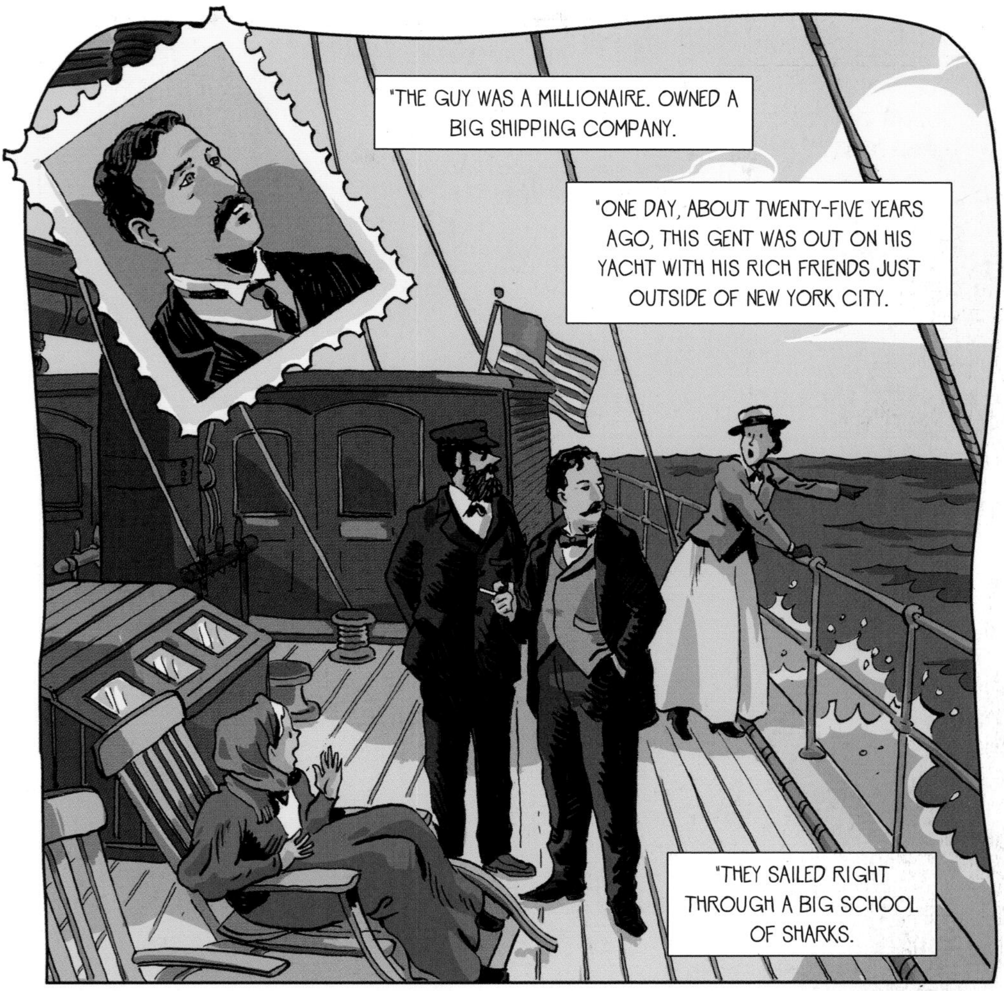
"THE GUY WAS A MILLIONAIRE. OWNED A BIG SHIPPING COMPANY.
"ONE DAY, ABOUT TWENTY-FIVE YEARS AGO, THIS GENT WAS OUT ON HIS YACHT WITH HIS RICH FRIENDS JUST OUTSIDE OF NEW YORK CITY.
"THEY SAILED RIGHT THROUGH A BIG SCHOOL OF SHARKS.

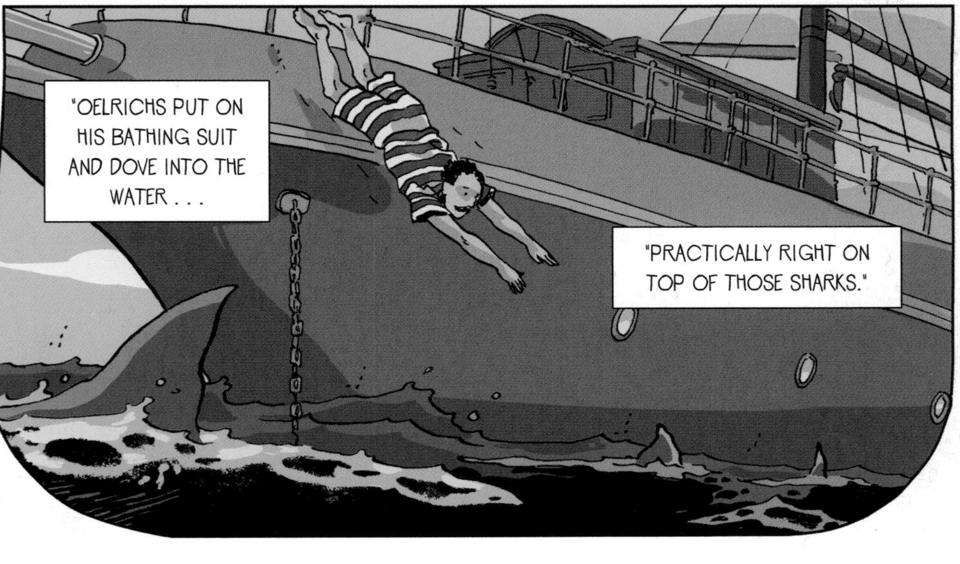
"OELRICHS PUT ON HIS BATHING SUIT AND DOVE INTO THE WATER . . .
"PRACTICALLY RIGHT ON TOP OF THOSE SHARKS."

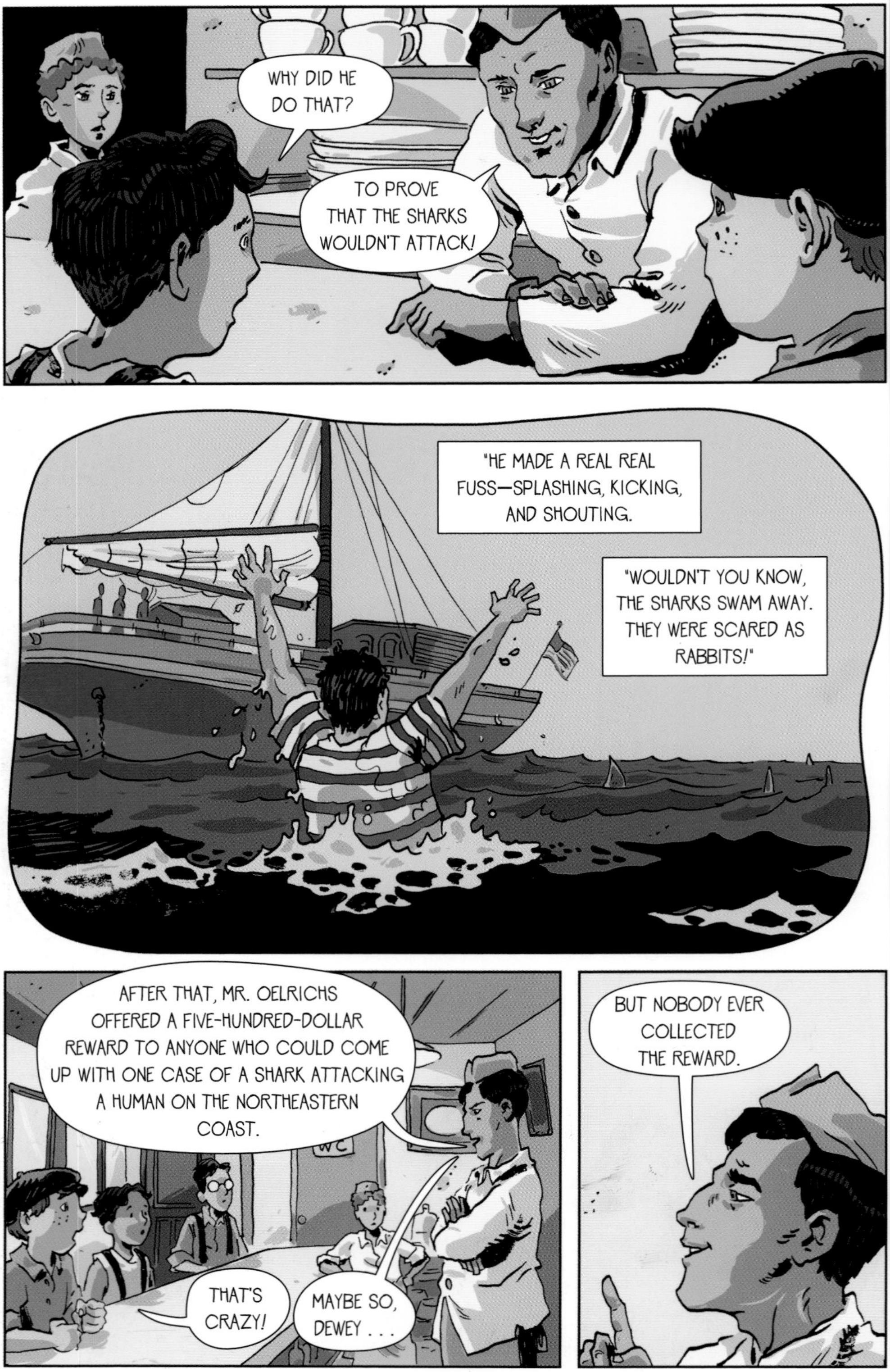
WHY DID HE DO THAT?
TO PROVE THAT THE SHARKS WOULDN'T ATTACK!
"HE MADE A REAL REAL FUSS—SPLASHING, KICKING, AND SHOUTING.
"WOULDN'T YOU KNOW, THE SHARKS SWAM AWAY. THEY WERE SCARED AS RABBITS!"
AFTER THAT, MR. OELRICHS OFFERED A FIVE-HUNDRED-DOLLAR REWARD TO ANYONE WHO COULD COME UP WITH ONE CASE OF A SHARK ATTACKING A HUMAN ON THE NORTHEASTERN COAST.
WC
THAT'S CRAZY!
MAYBE SO, DEWEY . . .
BUT NOBODY EVER COLLECTED THE REWARD.

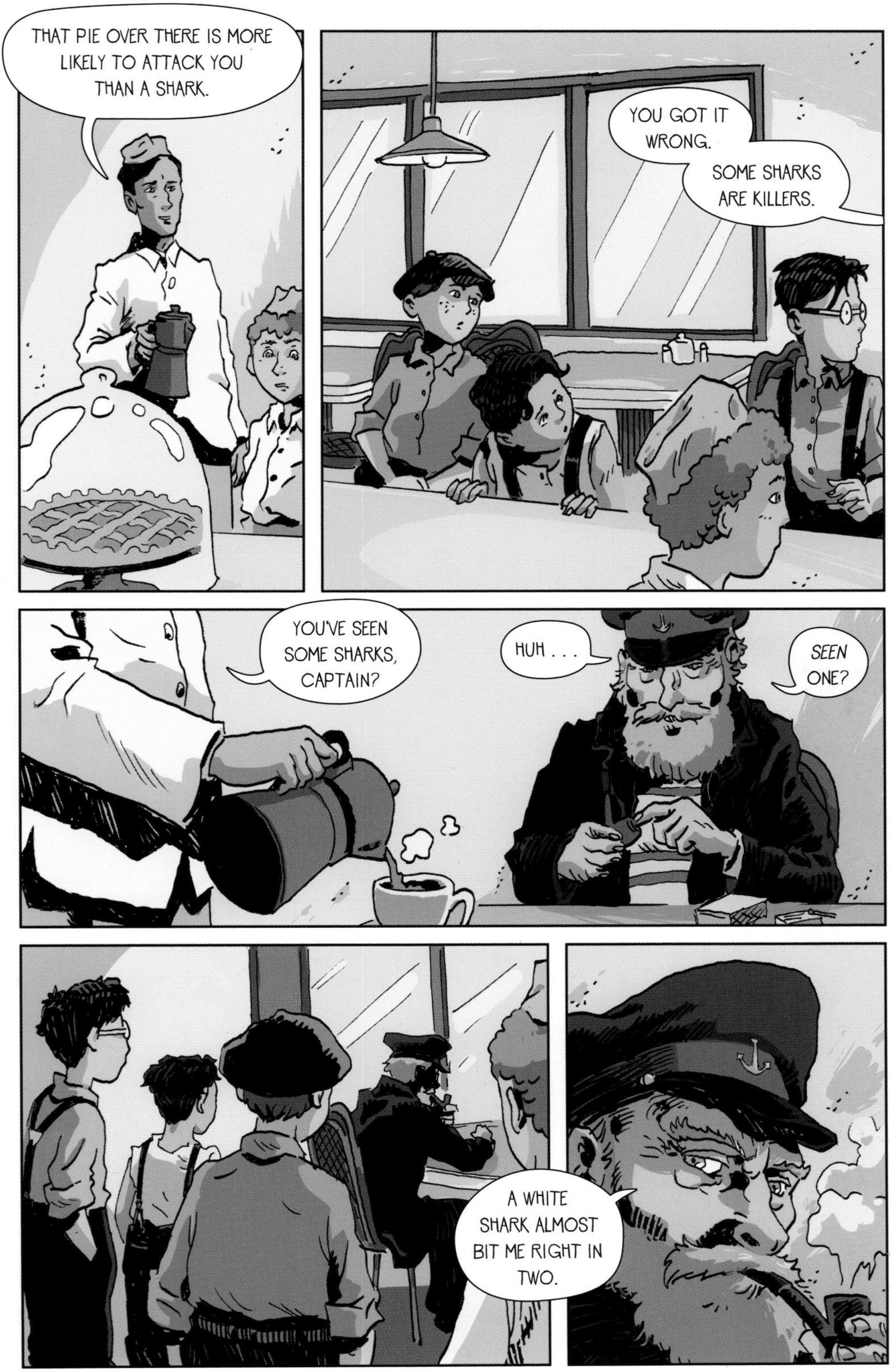
THAT PIE OVER THERE IS MORE LIKELY TO ATTACK YOU THAN A SHARK.
YOU GOT IT WRONG.
SOME SHARKS ARE KILLERS.
YOU'VE SEEN SOME SHARKS, CAPTAIN?
HUH . . .
SEEN ONE?
A WHITE SHARK ALMOST BIT ME RIGHT IN TWO.

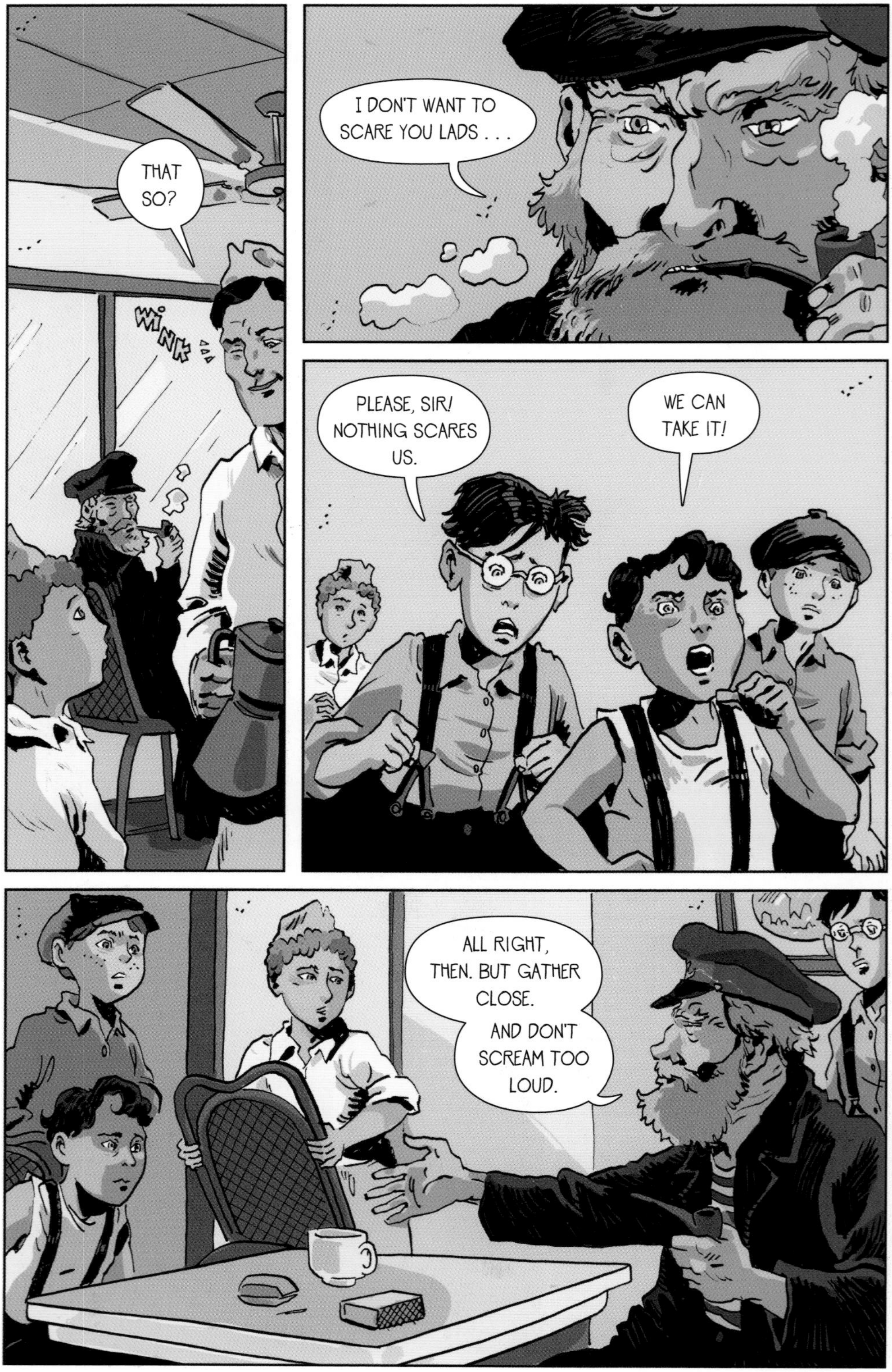
THAT SO?
WINK
I DON'T WANT TO SCARE YOU LADS . . .
PLEASE, SIR! NOTHING SCARES US.
WE CAN TAKE IT!
ALL RIGHT, THEN. BUT GATHER CLOSE.
AND DON'T SCREAM TOO LOUD.

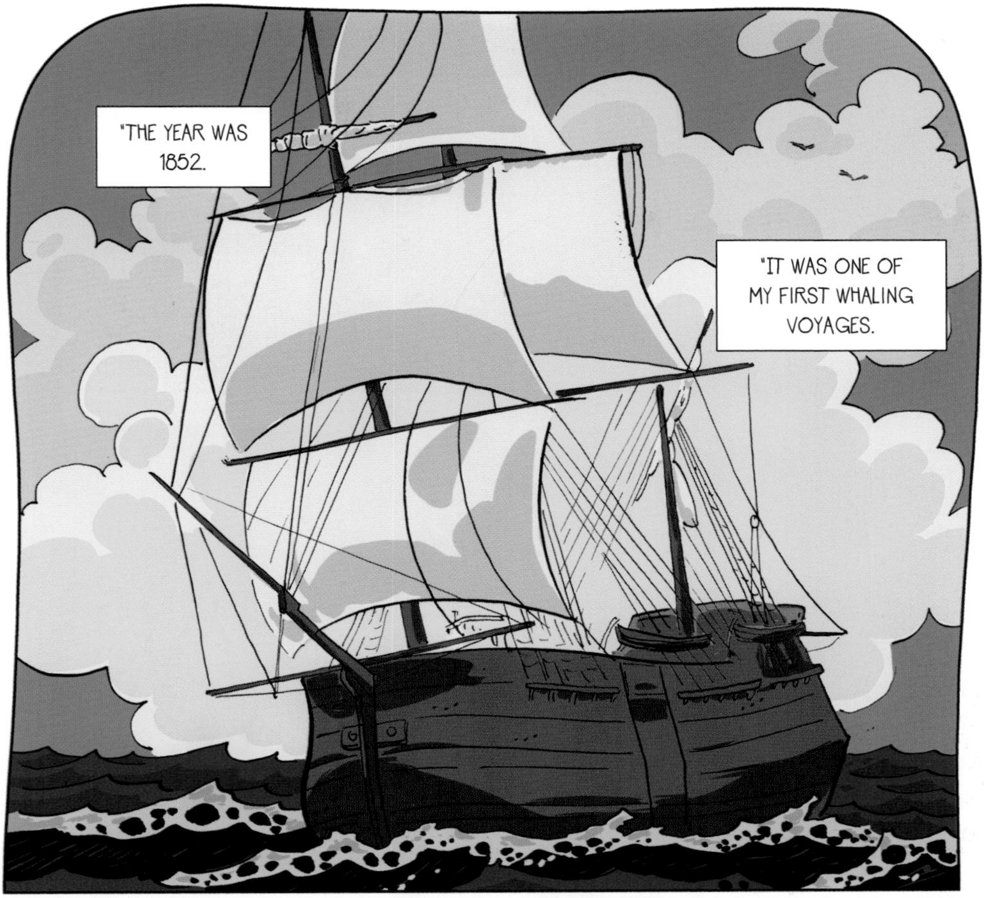
"THE YEAR WAS 1852.
"IT WAS ONE OF MY FIRST WHALING VOYAGES.

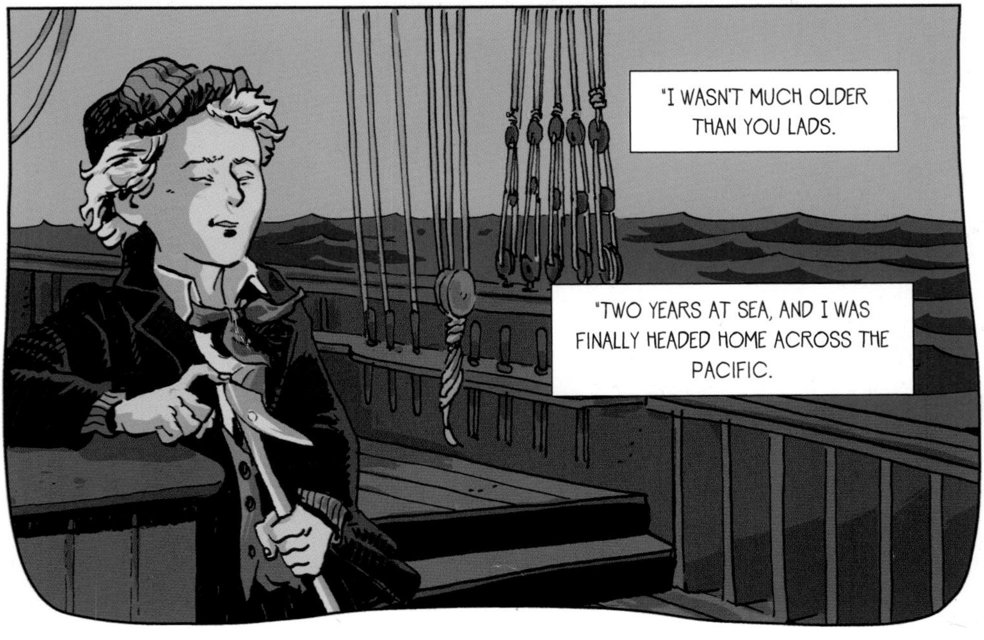
"I WASN'T MUCH OLDER THAN YOU LADS.
"TWO YEARS AT SEA, AND I WAS FINALLY HEADED HOME ACROSS THE PACIFIC.

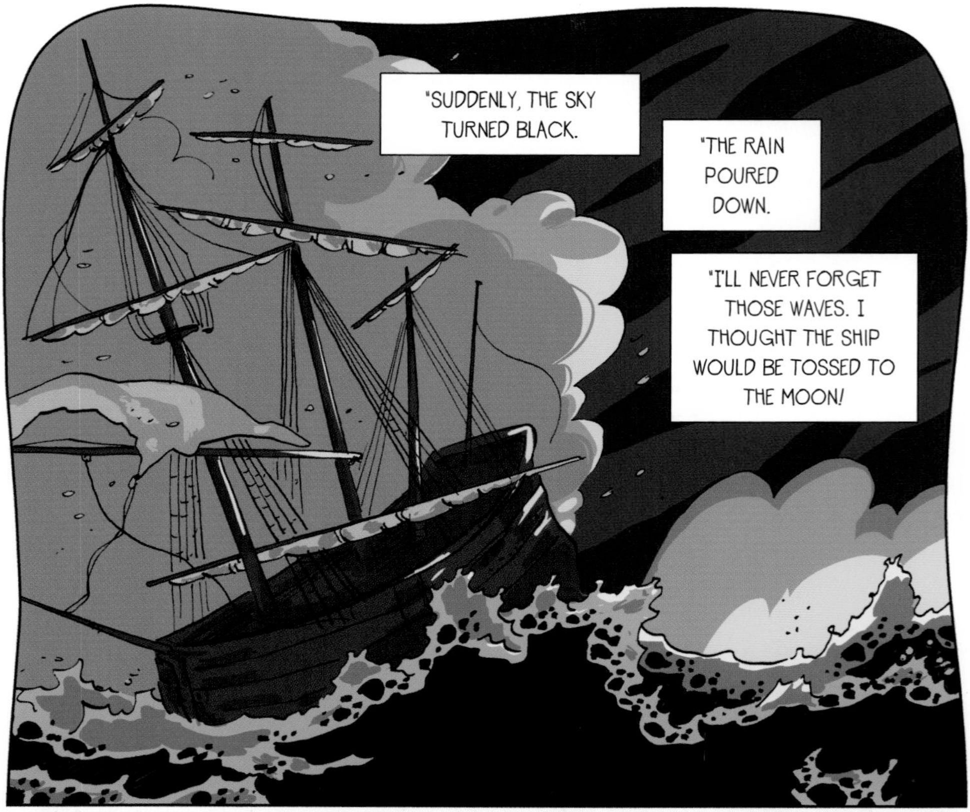
"SUDDENLY, THE SKY TURNED BLACK.
"THE RAIN POURED DOWN.
"I'LL NEVER FORGET THOSE WAVES. I THOUGHT THE SHIP WOULD BE TOSSED TO THE MOON!

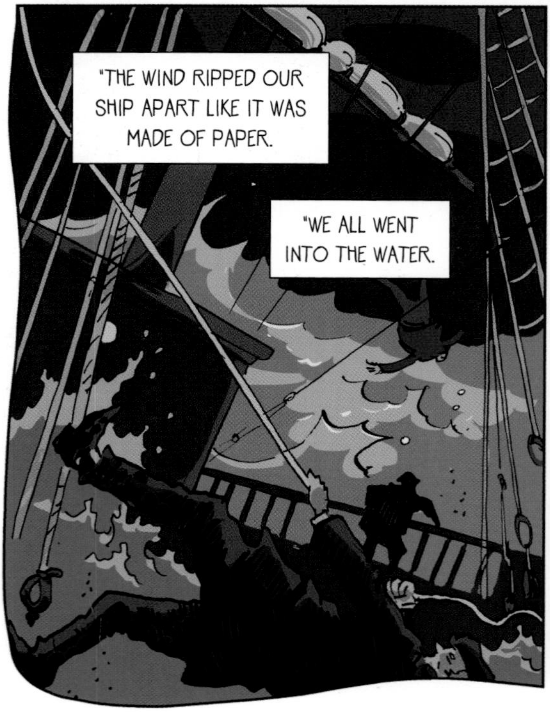
"THE WIND RIPPED OUR SHIP APART LIKE IT WAS MADE OF PAPER.
"WE ALL WENT INTO THE WATER.

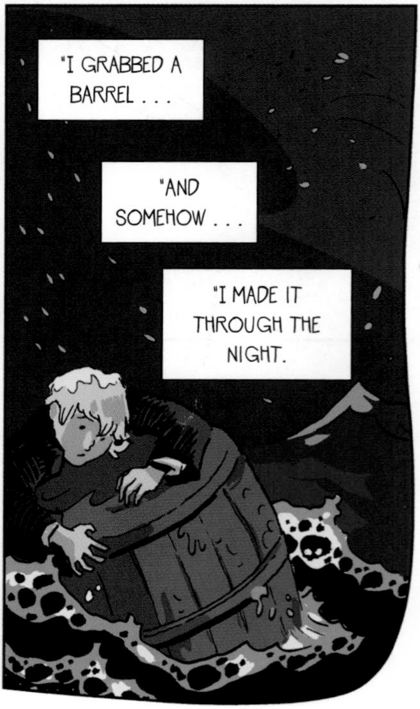
"I GRABBED A BARREL . . .
"AND SOMEHOW . . .
"I MADE IT THROUGH THE NIGHT.

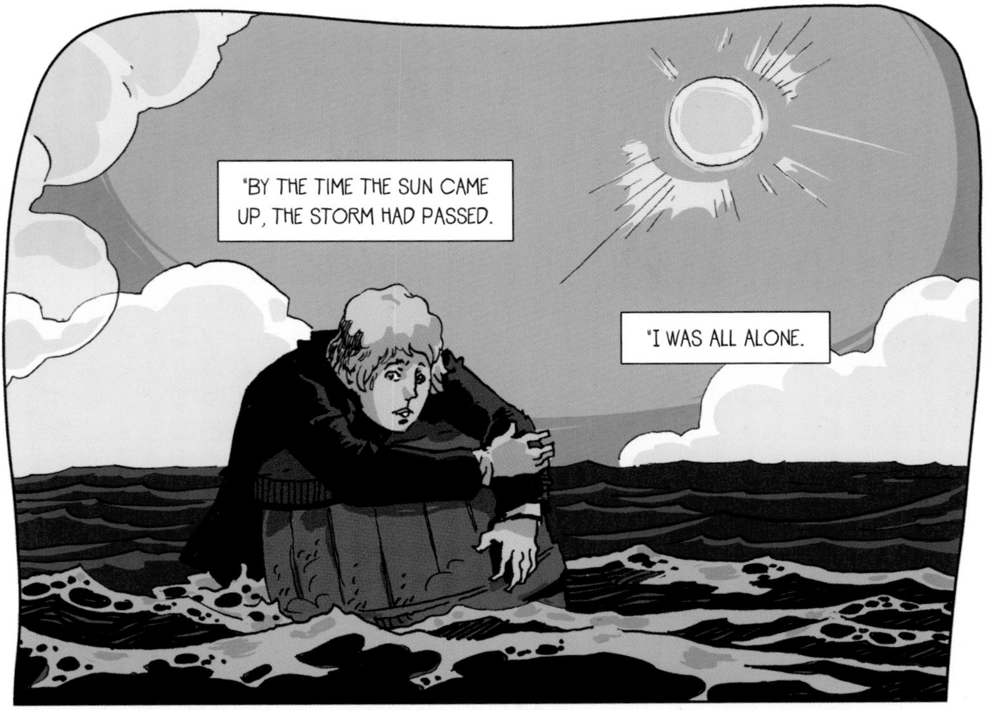
"BY THE TIME THE SUN CAME UP, THE STORM HAD PASSED.
"I WAS ALL ALONE.

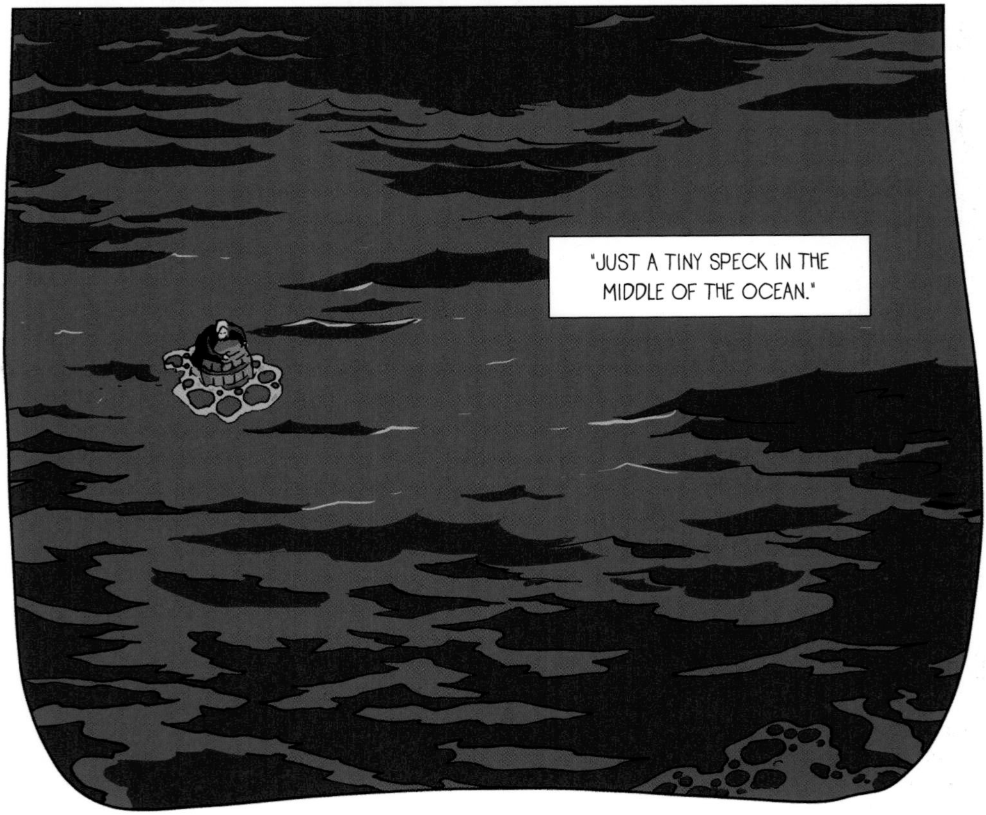
"JUST A TINY SPECK IN THE MIDDLE OF THE OCEAN."

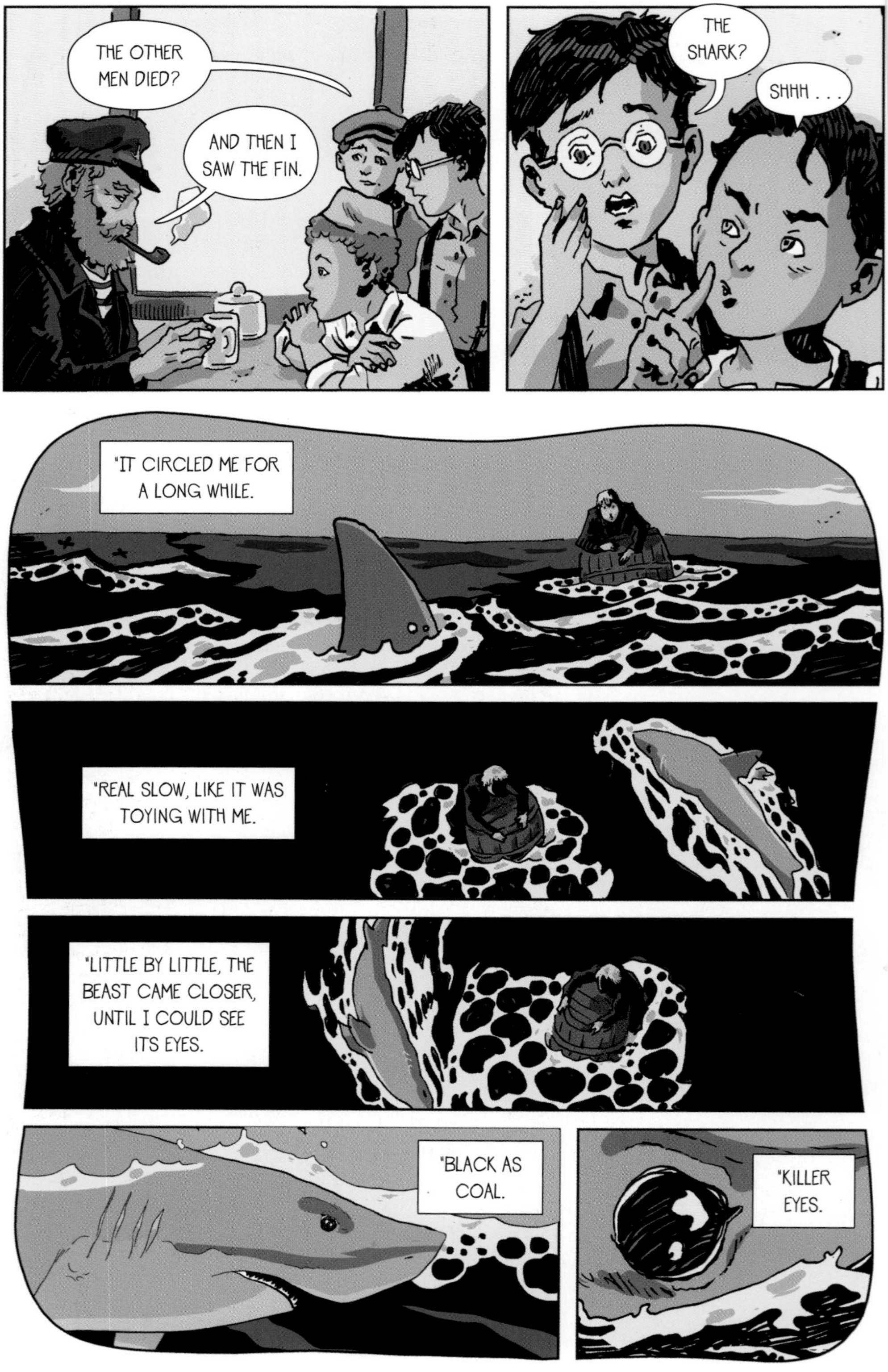
THE OTHER MEN DIED?
AND THEN I SAW THE FIN.
THE SHARK?
SHHH . . .
"IT CIRCLED ME FOR A LONG WHILE.
"REAL SLOW, LIKE IT WAS TOYING WITH ME.
"LITTLE BY LITTLE, THE BEAST CAME CLOSER, UNTIL I COULD SEE ITS EYES.
"BLACK AS COAL.
"KILLER EYES.

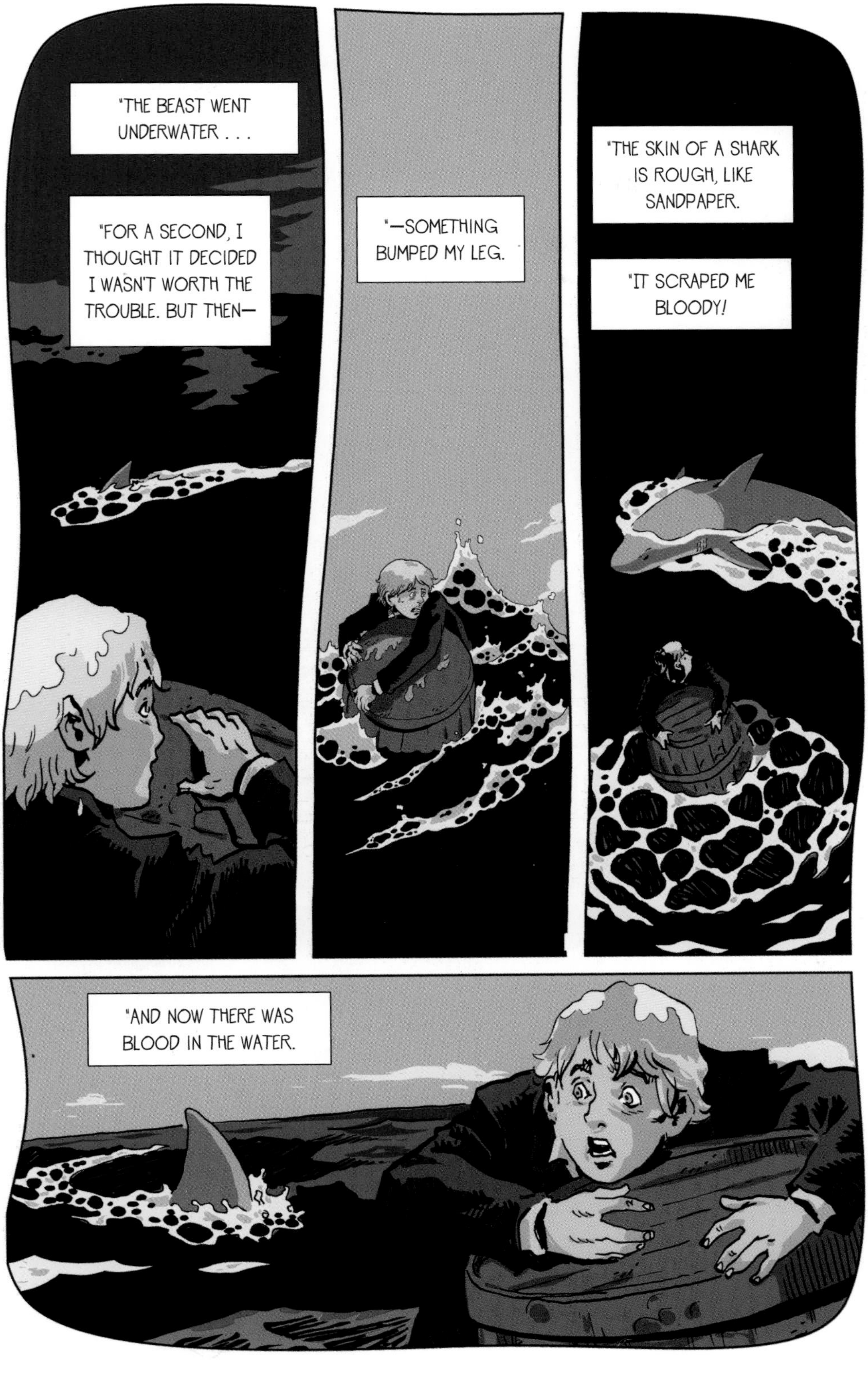
"THE BEAST WENT UNDERWATER . . .
"FOR A SECOND, I THOUGHT IT DECIDED I WASN'T WORTH THE TROUBLE. BUT THEN—
"—SOMETHING BUMPED MY LEG.
"THE SKIN OF A SHARK IS ROUGH, LIKE SANDPAPER.
"IT SCRAPED ME BLOODY!
"AND NOW THERE WAS BLOOD IN THE WATER.

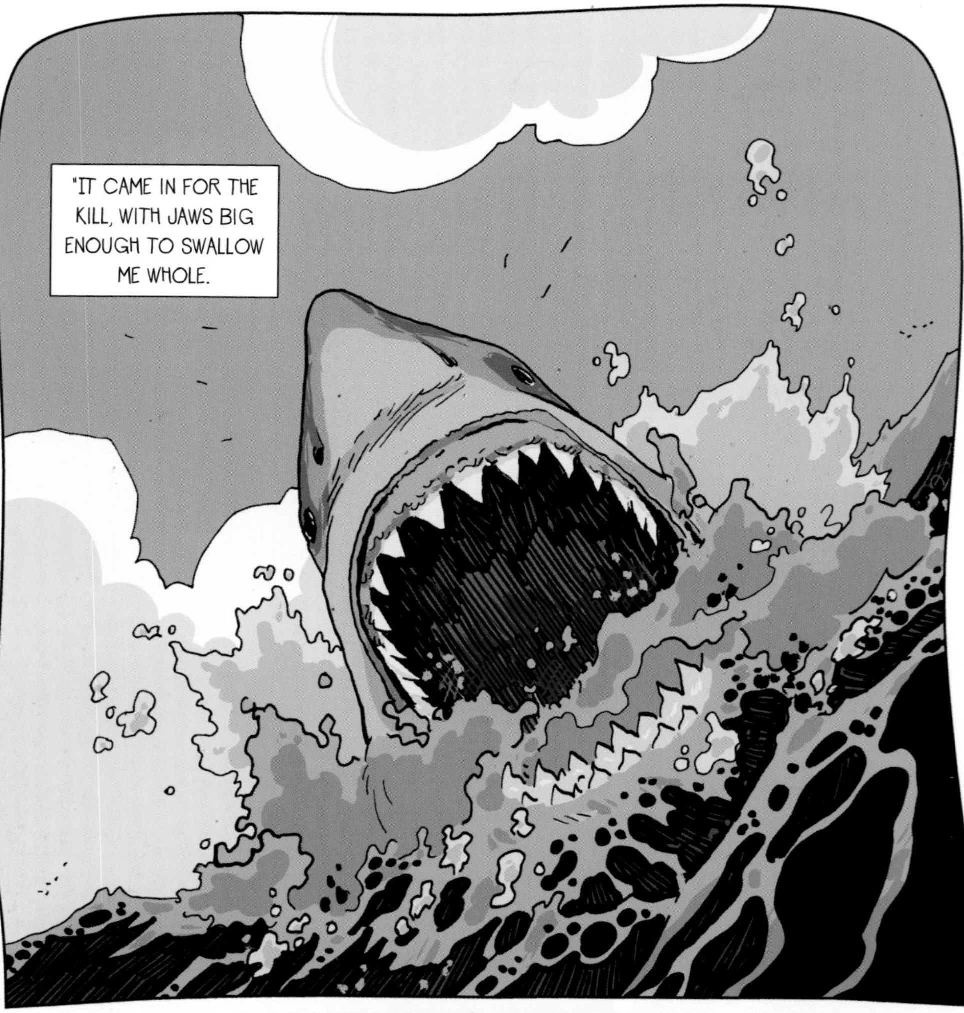
"IT CAME IN FOR THE KILL, WITH JAWS BIG ENOUGH TO SWALLOW ME WHOLE.

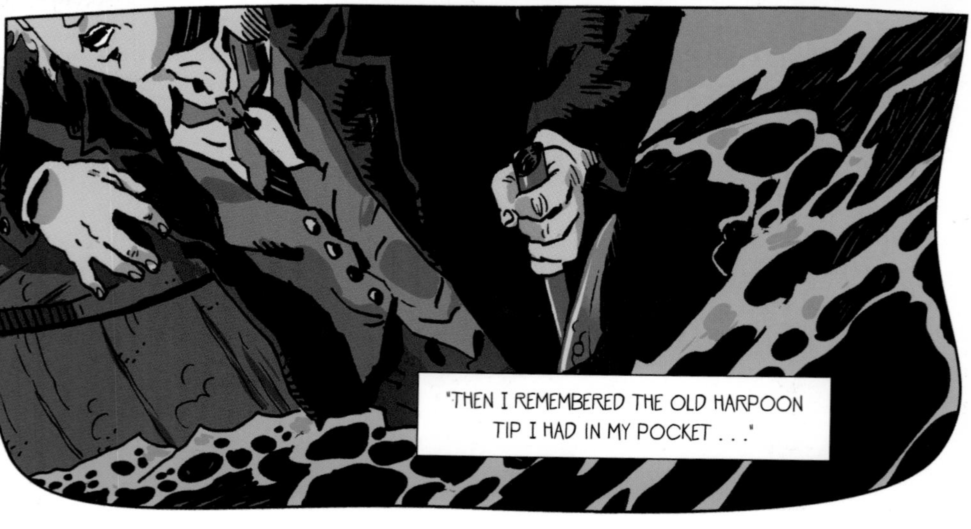
"THEN I REMEMBERED THE OLD HARPOON TIP I HAD IN MY POCKET . . ."

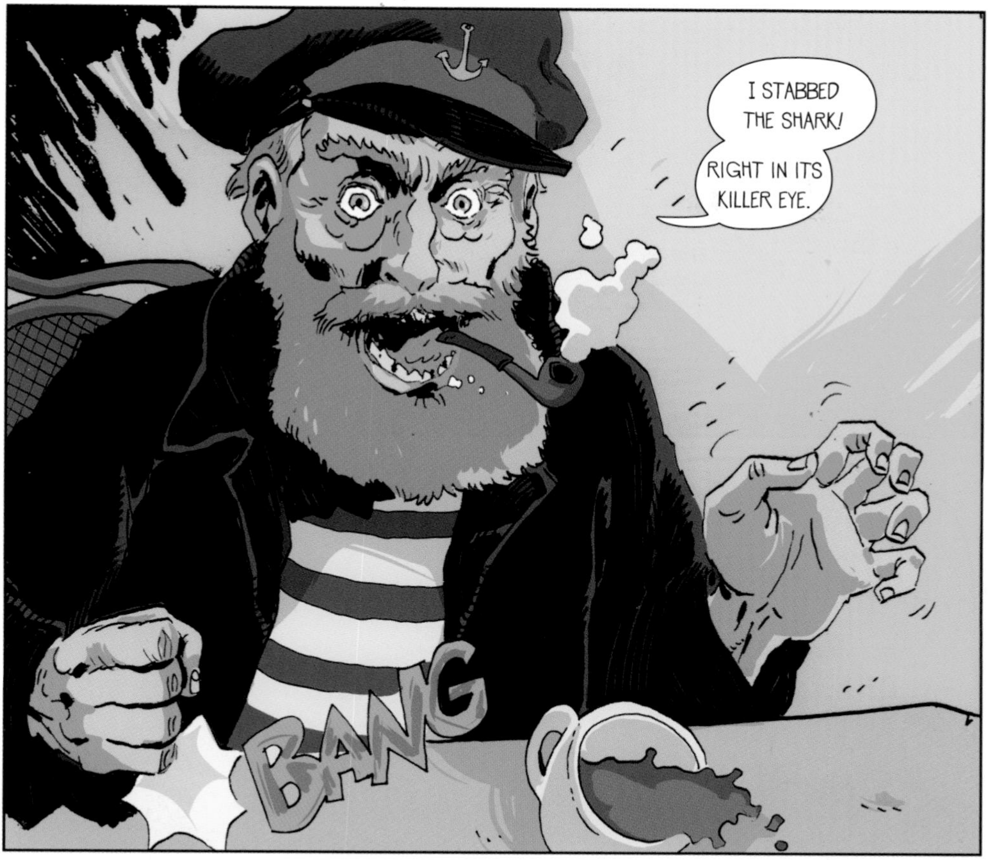
I STABBED THE SHARK!
RIGHT IN ITS KILLER EYE.
BANG

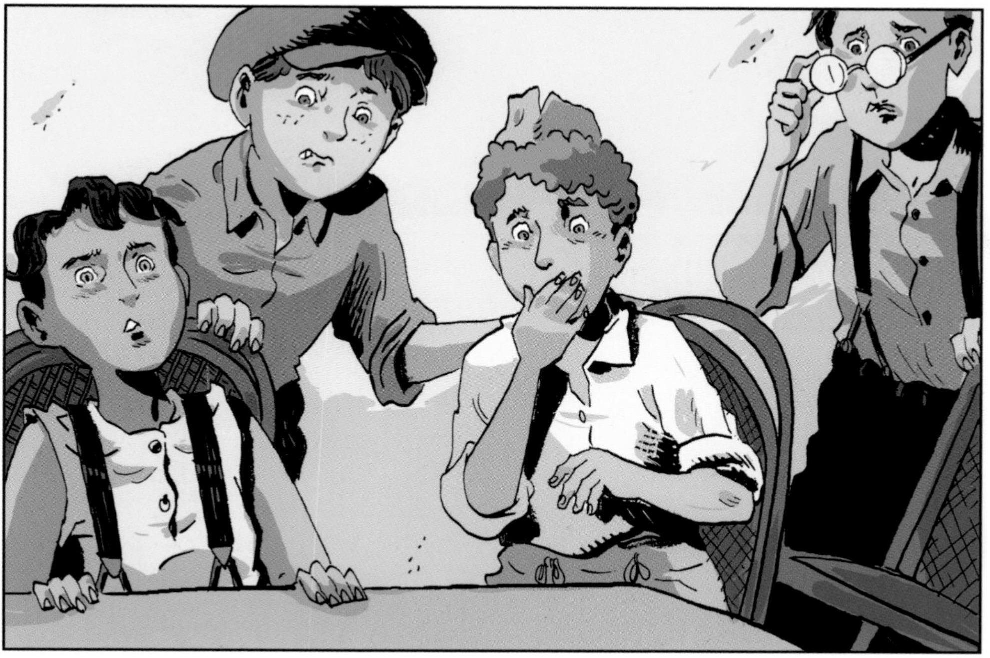

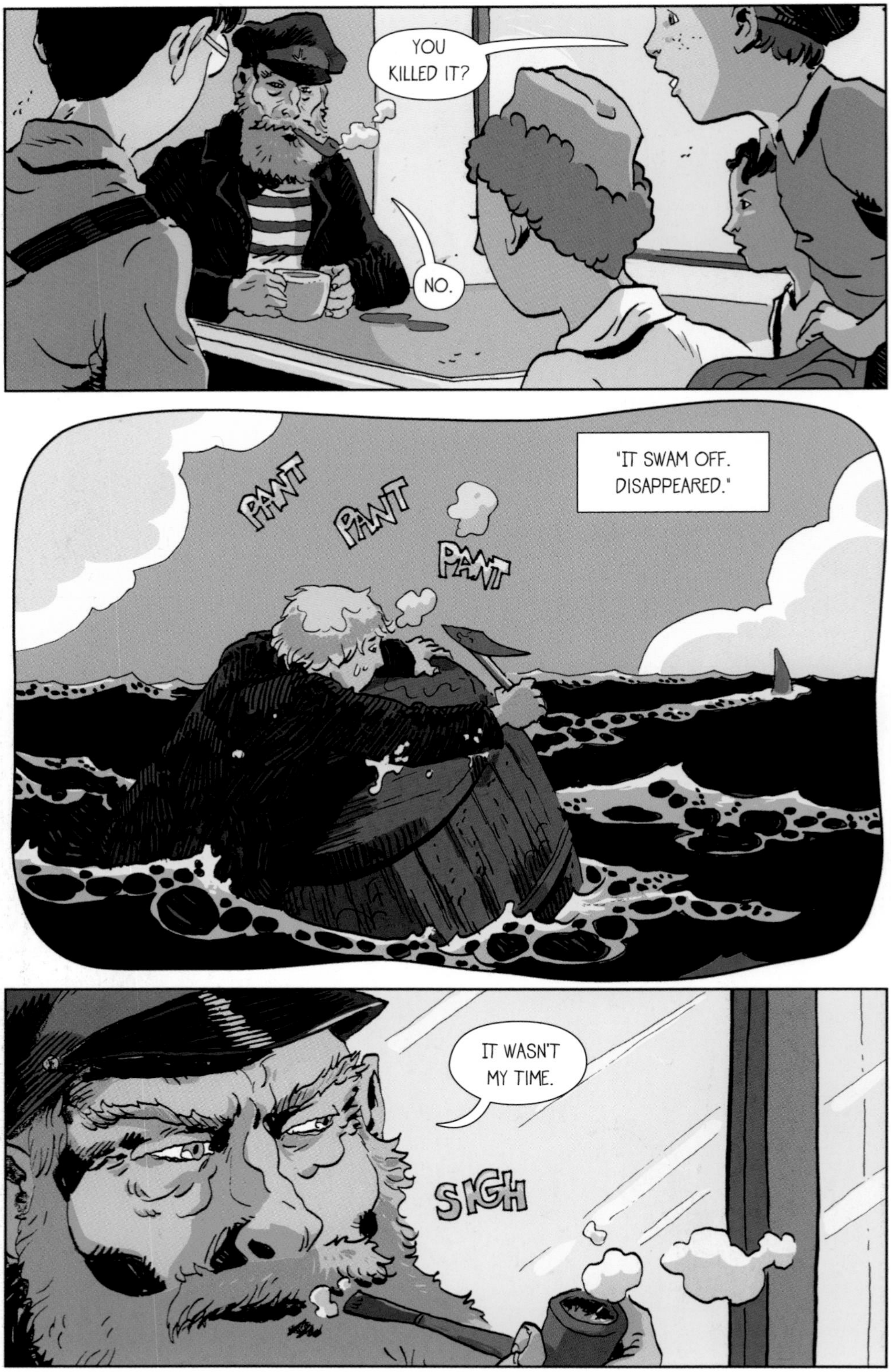
YOU KILLED IT?
NO.
"IT SWAM OFF. DISAPPEARED."
PANT
PANT
PANT
IT WASN'T MY TIME.
SIGH

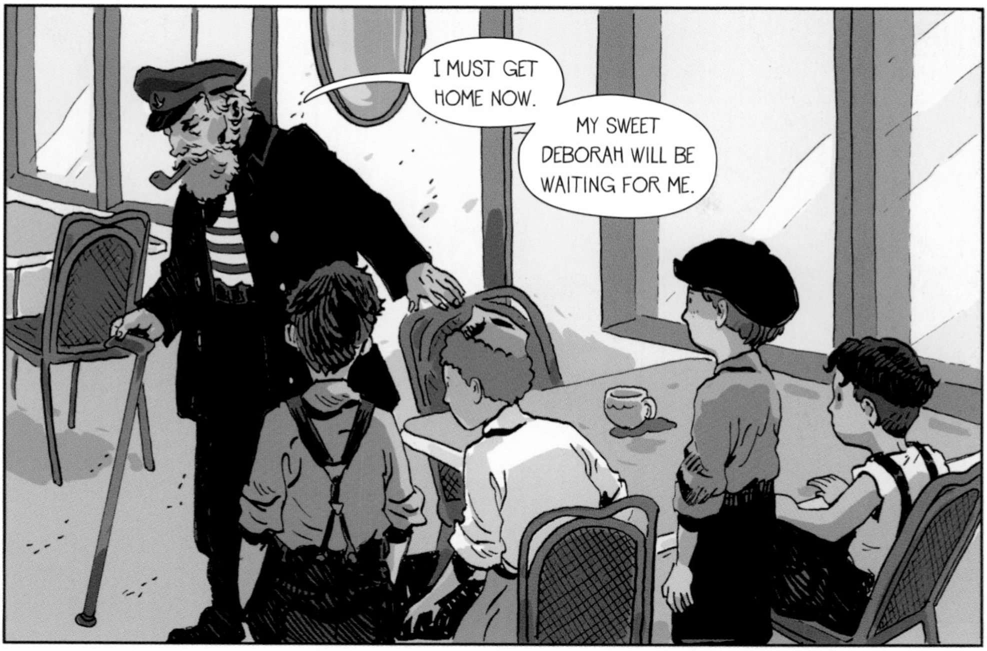
I MUST GET HOME NOW.
MY SWEET DEBORAH WILL BE WAITING FOR ME.

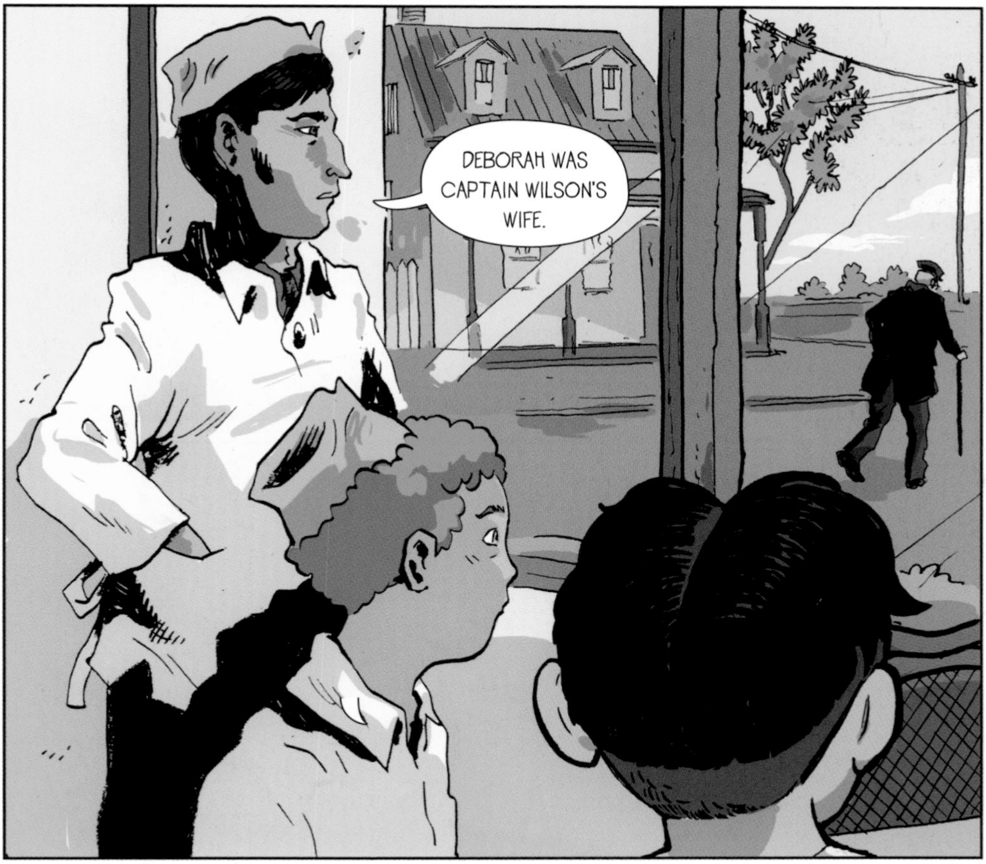
DEBORAH WAS CAPTAIN WILSON'S WIFE.

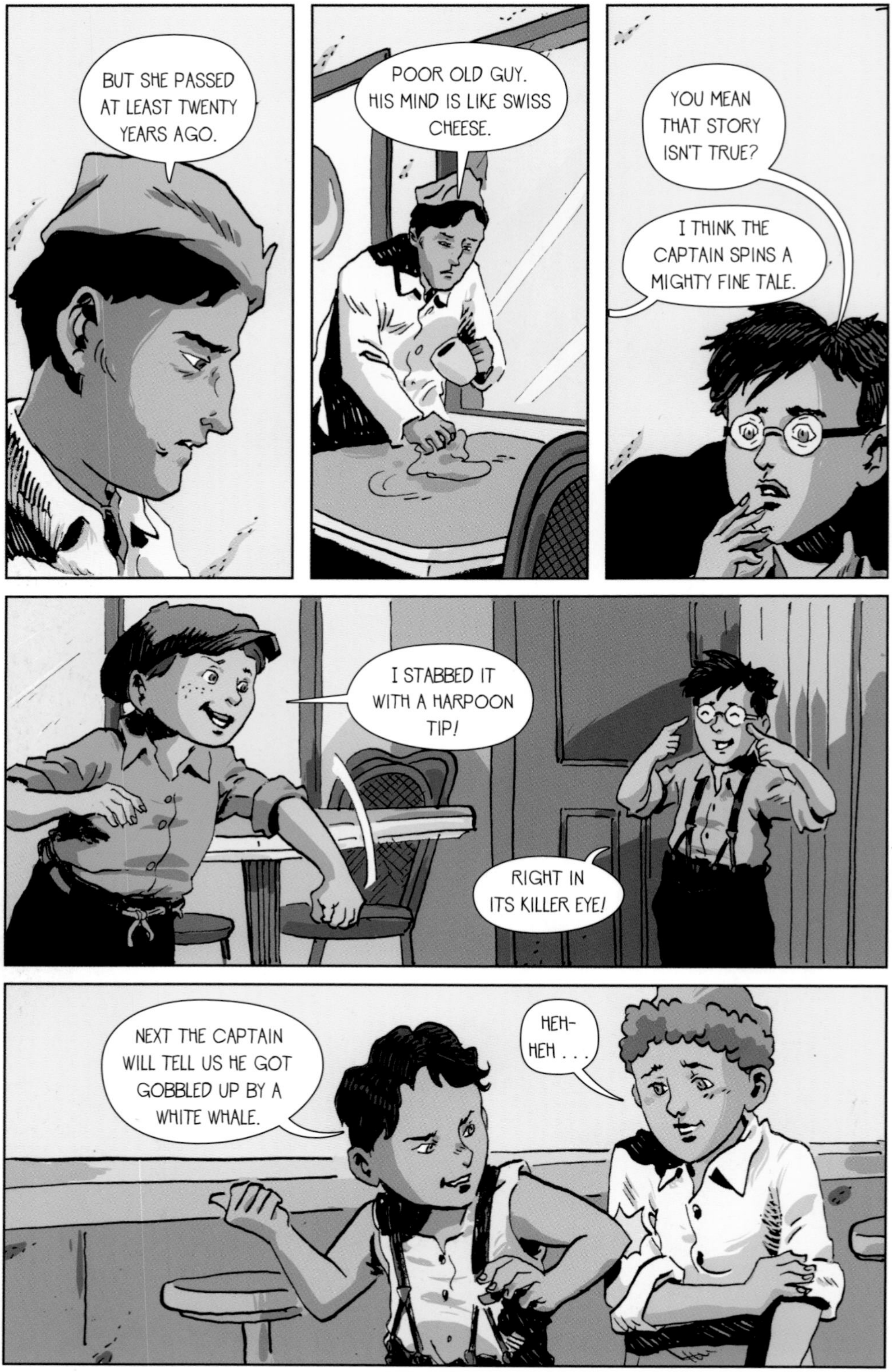

BUT SHE PASSED AT LEAST TWENTY YEARS AGO.
POOR OLD GUY. HIS MIND IS LIKE SWISS CHEESE.
YOU MEAN THAT STORY ISN'T TRUE?
I THINK THE CAPTAIN SPINS A MIGHTY FINE TALE.
I STABBED IT WITH A HARPOON TIP!
RIGHT IN ITS KILLER EYE!
NEXT THE CAPTAIN WILL TELL US HE GOT GOBBLED UP BY A WHITE WHALE.
HEH-HEH . . .

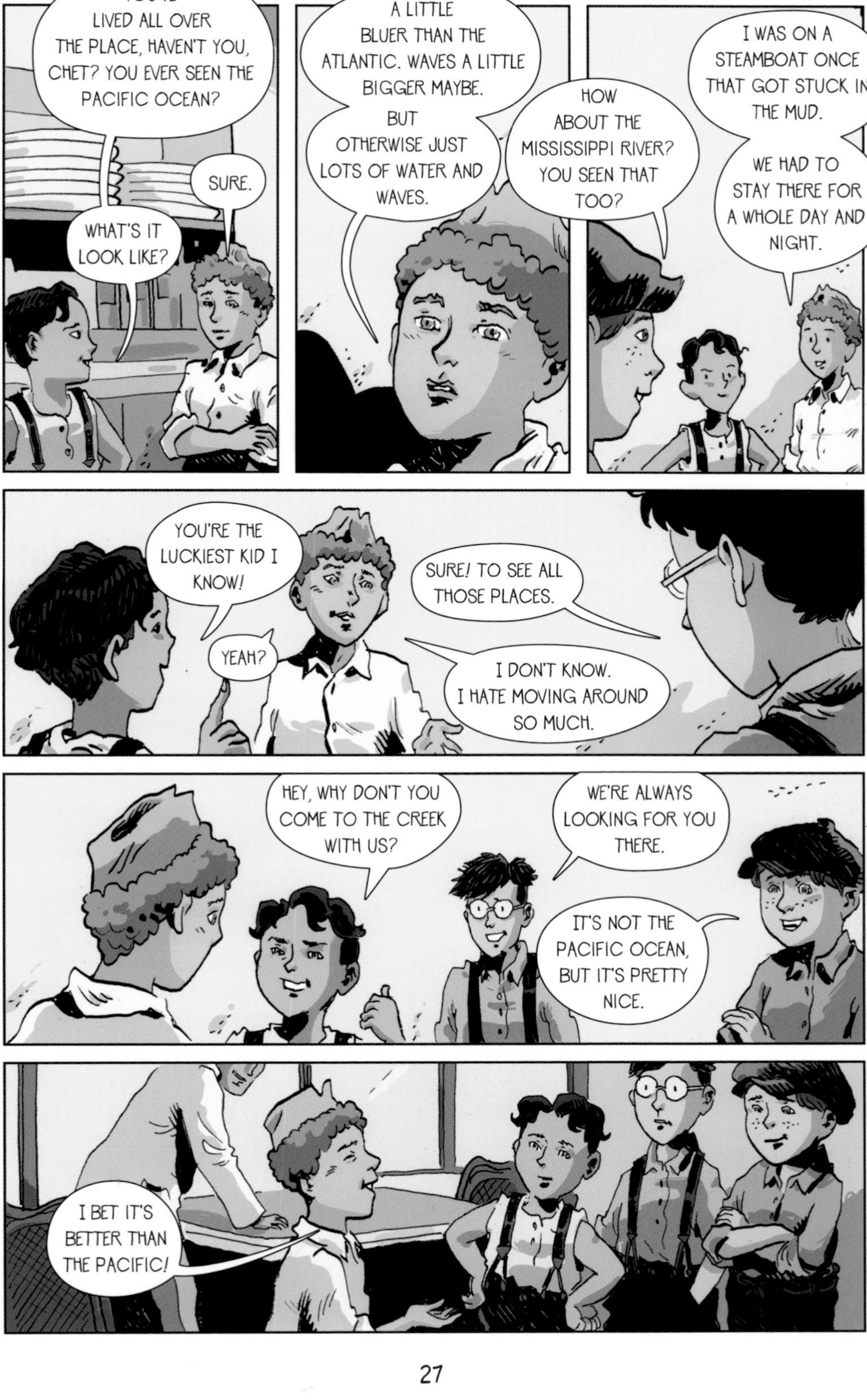

YOU'VE LIVED ALL OVER THE PLACE, HAVEN'T YOU, CHET? YOU EVER SEEN THE PACIFIC OCEAN?
SURE.
WHAT'S IT LOOK LIKE?
A LITTLE BLUER THAN THE ATLANTIC. WAVES A LITTLE BIGGER MAYBE.
BUT OTHERWISE JUST LOTS OF WATER AND WAVES.
HOW ABOUT THE MISSISSIPPI RIVER? YOU SEEN THAT TOO?
I WAS ON A STEAMBOAT ONCE THAT GOT STUCK IN THE MUD.
WE HAD TO STAY THERE FOR A WHOLE DAY AND NIGHT.
YOU'RE THE LUCKIEST KID I KNOW!
YEAH?
SURE! TO SEE ALL THOSE PLACES.
I DON'T KNOW. I HATE MOVING AROUND SO MUCH.
HEY, WHY DON'T YOU COME TO THE CREEK WITH US?
WE'RE ALWAYS LOOKING FOR YOU THERE.
IT'S NOT THE PACIFIC OCEAN, BUT IT'S PRETTY NICE.
I BET IT'S BETTER THAN THE PACIFIC!

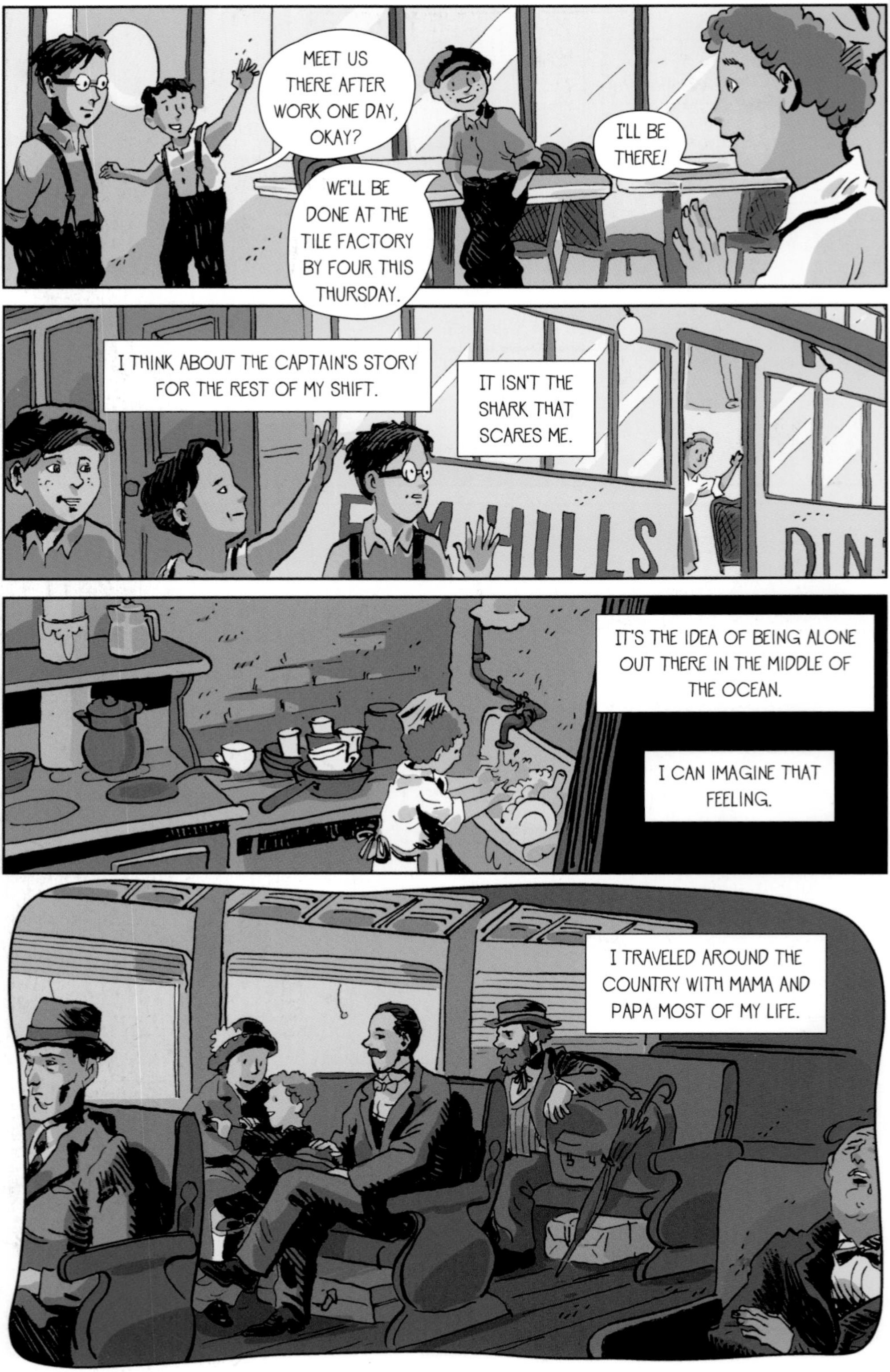
MEET US THERE AFTER WORK ONE DAY, OKAY?
WE'LL BE DONE AT THE TILE FACTORY BY FOUR THIS THURSDAY.
I'LL BE THERE!
I THINK ABOUT THE CAPTAIN'S STORY FOR THE REST OF MY SHIFT.
IT ISN'T THE SHARK THAT SCARES ME.
IT'S THE IDEA OF BEING ALONE OUT THERE IN THE MIDDLE OF THE OCEAN.
I CAN IMAGINE THAT FEELING.
I TRAVELED AROUND THE COUNTRY WITH MAMA AND PAPA MOST OF MY LIFE.

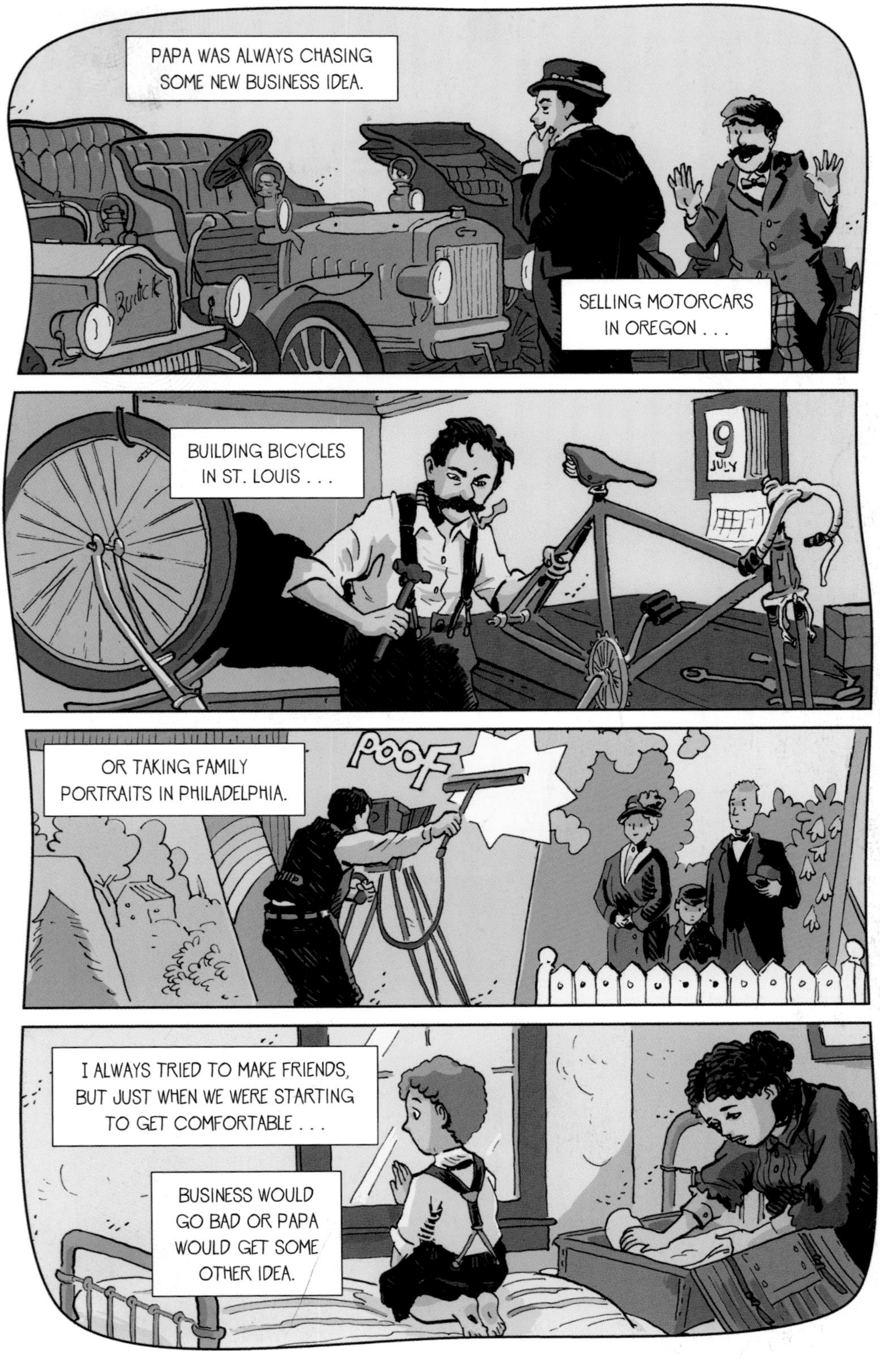

PAPA WAS ALWAYS CHASING SOME NEW BUSINESS IDEA.
Buick
SELLING MOTORCARS IN OREGON . . .
BUILDING BICYCLES IN ST. LOUIS . . .
9 JULY
OR TAKING FAMILY PORTRAITS IN PHILADELPHIA.
POOF
I ALWAYS TRIED TO MAKE FRIENDS, BUT JUST WHEN WE WERE STARTING TO GET COMFORTABLE . . .
BUSINESS WOULD GO BAD OR PAPA WOULD GET SOME OTHER IDEA.

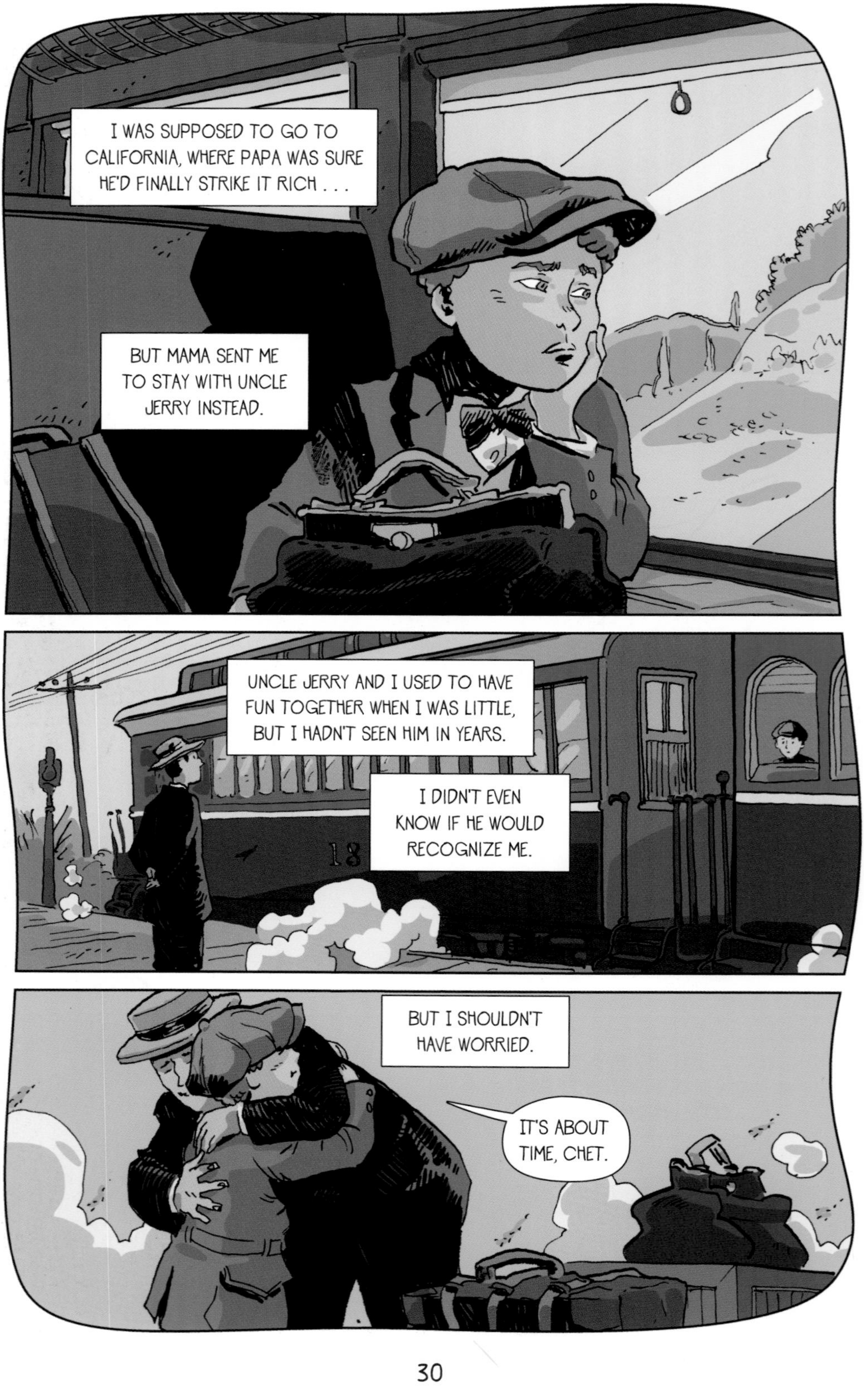
I WAS SUPPOSED TO GO TO CALIFORNIA, WHERE PAPA WAS SURE HE'D FINALLY STRIKE IT RICH . . .
BUT MAMA SENT ME TO STAY WITH UNCLE JERRY INSTEAD.
UNCLE JERRY AND I USED TO HAVE FUN TOGETHER WHEN I WAS LITTLE, BUT I HADN'T SEEN HIM IN YEARS.
I DIDN'T EVEN KNOW IF HE WOULD RECOGNIZE ME.
18
BUT I SHOULDN'T HAVE WORRIED.
IT'S ABOUT TIME, CHET.

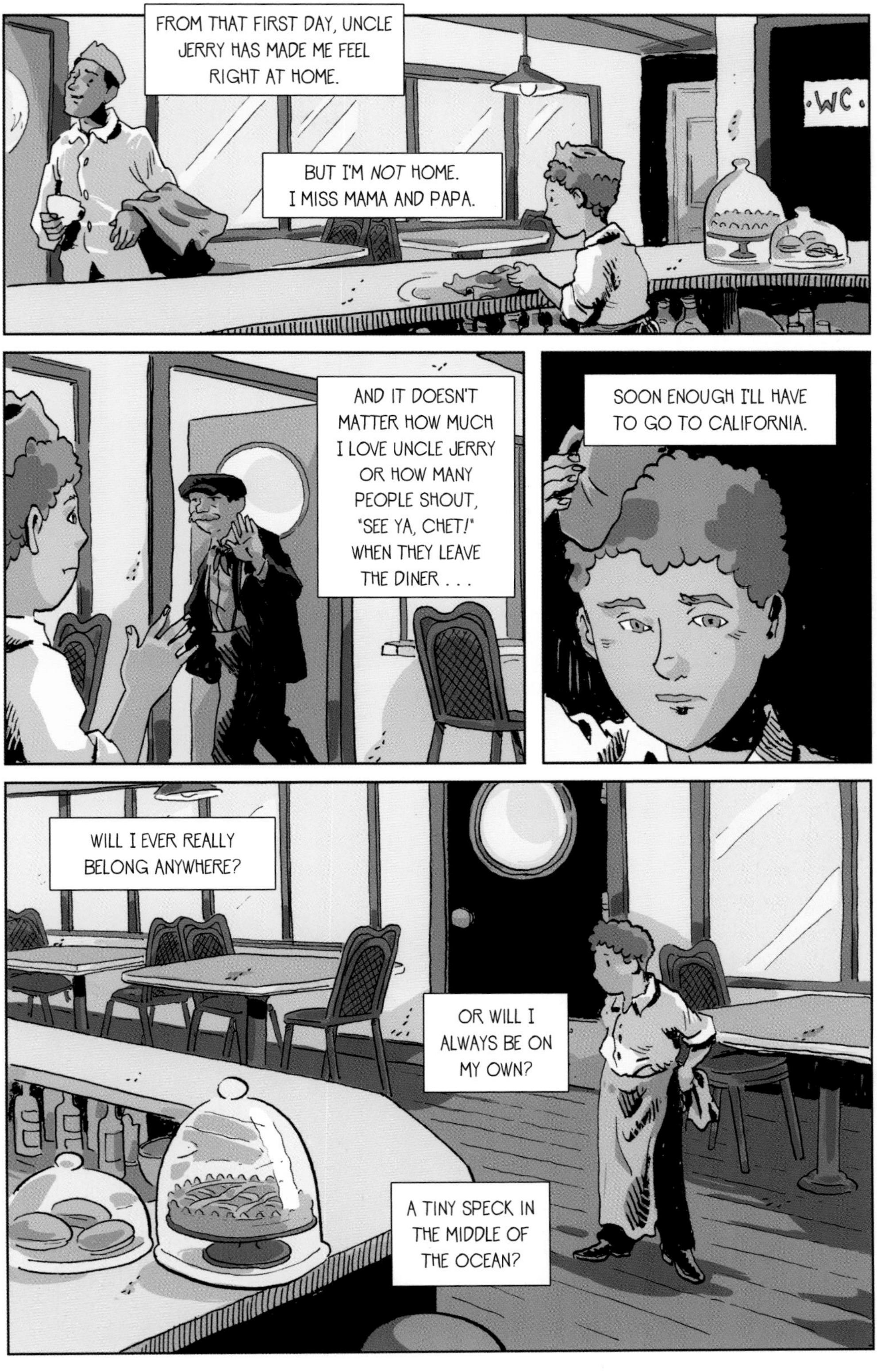
FROM THAT FIRST DAY, UNCLE JERRY HAS MADE ME FEEL RIGHT AT HOME.
·WC·
BUT I'M *NOT* HOME. I MISS MAMA AND PAPA.
AND IT DOESN'T MATTER HOW MUCH I LOVE UNCLE JERRY OR HOW MANY PEOPLE SHOUT, "SEE YA, CHET!" WHEN THEY LEAVE THE DINER . . .
SOON ENOUGH I'LL HAVE TO GO TO CALIFORNIA.
WILL I EVER REALLY BELONG ANYWHERE?
OR WILL I ALWAYS BE ON MY OWN?
A TINY SPECK IN THE MIDDLE OF THE OCEAN?

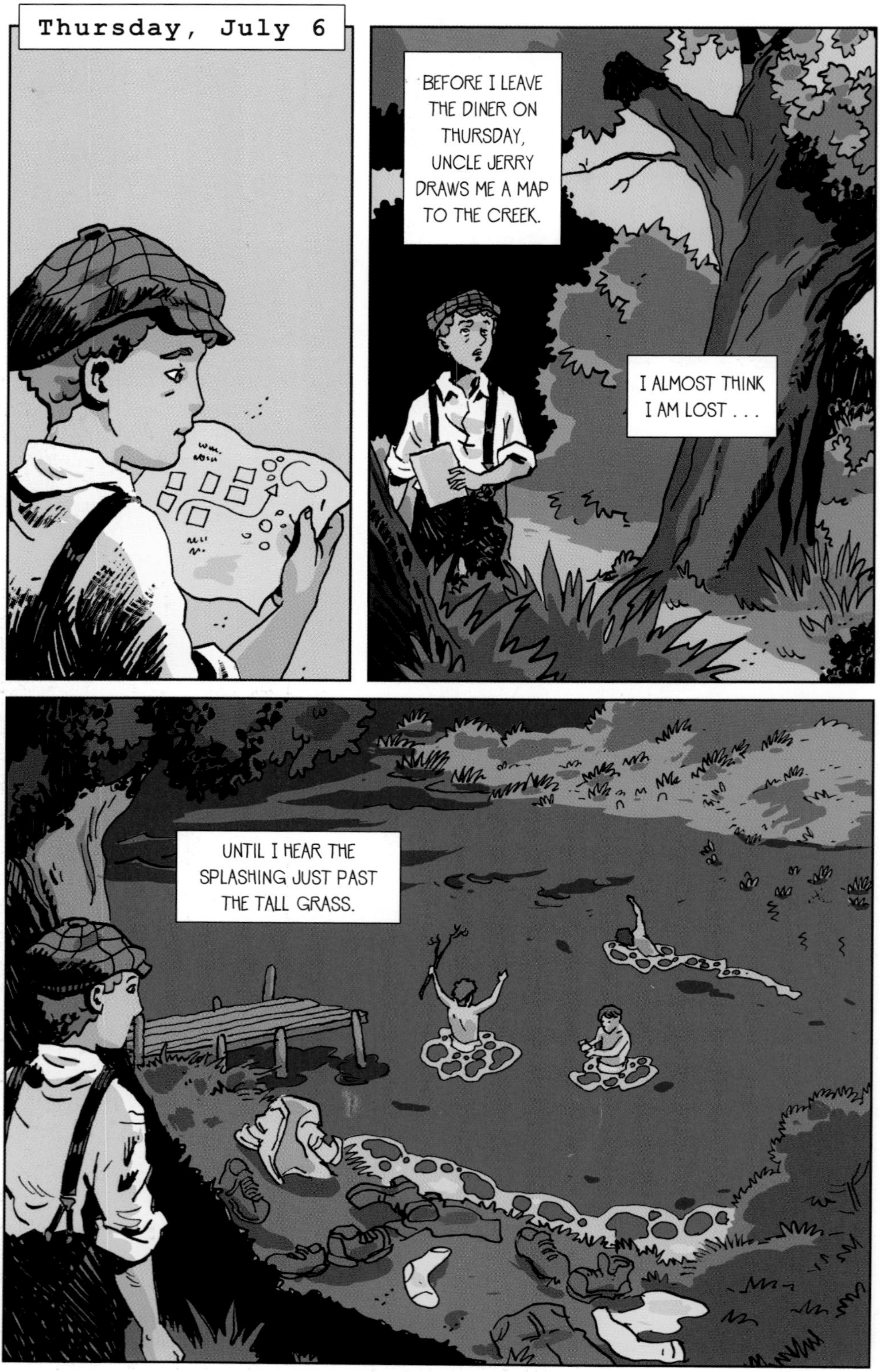
Thursday, July 6
BEFORE I LEAVE THE DINER ON THURSDAY, UNCLE JERRY DRAWS ME A MAP TO THE CREEK.
I ALMOST THINK I AM LOST . . .
UNTIL I HEAR THE SPLASHING JUST PAST THE TALL GRASS.

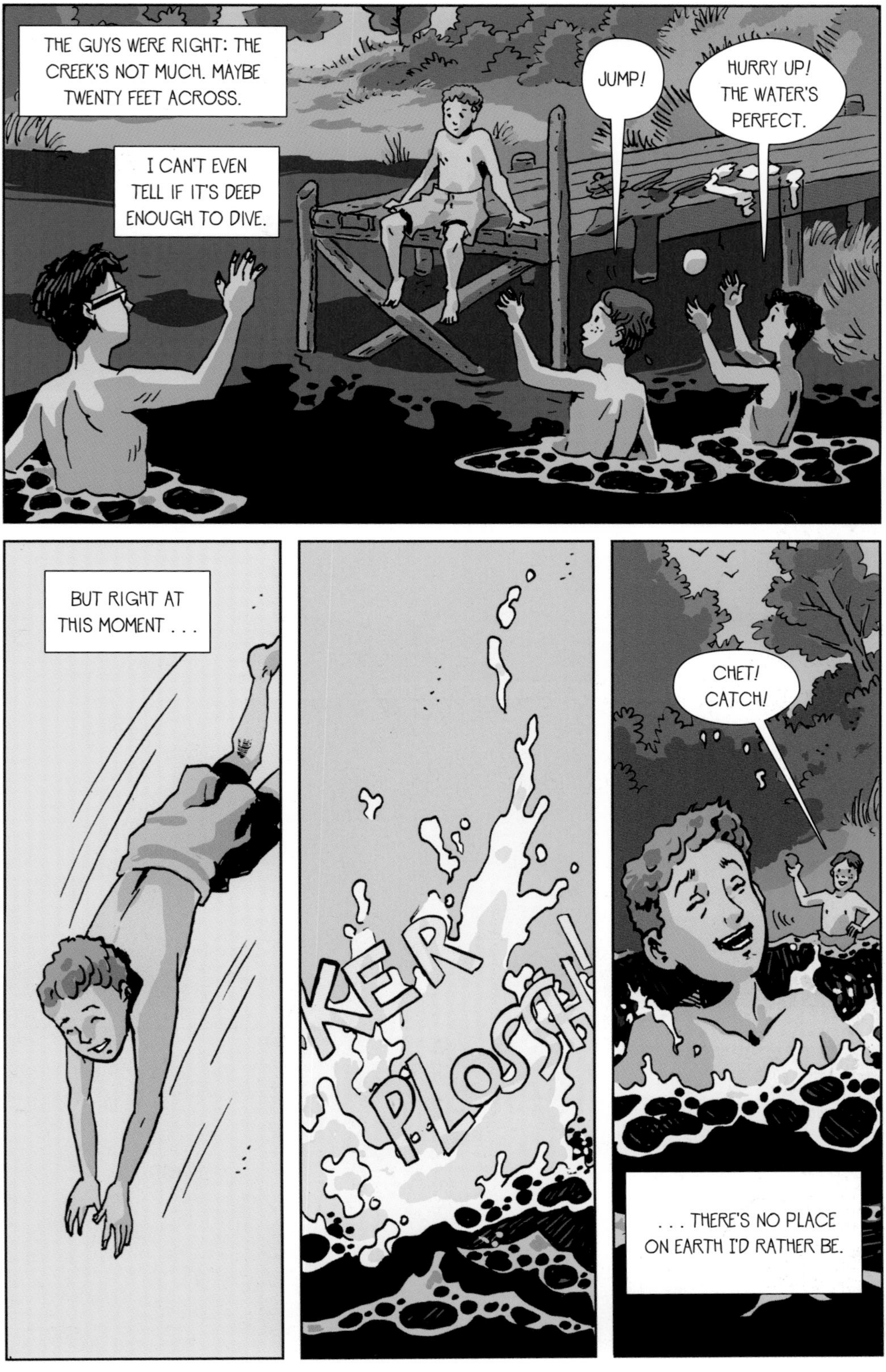
THE GUYS WERE RIGHT: THE CREEK'S NOT MUCH. MAYBE TWENTY FEET ACROSS.
I CAN'T EVEN TELL IF IT'S DEEP ENOUGH TO DIVE.
JUMP!
HURRY UP! THE WATER'S PERFECT.
BUT RIGHT AT THIS MOMENT . . .
KER PLOSSH!
CHET! CATCH!
. . . THERE'S NO PLACE ON EARTH I'D RATHER BE.

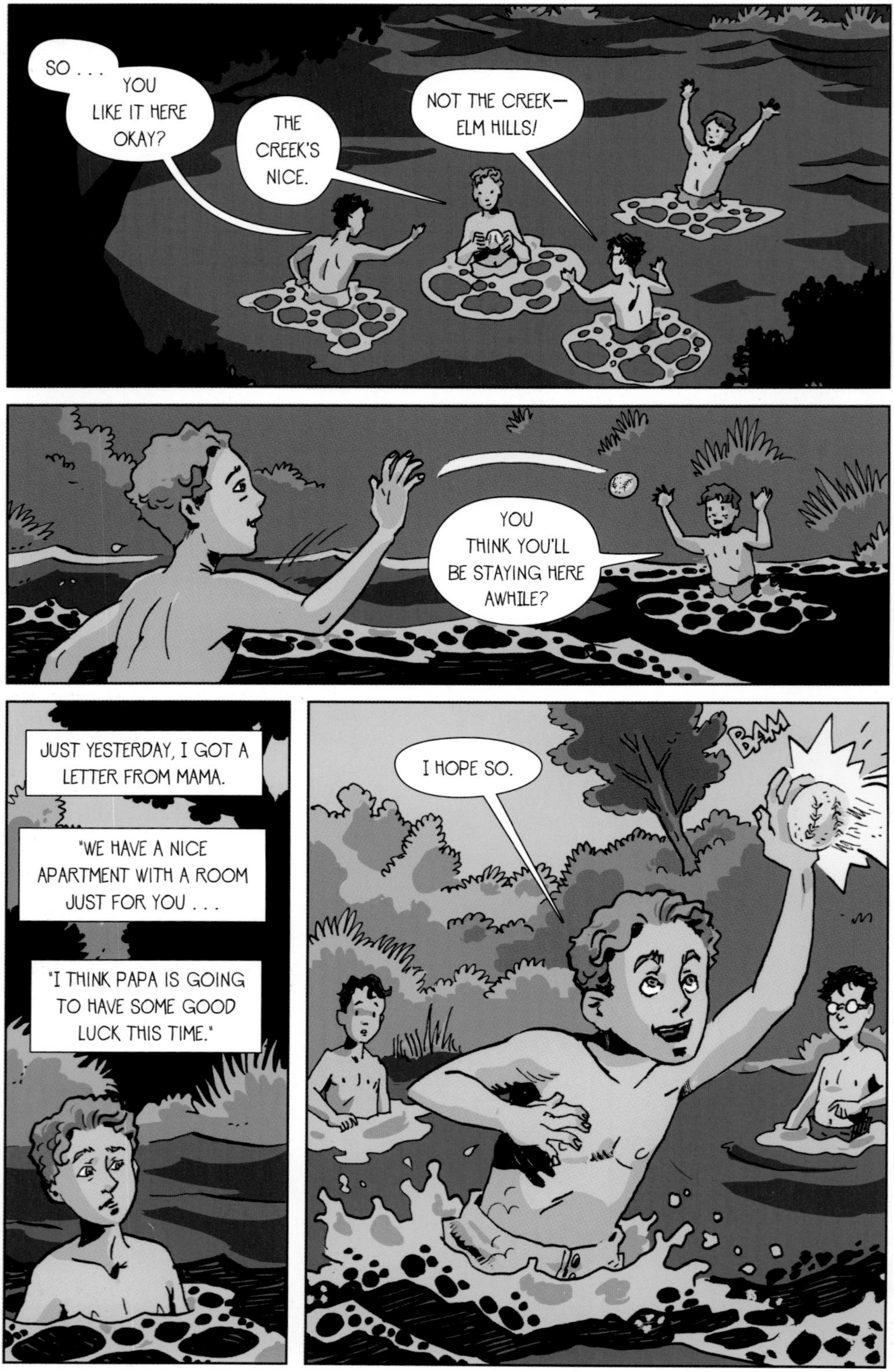
SO . . .
YOU LIKE IT HERE OKAY?
THE CREEK'S NICE.
NOT THE CREEK— ELM HILLS!
YOU THINK YOU'LL BE STAYING HERE AWHILE?
JUST YESTERDAY, I GOT A LETTER FROM MAMA.
"WE HAVE A NICE APARTMENT WITH A ROOM JUST FOR YOU . . .
"I THINK PAPA IS GOING TO HAVE SOME GOOD LUCK THIS TIME."
I HOPE SO.
BAM

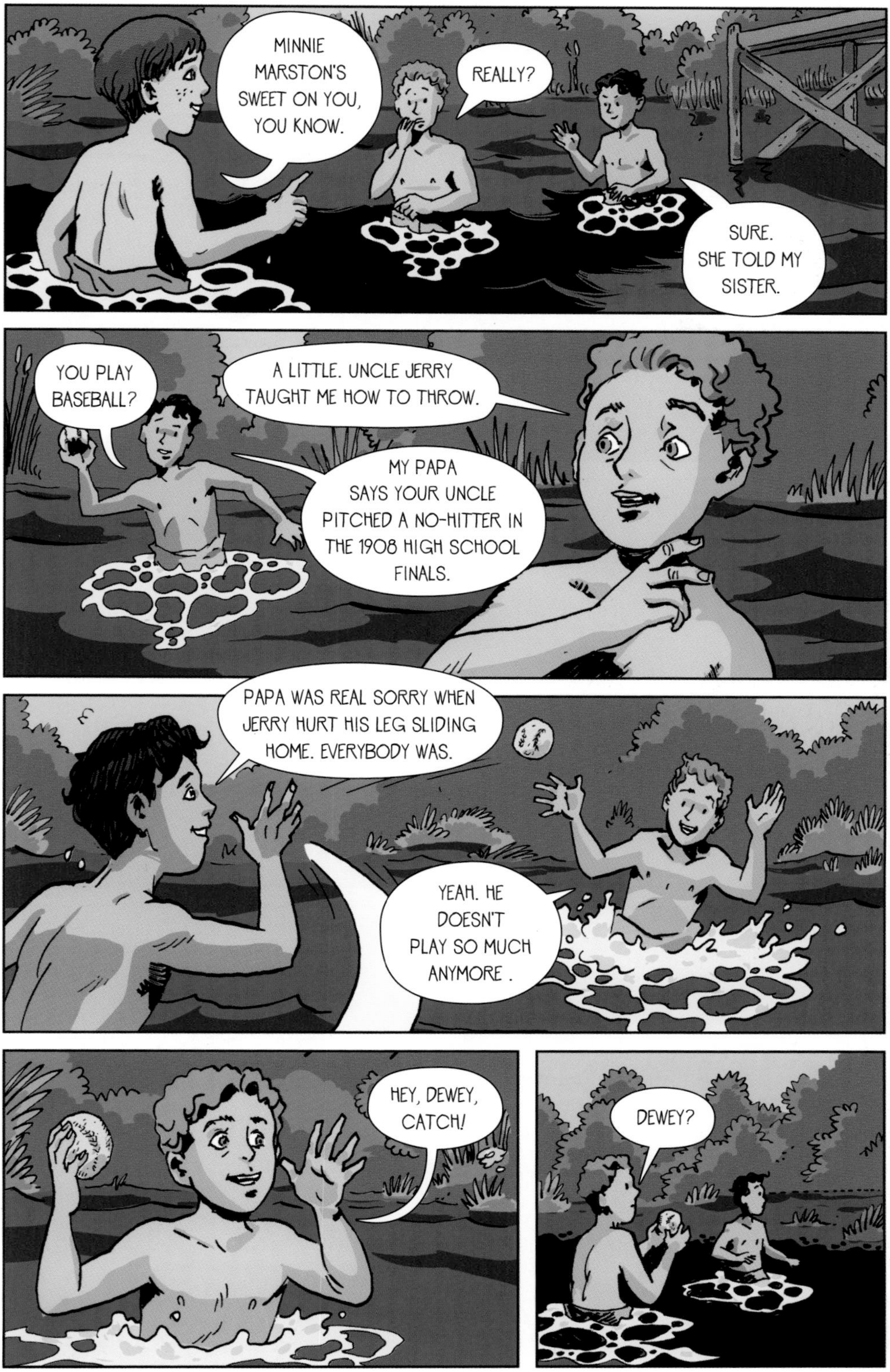
MINNIE MARSTON'S SWEET ON YOU, YOU KNOW.
REALLY?
SURE. SHE TOLD MY SISTER.
YOU PLAY BASEBALL?
A LITTLE. UNCLE JERRY TAUGHT ME HOW TO THROW.
MY PAPA SAYS YOUR UNCLE PITCHED A NO-HITTER IN THE 1908 HIGH SCHOOL FINALS.
PAPA WAS REAL SORRY WHEN JERRY HURT HIS LEG SLIDING HOME. EVERYBODY WAS.
YEAH. HE DOESN'T PLAY SO MUCH ANYMORE .
HEY, DEWEY, CATCH!
DEWEY?

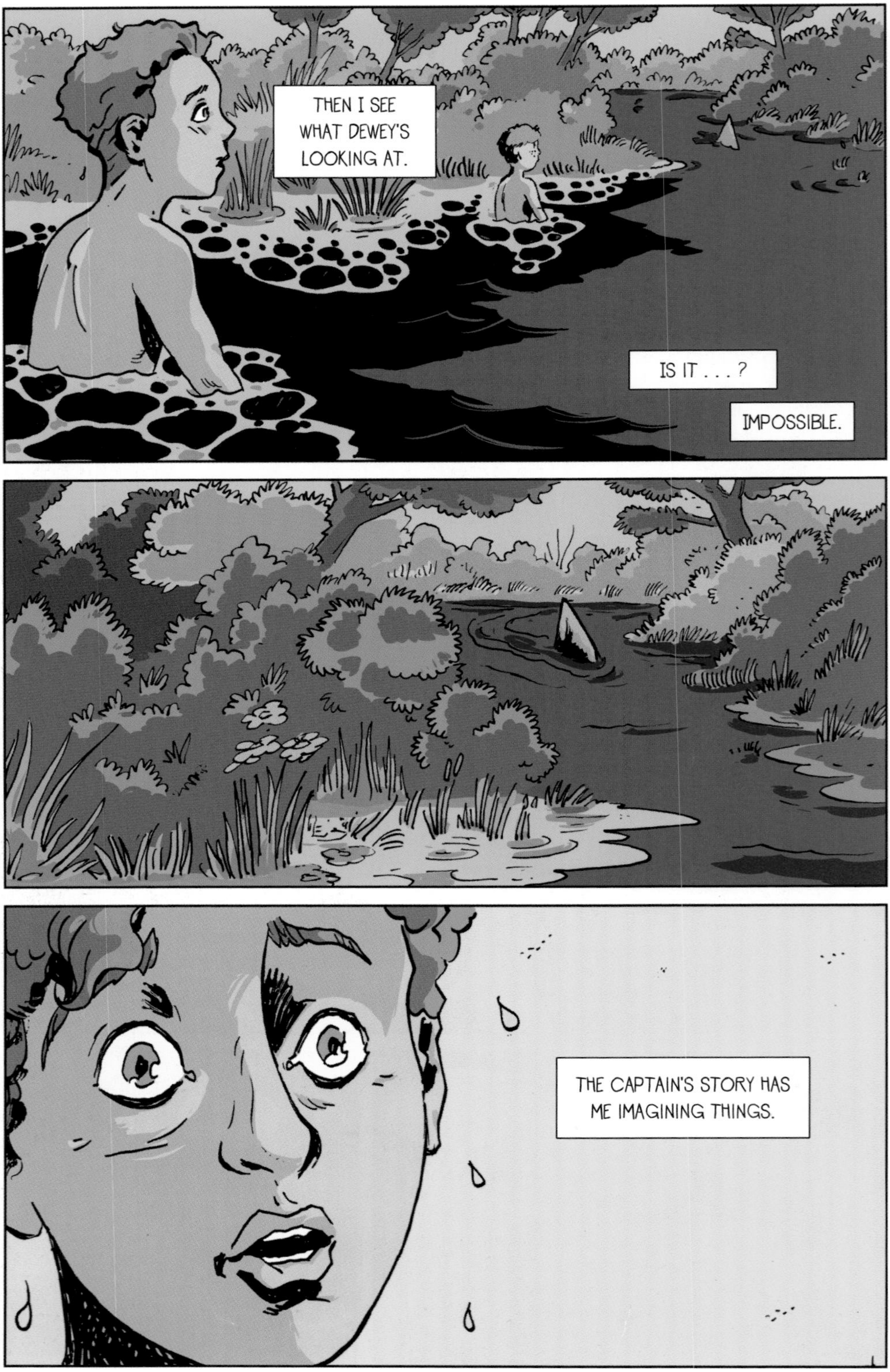
THEN I SEE WHAT DEWEY'S LOOKING AT.
IS IT . . . ?
IMPOSSIBLE.
THE CAPTAIN'S STORY HAS ME IMAGINING THINGS.

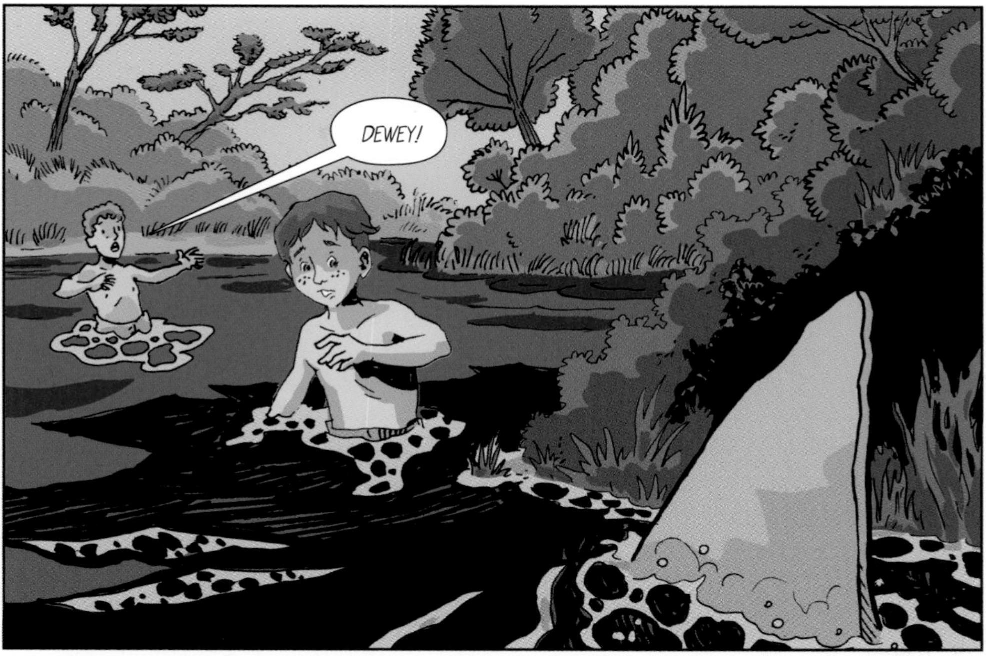
DEWEY!

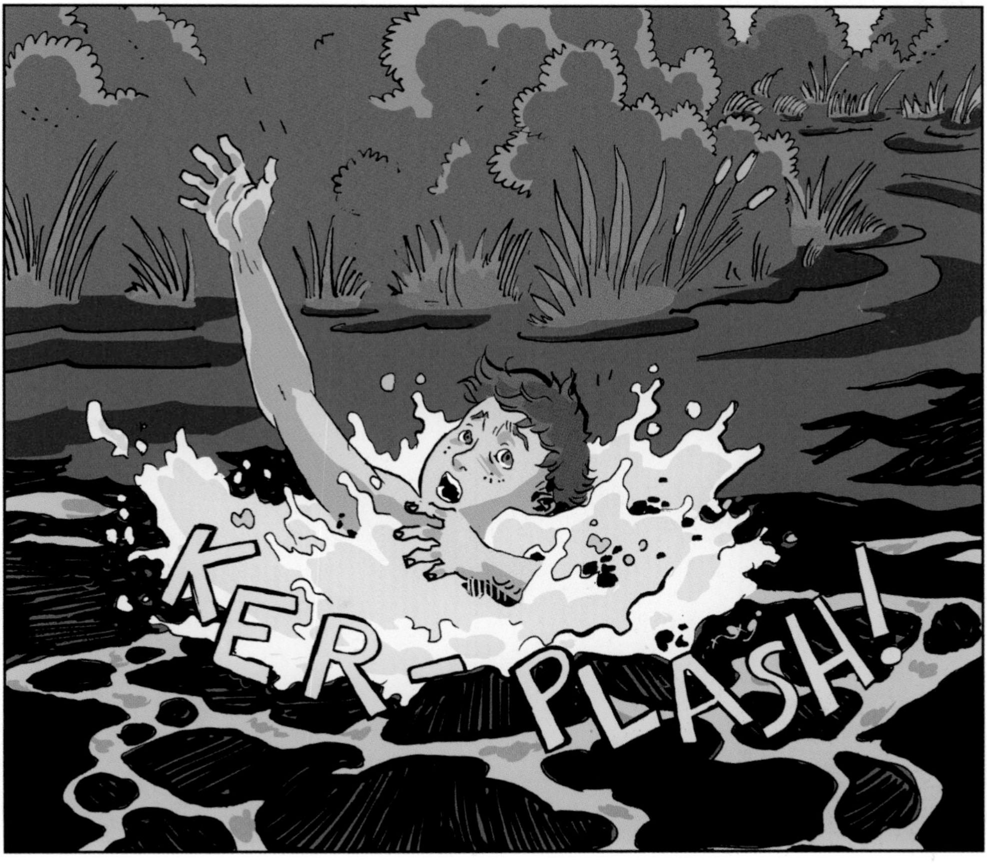
KER-PLASH!

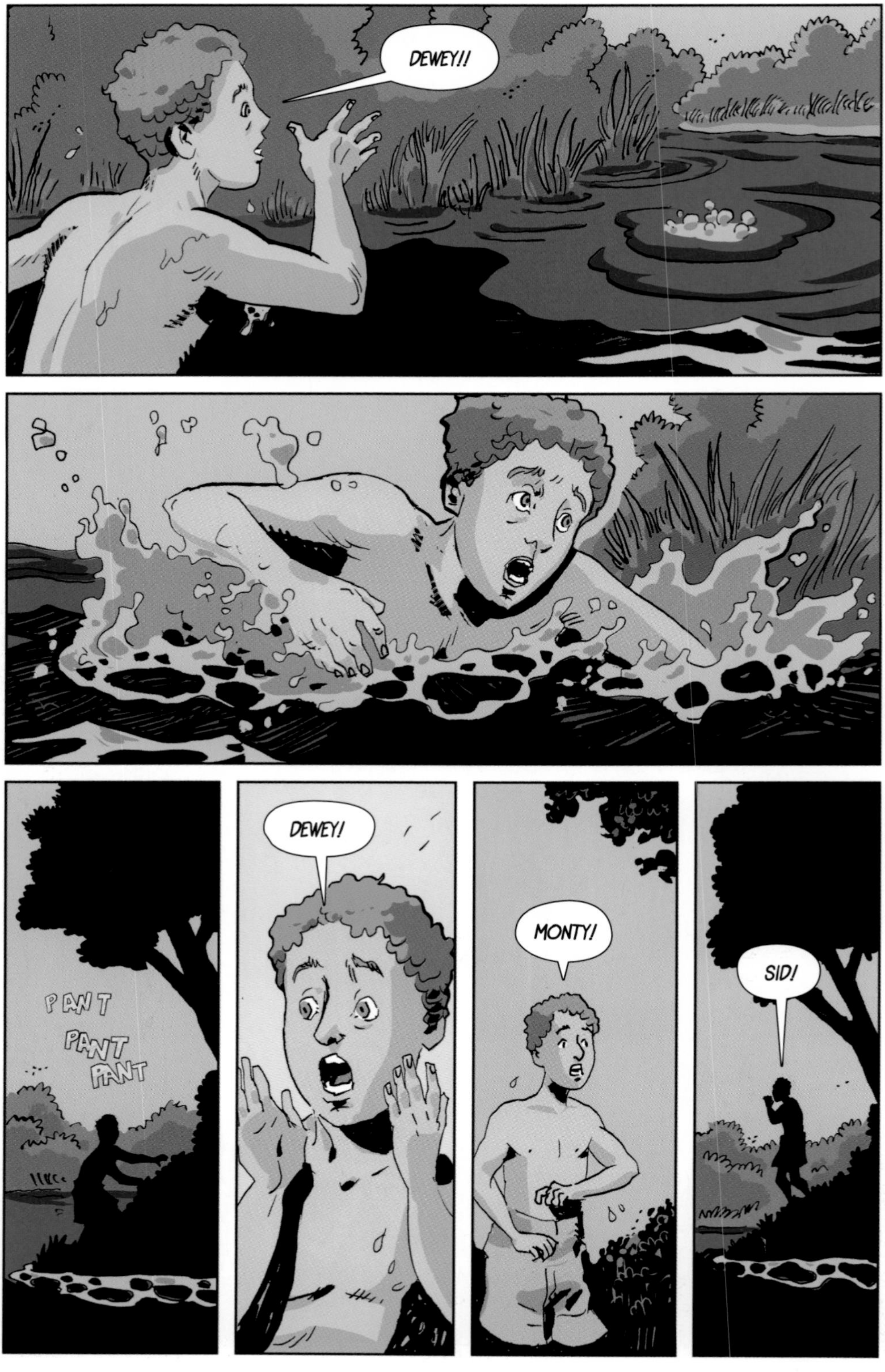
DEWEY!!
PANT
PANT
PANT
DEWEY!
MONTY!
SID!

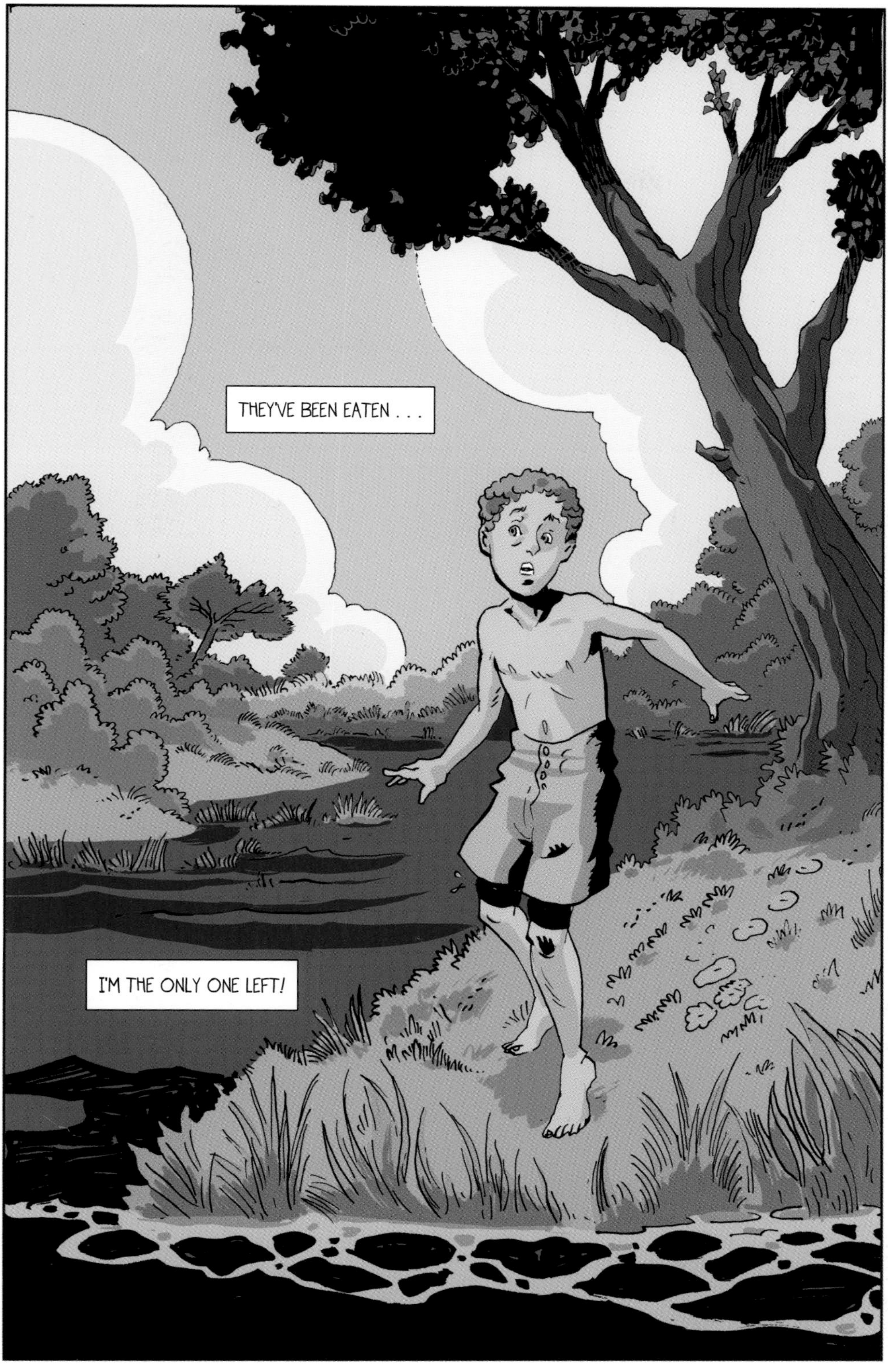
THEY'VE BEEN EATEN . . .
I'M THE ONLY ONE LEFT!

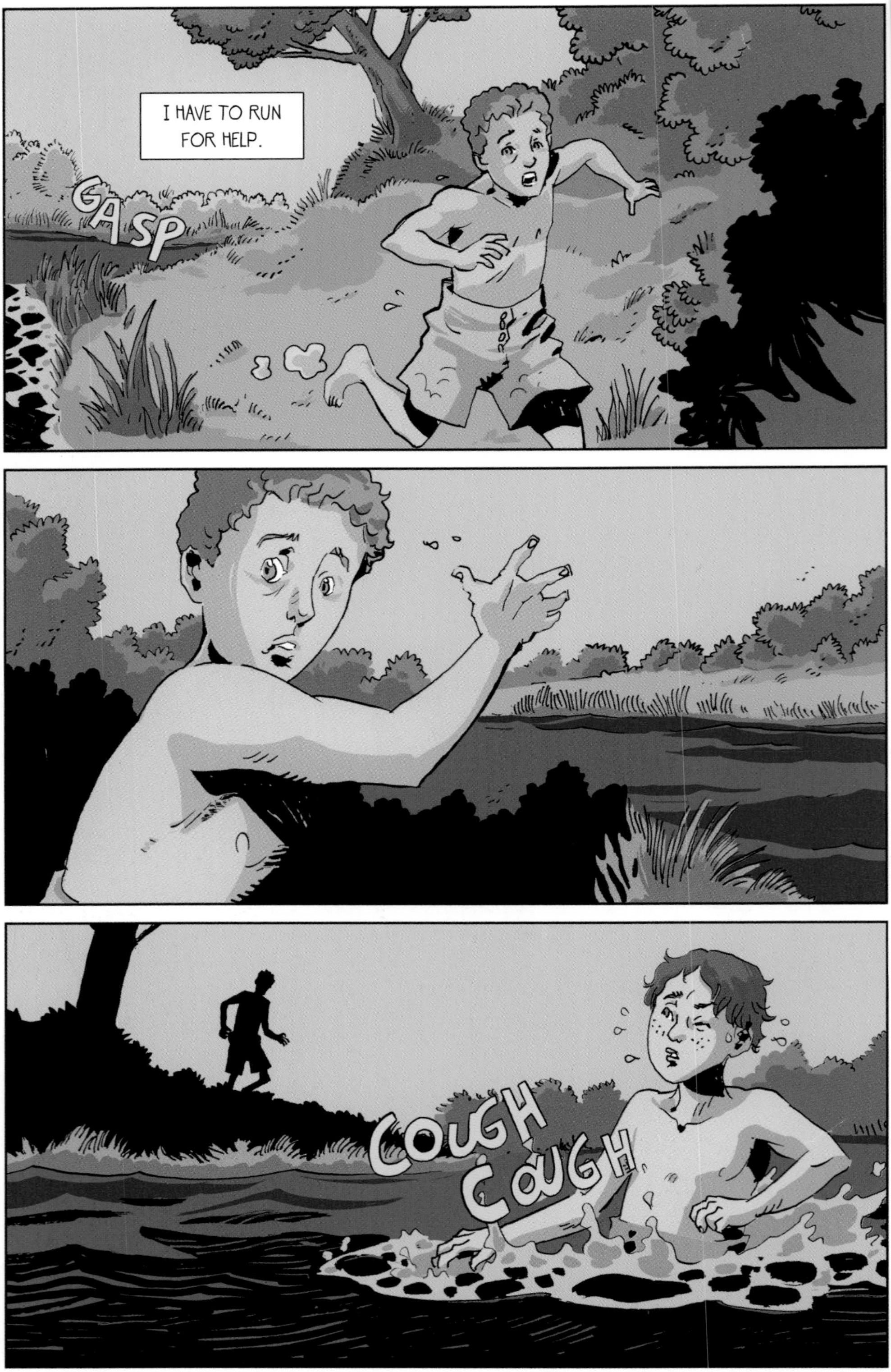
I HAVE TO RUN FOR HELP.
GASP
COUGH
COUGH

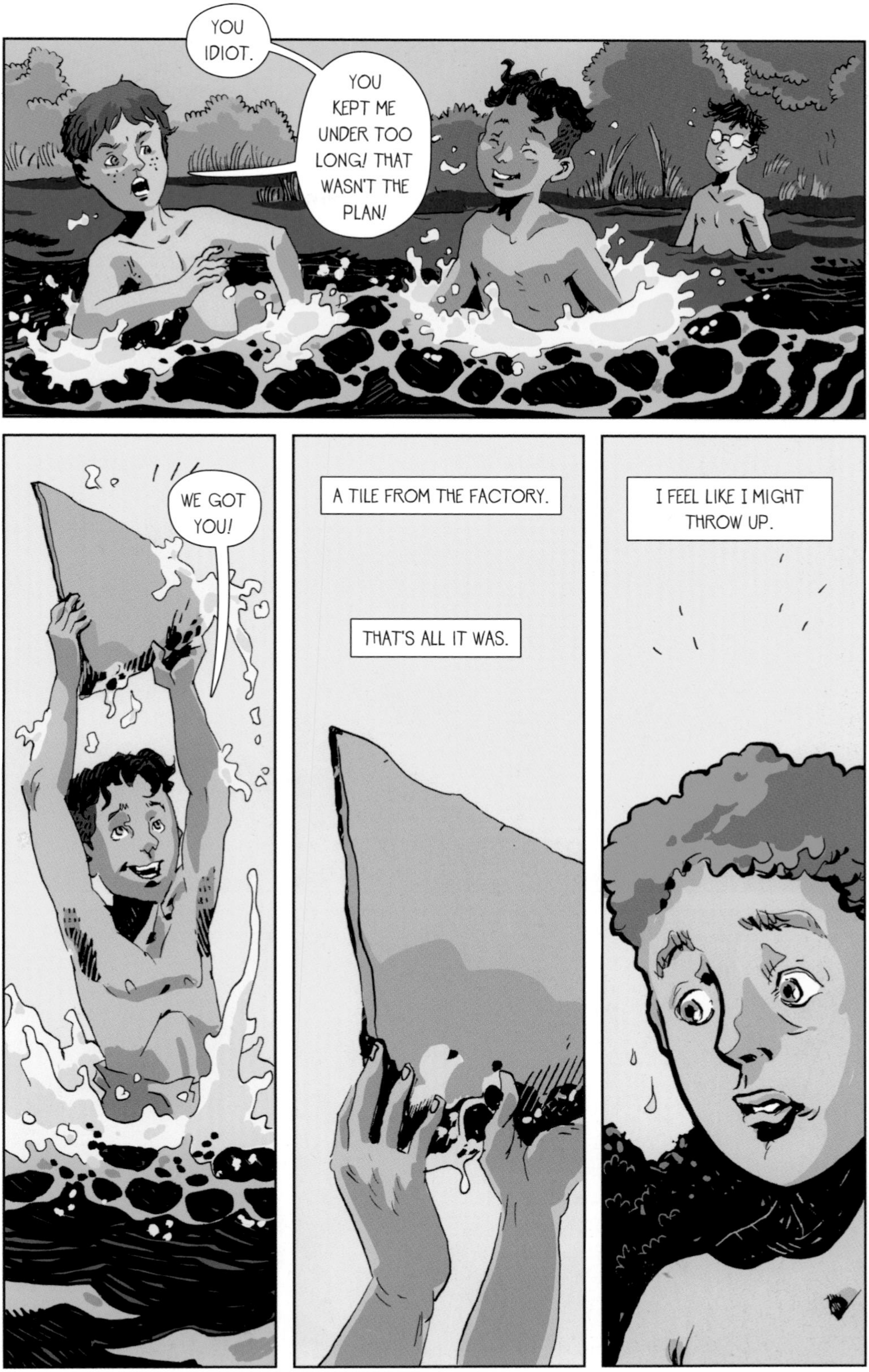
YOU IDIOT.
YOU KEPT ME UNDER TOO LONG! THAT WASN'T THE PLAN!
WE GOT YOU!
A TILE FROM THE FACTORY.
THAT'S ALL IT WAS.
I FEEL LIKE I MIGHT THROW UP.

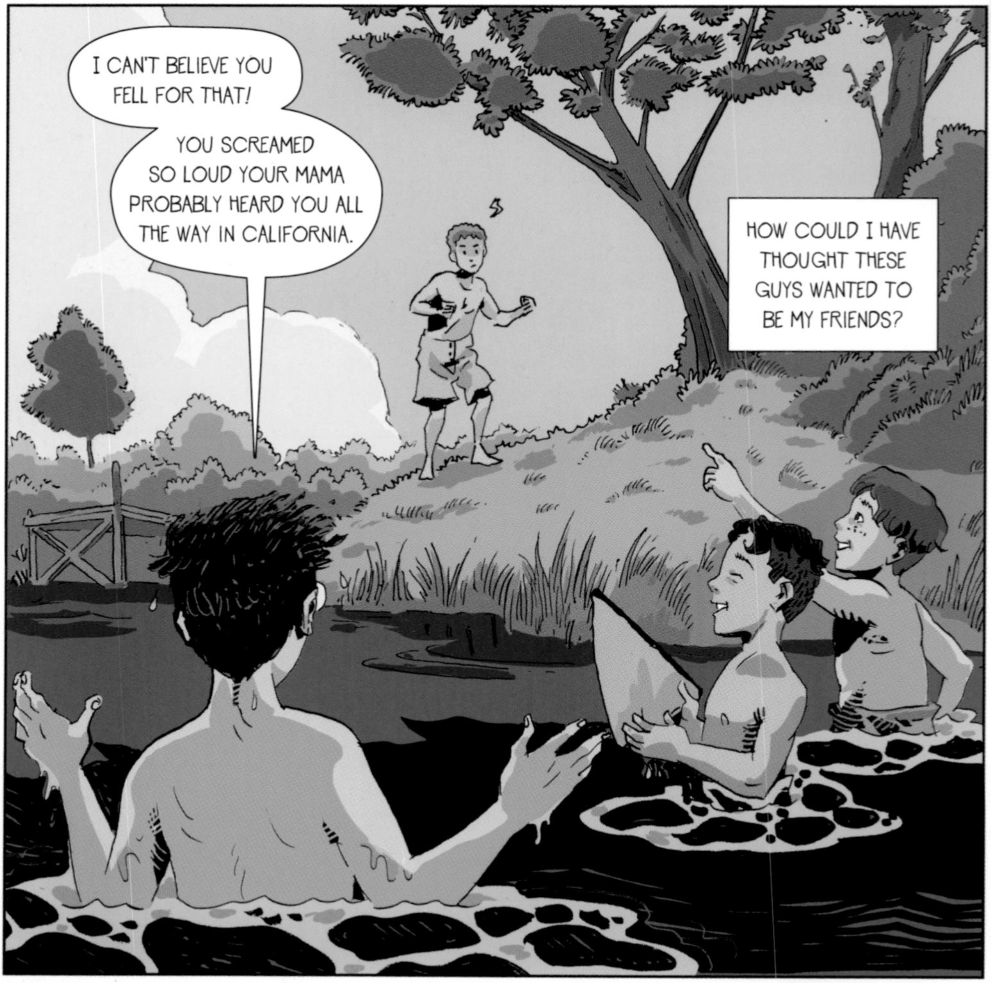
I CAN'T BELIEVE YOU FELL FOR THAT!
YOU SCREAMED SO LOUD YOUR MAMA PROBABLY HEARD YOU ALL THE WAY IN CALIFORNIA.
HOW COULD I HAVE THOUGHT THESE GUYS WANTED TO BE MY FRIENDS?

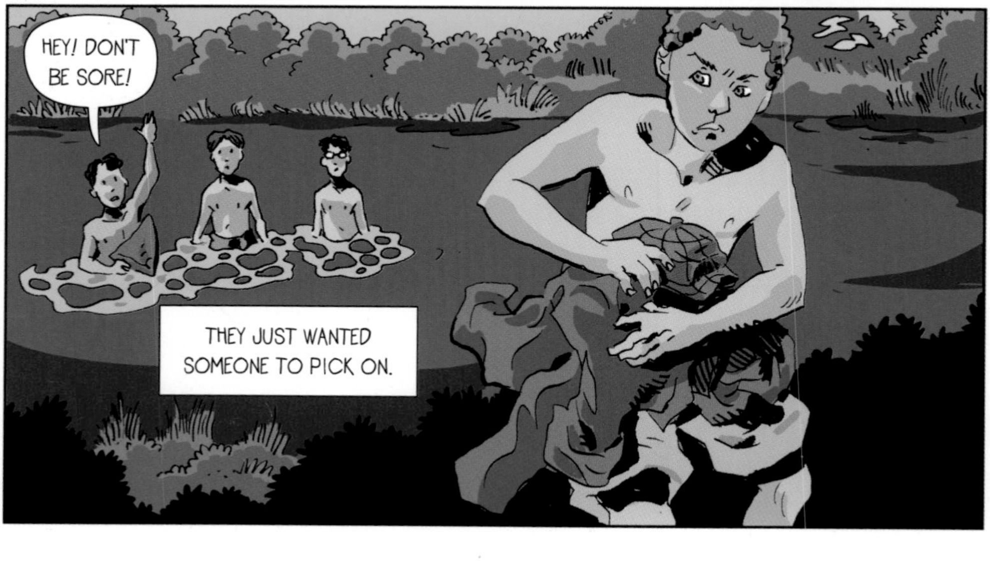
HEY! DON'T BE SORE!
THEY JUST WANTED SOMEONE TO PICK ON.

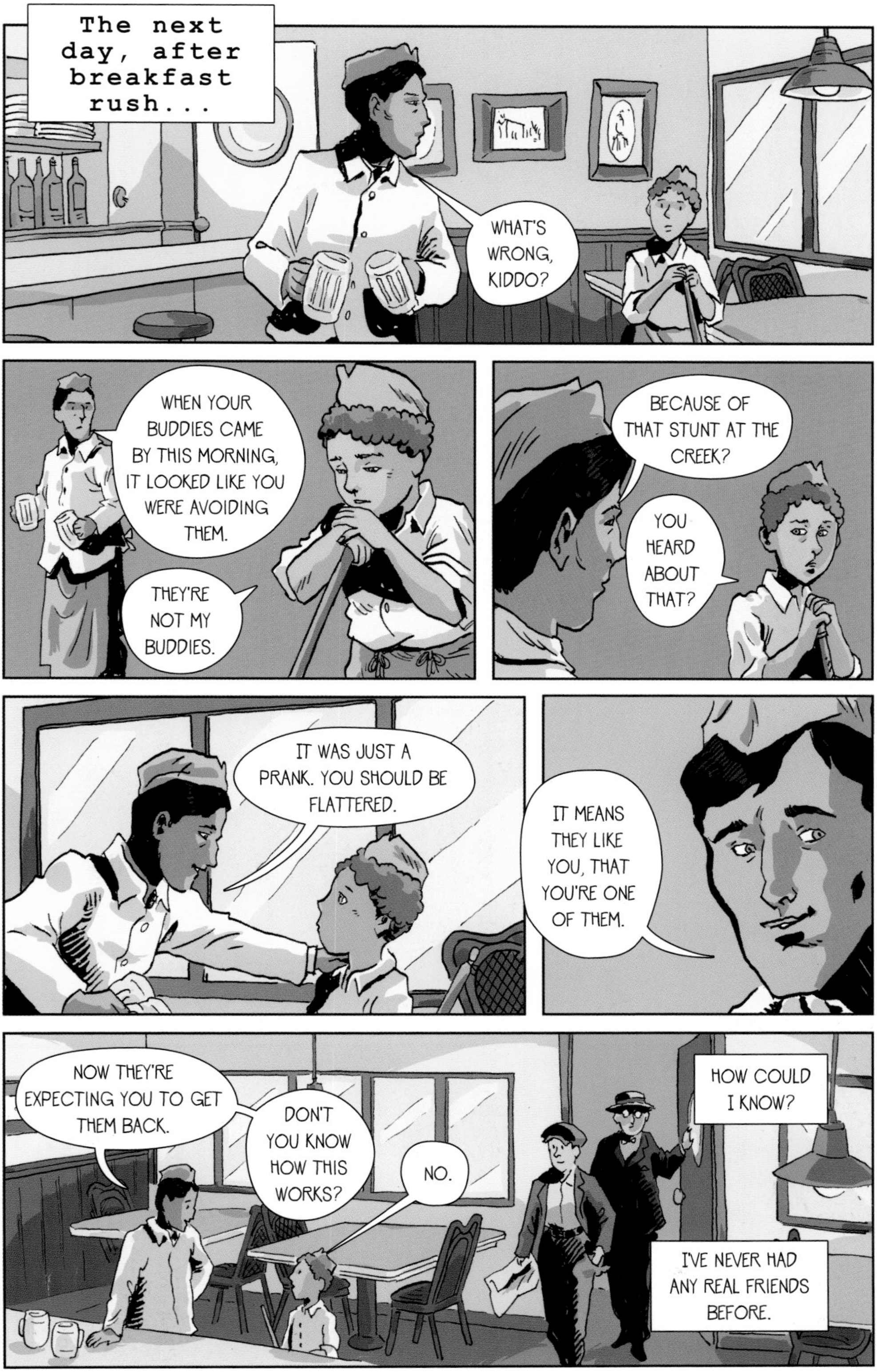
The next day, after breakfast rush...
WHAT'S WRONG, KIDDO?
WHEN YOUR BUDDIES CAME BY THIS MORNING, IT LOOKED LIKE YOU WERE AVOIDING THEM.
THEY'RE NOT MY BUDDIES.
BECAUSE OF THAT STUNT AT THE CREEK?
YOU HEARD ABOUT THAT?
IT WAS JUST A PRANK. YOU SHOULD BE FLATTERED.
IT MEANS THEY LIKE YOU, THAT YOU'RE ONE OF THEM.
NOW THEY'RE EXPECTING YOU TO GET THEM BACK.
DON'T YOU KNOW HOW THIS WORKS?
NO.
HOW COULD I KNOW?
I'VE NEVER HAD ANY REAL FRIENDS BEFORE.

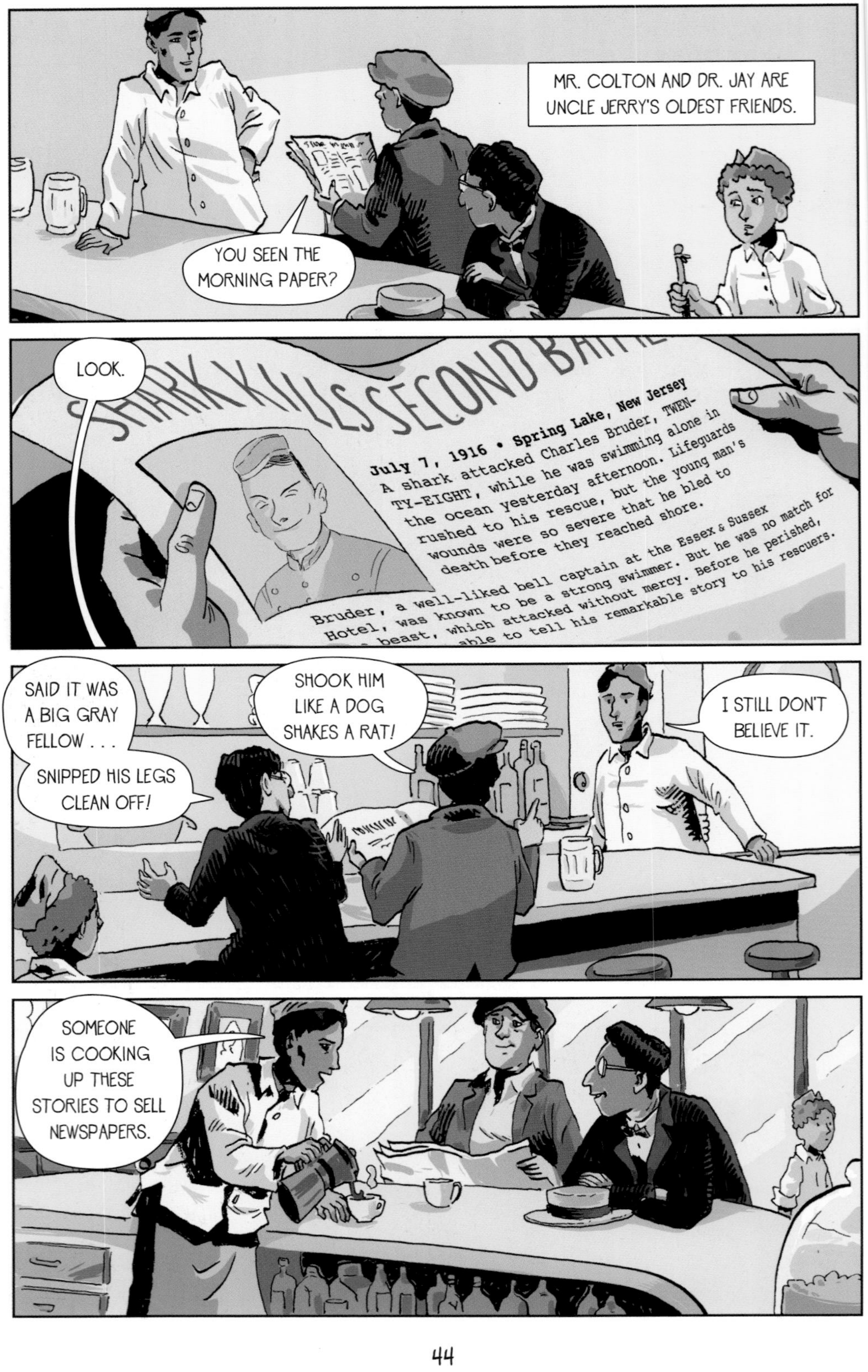

MR. COLTON AND DR. JAY ARE UNCLE JERRY'S OLDEST FRIENDS.
YOU SEEN THE MORNING PAPER?
LOOK.
SHARK KILLS SECOND
July 7, 1916 • Spring Lake, New Jersey
A shark attacked Charles Bruder, TWENTY-EIGHT, while he was swimming alone in the ocean yesterday afternoon. Lifeguards rushed to his rescue, but the young man's wounds were so severe that he bled to death before they reached shore.
Bruder, a well-liked bell captain at the Essex & Sussex Hotel, was known to be a strong swimmer. But he was no match for beast, which attacked without mercy. Before he perished, able to tell his remarkable story to his rescuers.
SAID IT WAS A BIG GRAY FELLOW . . .
SHOOK HIM LIKE A DOG SHAKES A RAT!
I STILL DON'T BELIEVE IT.
SNIPPED HIS LEGS CLEAN OFF!
SOMEONE IS COOKING UP THESE STORIES TO SELL NEWSPAPERS.

COULD BE.

BUT MY WIFE'S COUSIN LIVES OUT THERE AND SHE SAYS NOBODY WILL GO NEAR THE OCEAN.

THEY HAVE FISHERMEN WITH RIFLES SHOOTING ANYTHING THAT MOVES.

YOU KNOW WHAT THIS REMINDS ME OF?

THE CREEK DEVIL.

WHAT'S THAT?

OLD-TIMERS SAY THERE'S A MONSTER THAT LIVES DOWN NEAR THE CREEK.

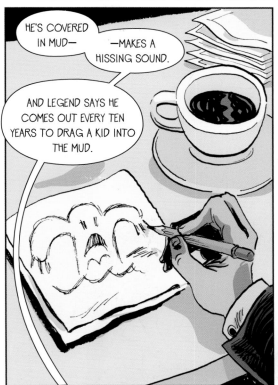

HE'S COVERED IN MUD—

—MAKES A HISSING SOUND.

AND LEGEND SAYS HE COMES OUT EVERY TEN YEARS TO DRAG A KID INTO THE MUD.

PEOPLE BELIEVE THAT?

EVERYONE IN TOWN KNOWS THE LEGEND.

BUT NOBODY REALLY BELIEVES IT.

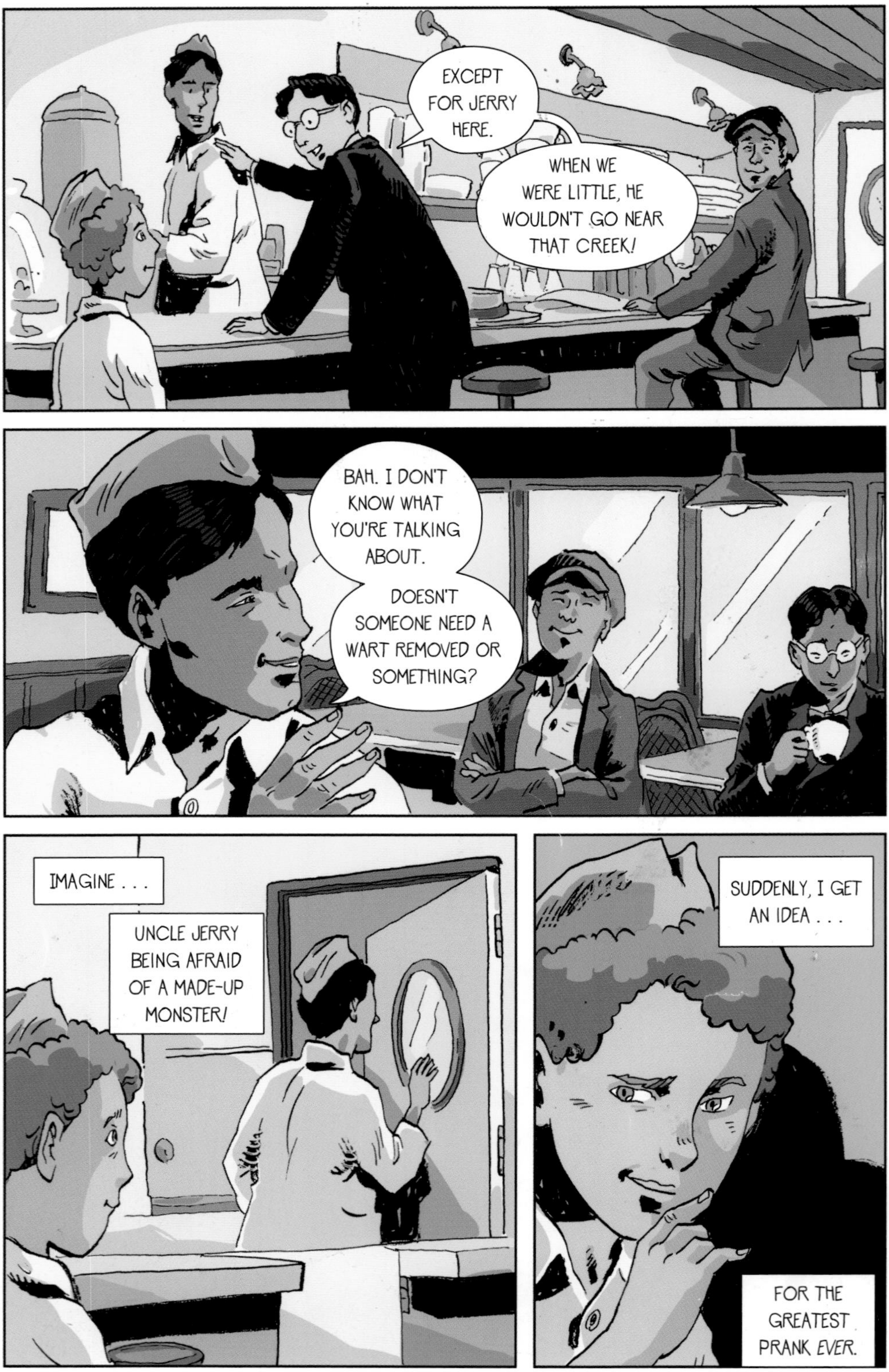
EXCEPT FOR JERRY HERE.
WHEN WE WERE LITTLE, HE WOULDN'T GO NEAR THAT CREEK!
BAH. I DON'T KNOW WHAT YOU'RE TALKING ABOUT.
DOESN'T SOMEONE NEED A WART REMOVED OR SOMETHING?
IMAGINE . . .
UNCLE JERRY BEING AFRAID OF A MADE-UP MONSTER!
SUDDENLY, I GET AN IDEA . . .
FOR THE GREATEST PRANK EVER.

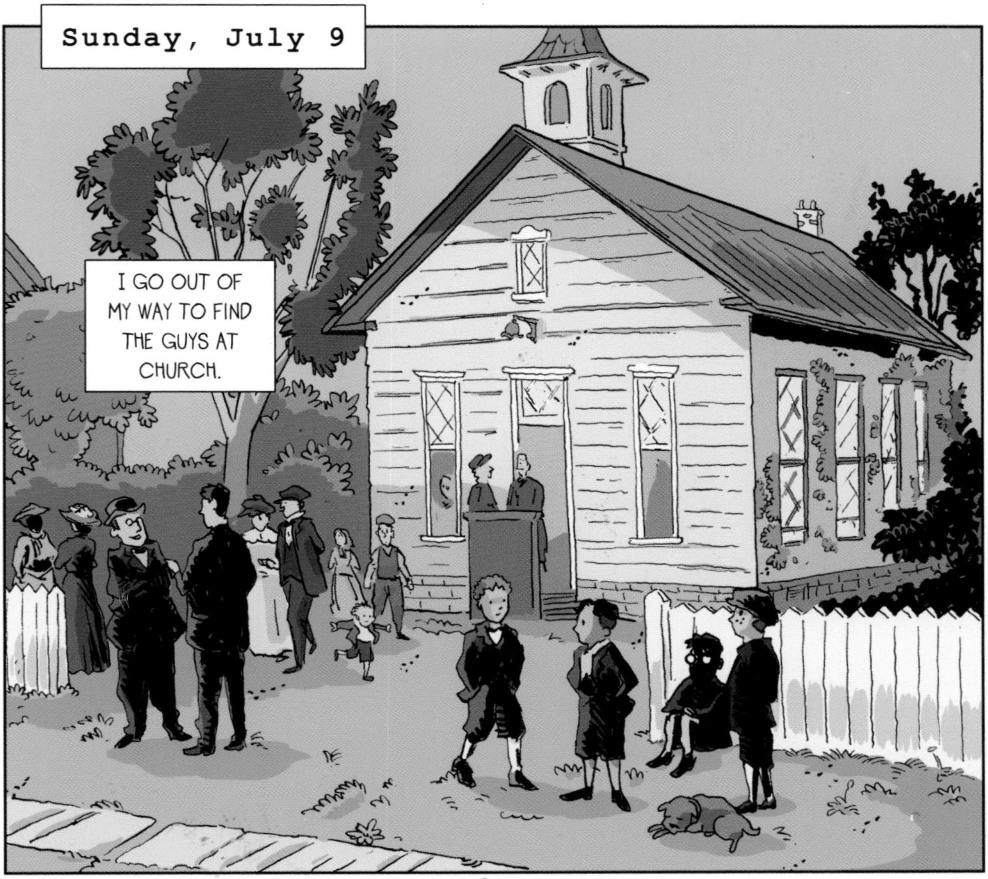
Sunday, July 9
I GO OUT OF MY WAY TO FIND THE GUYS AT CHURCH.

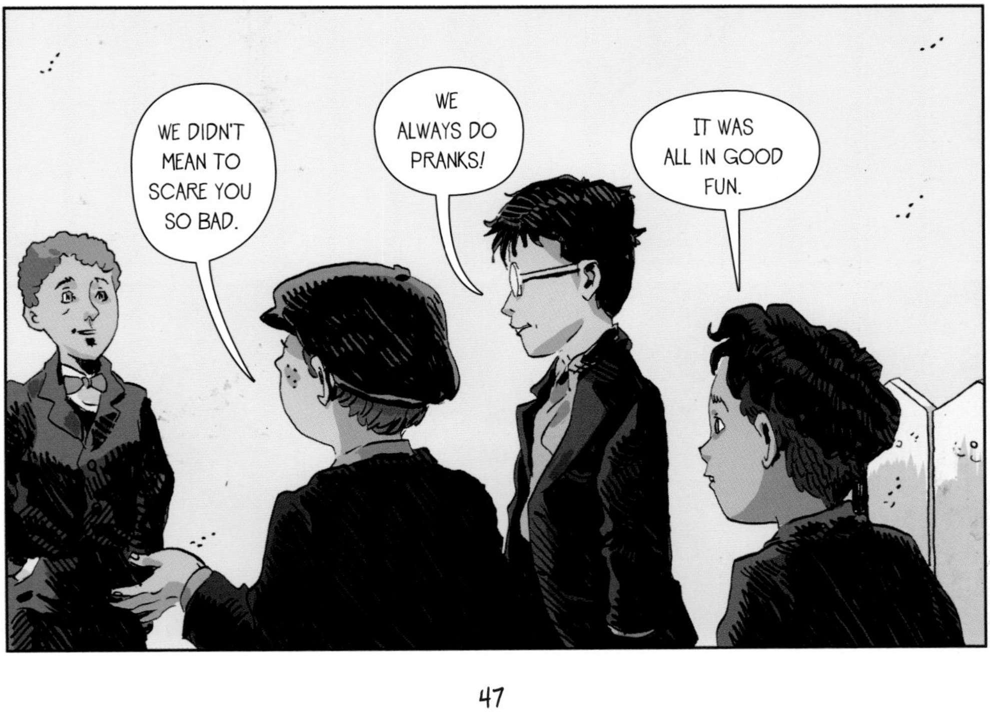
WE DIDN'T MEAN TO SCARE YOU SO BAD.
WE ALWAYS DO PRANKS!
IT WAS ALL IN GOOD FUN.

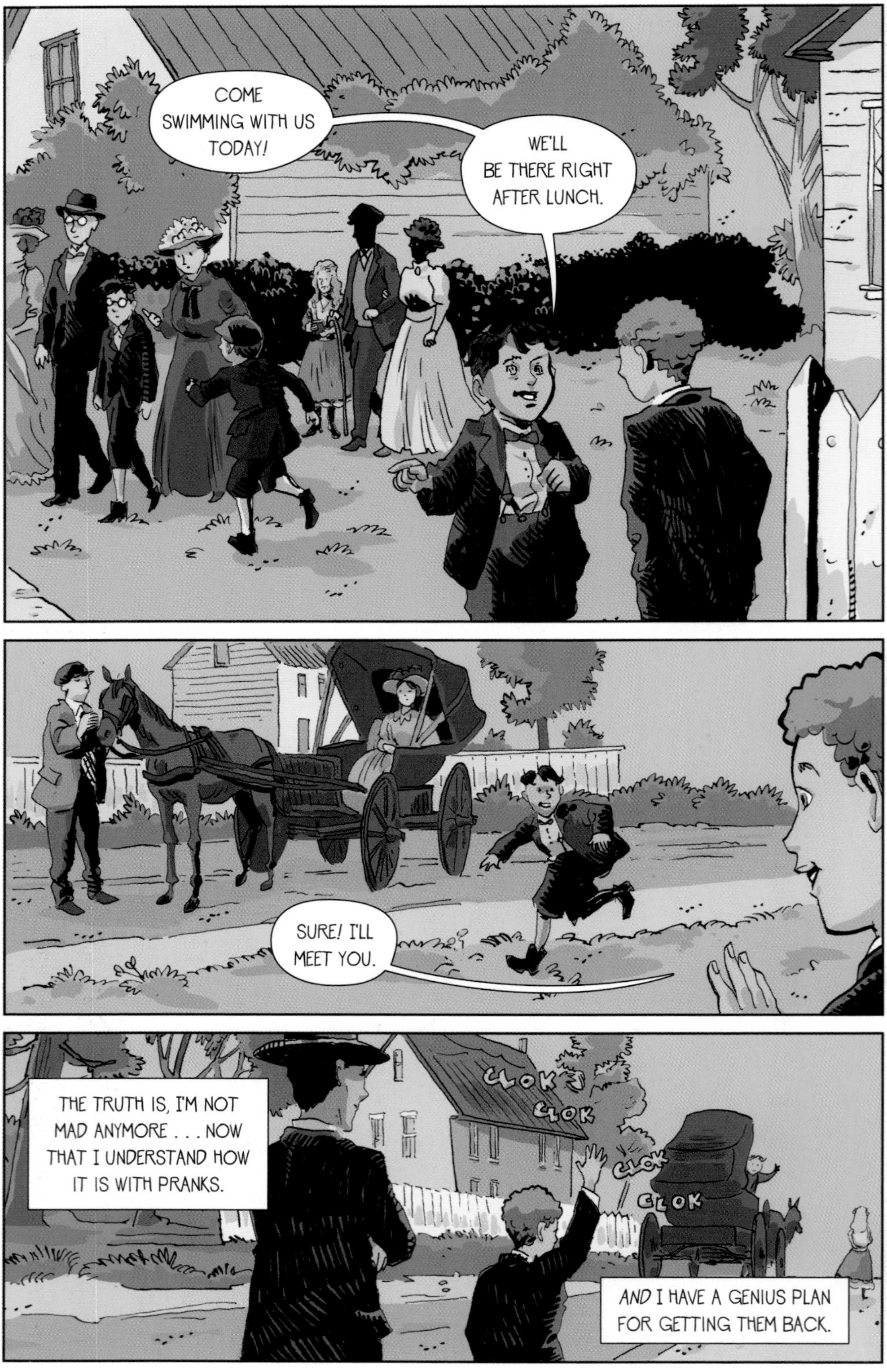
COME SWIMMING WITH US TODAY!
WE'LL BE THERE RIGHT AFTER LUNCH.
SURE! I'LL MEET YOU.
THE TRUTH IS, I'M NOT MAD ANYMORE . . . NOW THAT I UNDERSTAND HOW IT IS WITH PRANKS.
CLOK
CLOK
CLOK
CLOK
AND I HAVE A GENIUS PLAN FOR GETTING THEM BACK.

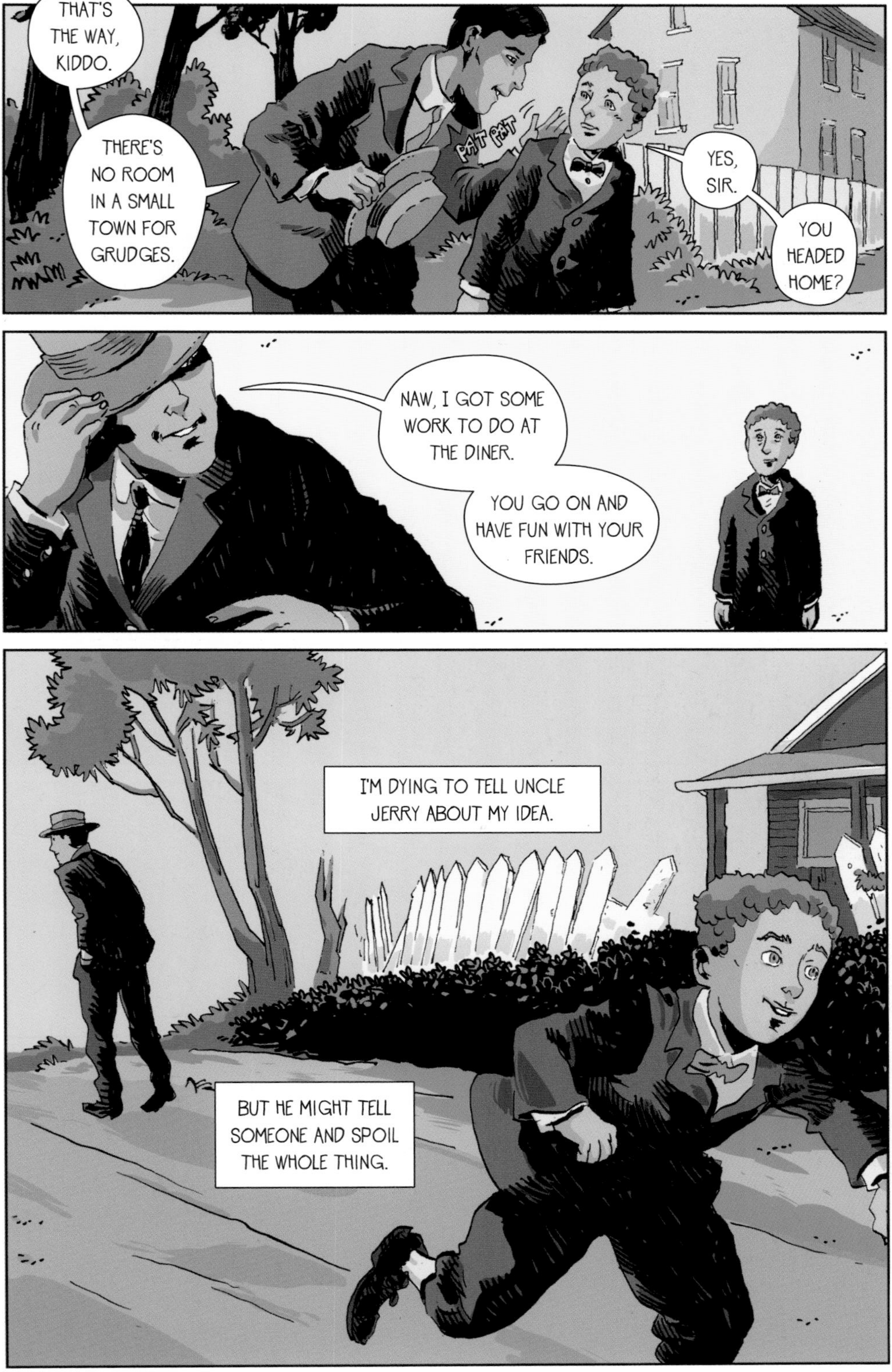
THAT'S THE WAY, KIDDO.
THERE'S NO ROOM IN A SMALL TOWN FOR GRUDGES.
PAT PAT
YES, SIR.
YOU HEADED HOME?
NAW, I GOT SOME WORK TO DO AT THE DINER.
YOU GO ON AND HAVE FUN WITH YOUR FRIENDS.
I'M DYING TO TELL UNCLE JERRY ABOUT MY IDEA.
BUT HE MIGHT TELL SOMEONE AND SPOIL THE WHOLE THING.

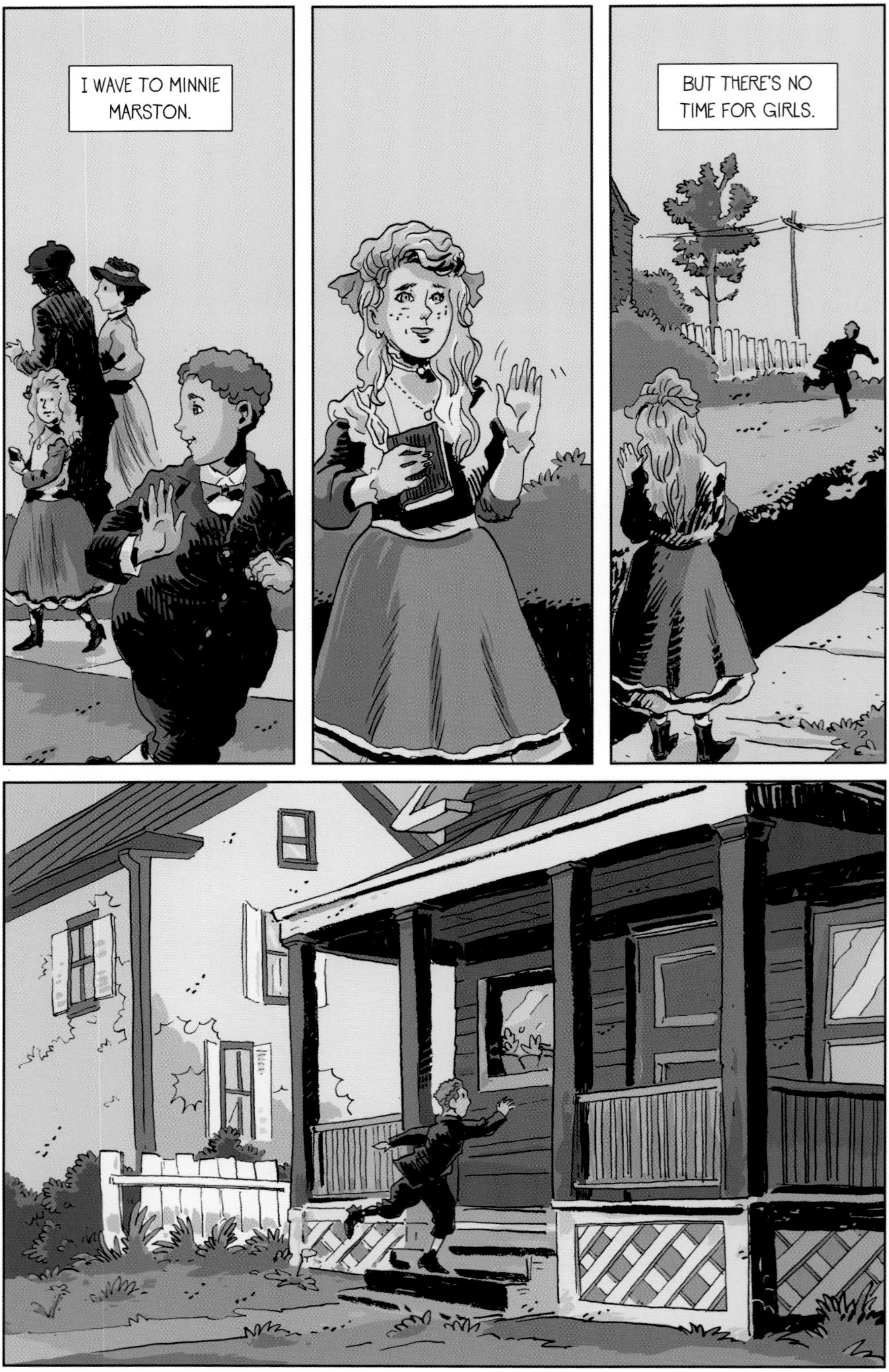
I WAVE TO MINNIE MARSTON.
BUT THERE'S NO TIME FOR GIRLS.

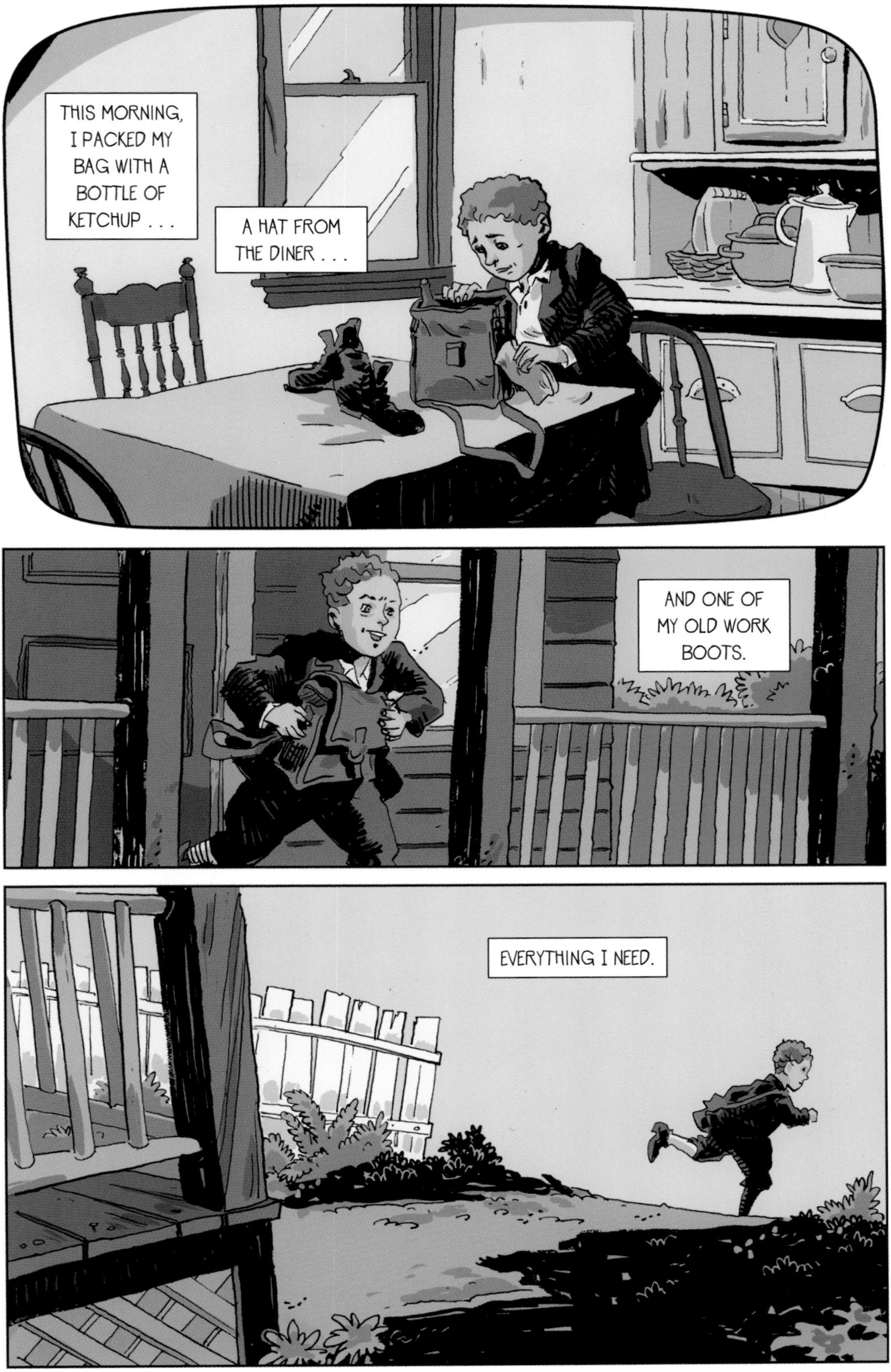
THIS MORNING, I PACKED MY BAG WITH A BOTTLE OF KETCHUP . . .
A HAT FROM THE DINER . . .
AND ONE OF MY OLD WORK BOOTS.
EVERYTHING I NEED.

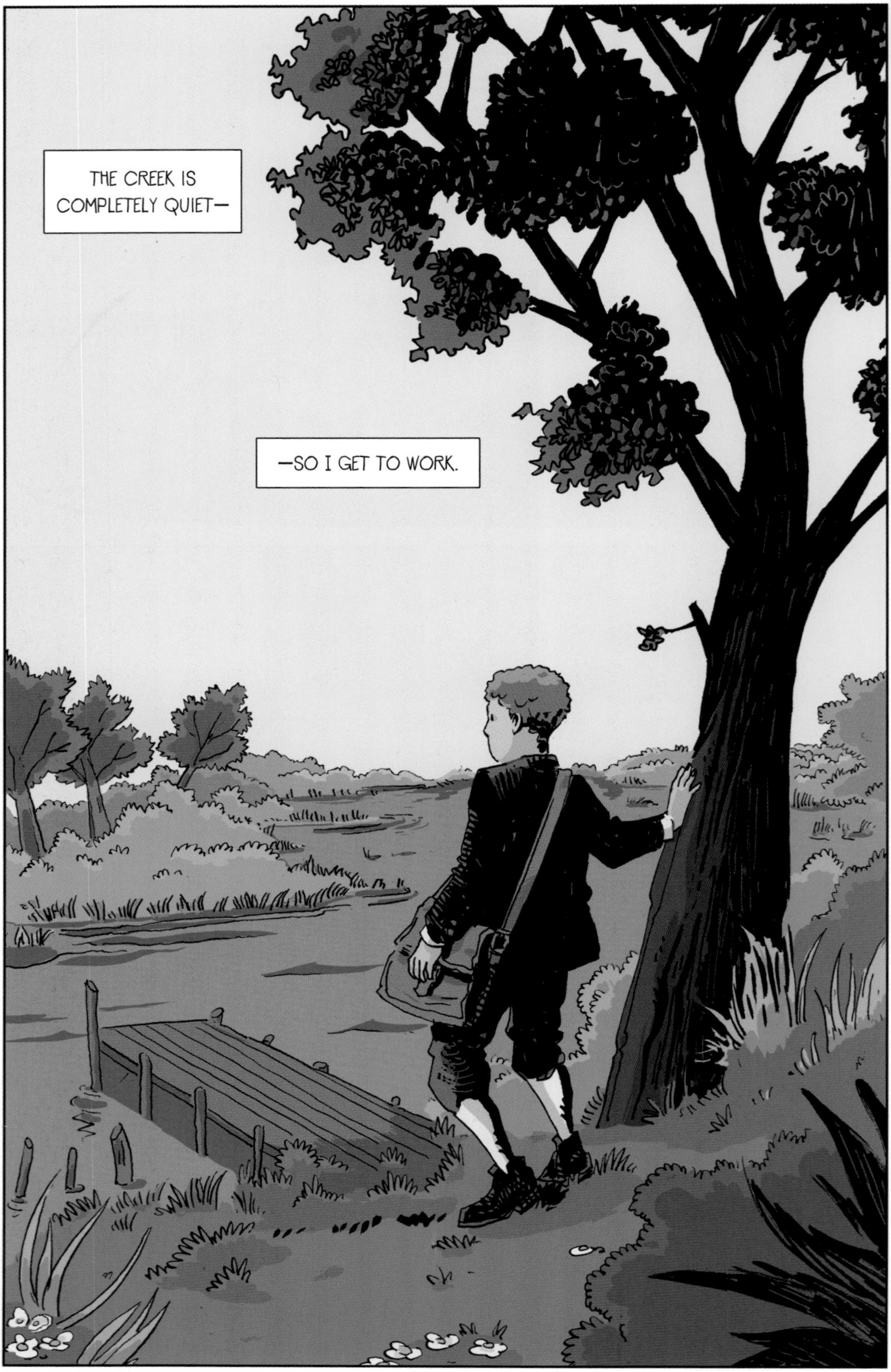
THE CREEK IS COMPLETELY QUIET—
—SO I GET TO WORK.

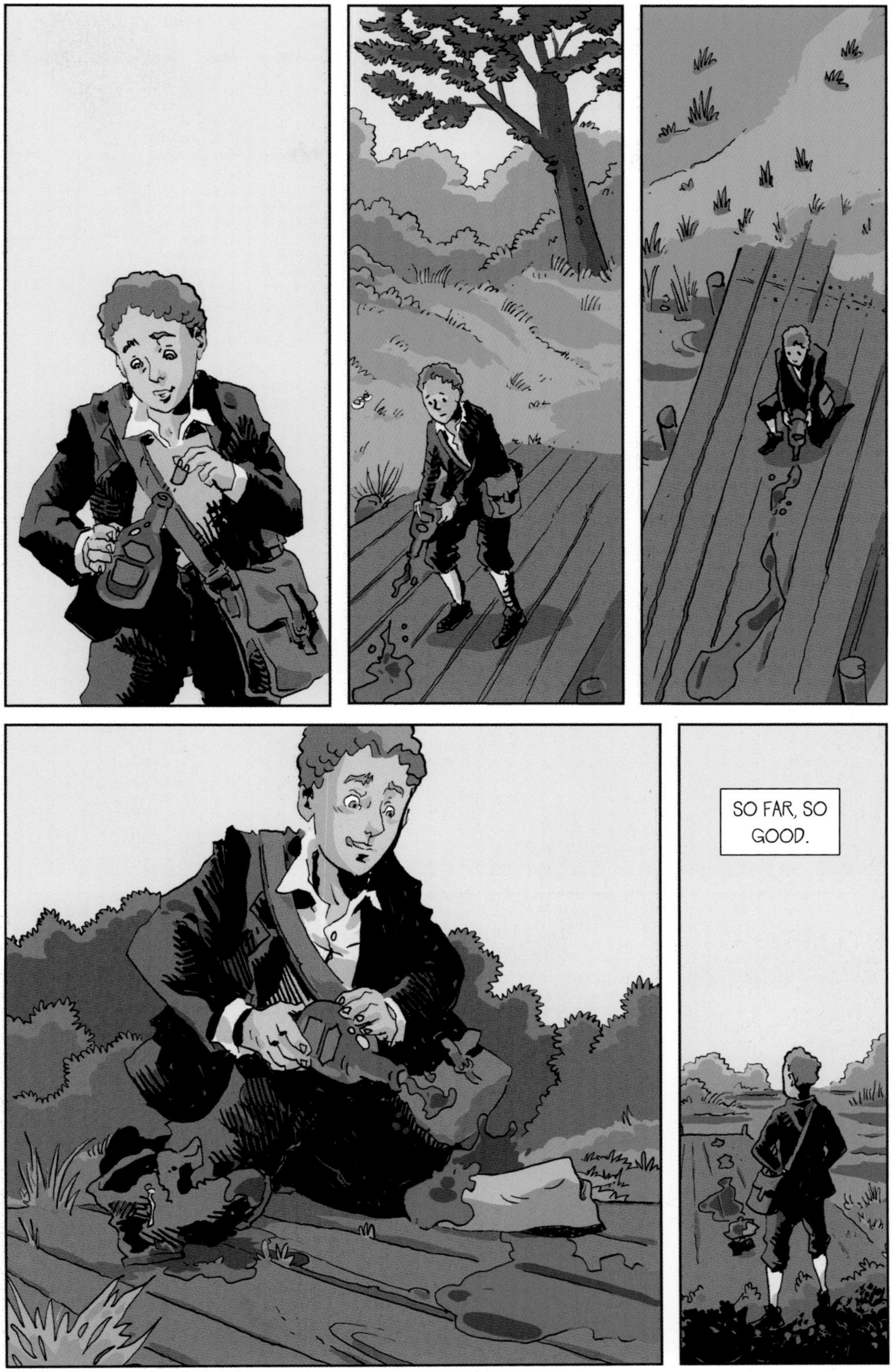
SO FAR, SO GOOD.

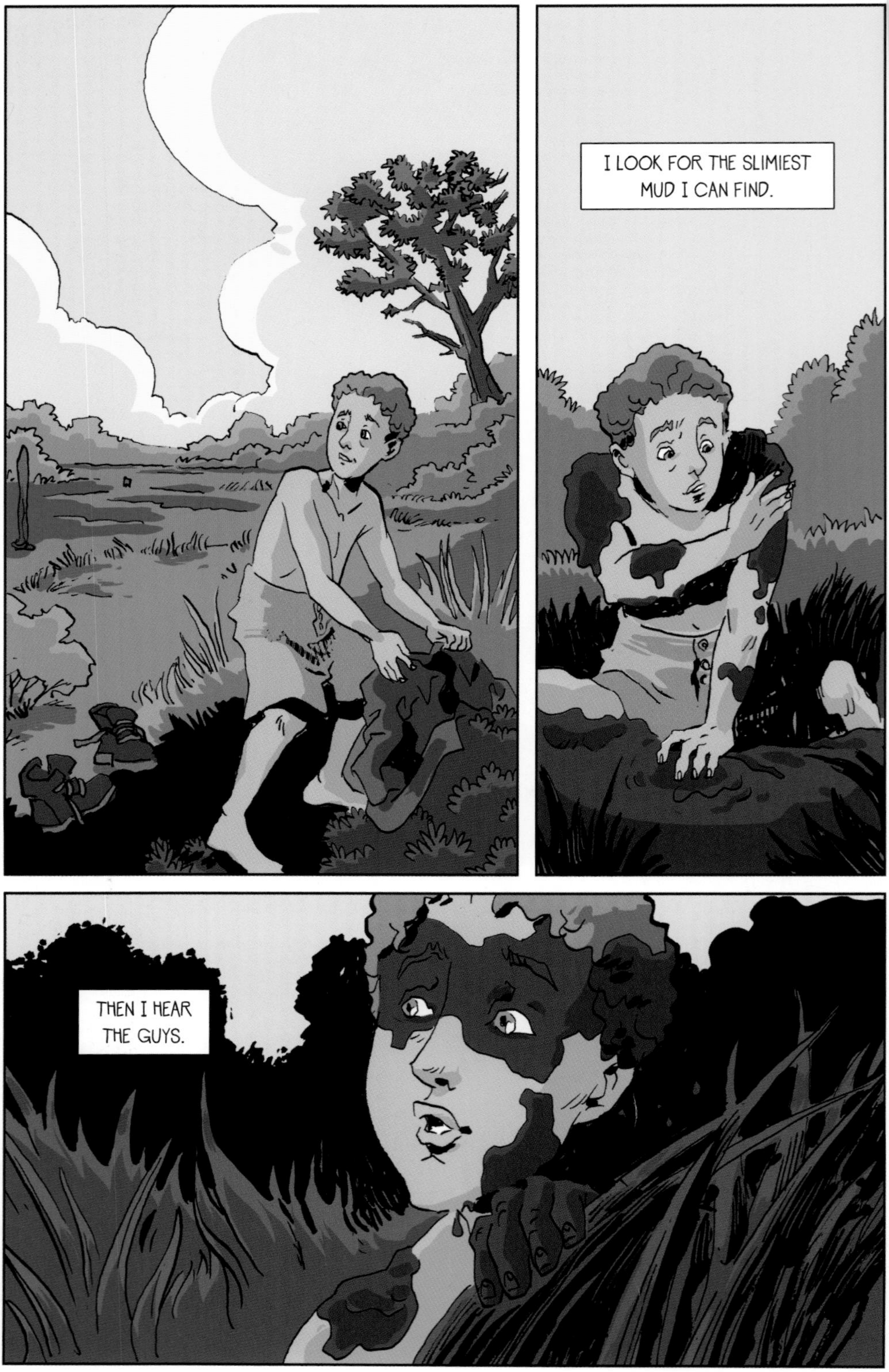
I LOOK FOR THE SLIMIEST
MUD I CAN FIND.
THEN I HEAR
THE GUYS.

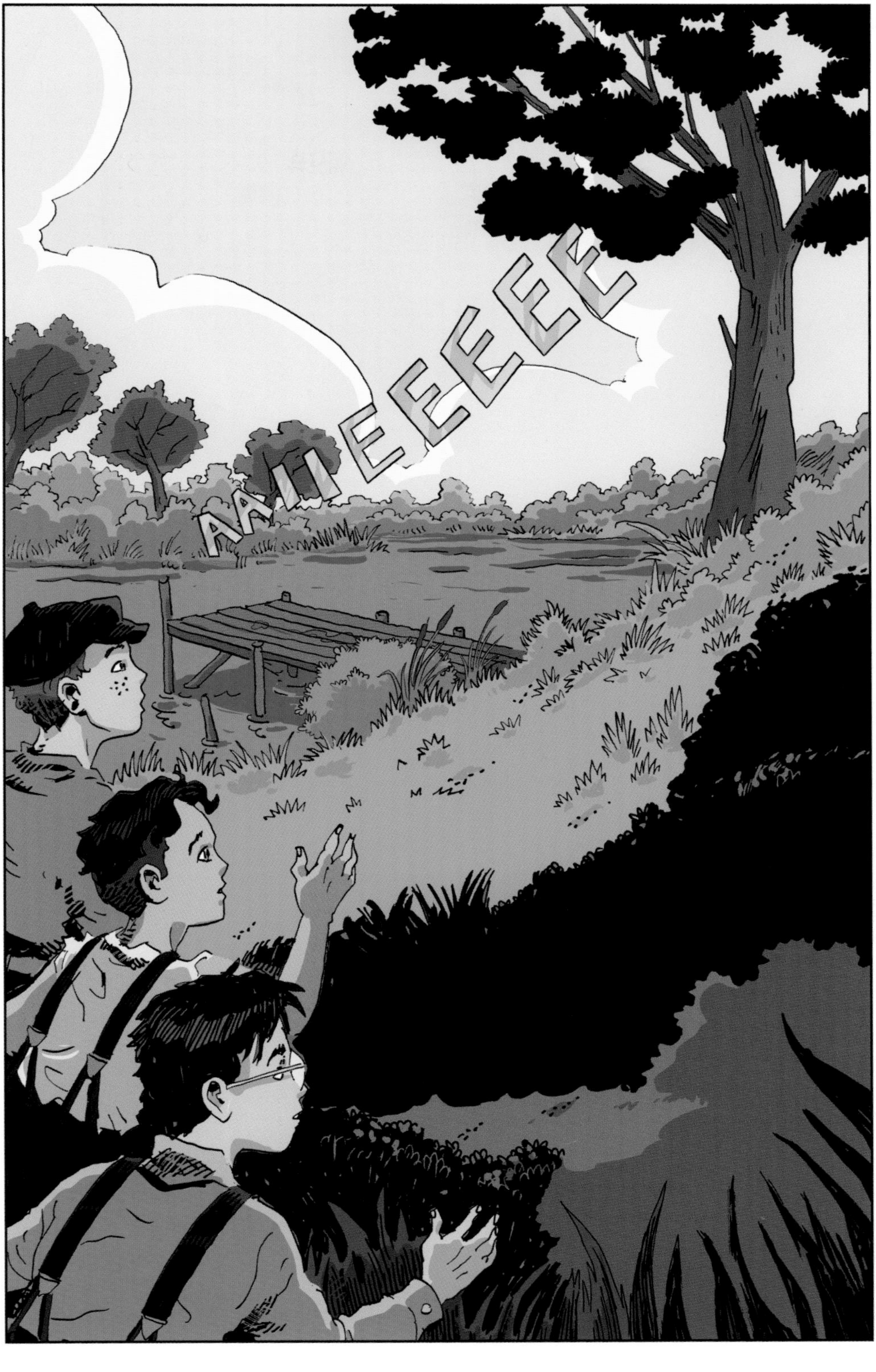
AAIIEEEEEE

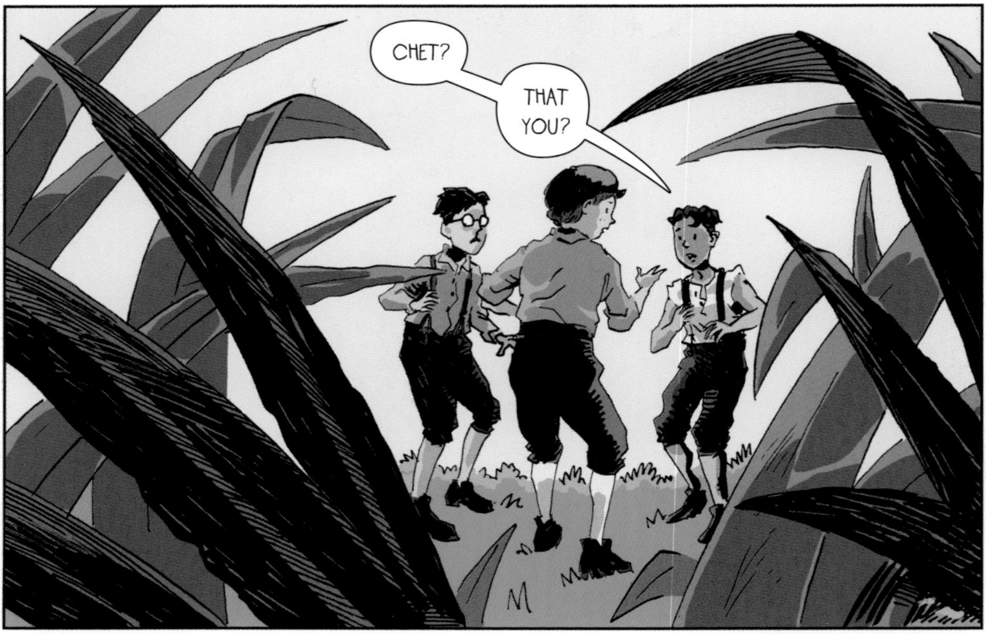
CHET?
THAT YOU?

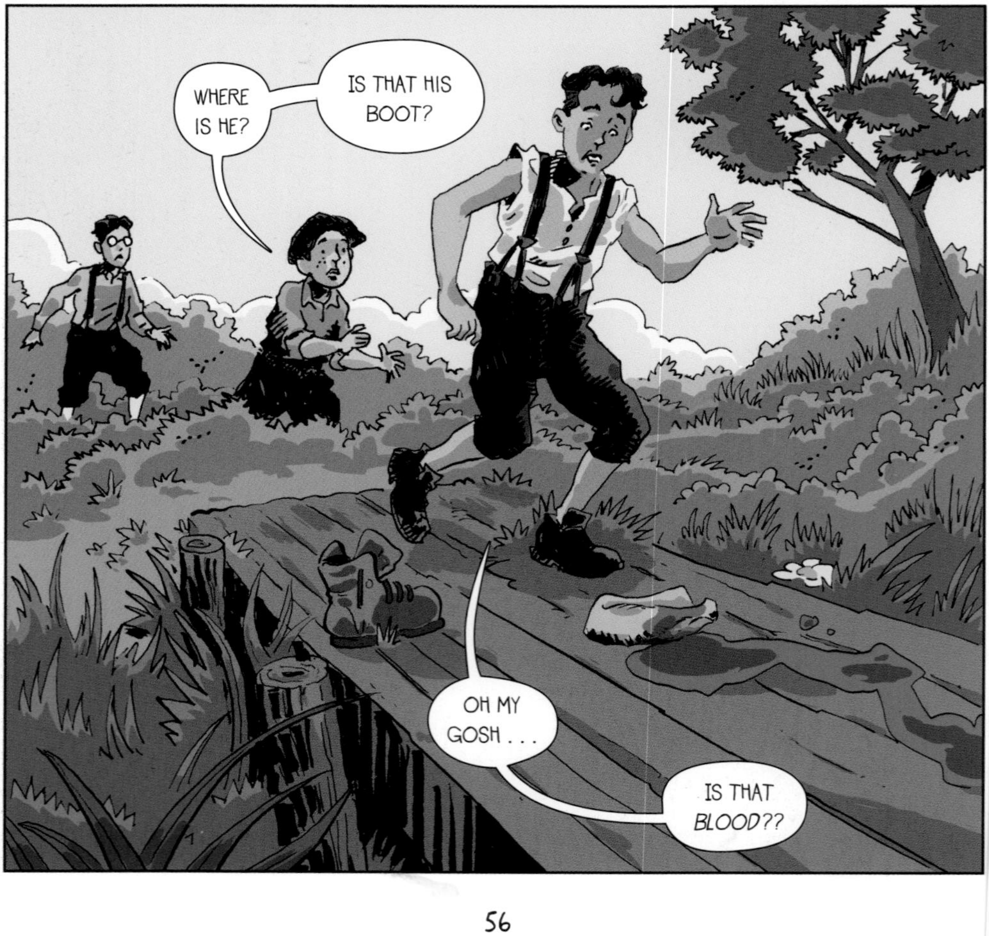
WHERE IS HE?
IS THAT HIS BOOT?
OH MY GOSH . . .
IS THAT *BLOOD??*

WHAT WAS THAT?!

QUIET!

SHOULD WE GET SOMEONE?

WHAT'S HAPPENING?

MOOAANNN

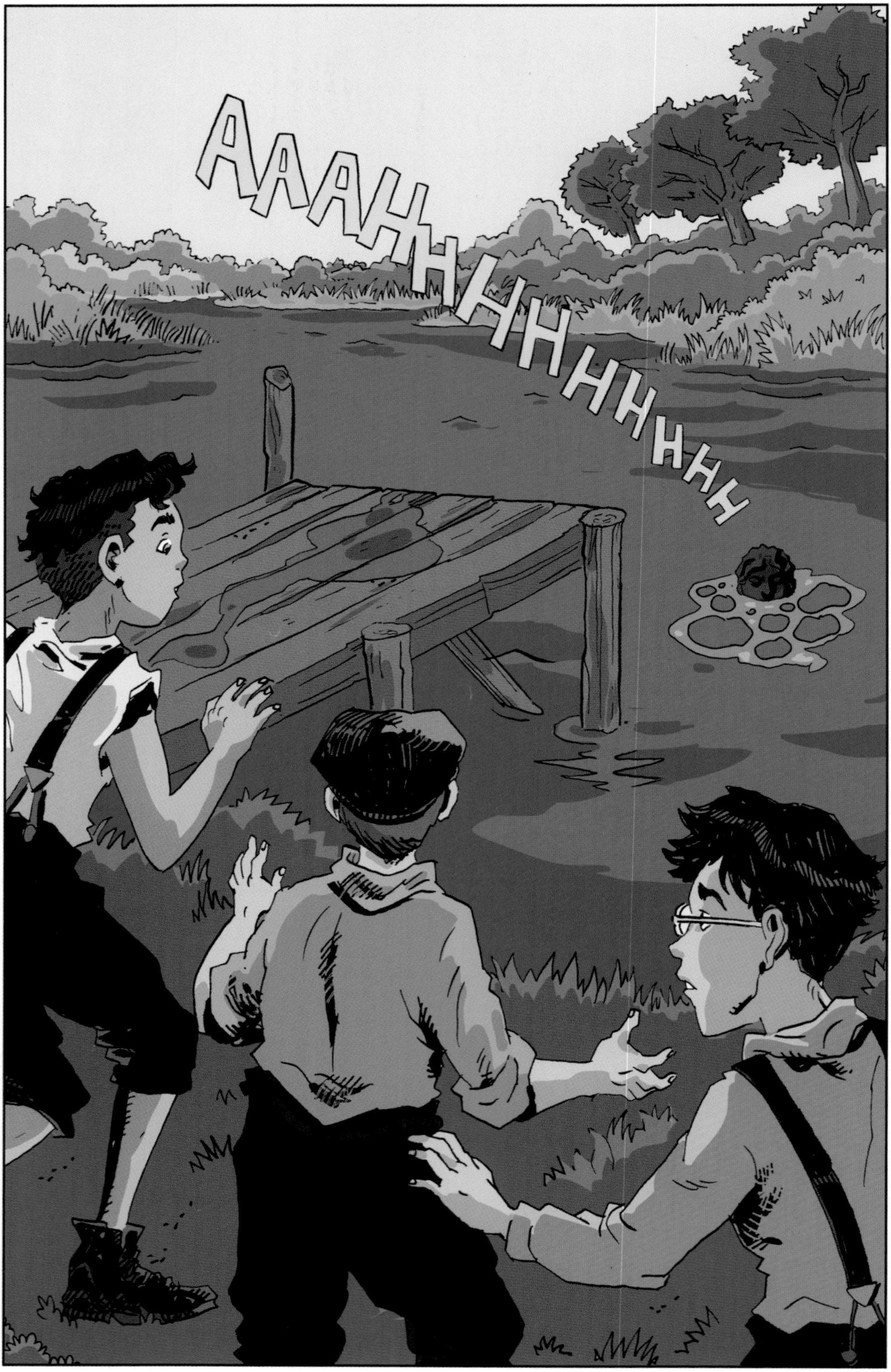
AAAHHHHHHHHHHH

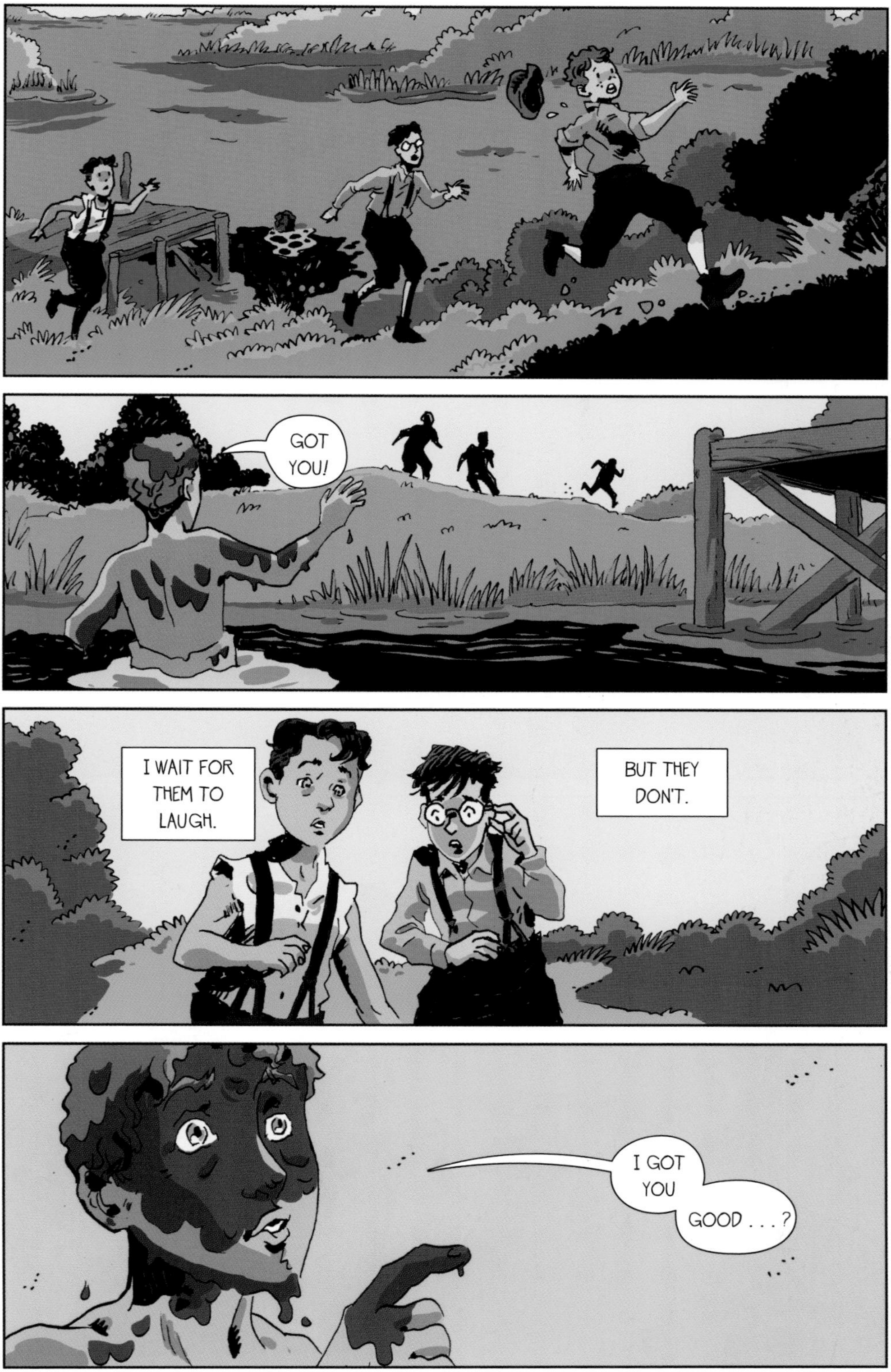
GOT YOU!
I WAIT FOR THEM TO LAUGH.
BUT THEY DON'T.
I GOT YOU GOOD . . . ?

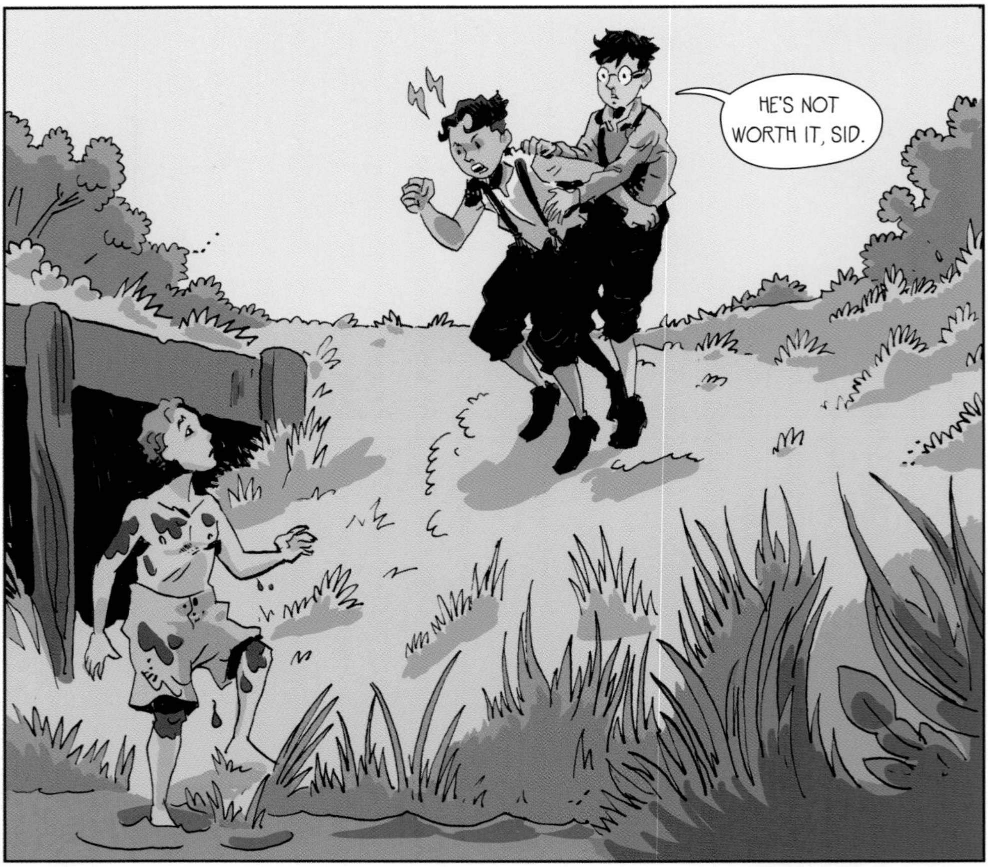
HE'S NOT WORTH IT, SID.

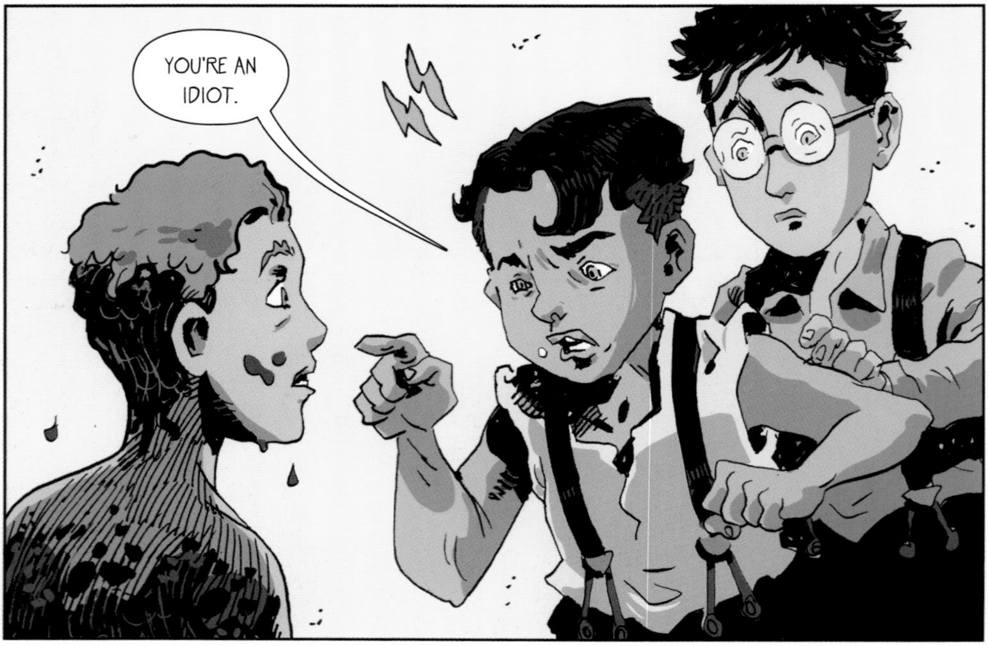
YOU'RE AN IDIOT.

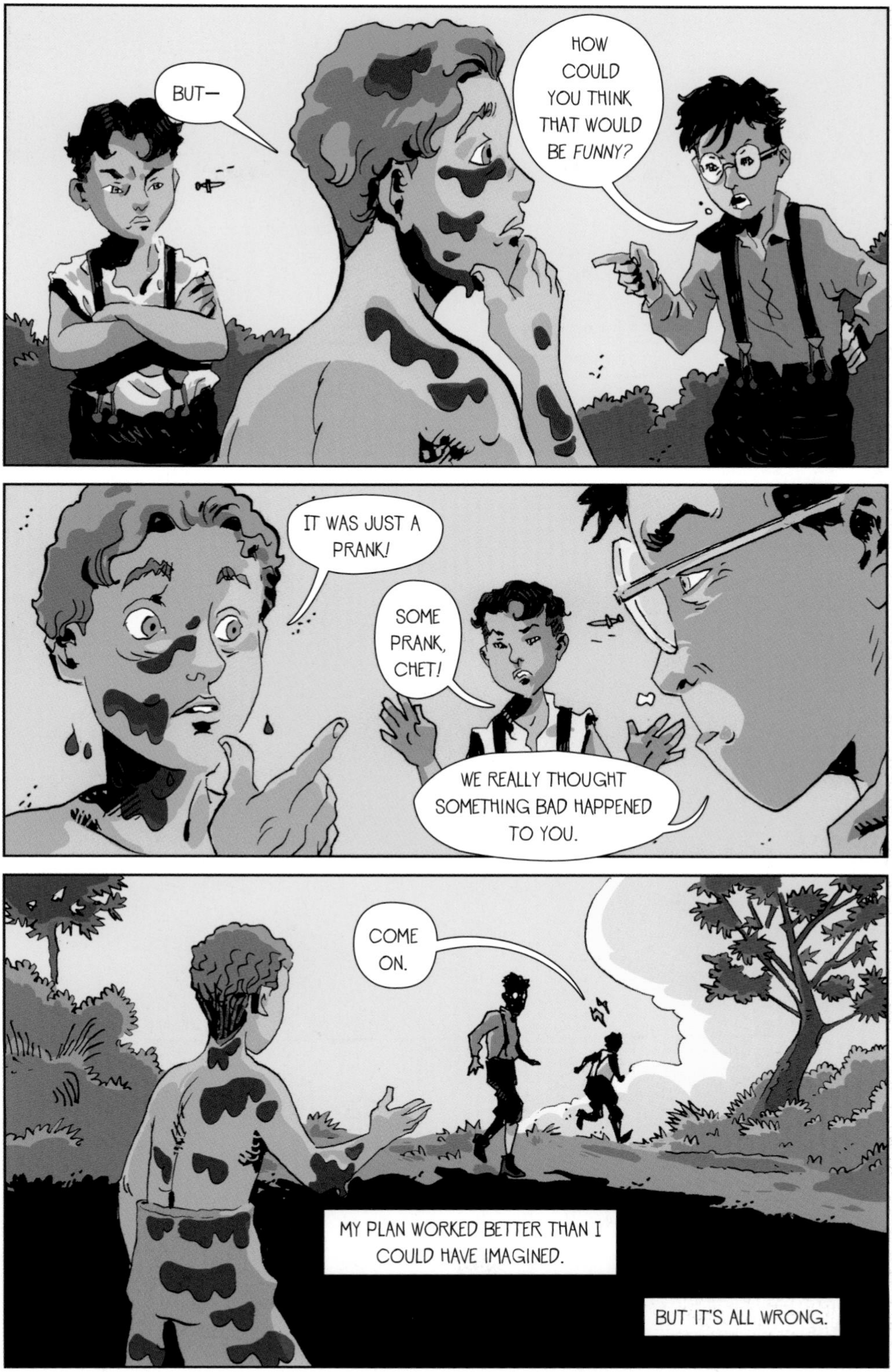
BUT—
HOW COULD YOU THINK THAT WOULD BE *FUNNY?*
IT WAS JUST A PRANK!
SOME PRANK, CHET!
WE REALLY THOUGHT SOMETHING BAD HAPPENED TO YOU.
COME ON.
MY PLAN WORKED BETTER THAN I COULD HAVE IMAGINED.
BUT IT'S ALL WRONG.

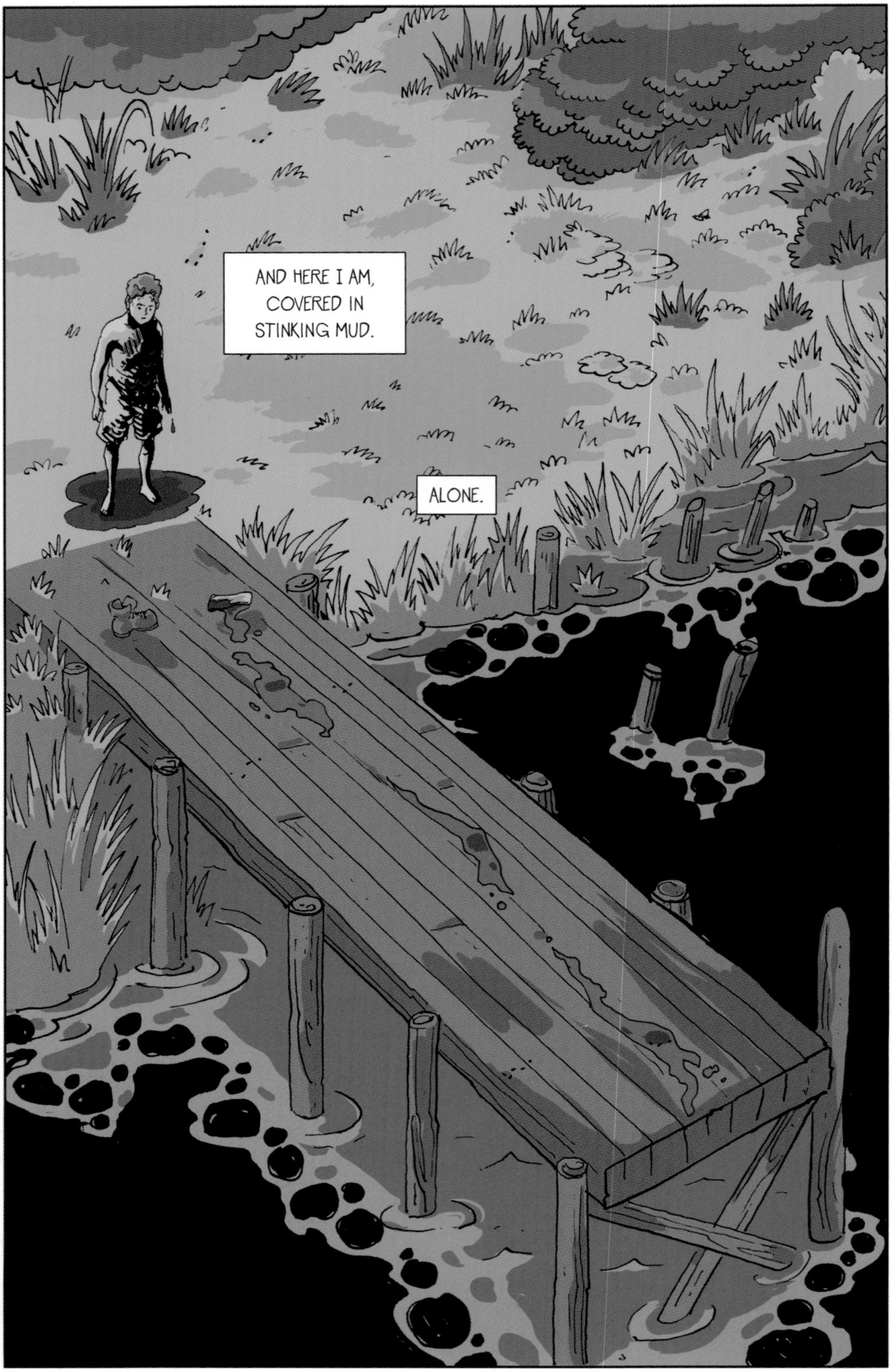
AND HERE I AM, COVERED IN STINKING MUD.
ALONE.

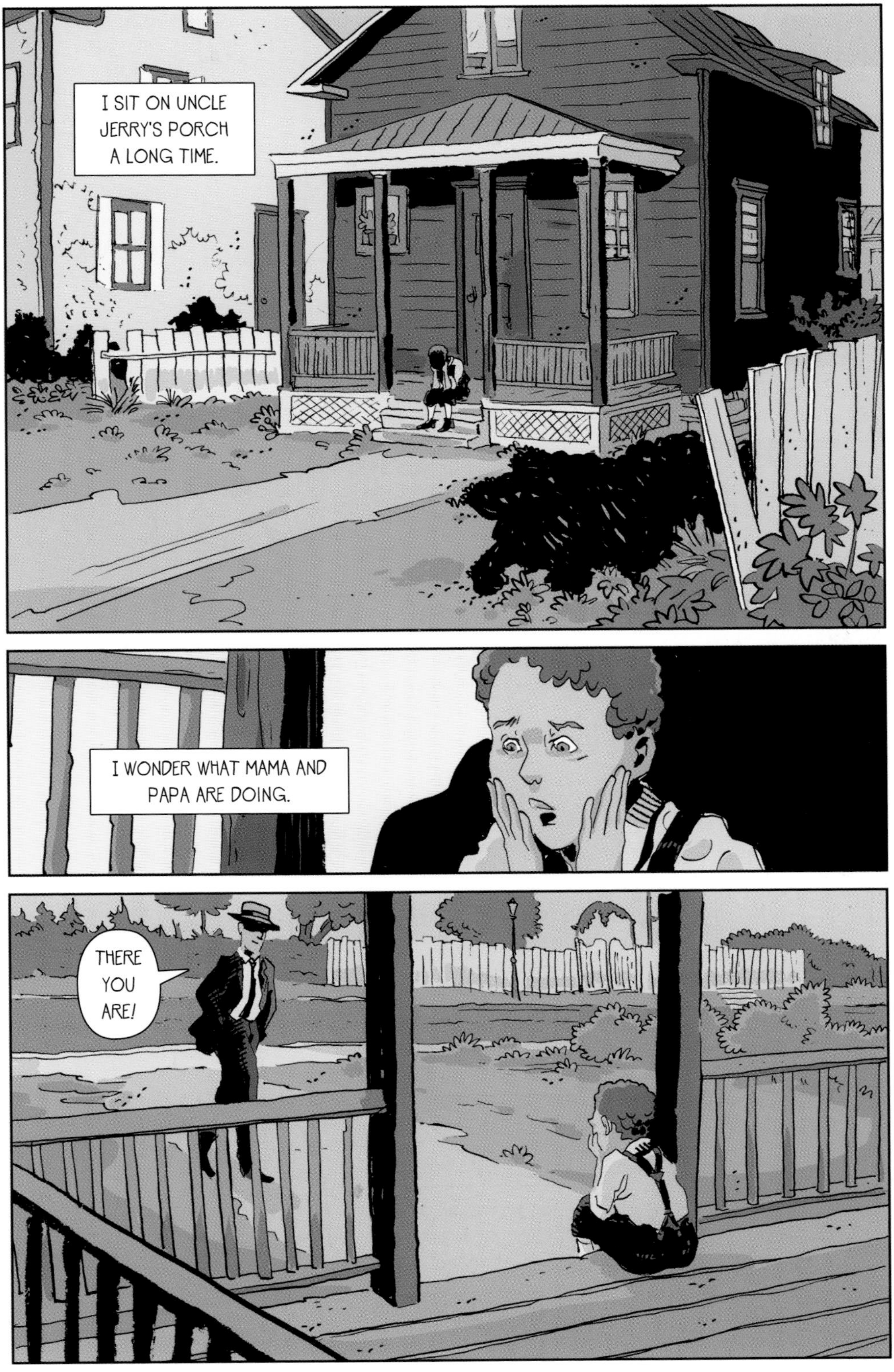
I SIT ON UNCLE JERRY'S PORCH A LONG TIME.
I WONDER WHAT MAMA AND PAPA ARE DOING.
THERE YOU ARE!

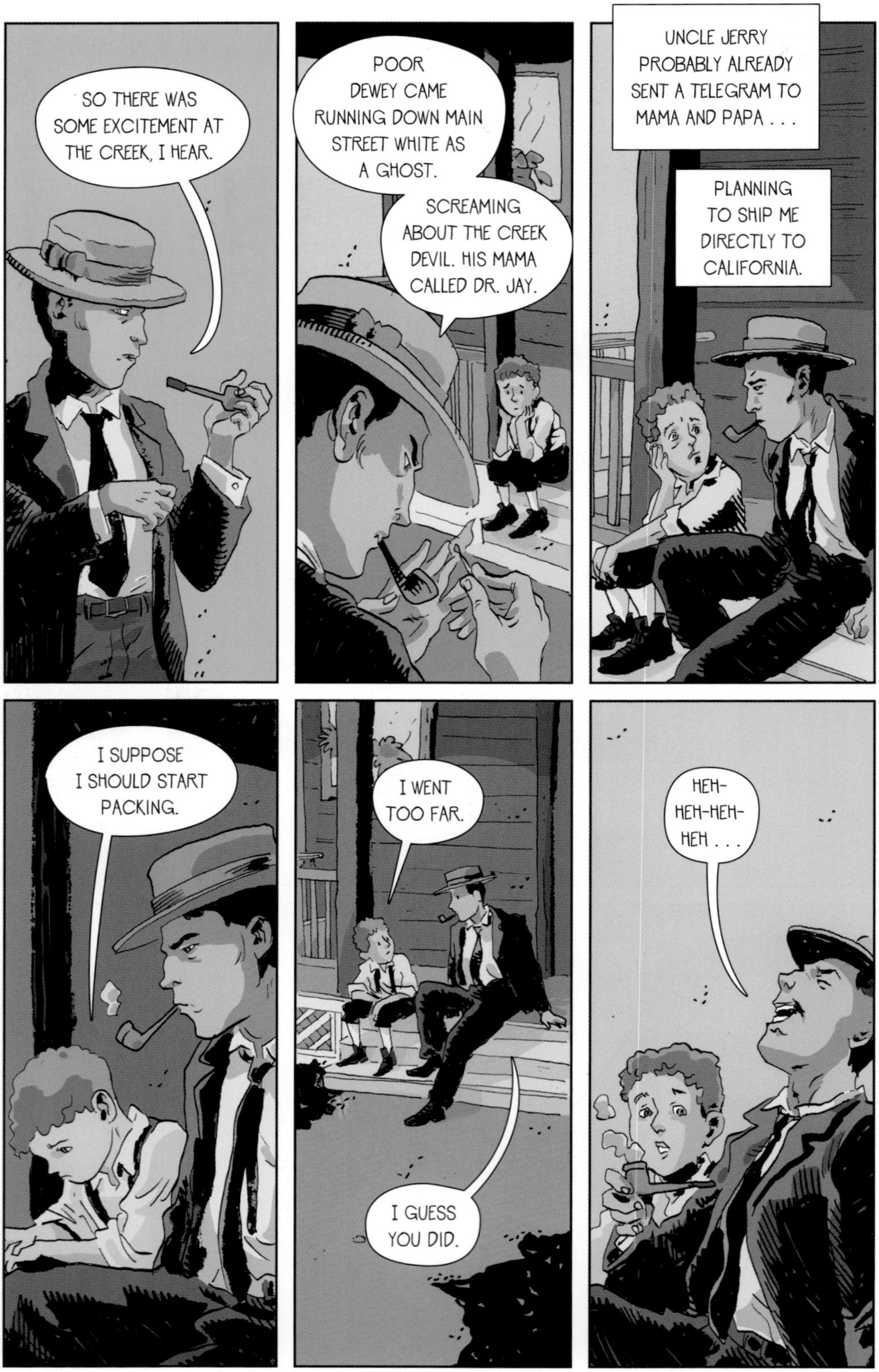
SO THERE WAS SOME EXCITEMENT AT THE CREEK, I HEAR.
POOR DEWEY CAME RUNNING DOWN MAIN STREET WHITE AS A GHOST.
SCREAMING ABOUT THE CREEK DEVIL. HIS MAMA CALLED DR. JAY.
UNCLE JERRY PROBABLY ALREADY SENT A TELEGRAM TO MAMA AND PAPA . . .
PLANNING TO SHIP ME DIRECTLY TO CALIFORNIA.
I SUPPOSE I SHOULD START PACKING.
I WENT TOO FAR.
I GUESS YOU DID.
HEH-HEH-HEH-HEH . . .

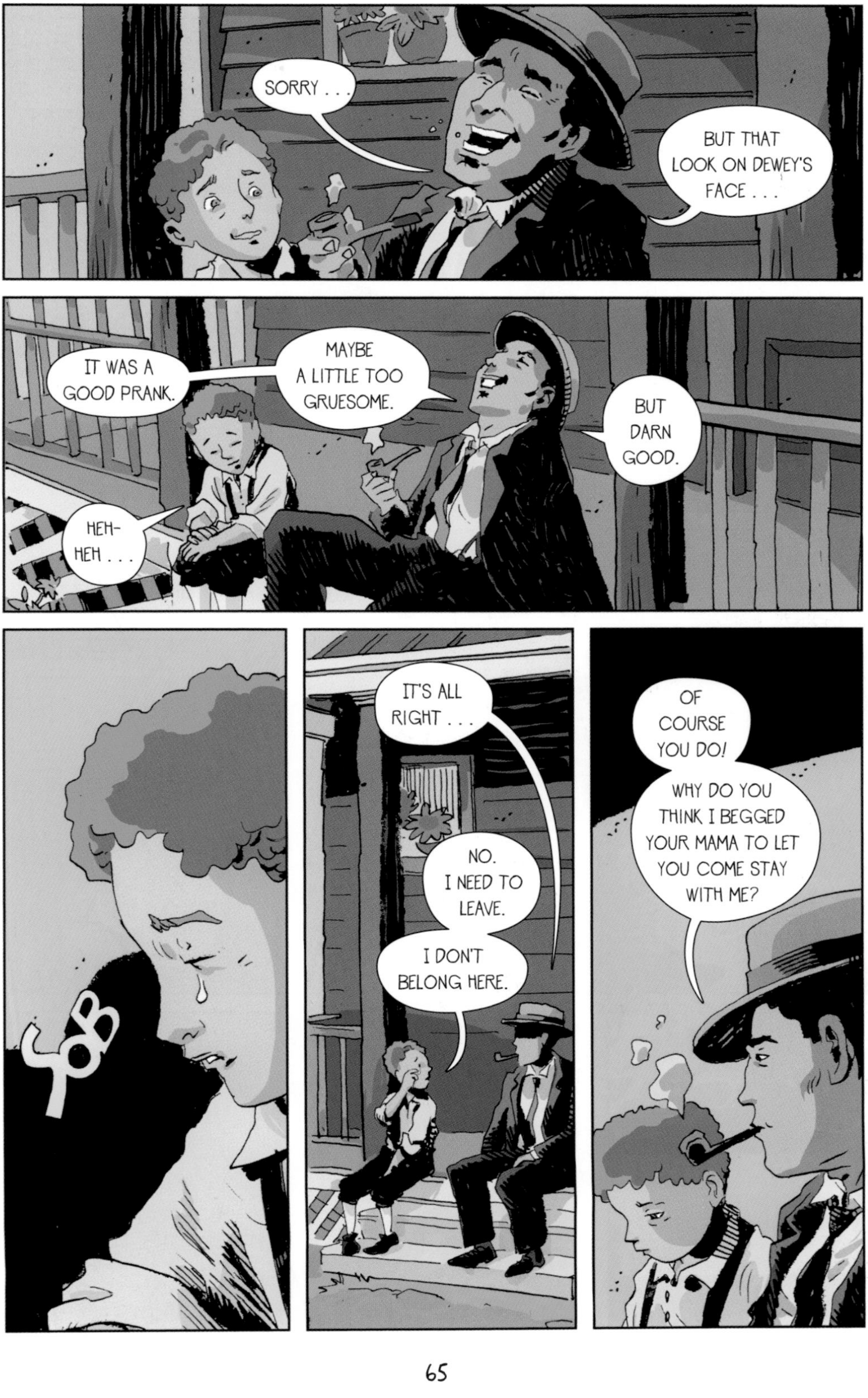

SORRY . . .
BUT THAT LOOK ON DEWEY'S FACE . . .
IT WAS A GOOD PRANK.
MAYBE A LITTLE TOO GRUESOME.
BUT DARN GOOD.
HEH-HEH . . .
SOB
IT'S ALL RIGHT . . .
NO. I NEED TO LEAVE.
I DON'T BELONG HERE.
OF COURSE YOU DO!
WHY DO YOU THINK I BEGGED YOUR MAMA TO LET YOU COME STAY WITH ME?

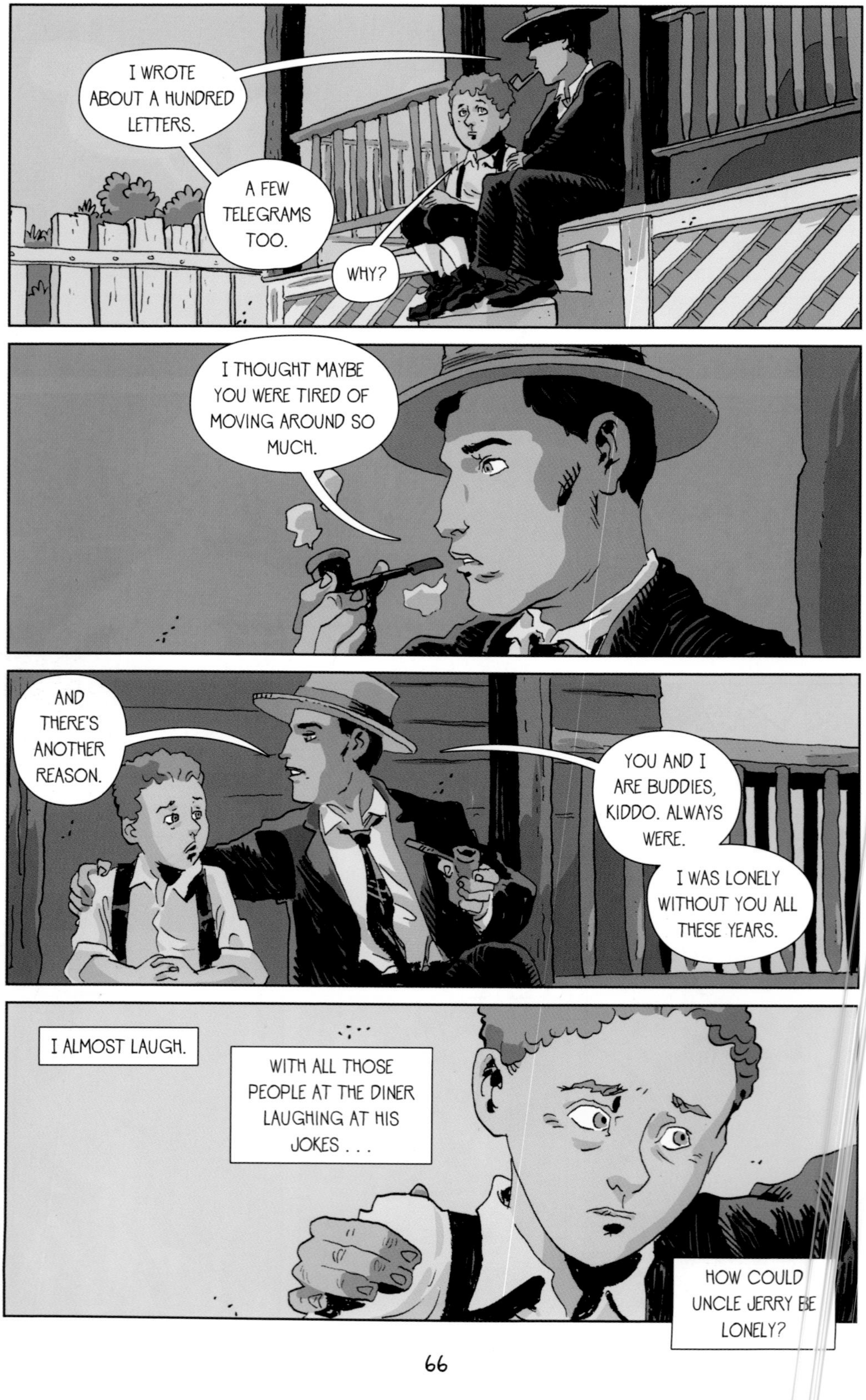
I WROTE ABOUT A HUNDRED LETTERS.
A FEW TELEGRAMS TOO.
WHY?
I THOUGHT MAYBE YOU WERE TIRED OF MOVING AROUND SO MUCH.
AND THERE'S ANOTHER REASON.
YOU AND I ARE BUDDIES, KIDDO. ALWAYS WERE.
I WAS LONELY WITHOUT YOU ALL THESE YEARS.
I ALMOST LAUGH.
WITH ALL THOSE PEOPLE AT THE DINER LAUGHING AT HIS JOKES . . .
HOW COULD UNCLE JERRY BE LONELY?

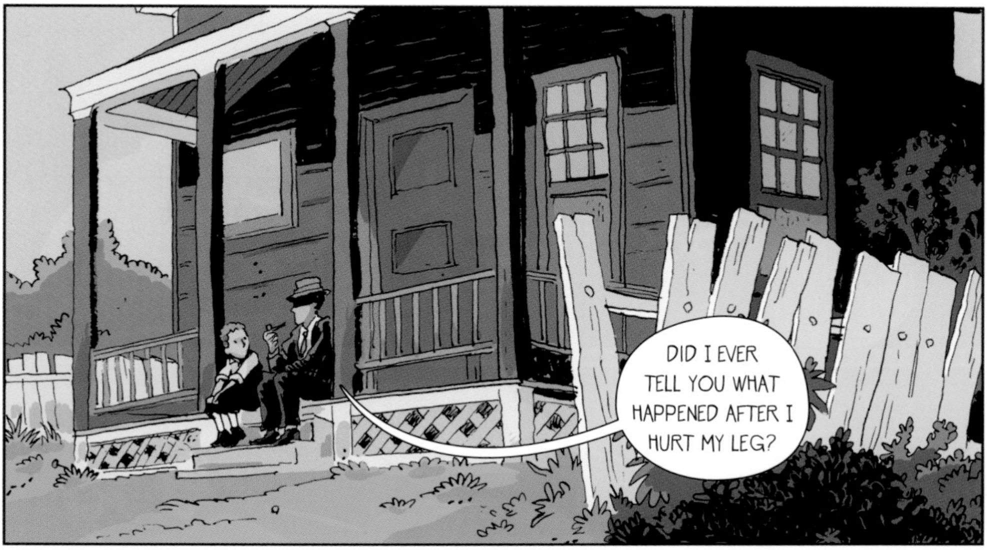
DID I EVER TELL YOU WHAT HAPPENED AFTER I HURT MY LEG?

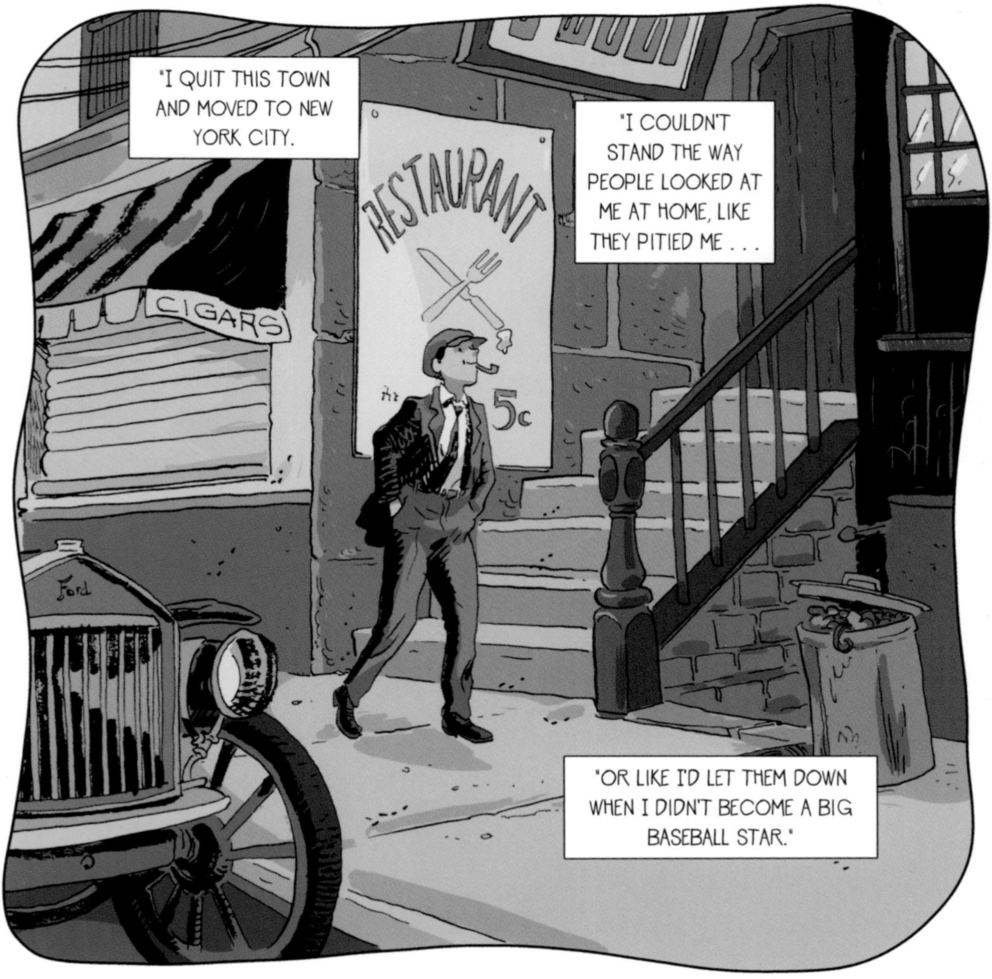
"I QUIT THIS TOWN AND MOVED TO NEW YORK CITY.
"I COULDN'T STAND THE WAY PEOPLE LOOKED AT ME AT HOME, LIKE THEY PITIED ME . . .
RESTAURANT
CIGARS
5c
Ford
"OR LIKE I'D LET THEM DOWN WHEN I DIDN'T BECOME A BIG BASEBALL STAR."

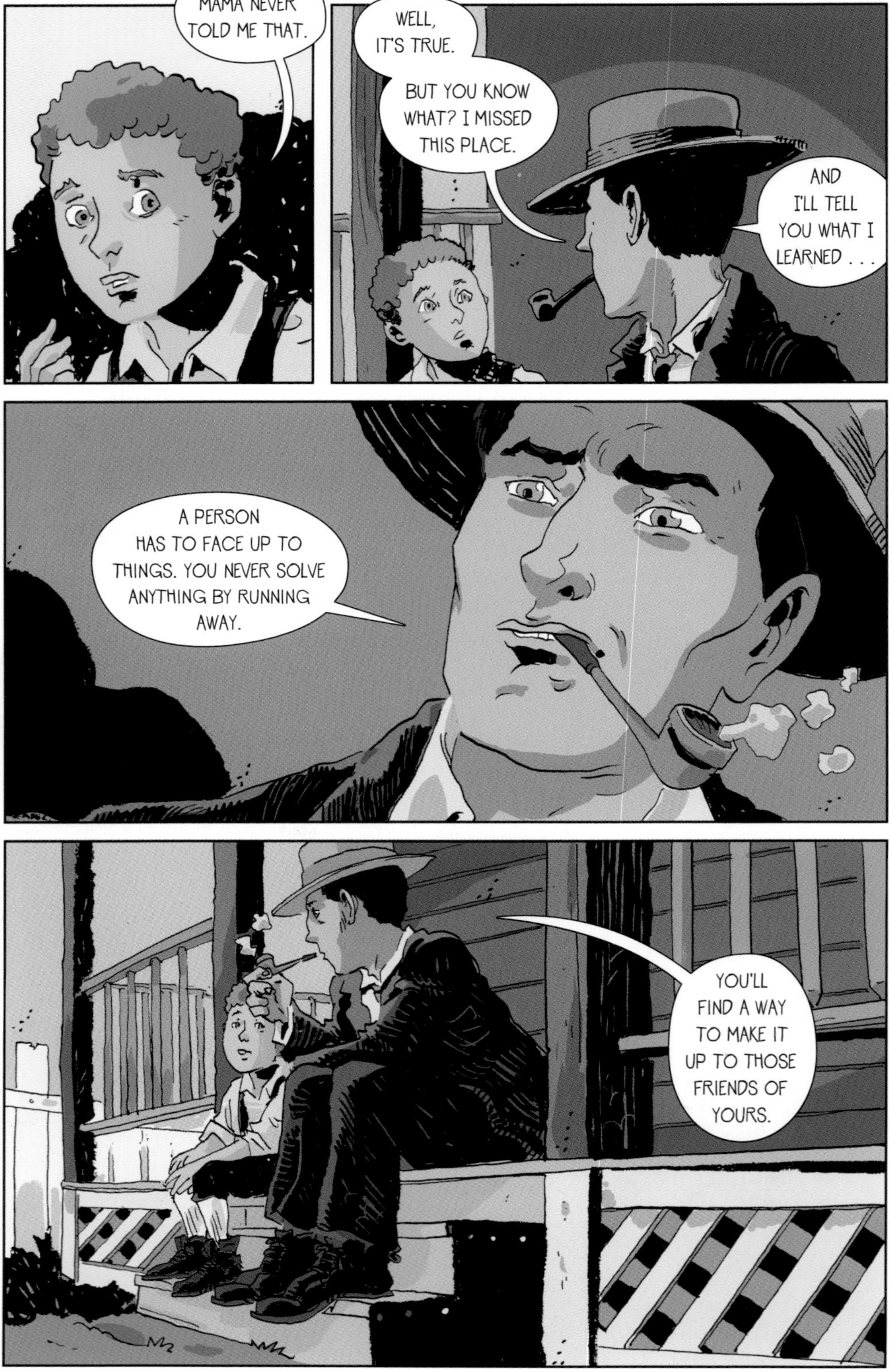
MAMA NEVER TOLD ME THAT.
WELL, IT'S TRUE.
BUT YOU KNOW WHAT? I MISSED THIS PLACE.
AND I'LL TELL YOU WHAT I LEARNED . . .
A PERSON HAS TO FACE UP TO THINGS. YOU NEVER SOLVE ANYTHING BY RUNNING AWAY.
YOU'LL FIND A WAY TO MAKE IT UP TO THOSE FRIENDS OF YOURS.

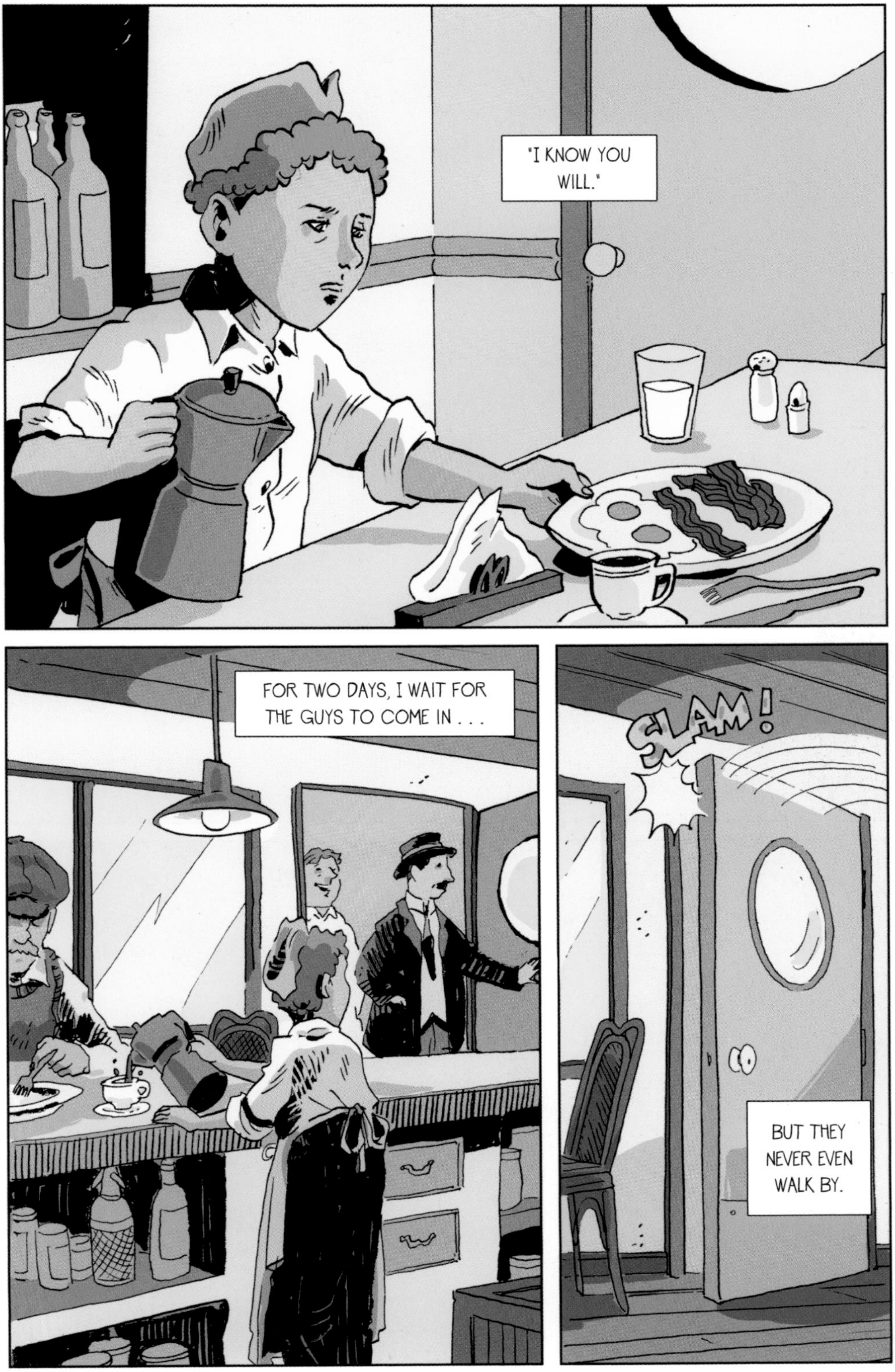
"I KNOW YOU WILL."
FOR TWO DAYS, I WAIT FOR THE GUYS TO COME IN . . .
SLAM!
BUT THEY NEVER EVEN WALK BY.

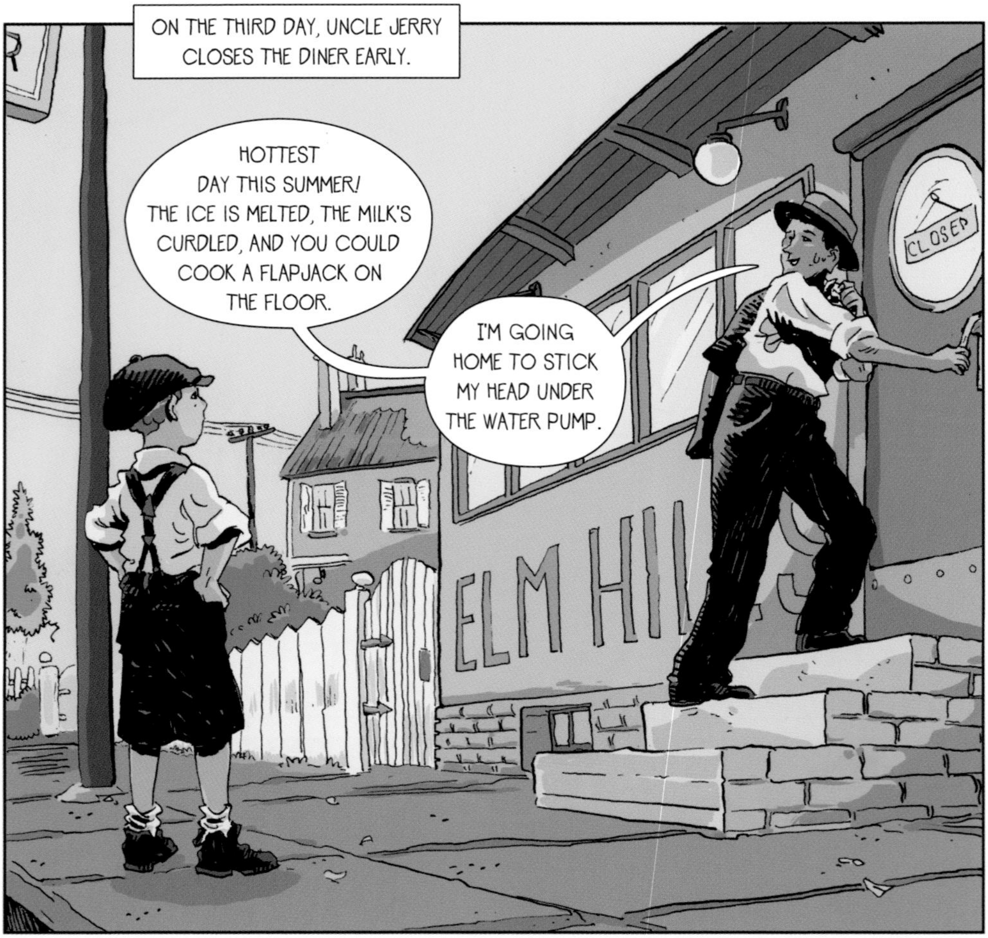
ON THE THIRD DAY, UNCLE JERRY CLOSES THE DINER EARLY.
HOTTEST DAY THIS SUMMER! THE ICE IS MELTED, THE MILK'S CURDLED, AND YOU COULD COOK A FLAPJACK ON THE FLOOR.
I'M GOING HOME TO STICK MY HEAD UNDER THE WATER PUMP.
CLOSED
ELM HIL

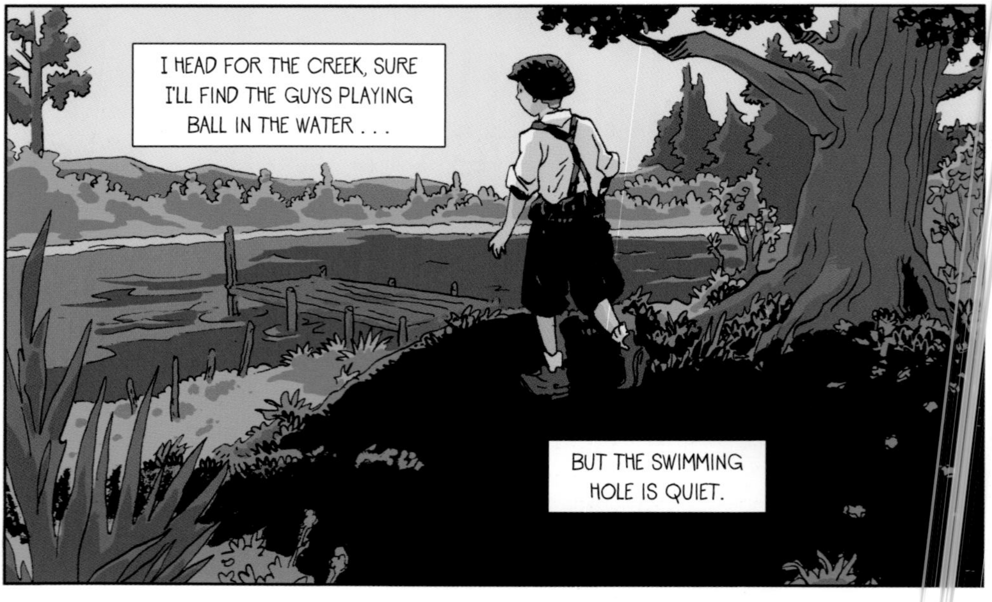
I HEAD FOR THE CREEK, SURE I'LL FIND THE GUYS PLAYING BALL IN THE WATER . . .
BUT THE SWIMMING HOLE IS QUIET.

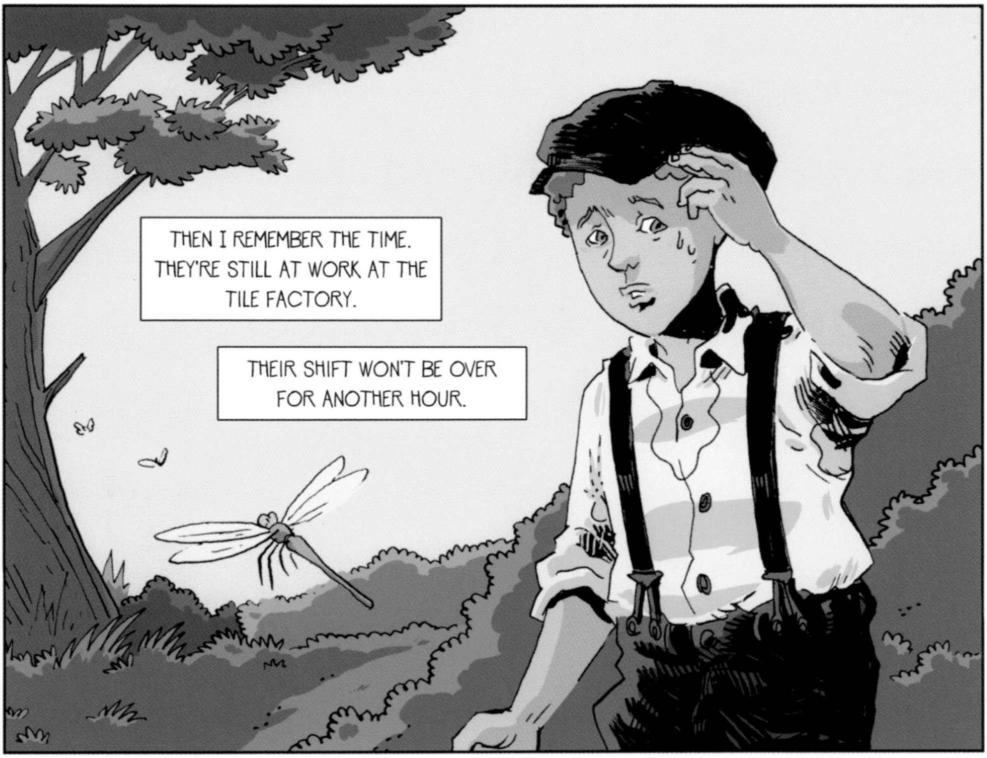
THEN I REMEMBER THE TIME. THEY'RE STILL AT WORK AT THE TILE FACTORY.
THEIR SHIFT WON'T BE OVER FOR ANOTHER HOUR.

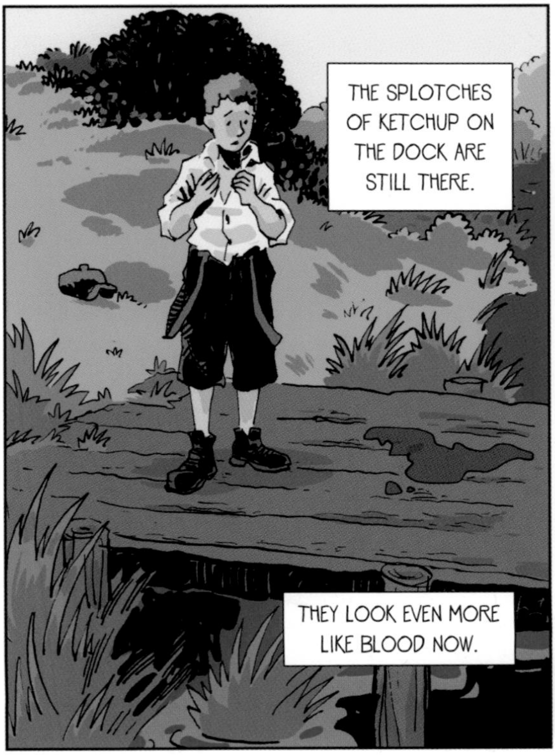
THE SPLOTCHES OF KETCHUP ON THE DOCK ARE STILL THERE.
THEY LOOK EVEN MORE LIKE BLOOD NOW.

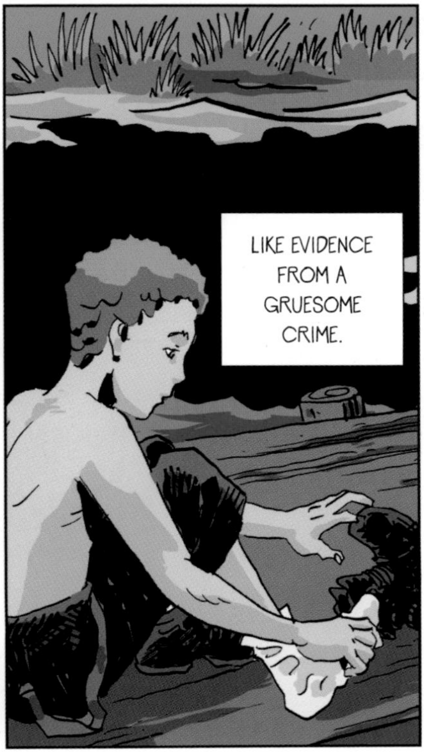
LIKE EVIDENCE FROM A GRUESOME CRIME.

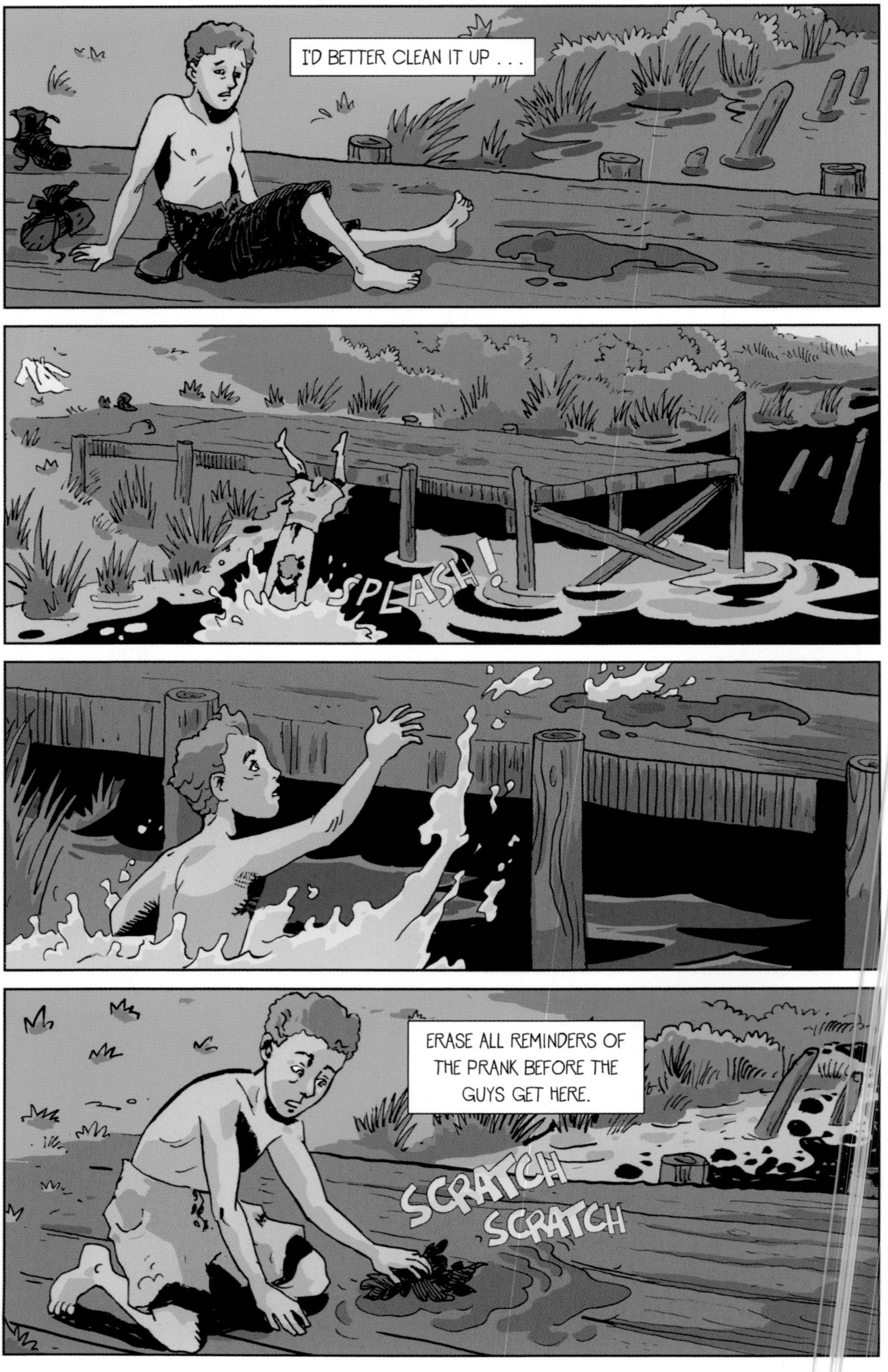
I'D BETTER CLEAN IT UP . . .
SPLASH!
ERASE ALL REMINDERS OF THE PRANK BEFORE THE GUYS GET HERE.
SCRATCH
SCRATCH

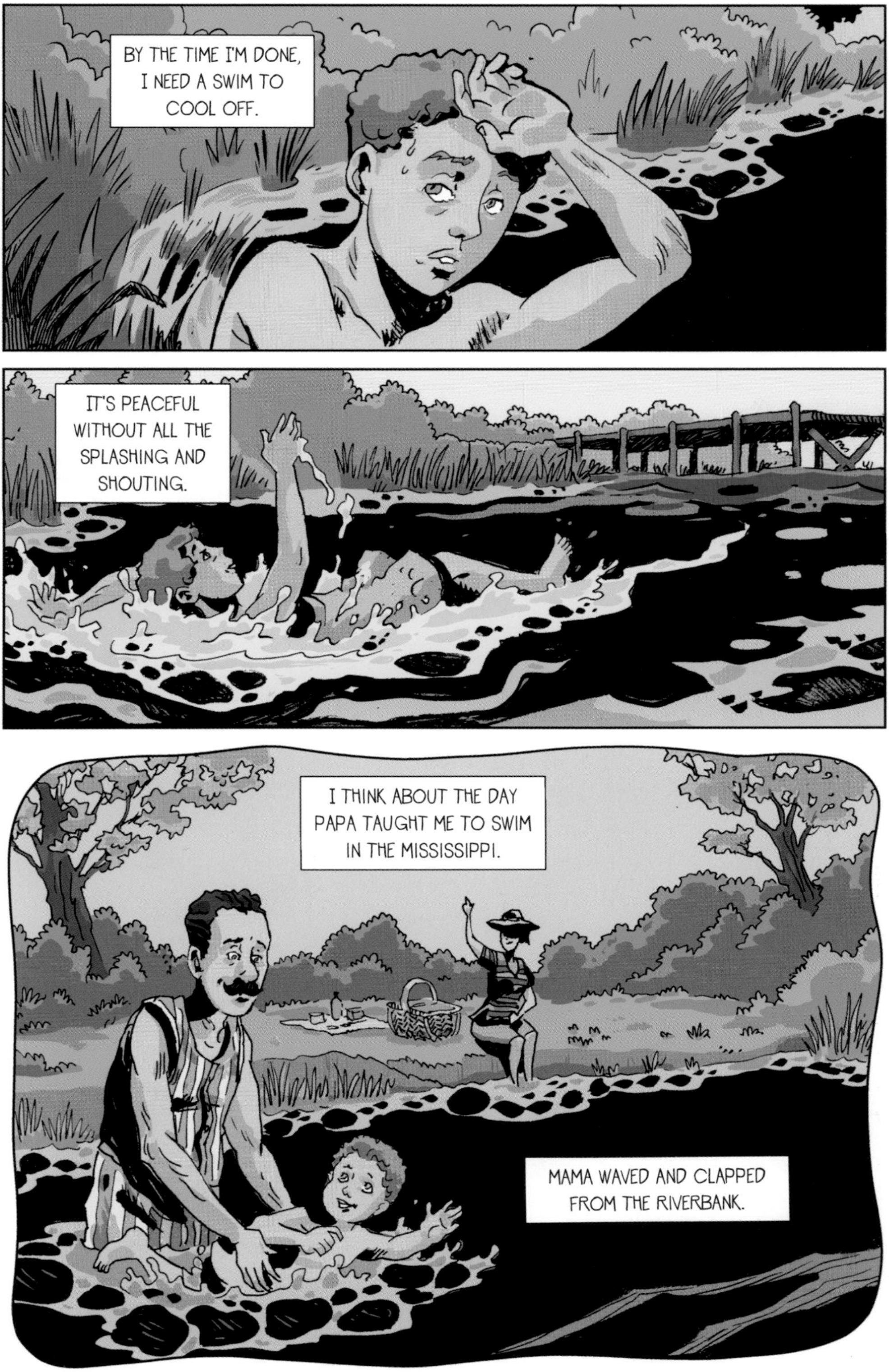
BY THE TIME I'M DONE, I NEED A SWIM TO COOL OFF.
IT'S PEACEFUL WITHOUT ALL THE SPLASHING AND SHOUTING.
I THINK ABOUT THE DAY PAPA TAUGHT ME TO SWIM IN THE MISSISSIPPI.
MAMA WAVED AND CLAPPED FROM THE RIVERBANK.

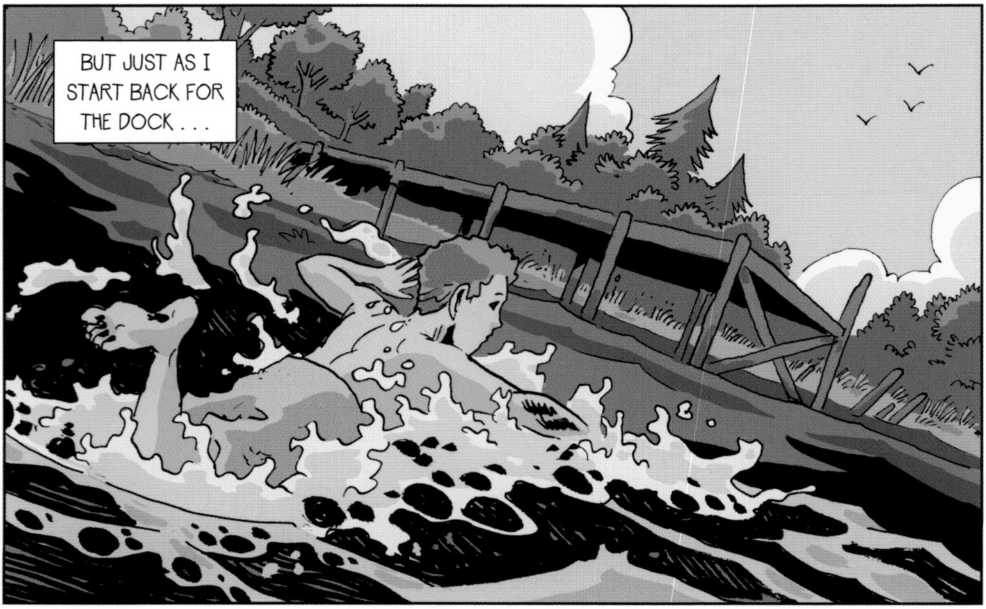
BUT JUST AS I START BACK FOR THE DOCK . . .

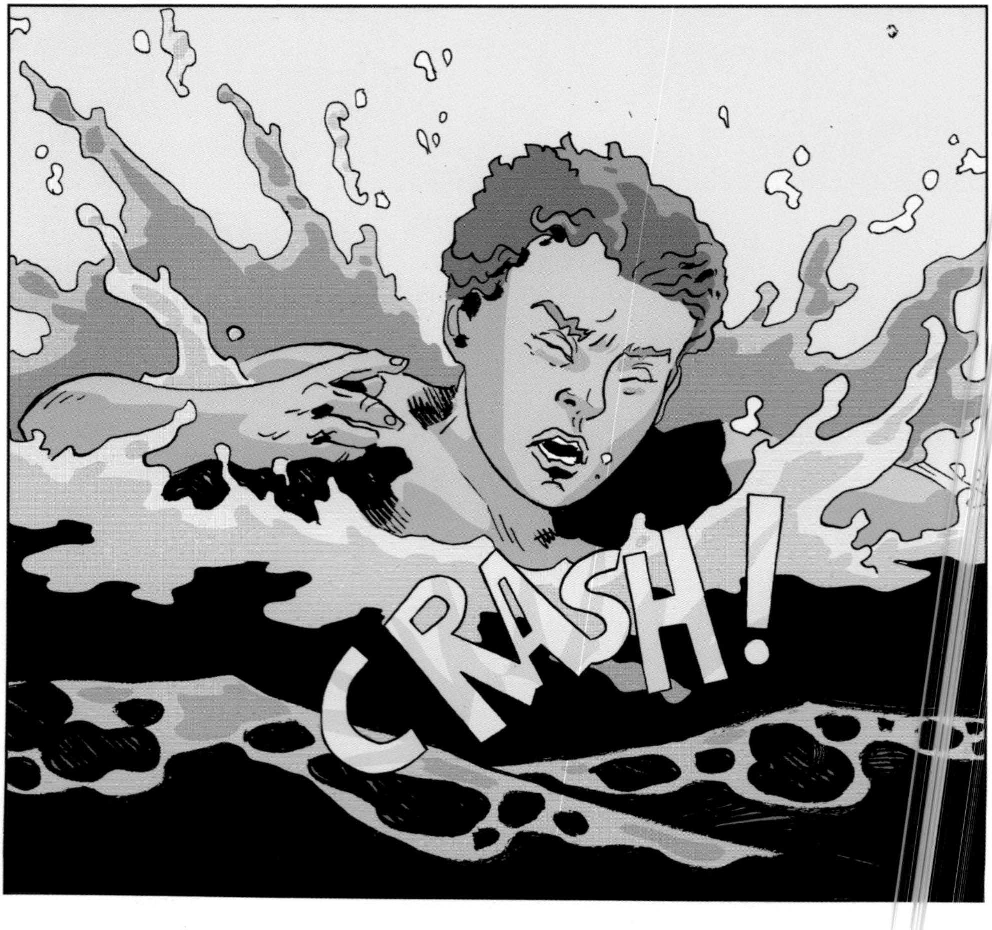
CRASH!

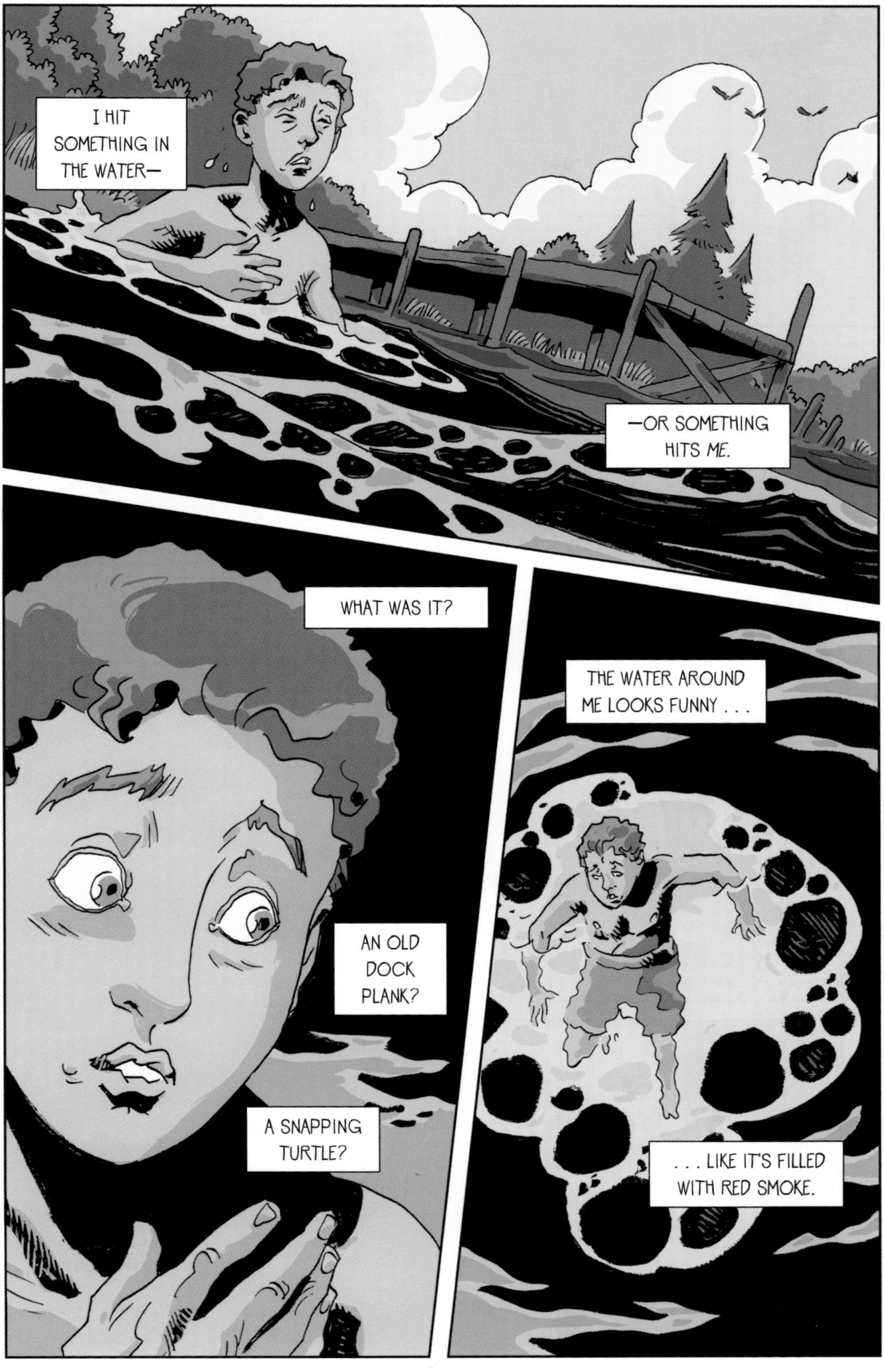
I HIT SOMETHING IN THE WATER—
—OR SOMETHING HITS *ME.*
WHAT WAS IT?
AN OLD DOCK PLANK?
A SNAPPING TURTLE?
THE WATER AROUND ME LOOKS FUNNY . . .
. . . LIKE IT'S FILLED WITH RED SMOKE.

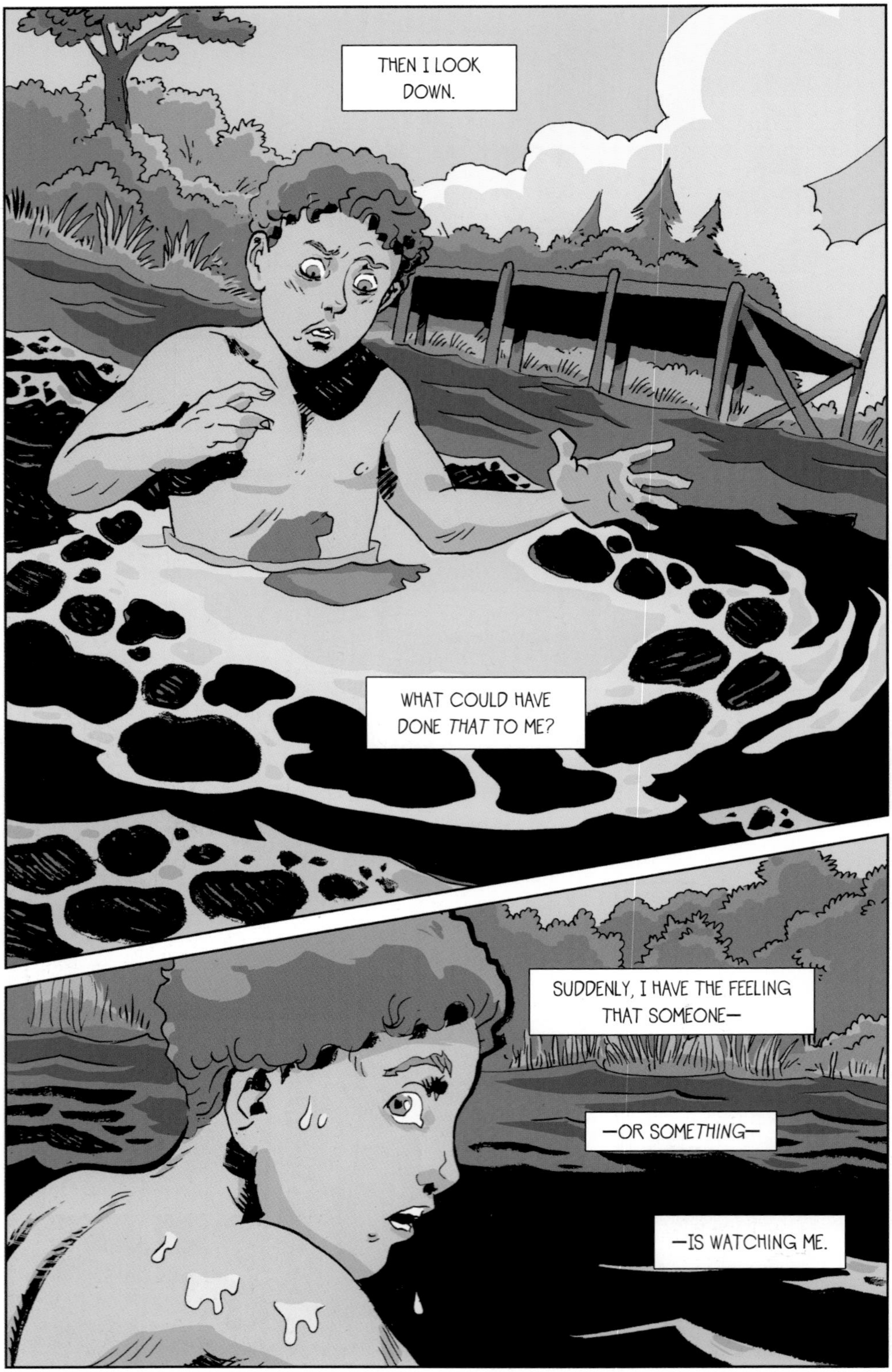
THEN I LOOK DOWN.
WHAT COULD HAVE DONE *THAT* TO ME?
SUDDENLY, I HAVE THE FEELING THAT SOMEONE—
—OR SOME*THING*—
—IS WATCHING ME.

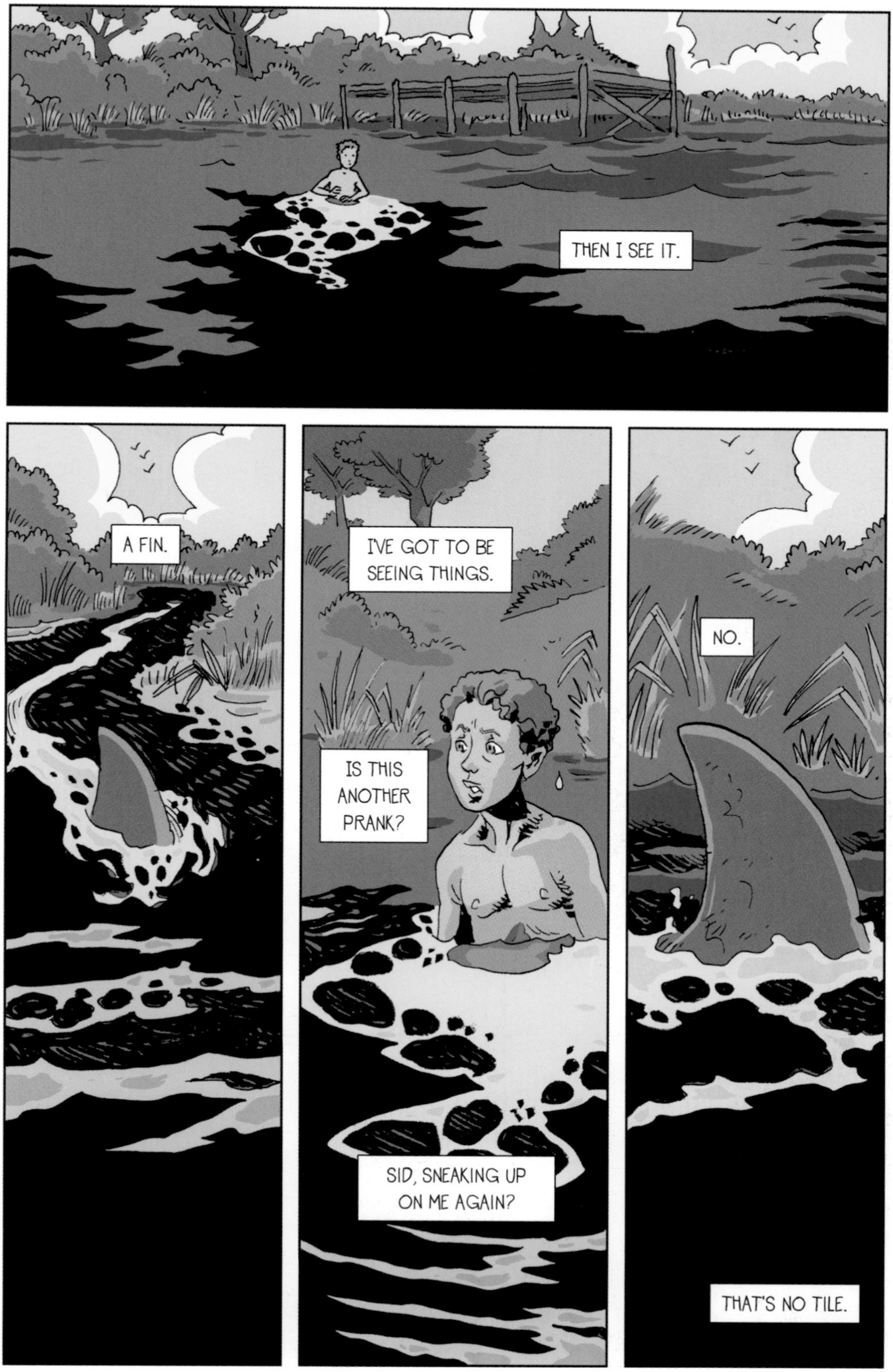
THEN I SEE IT.
A FIN.
I'VE GOT TO BE SEEING THINGS.
IS THIS ANOTHER PRANK?
SID, SNEAKING UP ON ME AGAIN?
NO.
THAT'S NO TILE.

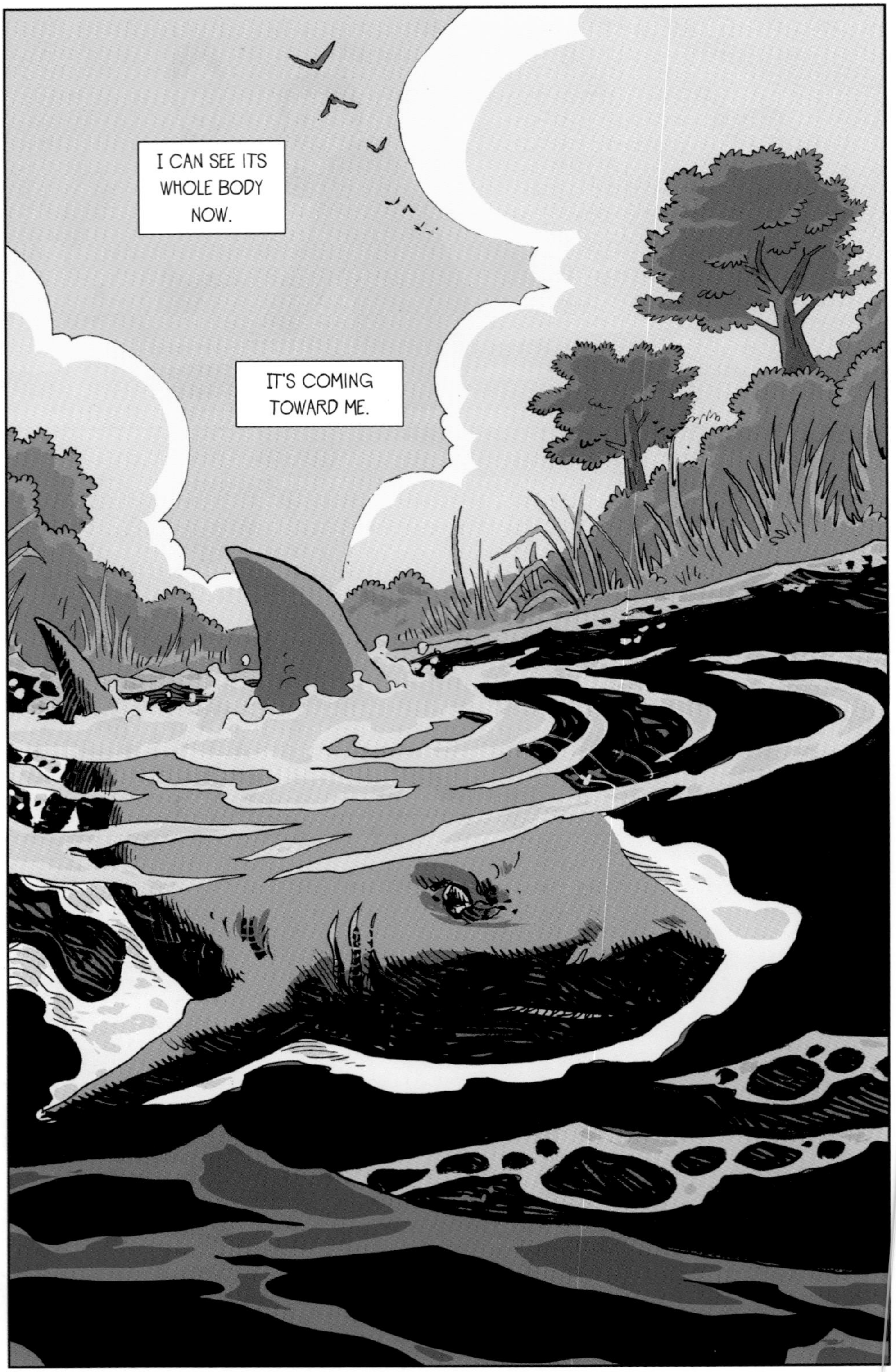
I CAN SEE ITS WHOLE BODY NOW.
IT'S COMING TOWARD ME.

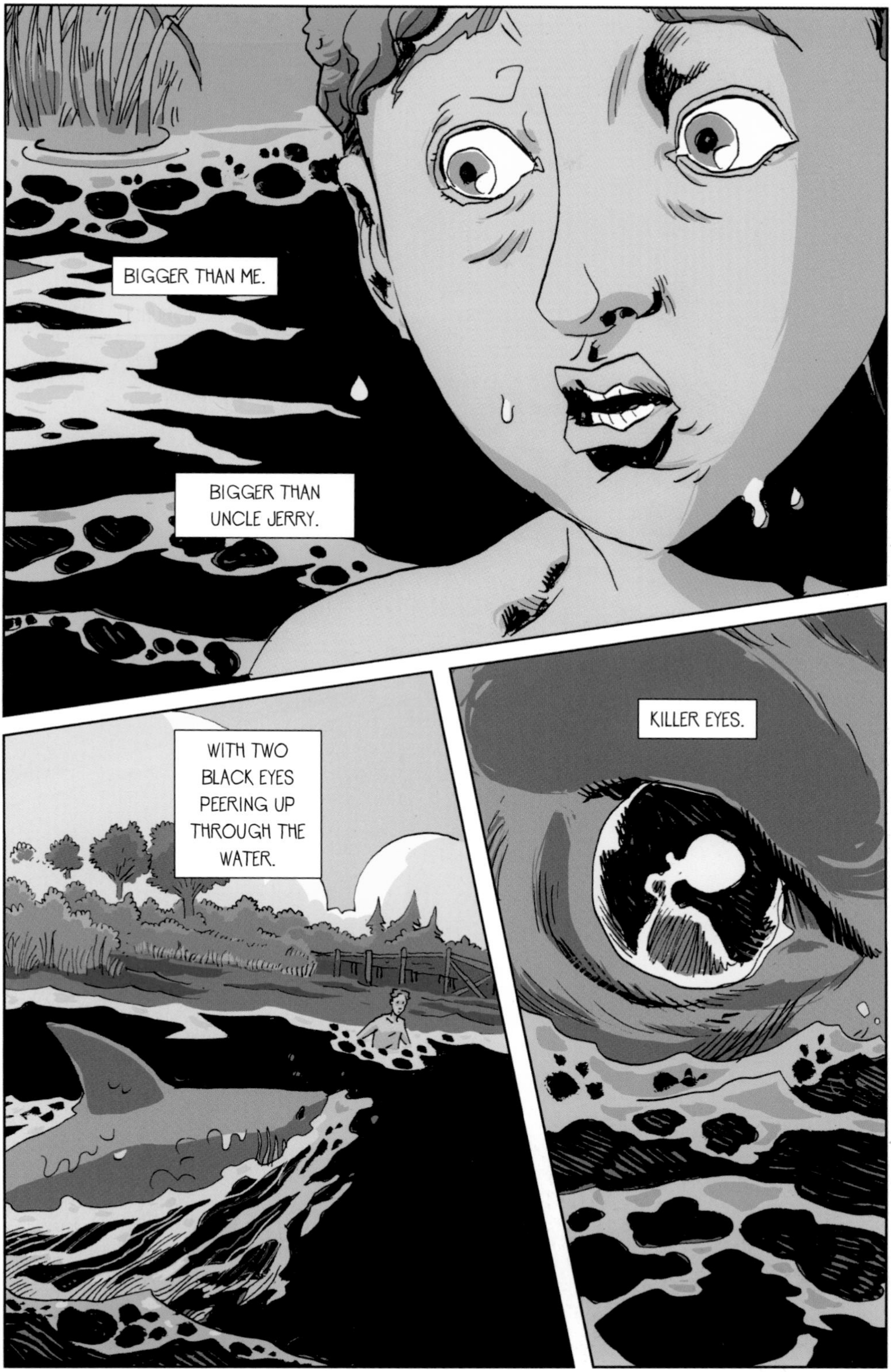
BIGGER THAN ME.
BIGGER THAN UNCLE JERRY.
WITH TWO BLACK EYES PEERING UP THROUGH THE WATER.
KILLER EYES.

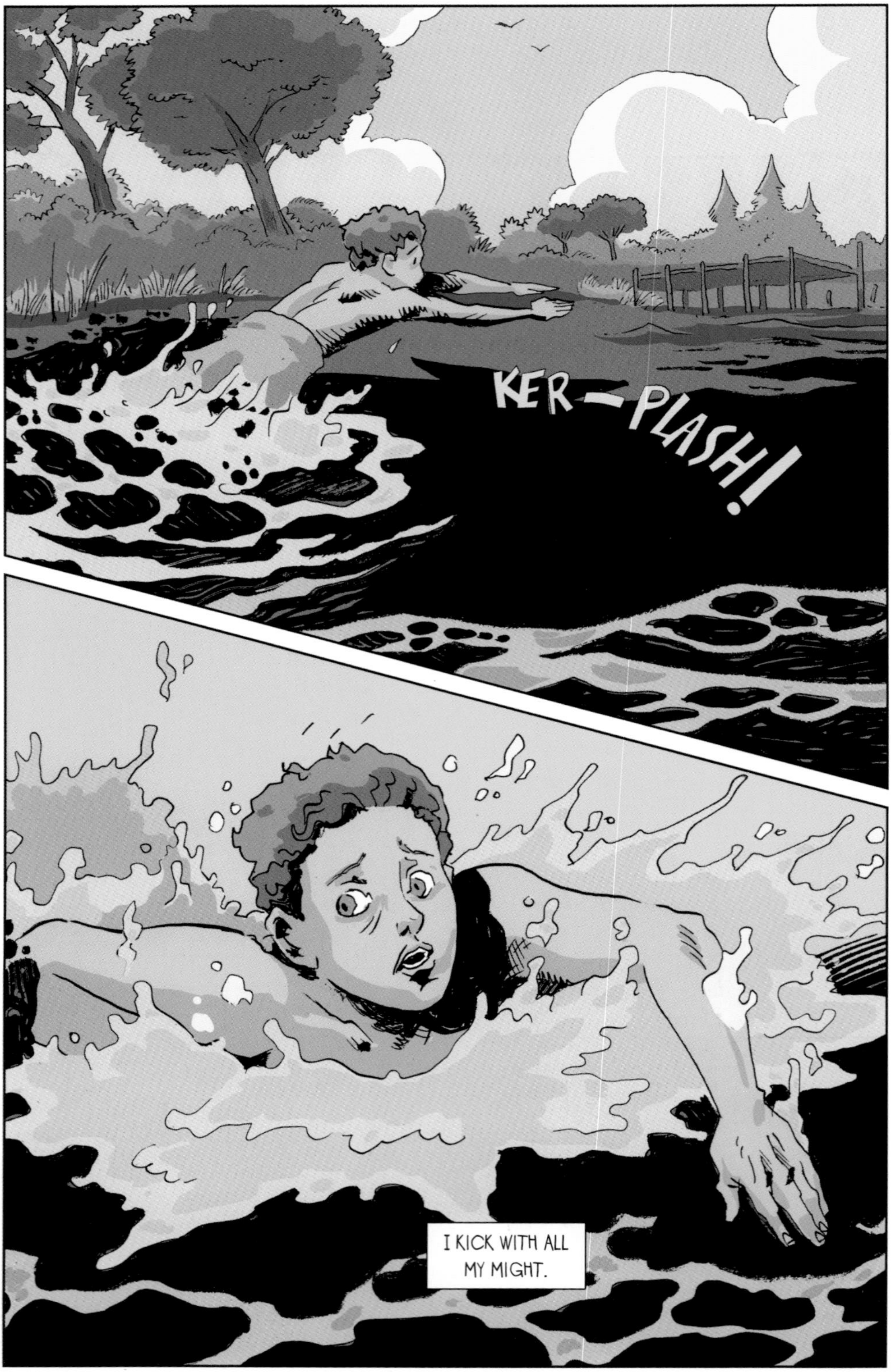
KER-PLASH!
I KICK WITH ALL MY MIGHT.

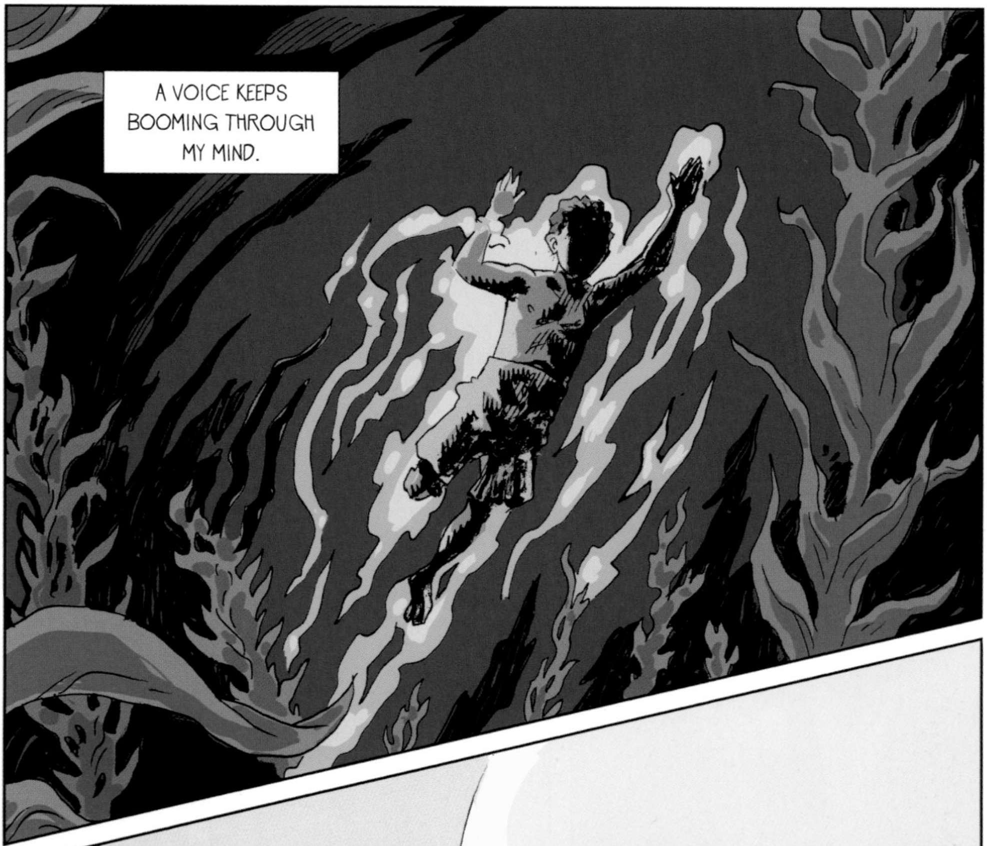
A VOICE KEEPS BOOMING THROUGH MY MIND.

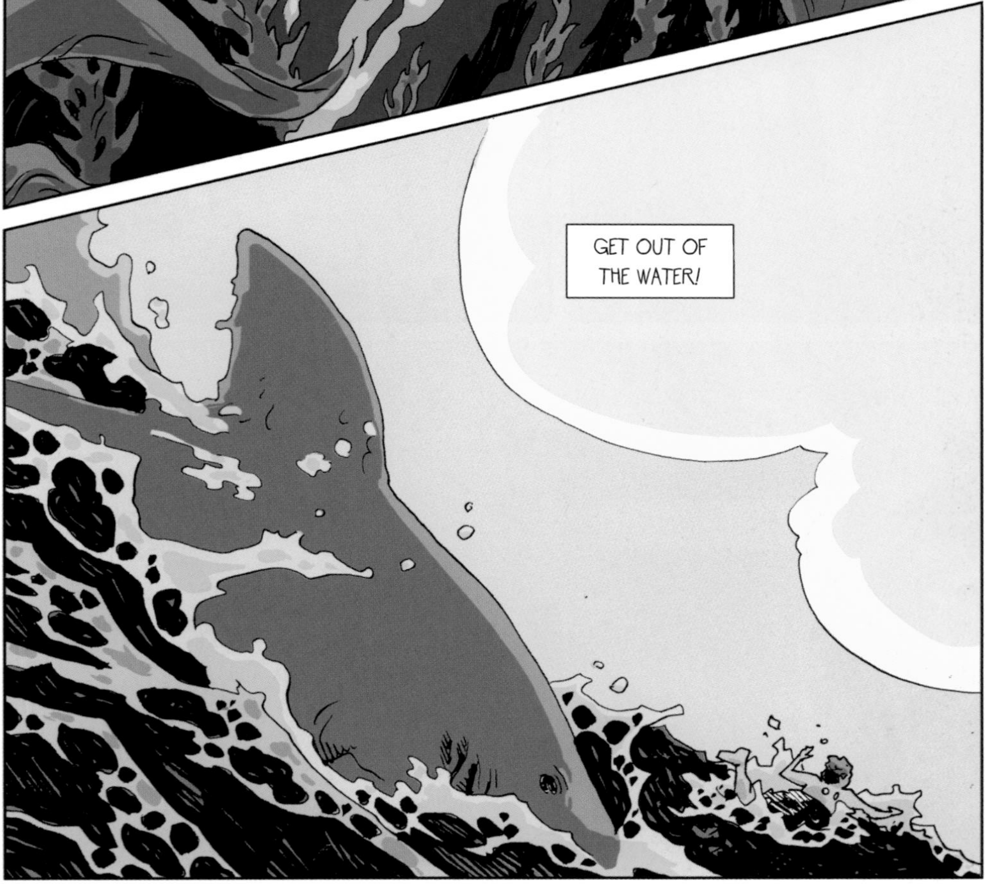
GET OUT OF THE WATER!

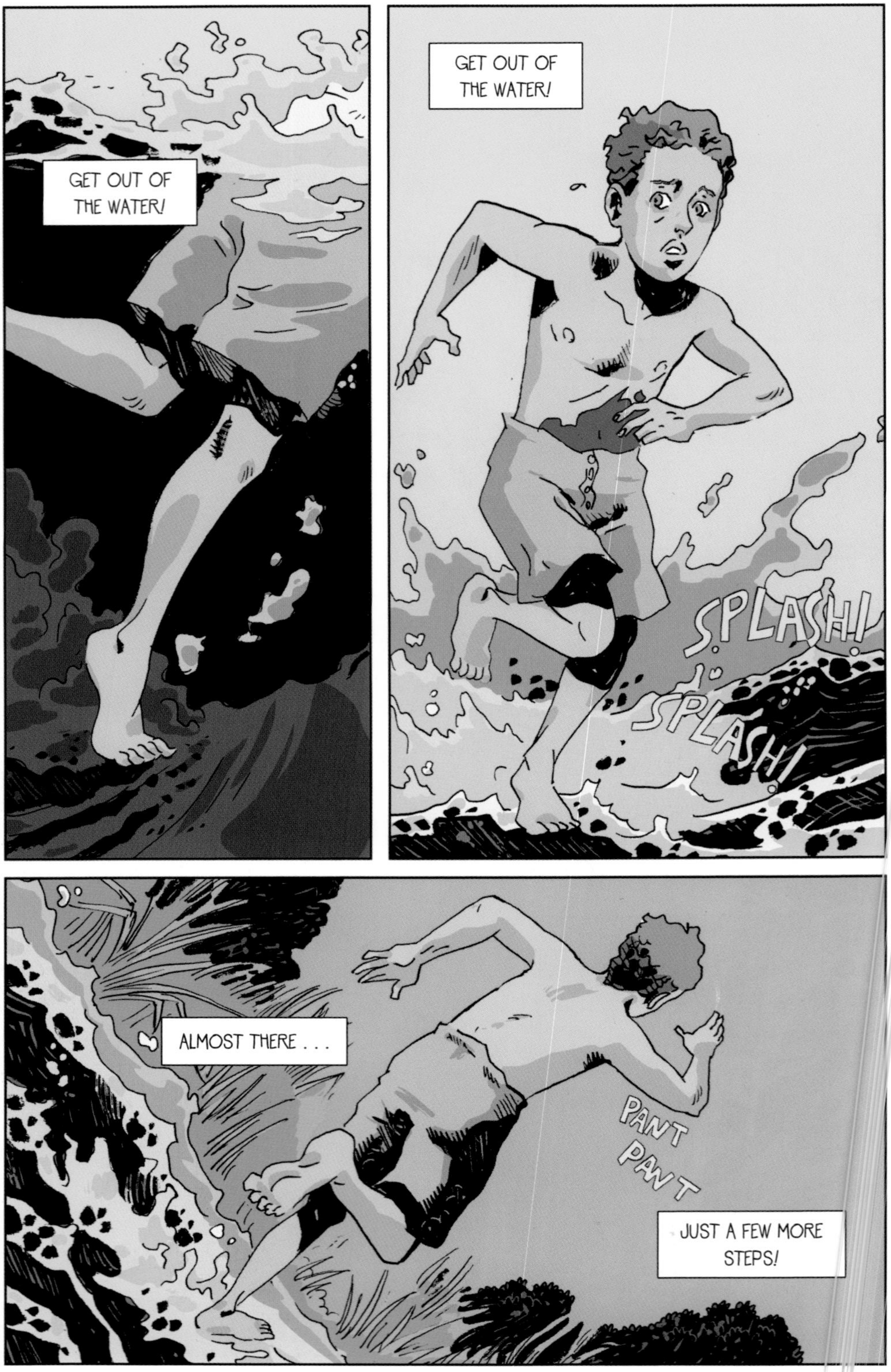
GET OUT OF THE WATER!
GET OUT OF THE WATER!
SPLASH!
SPLASH!
ALMOST THERE . . .
PANT PANT
JUST A FEW MORE STEPS!

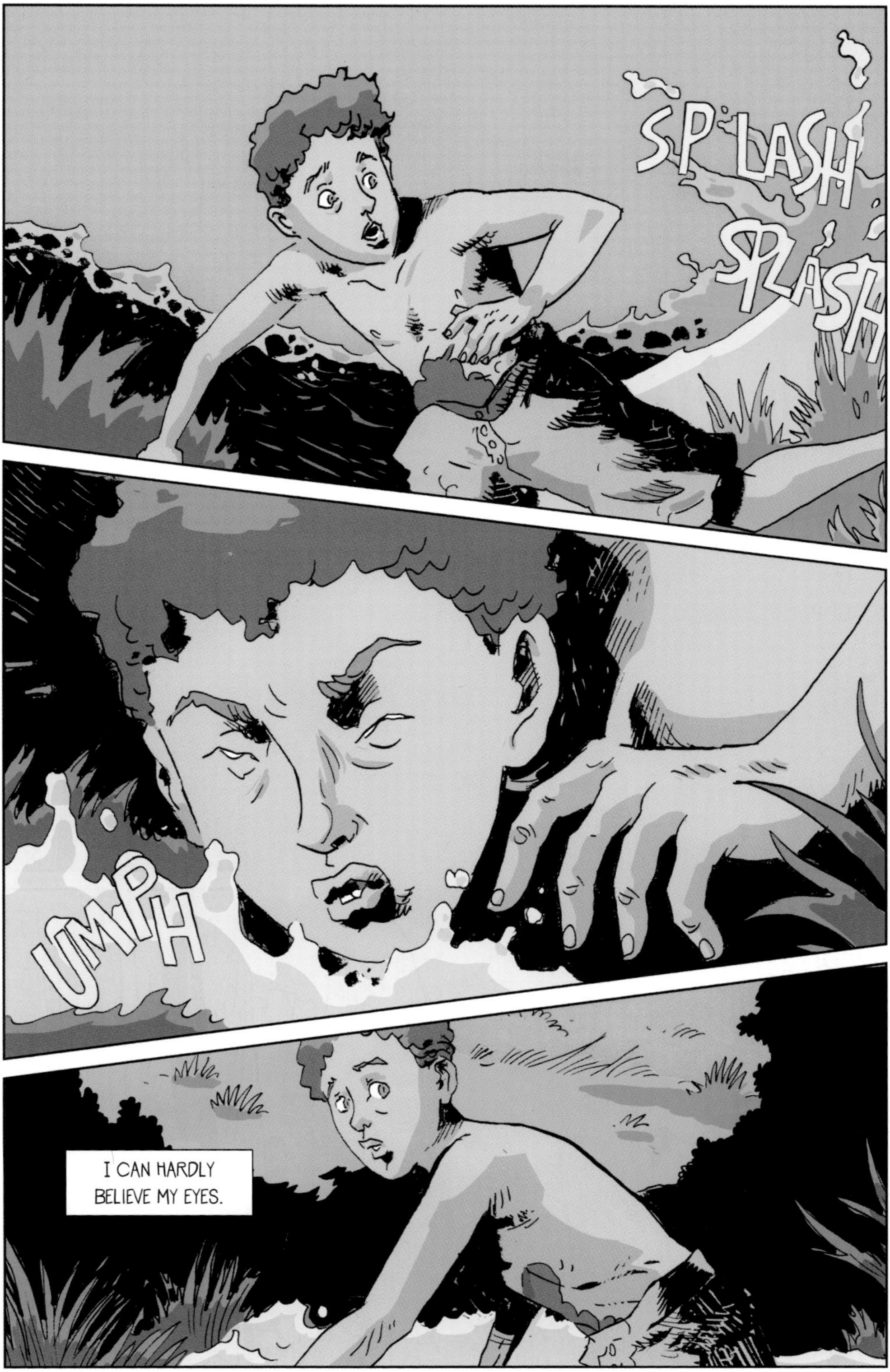
SPLASH
SPLASH
UMPH
I CAN HARDLY BELIEVE MY EYES.

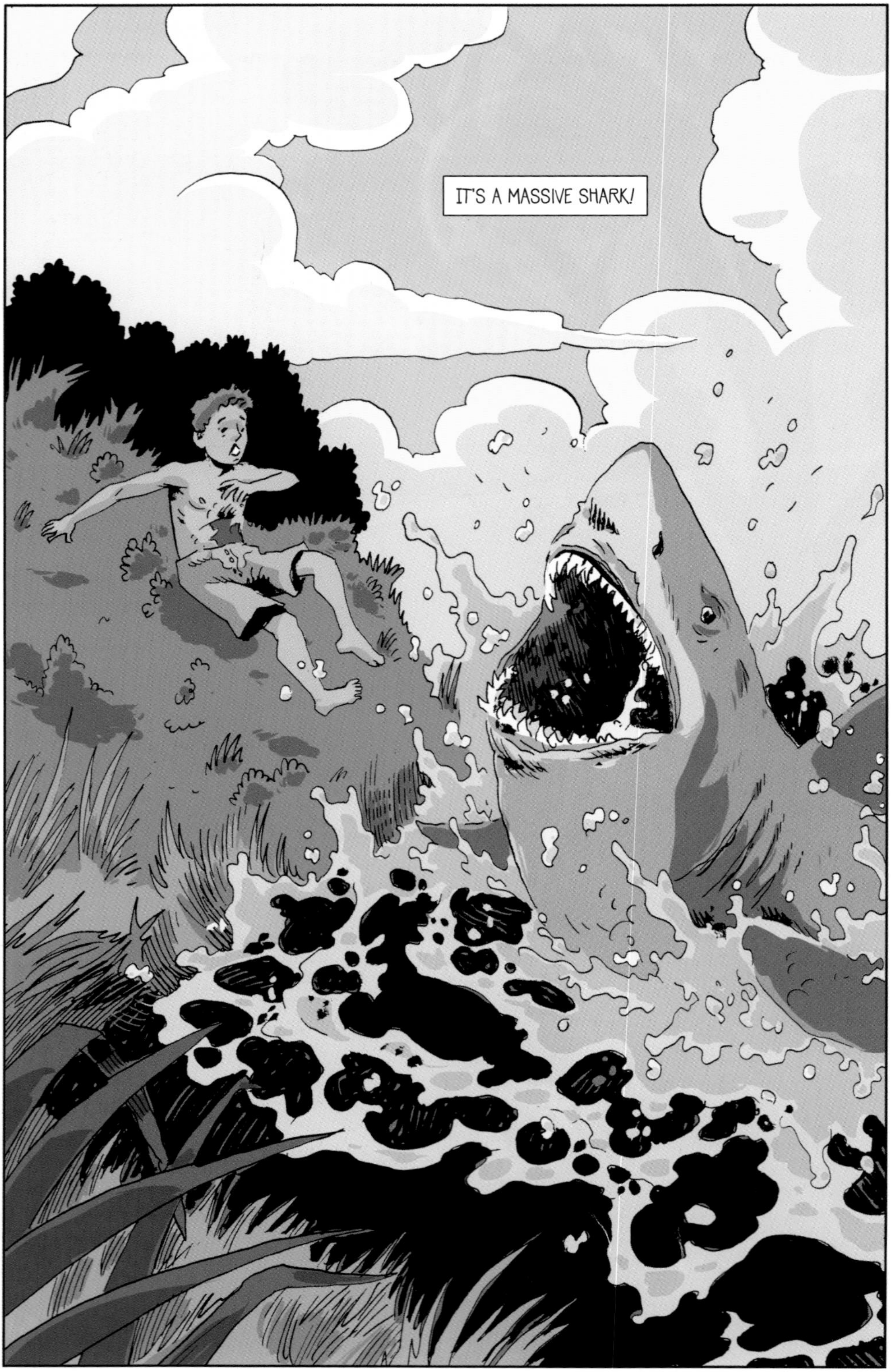
IT'S A MASSIVE SHARK!

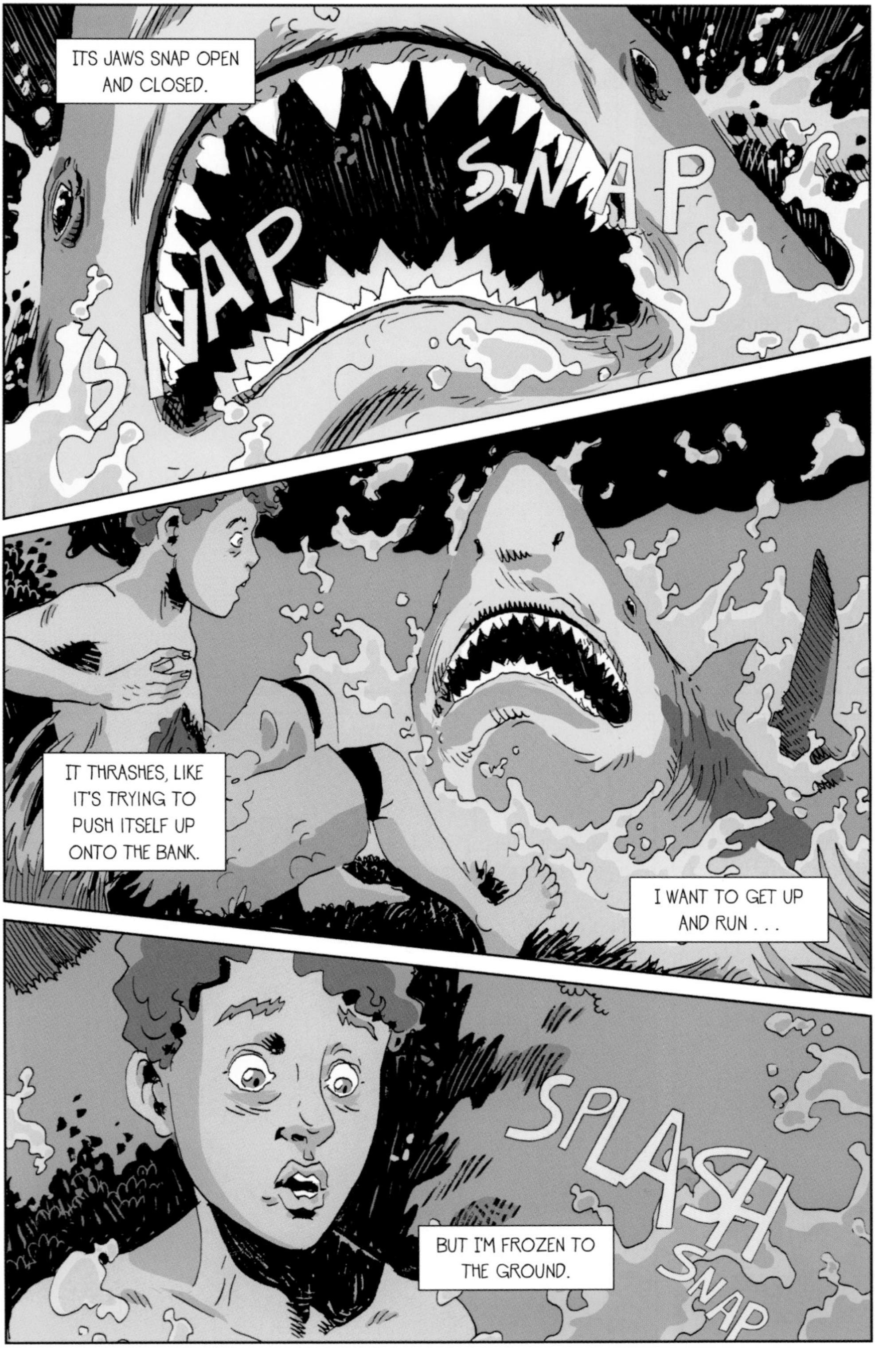
ITS JAWS SNAP OPEN AND CLOSED.
SNAP SNAP
IT THRASHES, LIKE IT'S TRYING TO PUSH ITSELF UP ONTO THE BANK.
I WANT TO GET UP AND RUN . . .
BUT I'M FROZEN TO THE GROUND.
SPLASH
SNAP

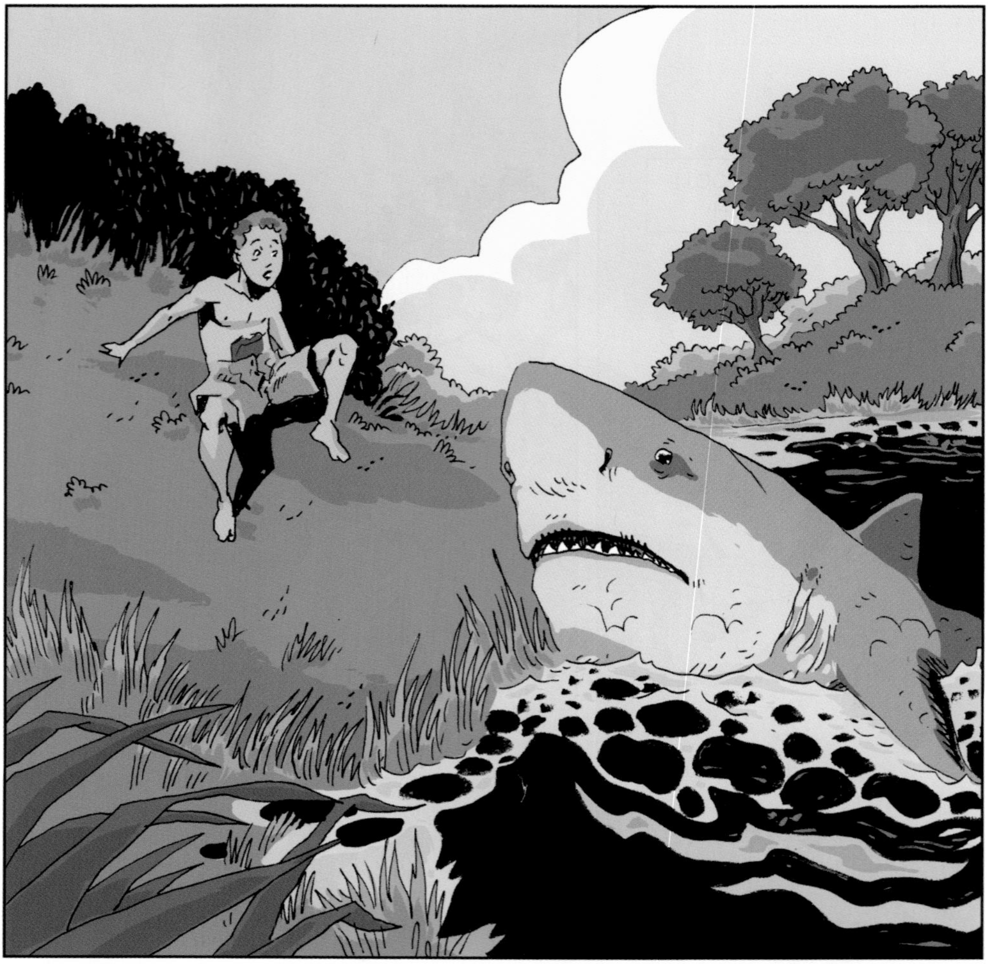

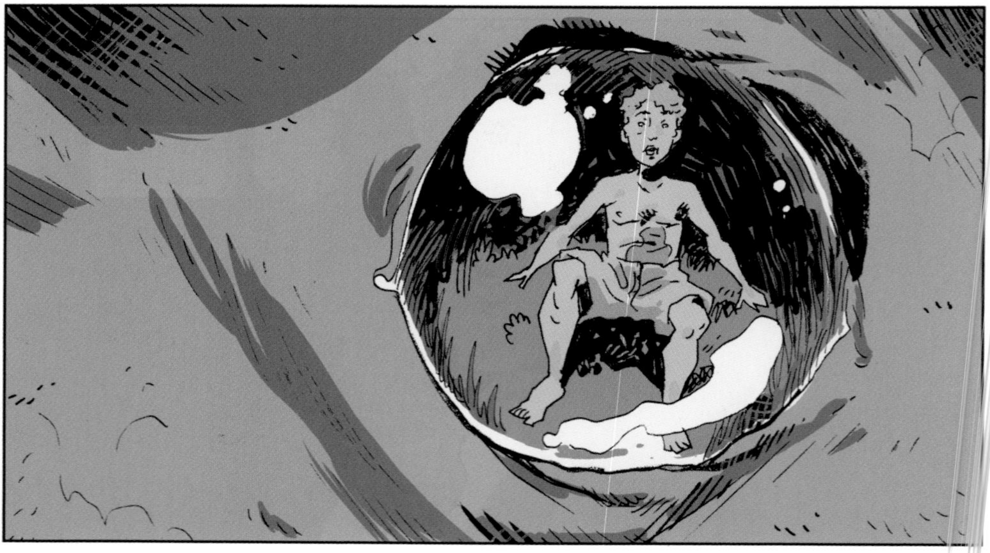

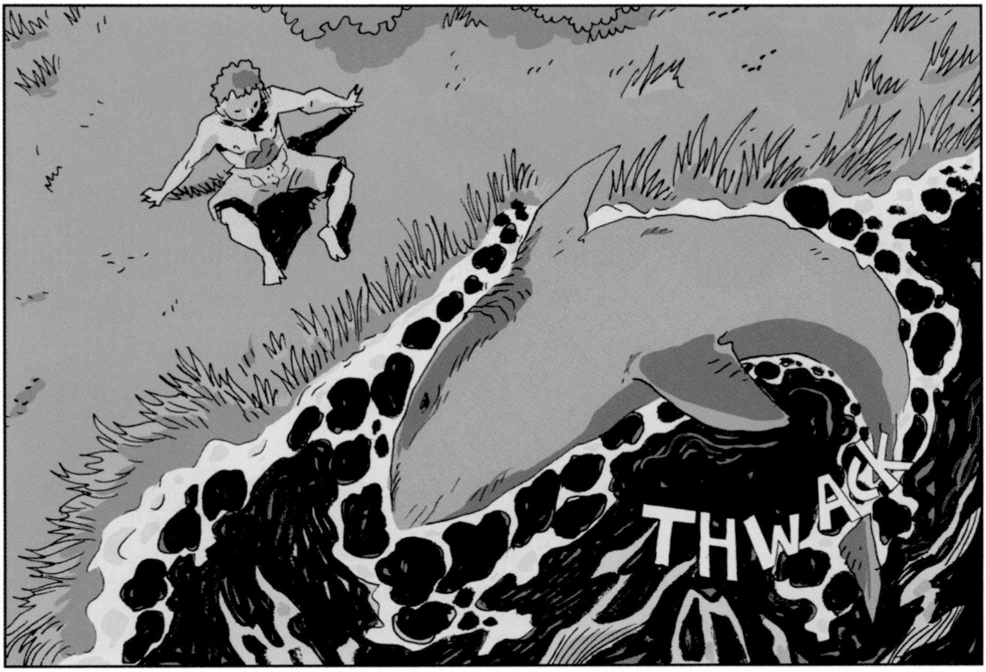
THWACK

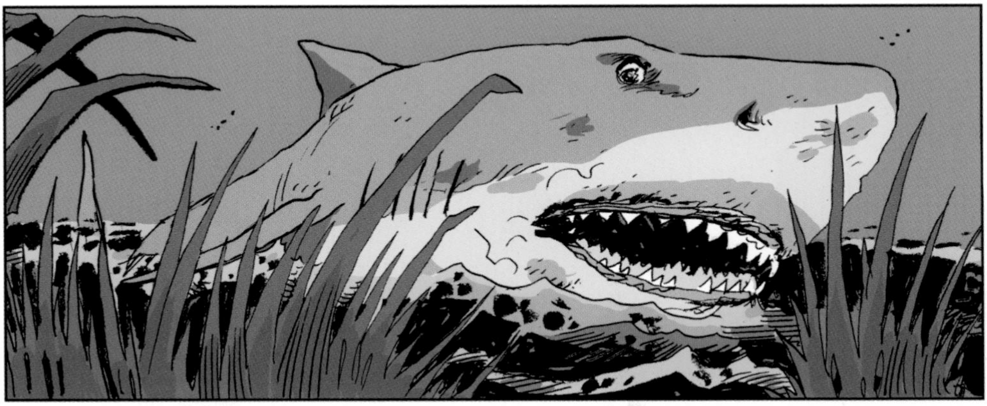

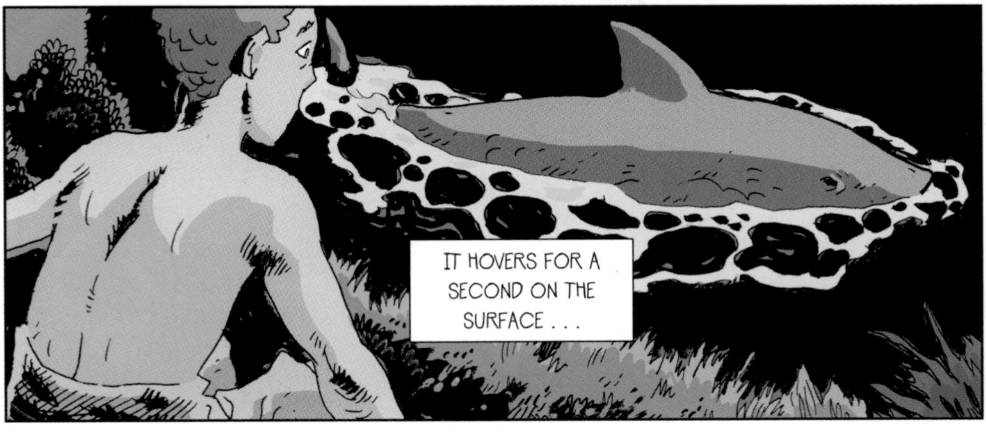
IT HOVERS FOR A
SECOND ON THE
SURFACE . . .

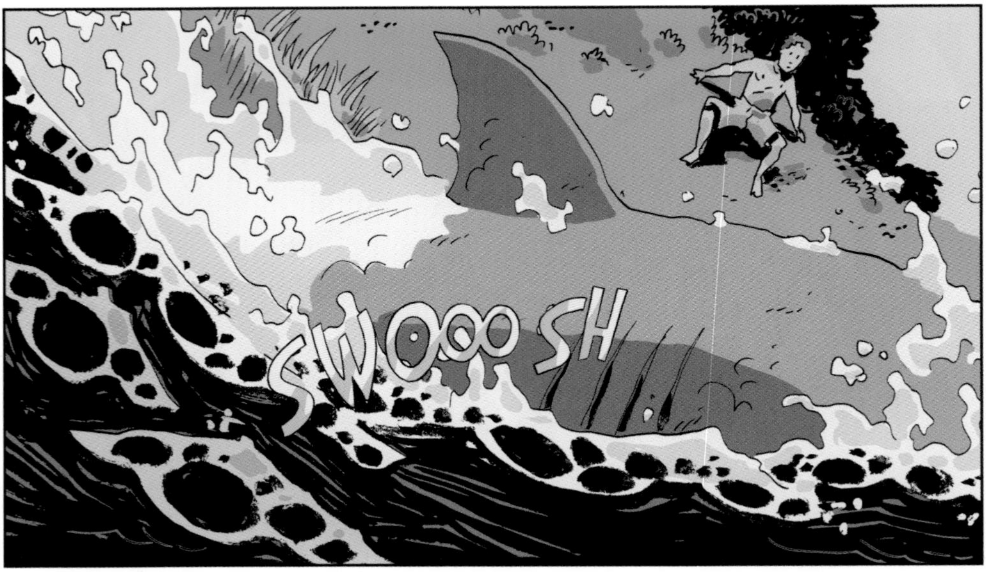
SWOOOSH

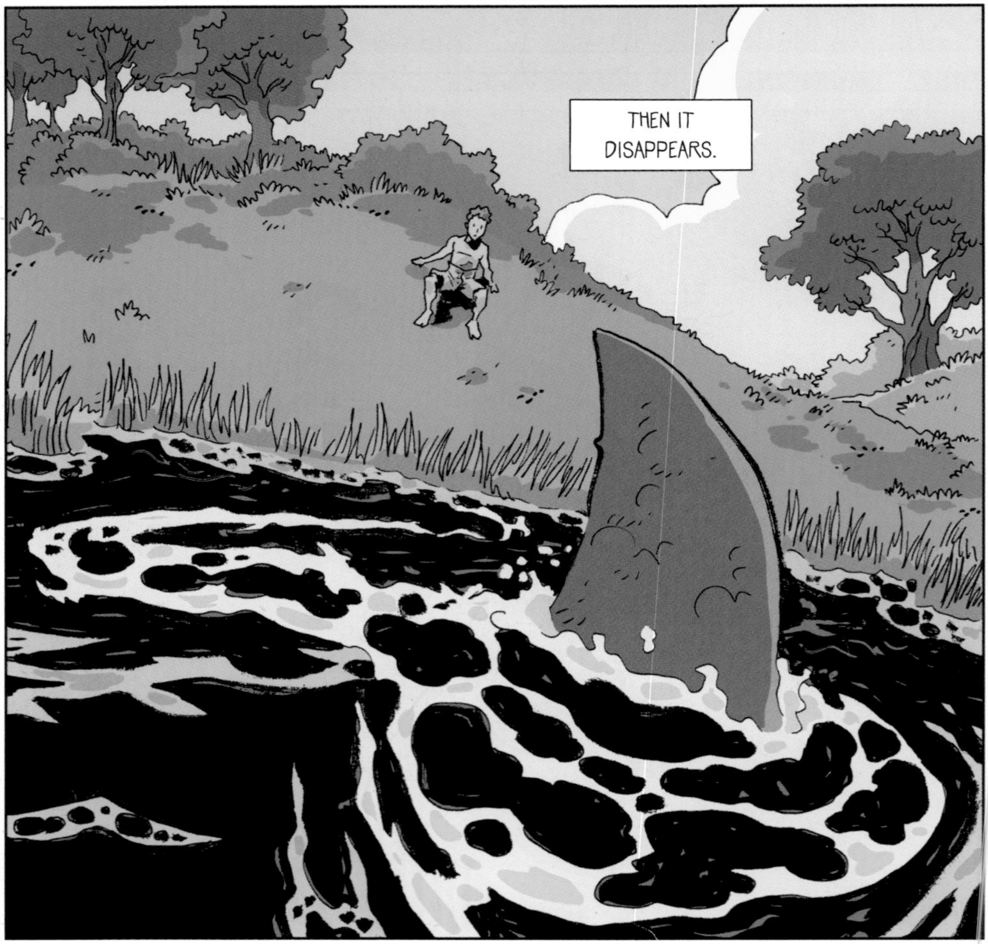
THEN IT DISAPPEARS.

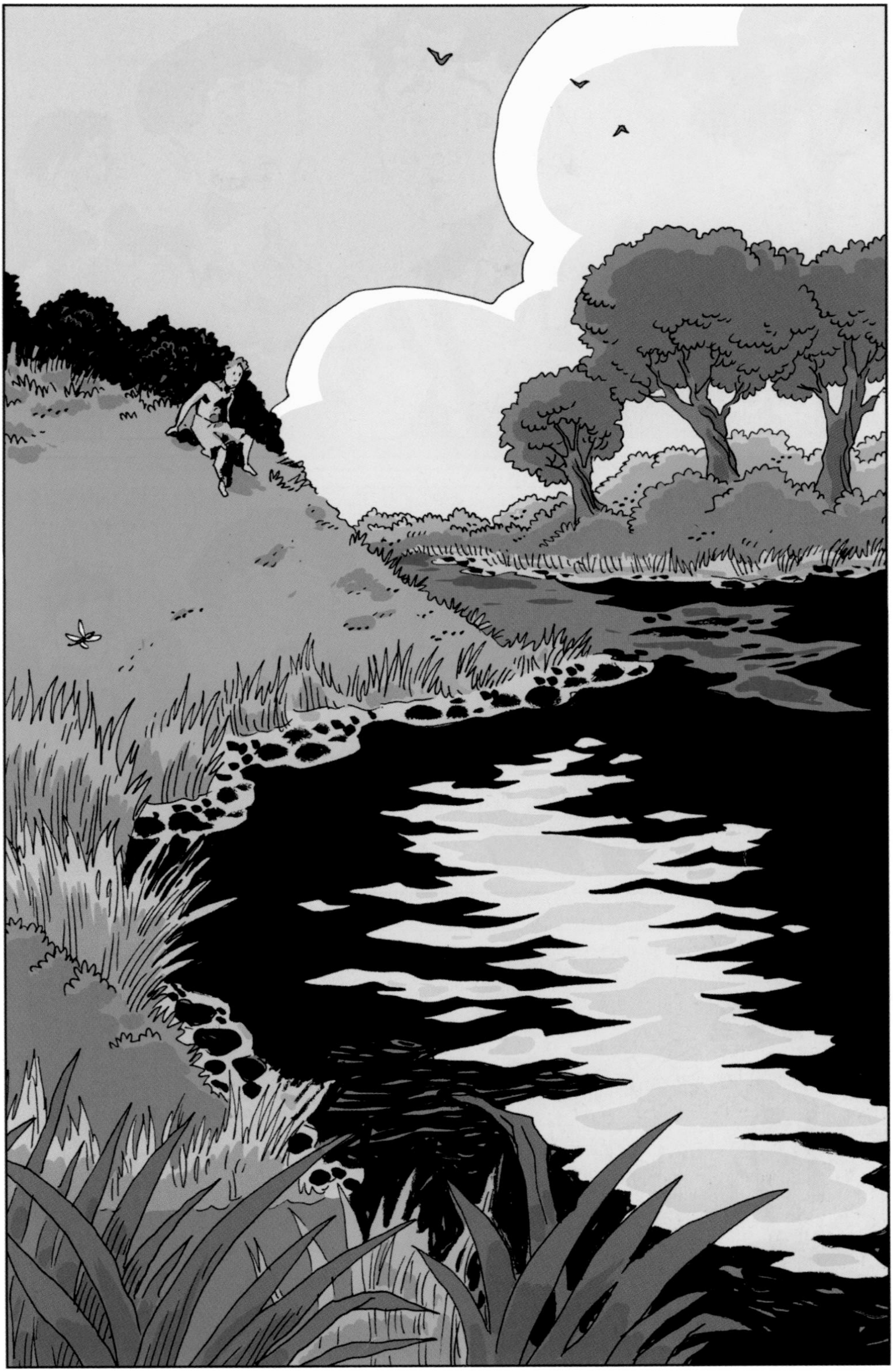

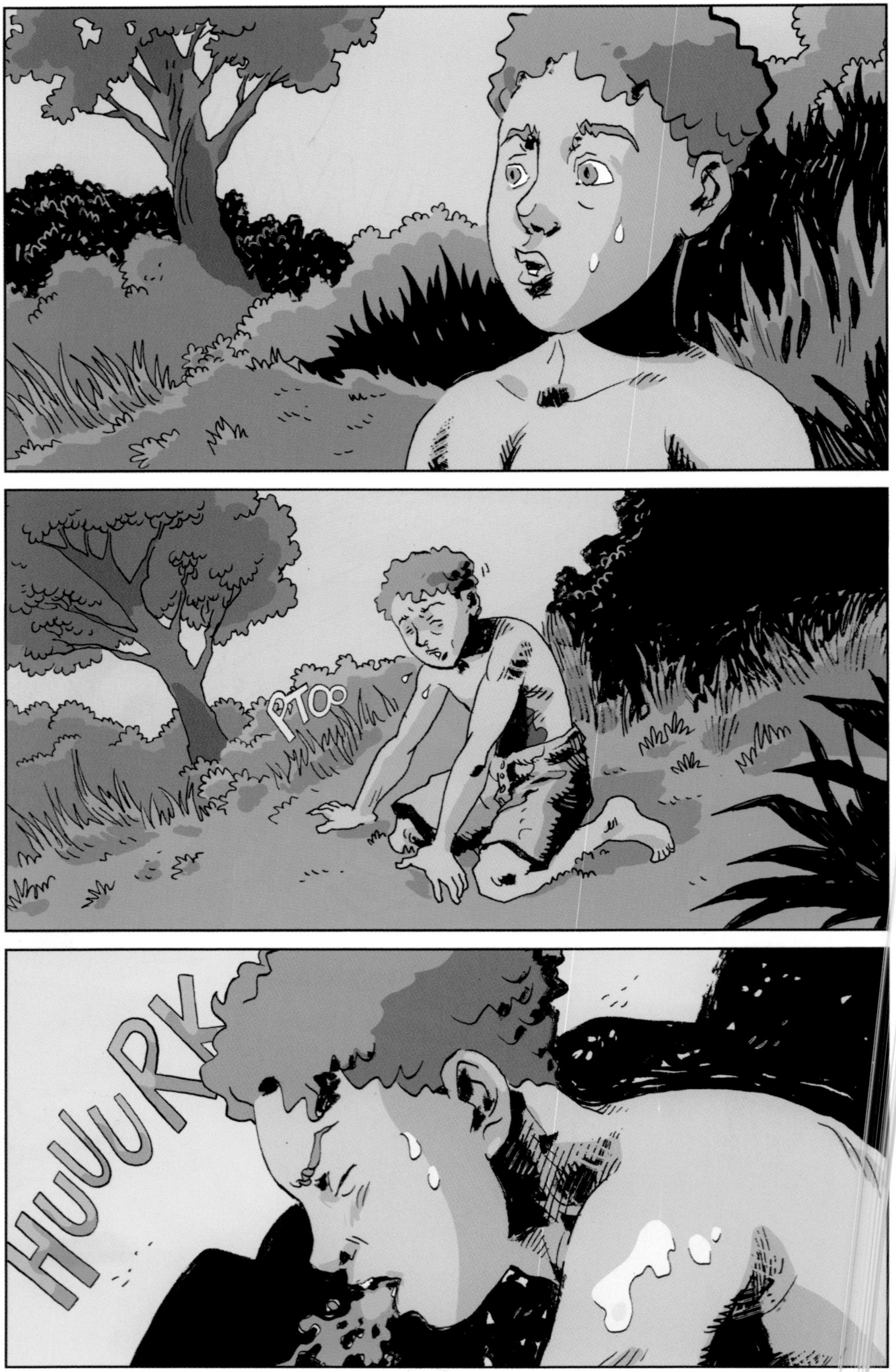
PTOO
HUUURK

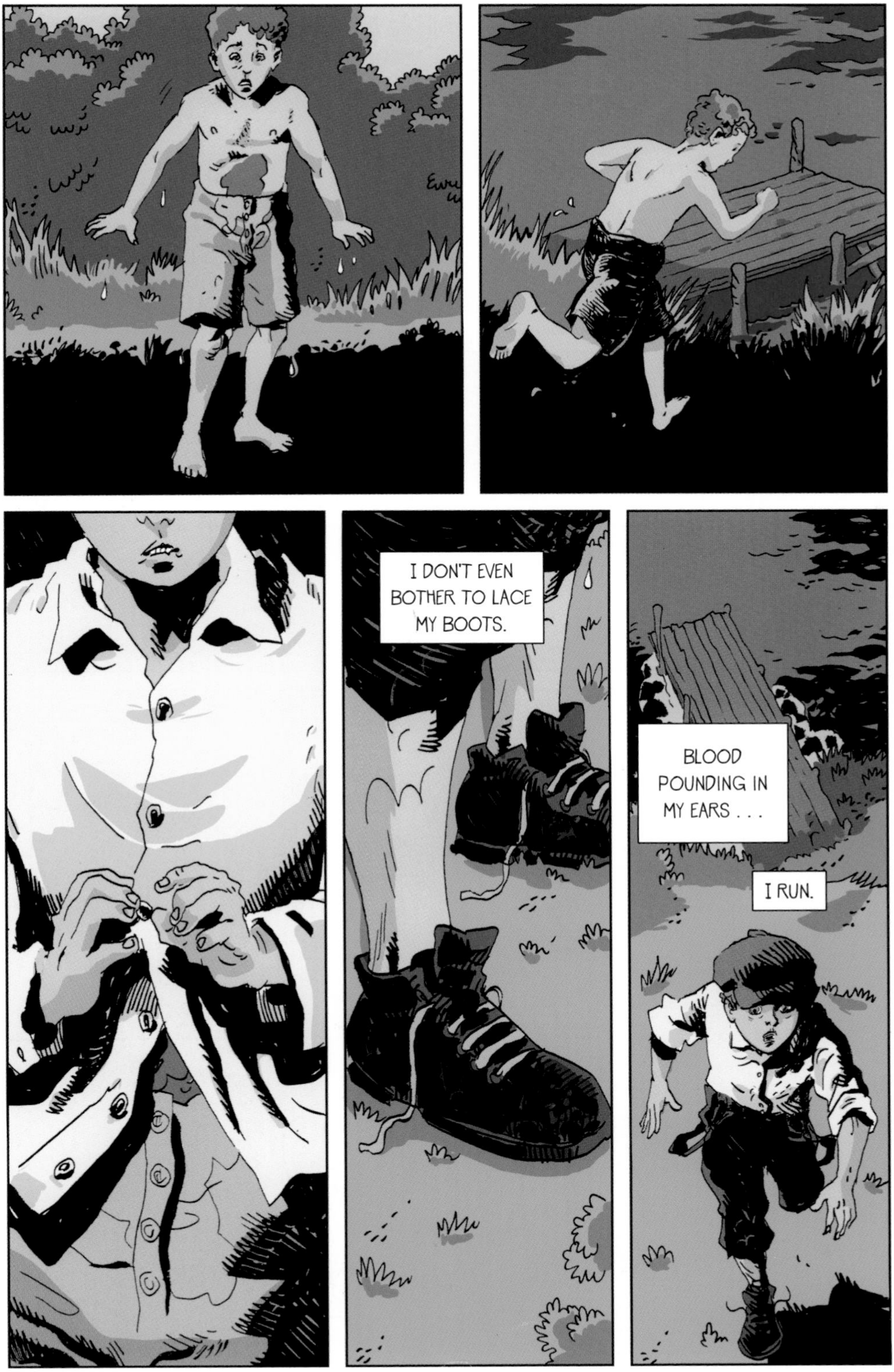
I DON'T EVEN BOTHER TO LACE MY BOOTS.
BLOOD POUNDING IN MY EARS . . .
I RUN.

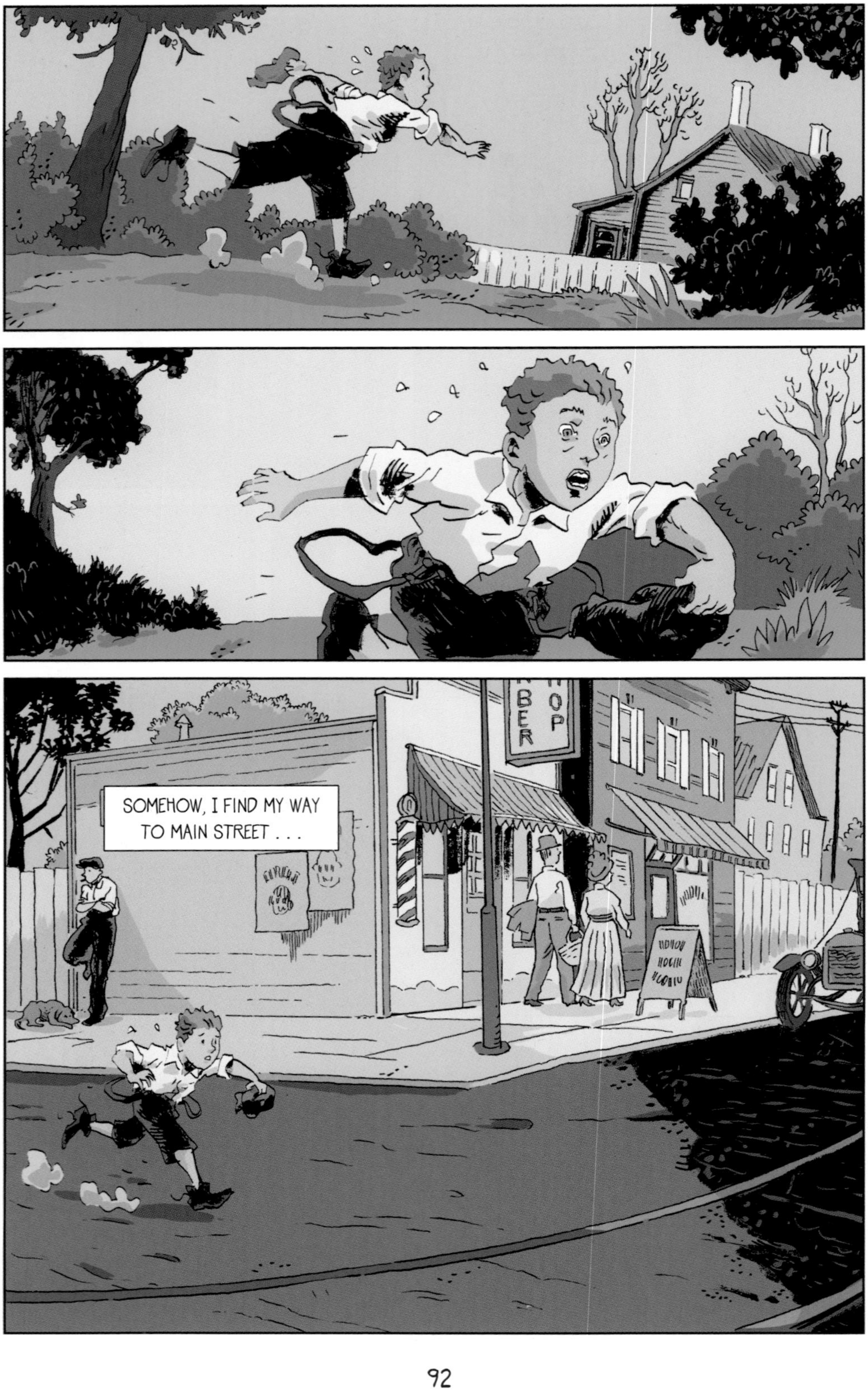
SOMEHOW, I FIND MY WAY TO MAIN STREET . . .

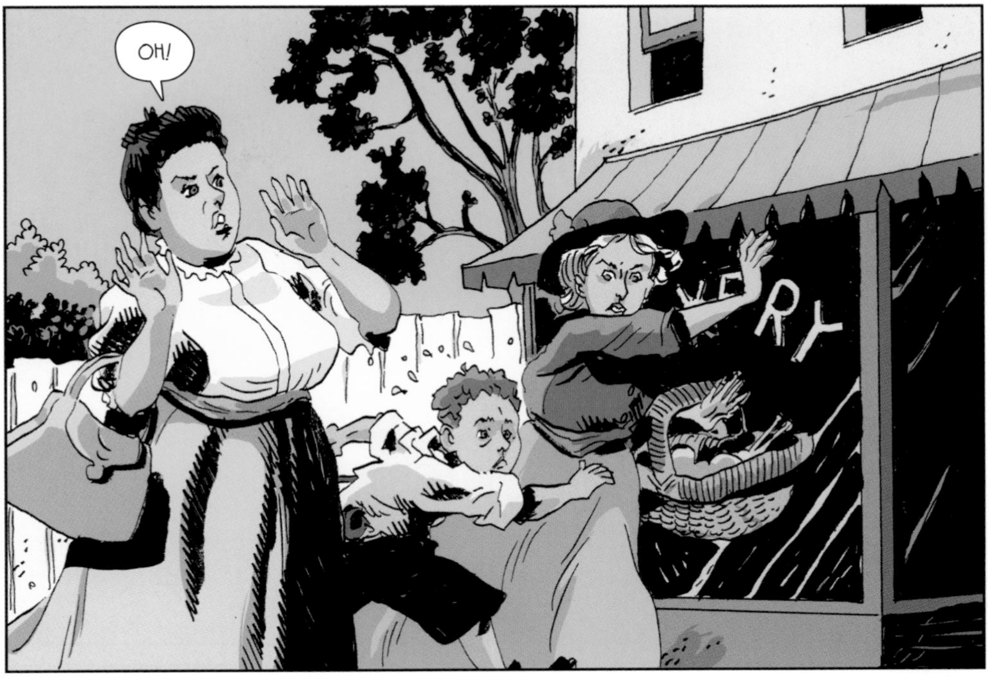
OH!

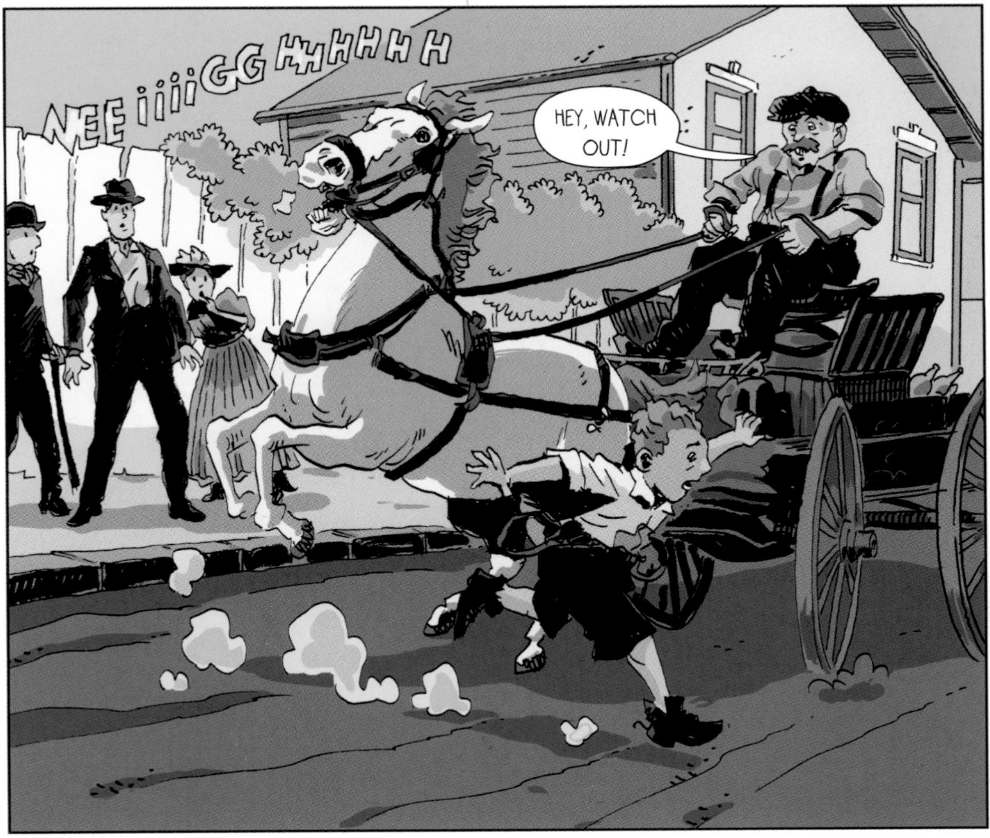
NEEiiiiGGHHHHHH
HEY, WATCH OUT!

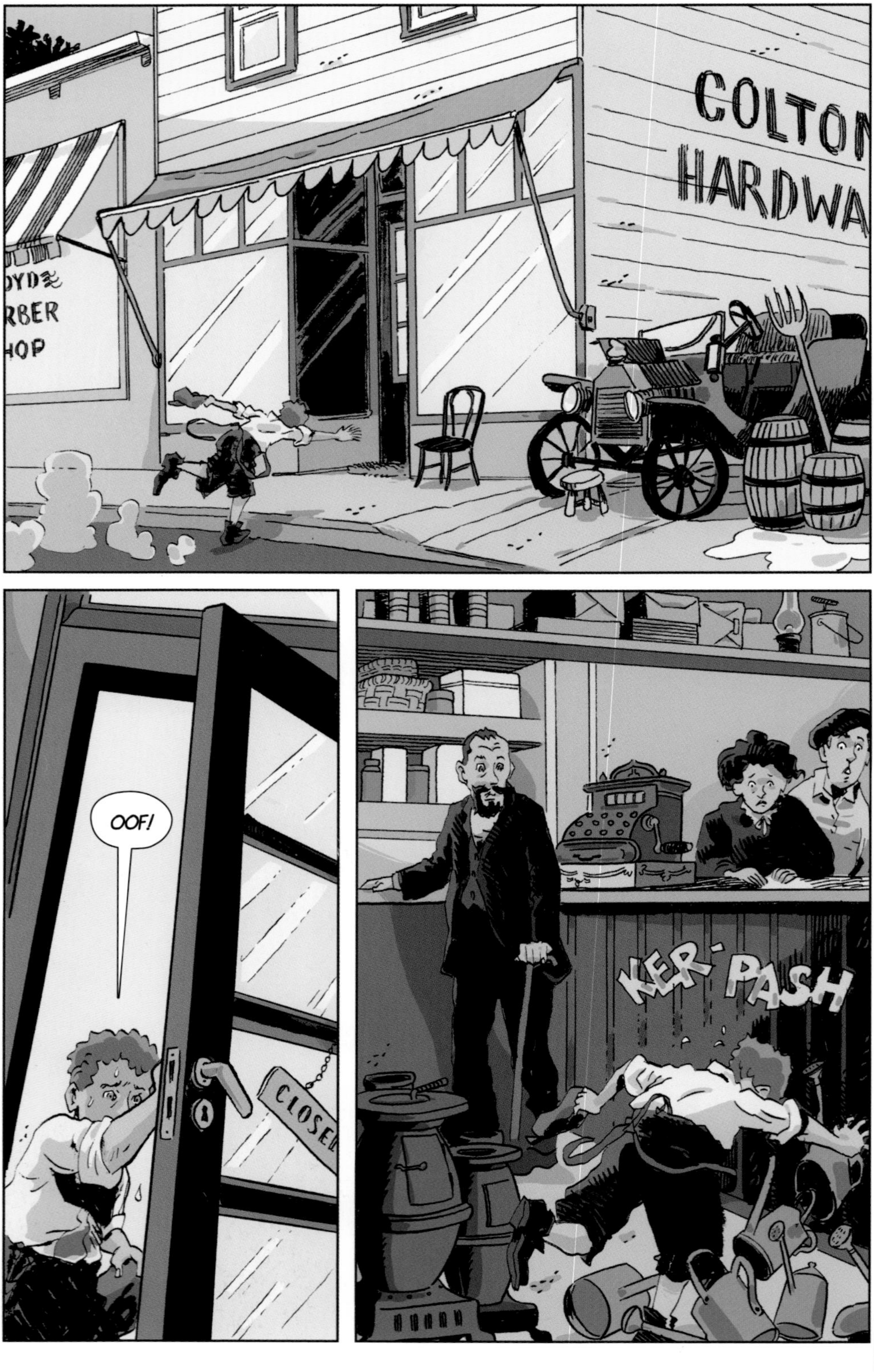
COLTON
HARDWA
OYDE
RBER
HOP
OOF!
CLOSE
KER-PASH

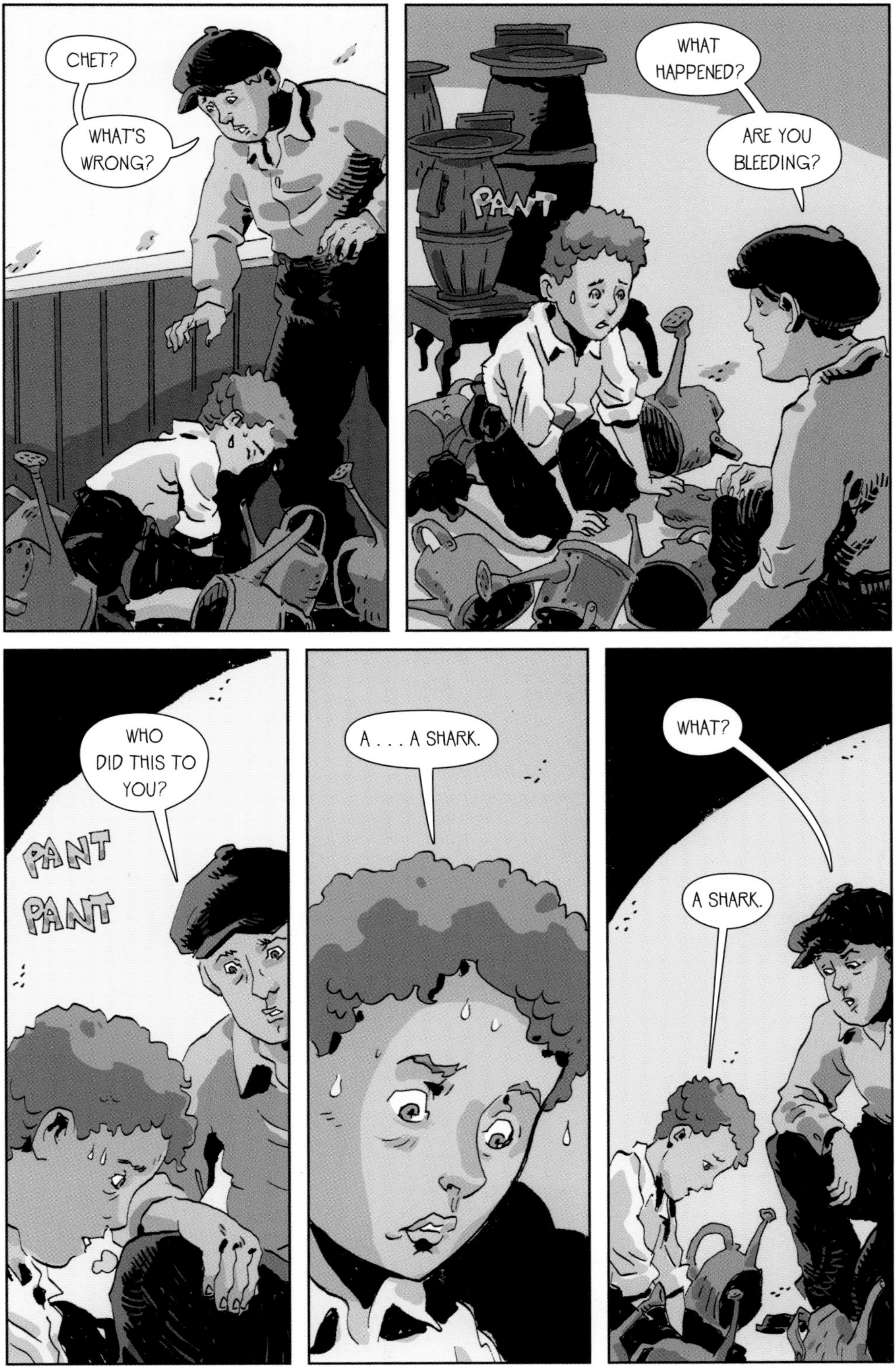
CHET?
WHAT'S WRONG?
WHAT HAPPENED?
ARE YOU BLEEDING?
PANT
WHO DID THIS TO YOU?
PANT
PANT
A . . . A SHARK.
WHAT?
A SHARK.

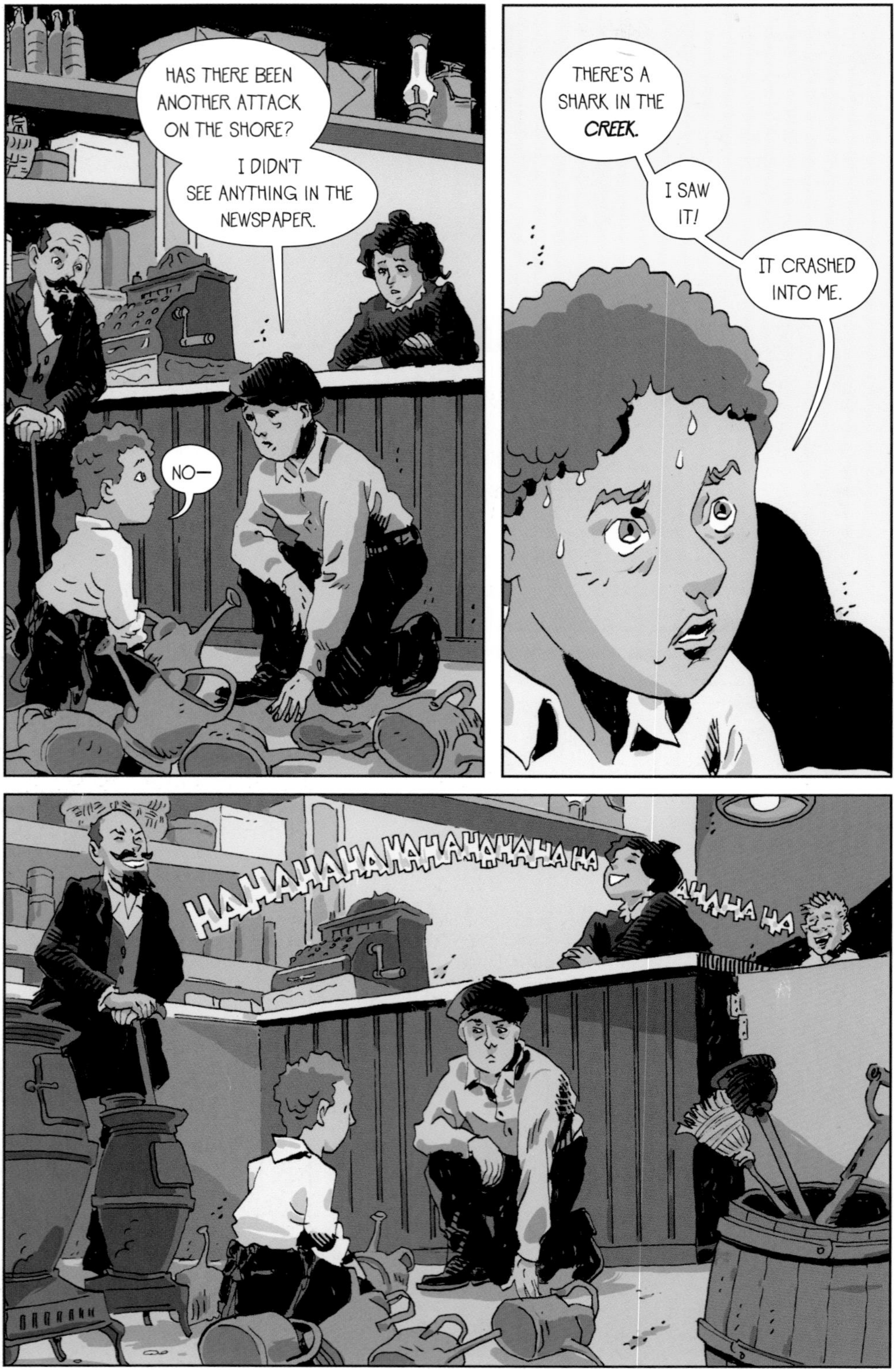
HAS THERE BEEN ANOTHER ATTACK ON THE SHORE?
I DIDN'T SEE ANYTHING IN THE NEWSPAPER.
NO—
THERE'S A SHARK IN THE *CREEK.*
I SAW IT!
IT CRASHED INTO ME.
HAHAHAHAHAHAHAHAHAHAHA HA
HAHAHA HA

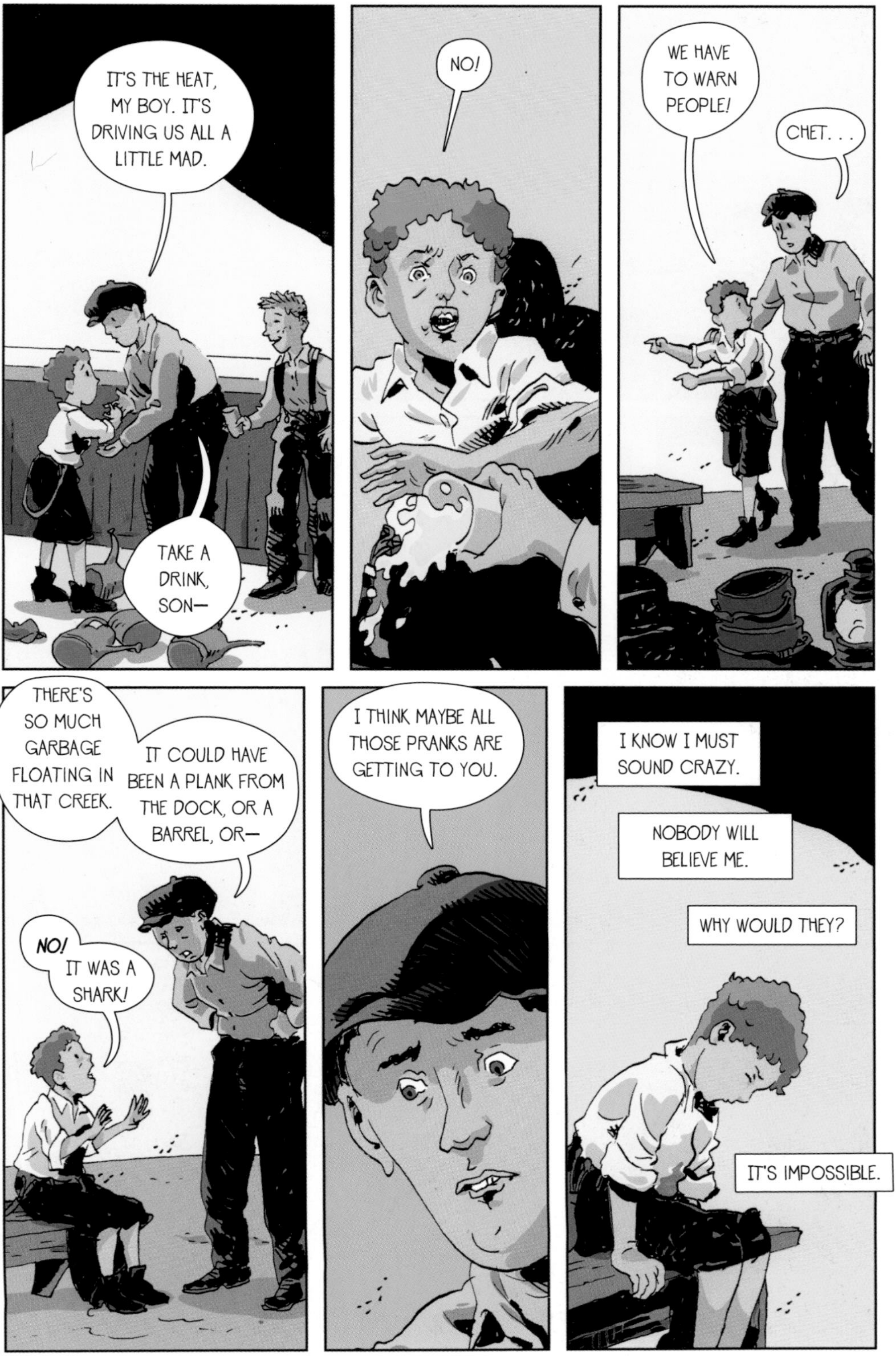
IT'S THE HEAT, MY BOY. IT'S DRIVING US ALL A LITTLE MAD.
TAKE A DRINK, SON—
NO!
WE HAVE TO WARN PEOPLE!
CHET. . .
THERE'S SO MUCH GARBAGE FLOATING IN THAT CREEK.
IT COULD HAVE BEEN A PLANK FROM THE DOCK, OR A BARREL, OR—
NO! IT WAS A SHARK!
I THINK MAYBE ALL THOSE PRANKS ARE GETTING TO YOU.
I KNOW I MUST SOUND CRAZY.
NOBODY WILL BELIEVE ME.
WHY WOULD THEY?
IT'S IMPOSSIBLE.

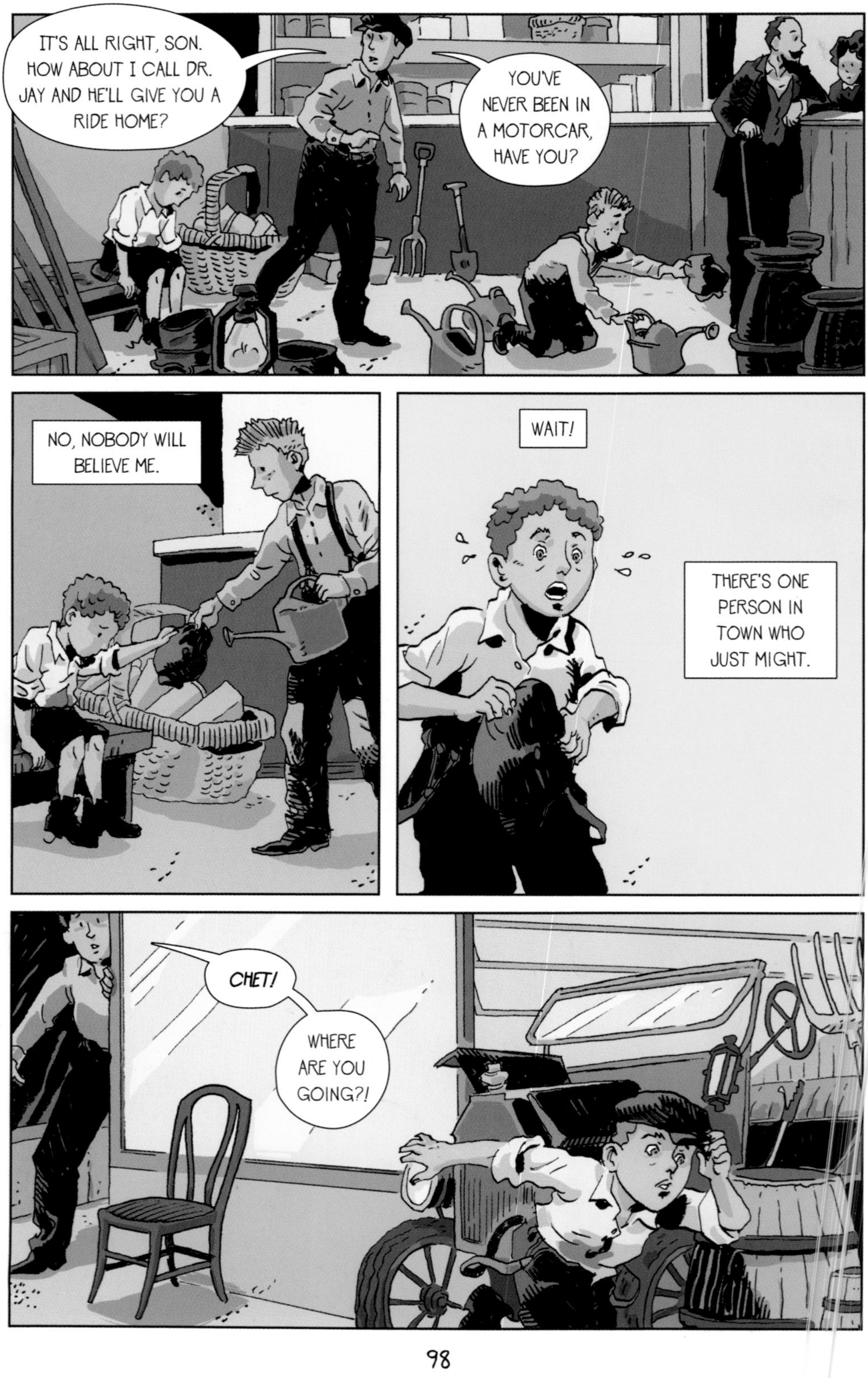
IT'S ALL RIGHT, SON. HOW ABOUT I CALL DR. JAY AND HE'LL GIVE YOU A RIDE HOME?
YOU'VE NEVER BEEN IN A MOTORCAR, HAVE YOU?
NO, NOBODY WILL BELIEVE ME.
WAIT!
THERE'S ONE PERSON IN TOWN WHO JUST MIGHT.
CHET!
WHERE ARE YOU GOING?!

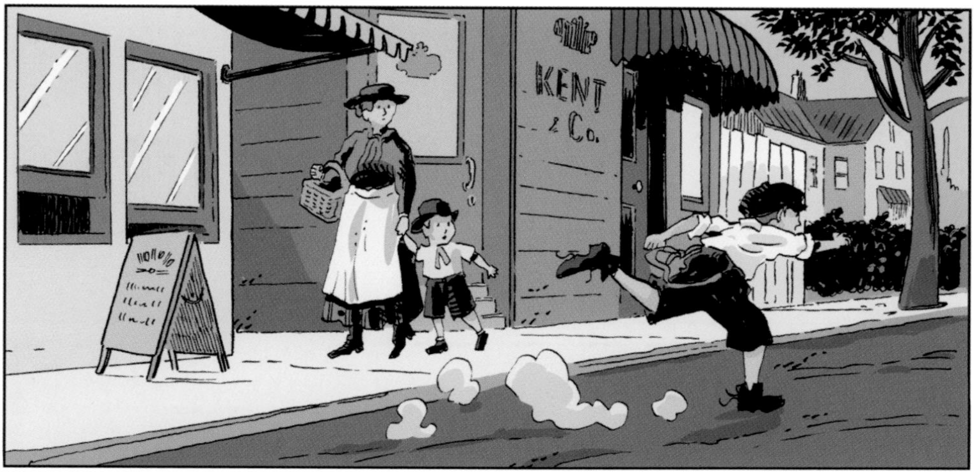
KENT
& Co.

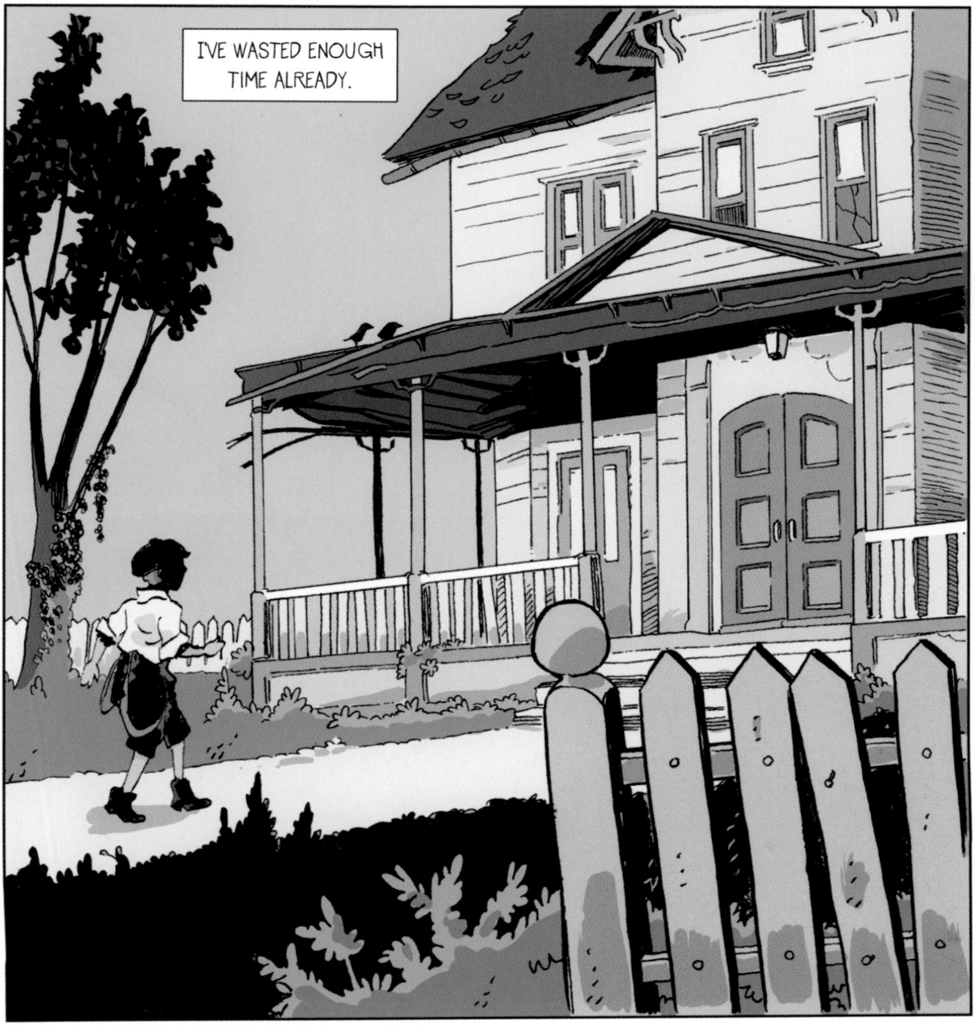
I'VE WASTED ENOUGH TIME ALREADY.

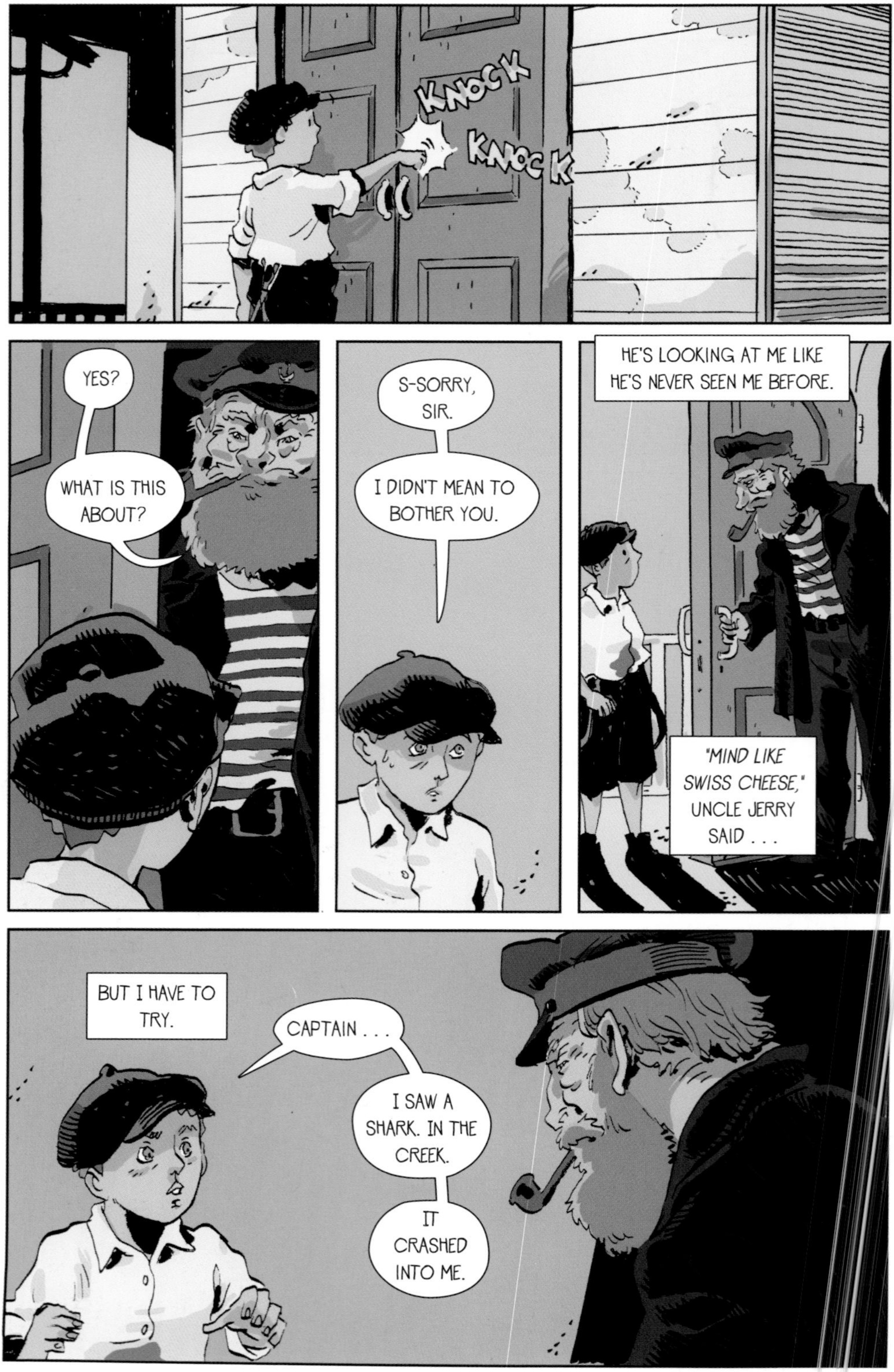
KNOCK
KNOCK
YES?
WHAT IS THIS ABOUT?
S-SORRY, SIR.
I DIDN'T MEAN TO BOTHER YOU.
HE'S LOOKING AT ME LIKE HE'S NEVER SEEN ME BEFORE.
"MIND LIKE SWISS CHEESE," UNCLE JERRY SAID . . .
BUT I HAVE TO TRY.
CAPTAIN . . .
I SAW A SHARK. IN THE CREEK.
IT CRASHED INTO ME.

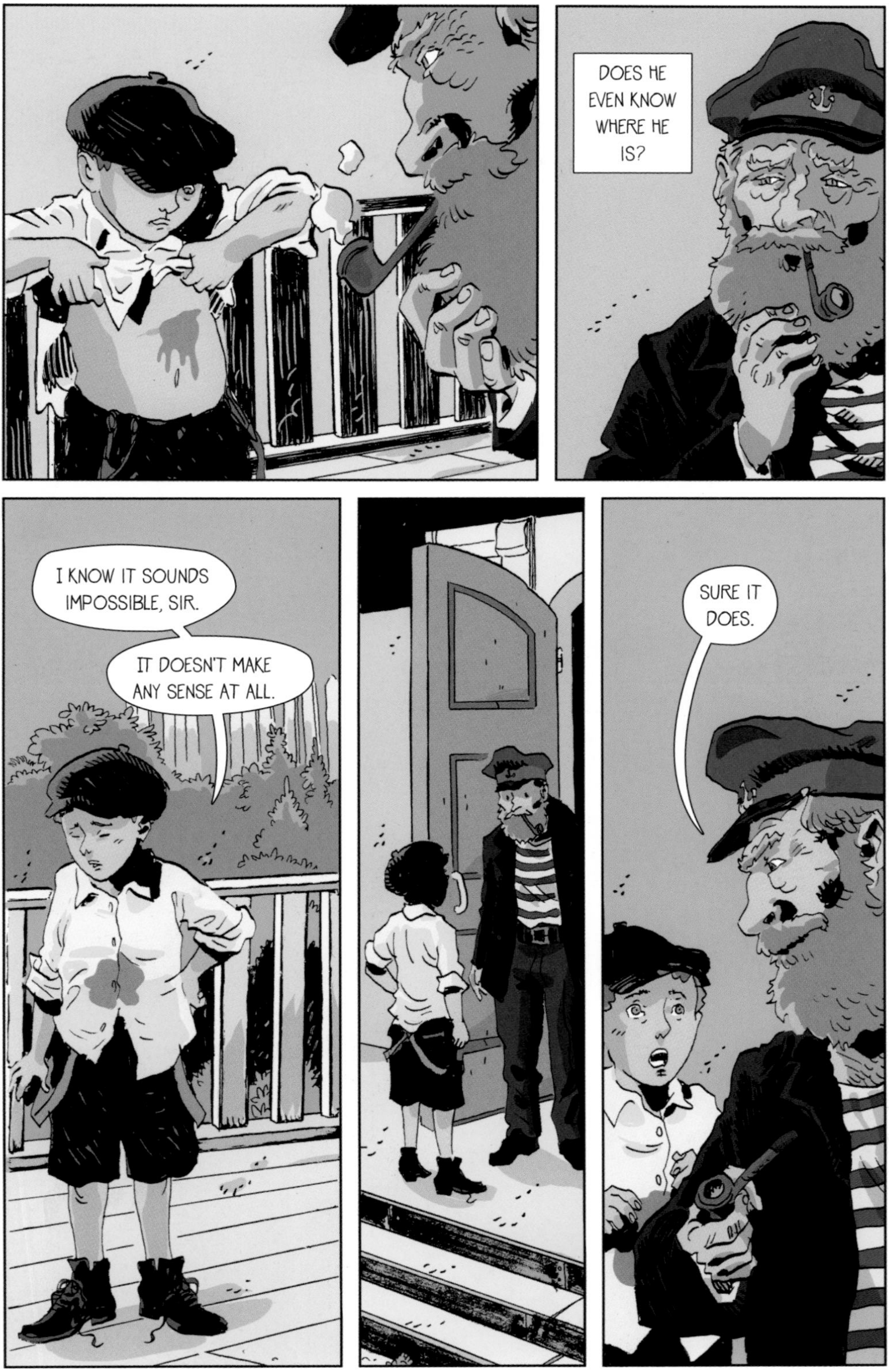
DOES HE
EVEN KNOW
WHERE HE
IS?
I KNOW IT SOUNDS IMPOSSIBLE, SIR.
IT DOESN'T MAKE ANY SENSE AT ALL.
SURE IT DOES.

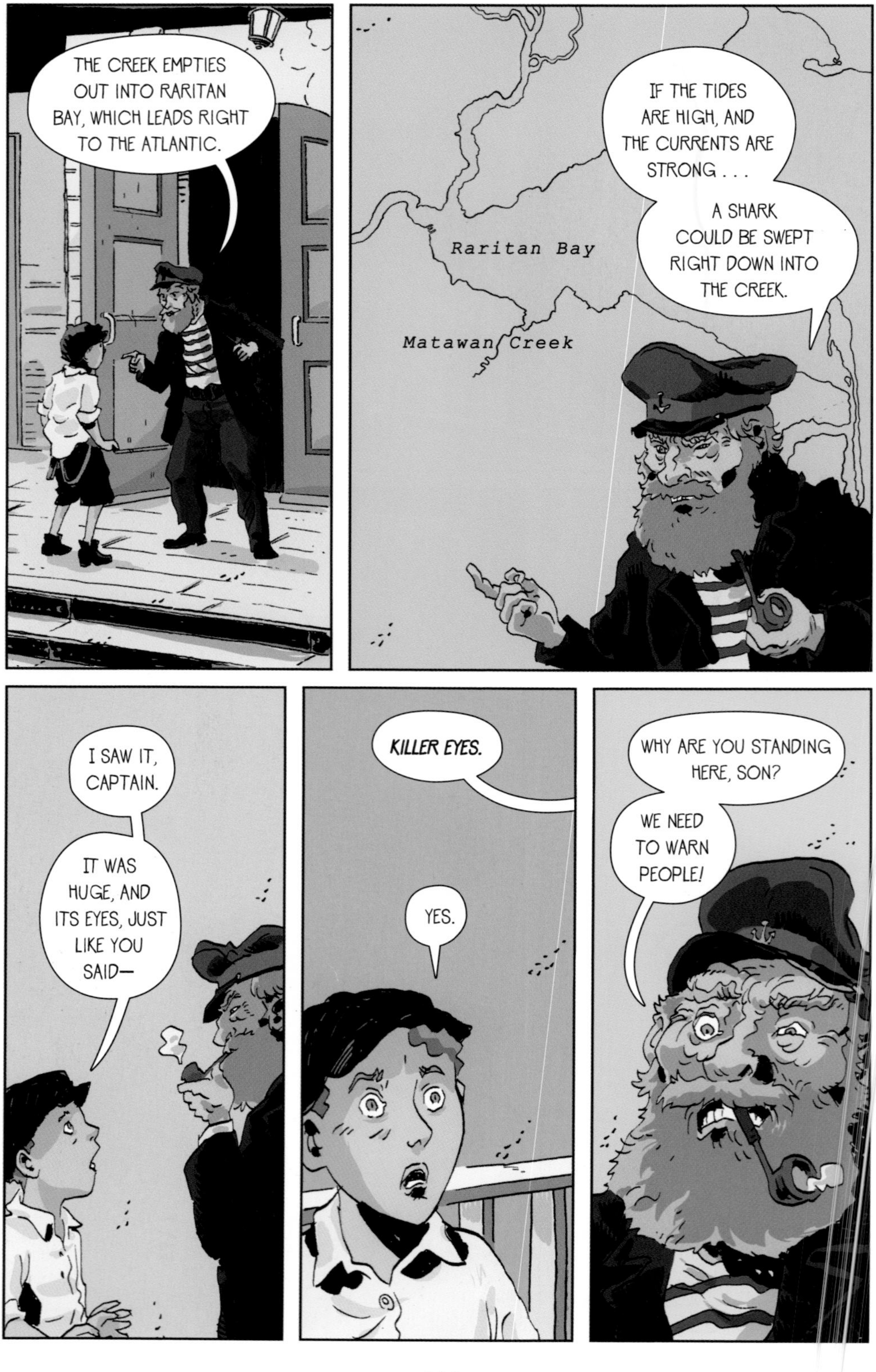
THE CREEK EMPTIES OUT INTO RARITAN BAY, WHICH LEADS RIGHT TO THE ATLANTIC.
IF THE TIDES ARE HIGH, AND THE CURRENTS ARE STRONG . . .
A SHARK COULD BE SWEPT RIGHT DOWN INTO THE CREEK.
Raritan Bay
Matawan Creek
I SAW IT, CAPTAIN.
IT WAS HUGE, AND ITS EYES, JUST LIKE YOU SAID—
KILLER EYES.
YES.
WHY ARE YOU STANDING HERE, SON?
WE NEED TO WARN PEOPLE!

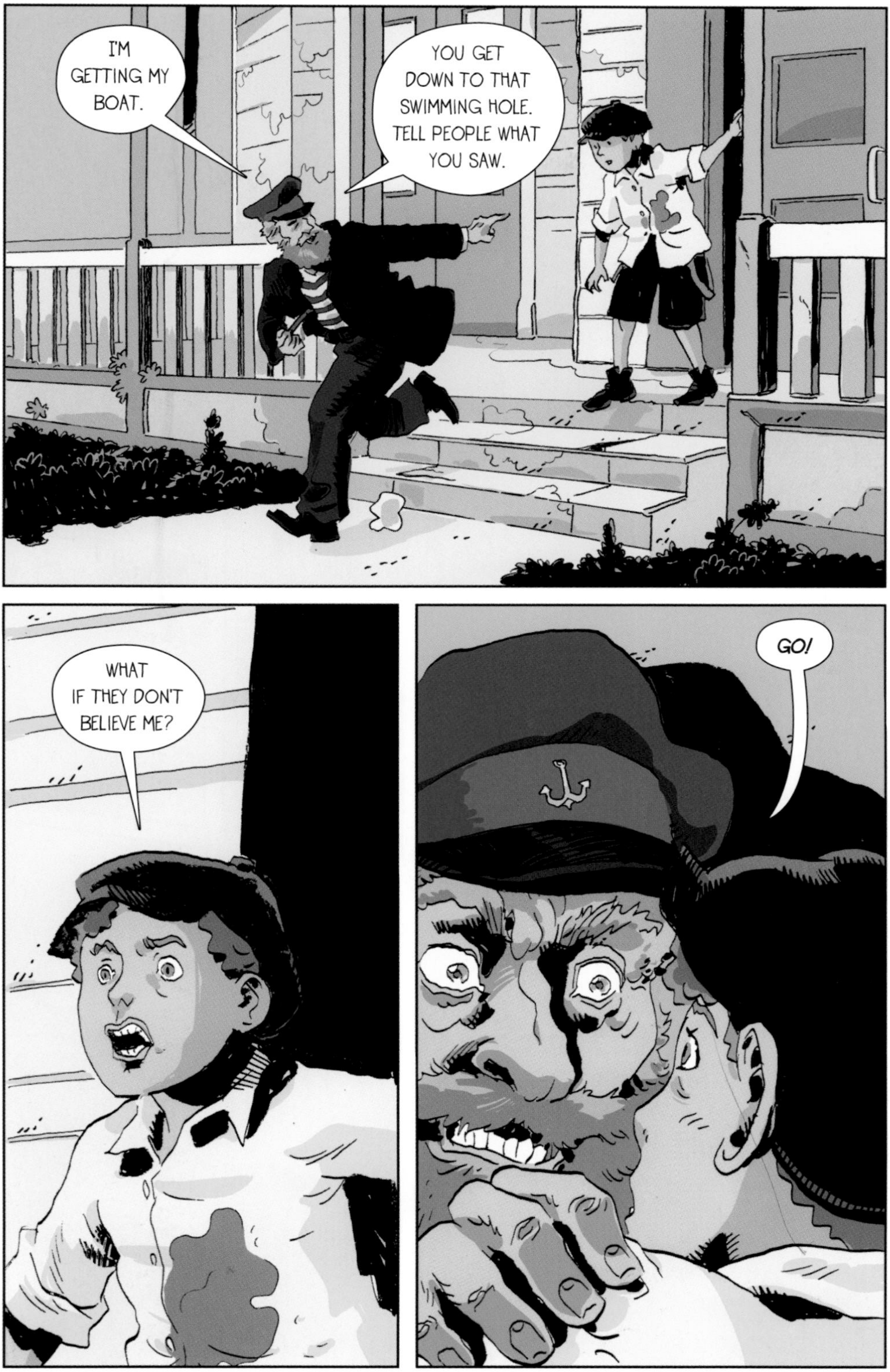
I'M GETTING MY BOAT.
YOU GET DOWN TO THAT SWIMMING HOLE. TELL PEOPLE WHAT YOU SAW.
WHAT IF THEY DON'T BELIEVE ME?
GO!

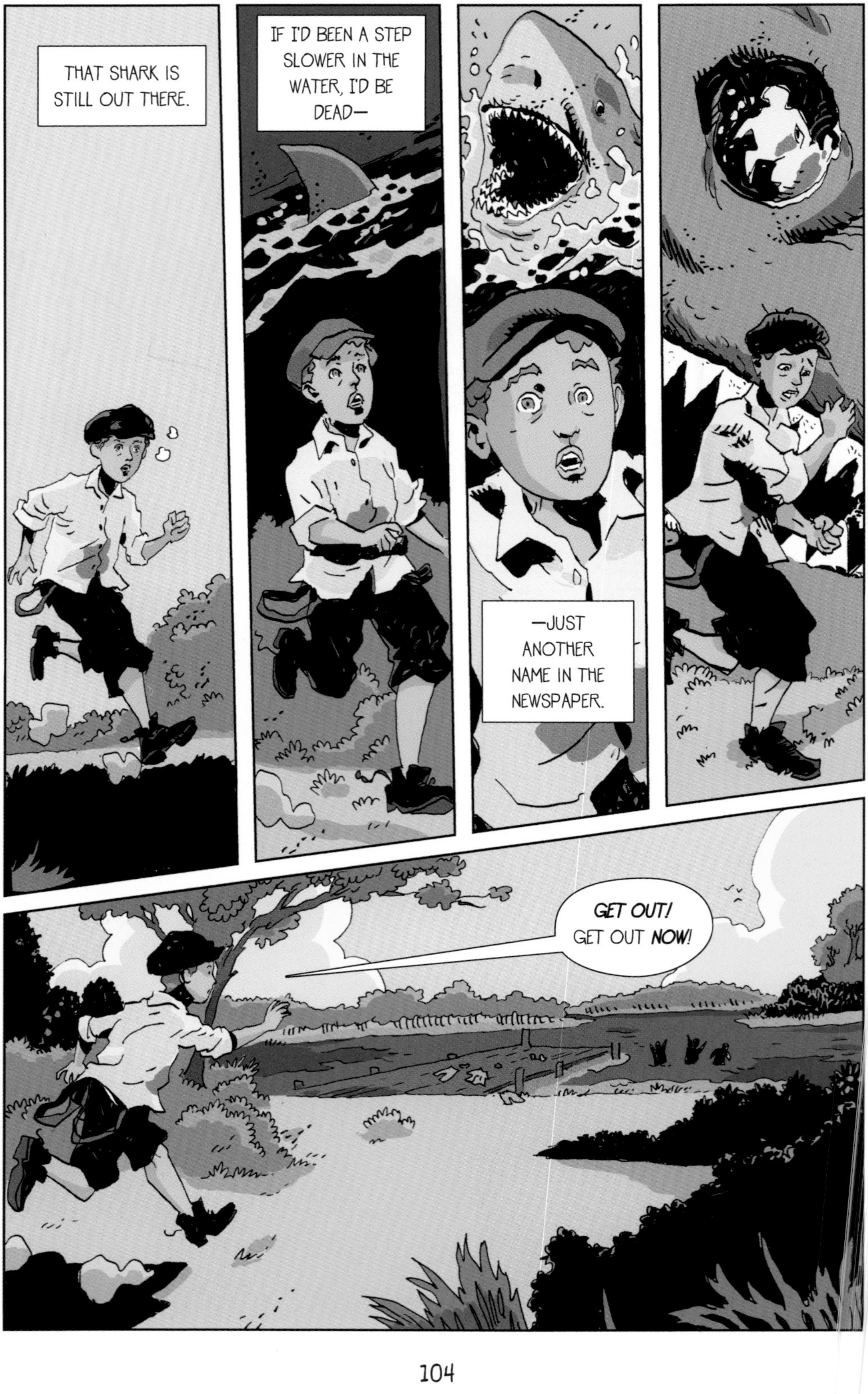
THAT SHARK IS STILL OUT THERE.
IF I'D BEEN A STEP SLOWER IN THE WATER, I'D BE DEAD—
—JUST ANOTHER NAME IN THE NEWSPAPER.
GET OUT! GET OUT NOW!

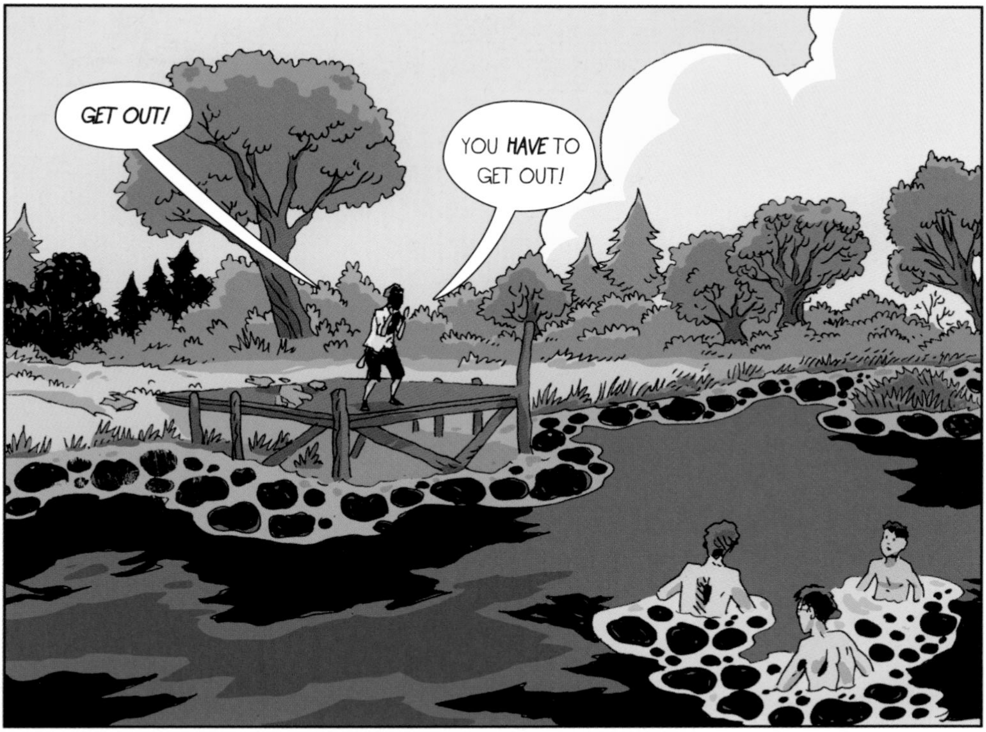
GET OUT!
YOU HAVE TO GET OUT!

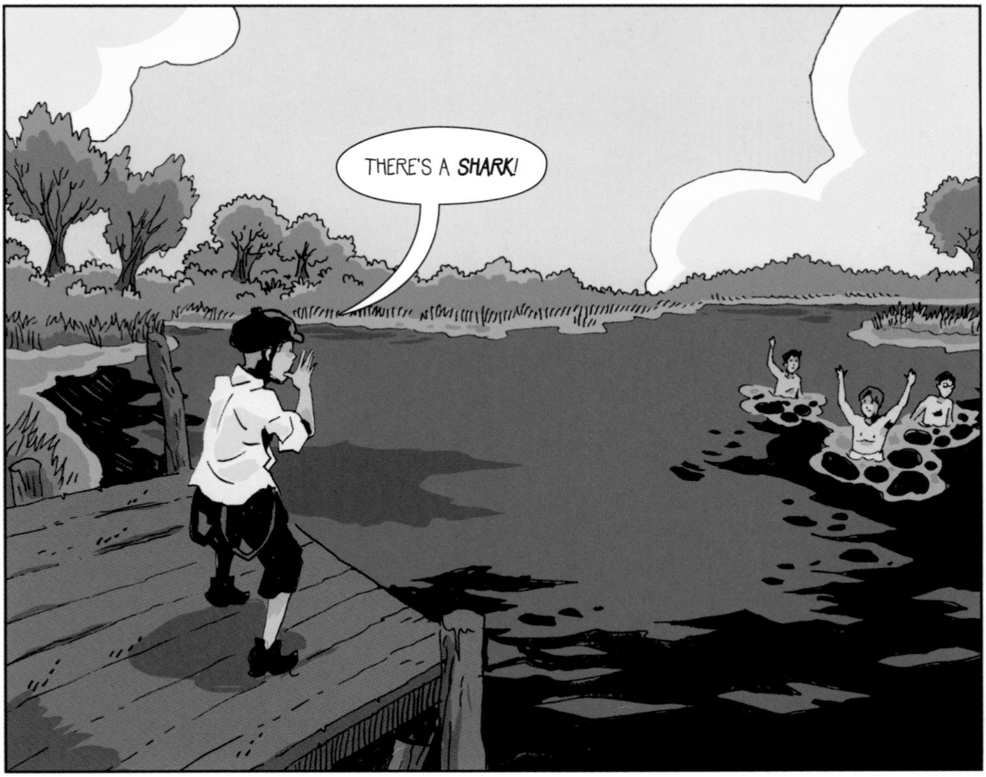
THERE'S A SHARK!

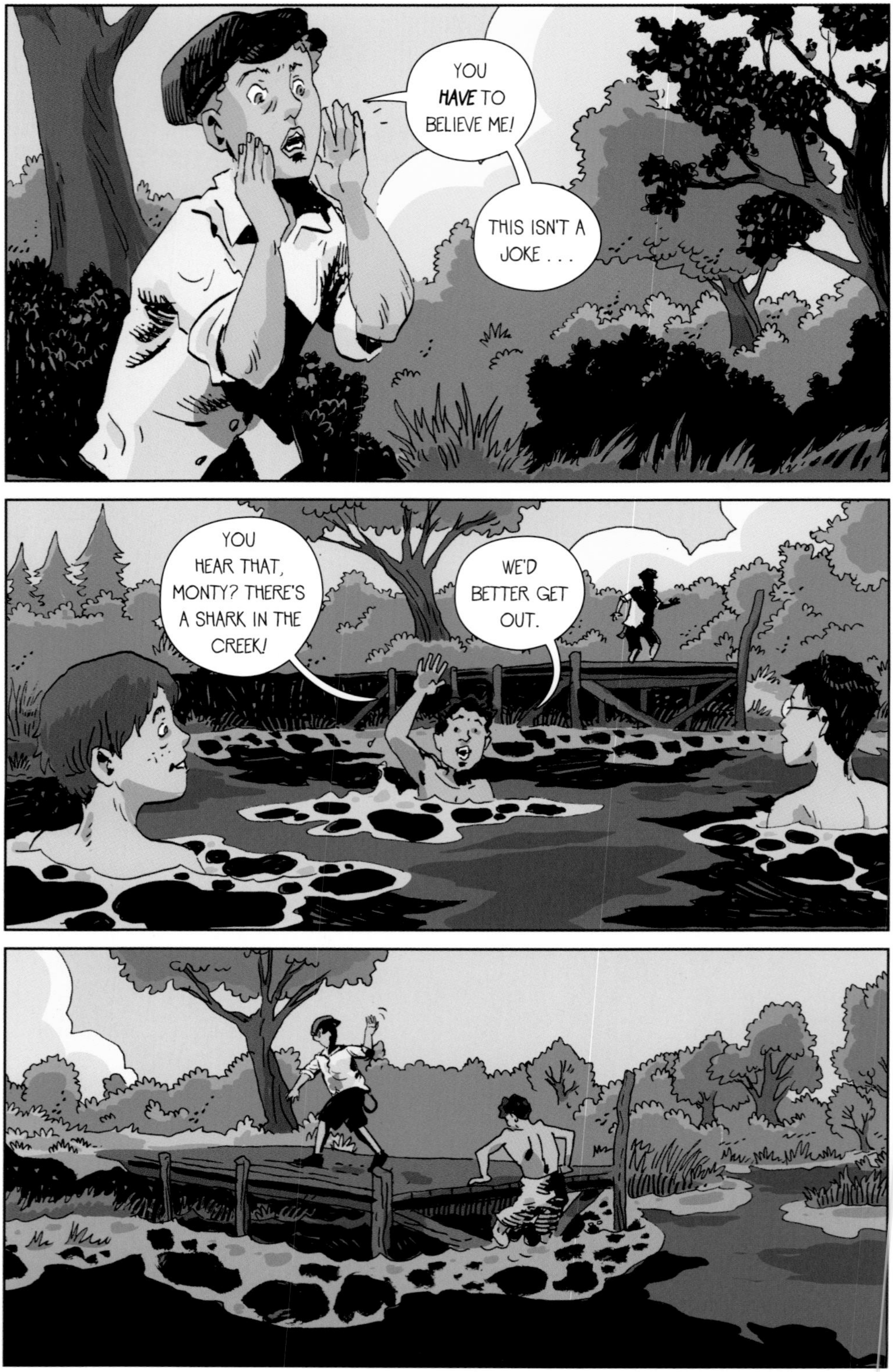
YOU **HAVE** TO BELIEVE ME!
THIS ISN'T A JOKE . . .
YOU HEAR THAT, MONTY? THERE'S A SHARK IN THE CREEK!
WE'D BETTER GET OUT.

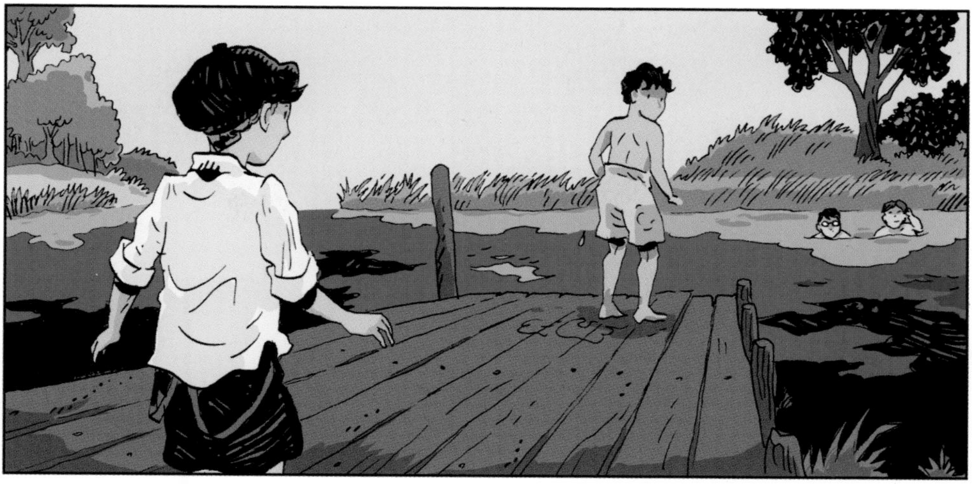

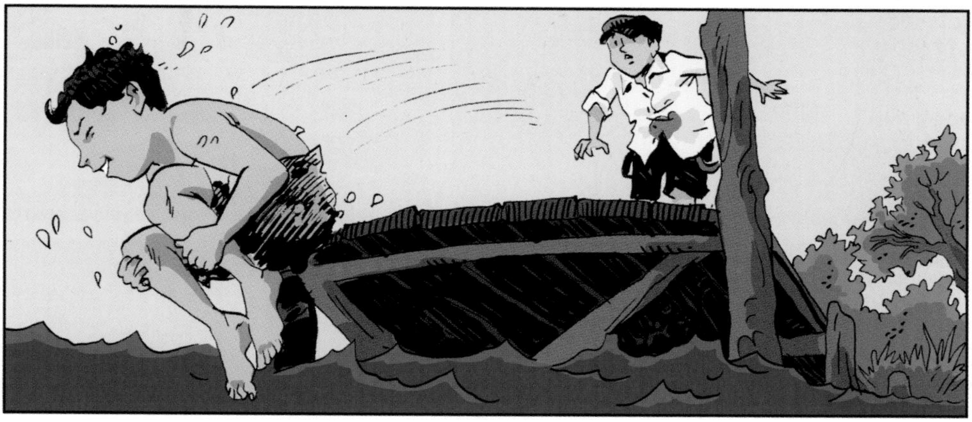

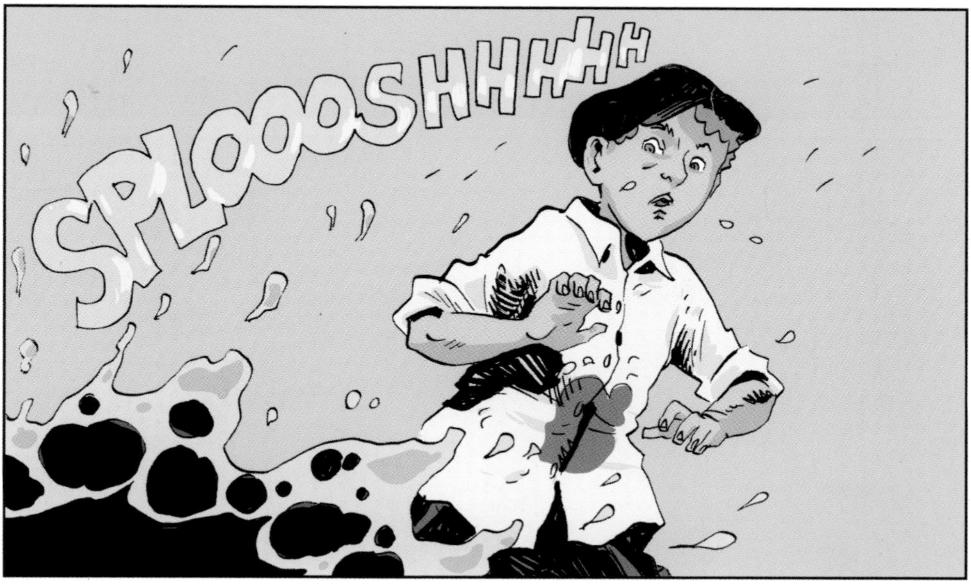
SPLOOOSHHHHHH

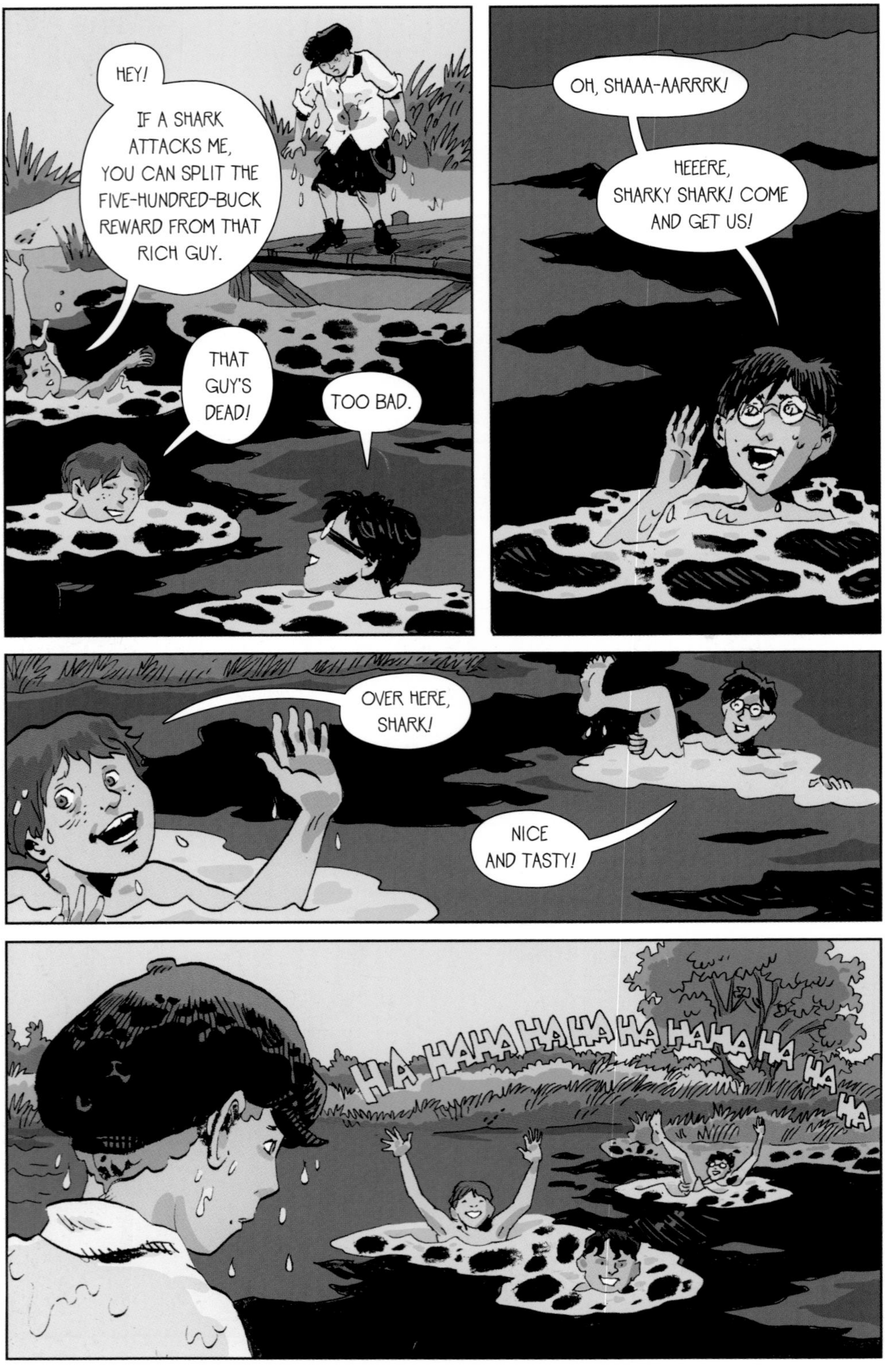
HEY!
IF A SHARK ATTACKS ME, YOU CAN SPLIT THE FIVE-HUNDRED-BUCK REWARD FROM THAT RICH GUY.
THAT GUY'S DEAD!
TOO BAD.
OH, SHAAA-AARRRK!
HEEERE, SHARKY SHARK! COME AND GET US!
OVER HERE, SHARK!
NICE AND TASTY!
HA HAHA HA HA HA HAHA HA HA HA HA

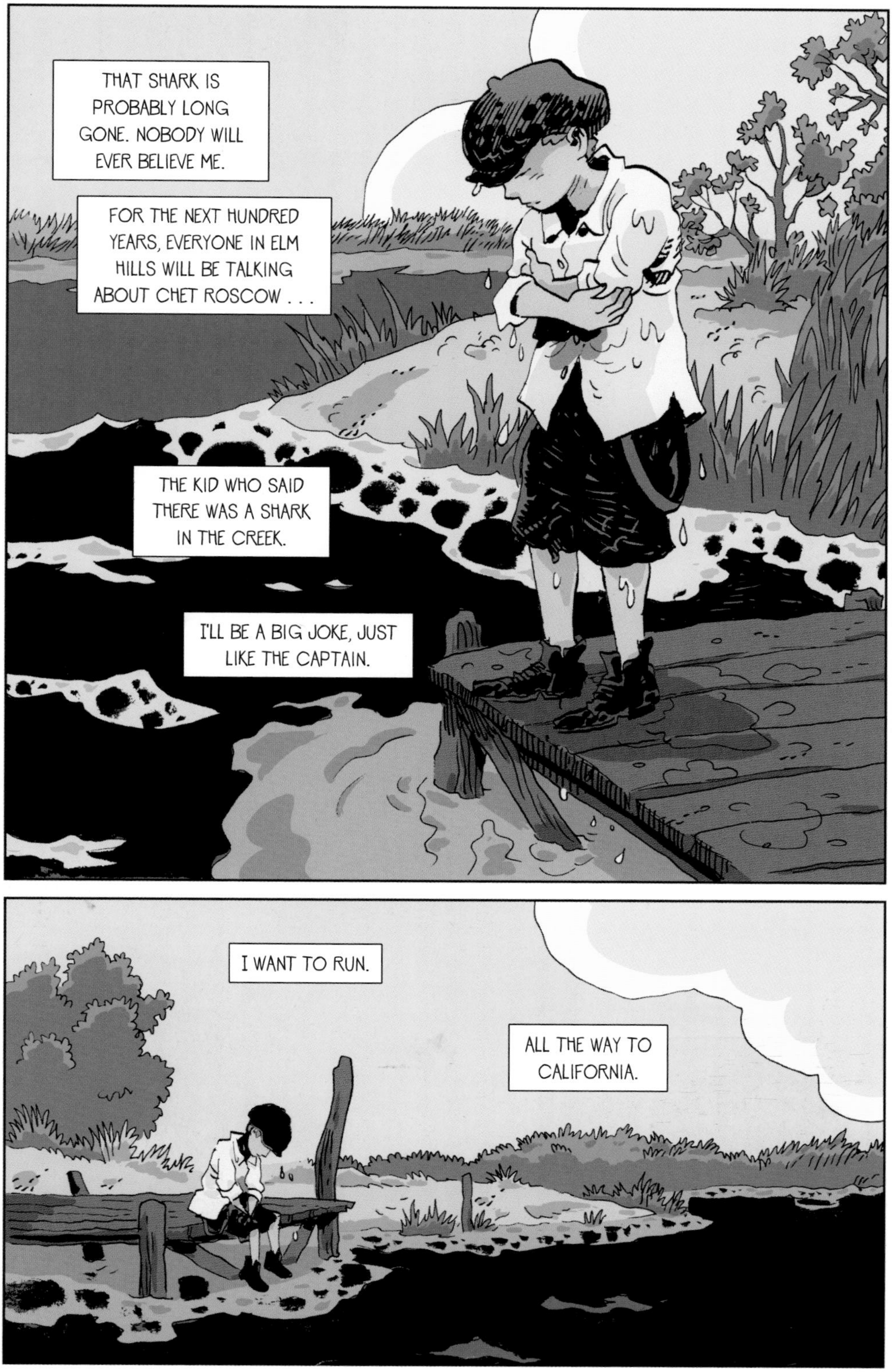
THAT SHARK IS PROBABLY LONG GONE. NOBODY WILL EVER BELIEVE ME.
FOR THE NEXT HUNDRED YEARS, EVERYONE IN ELM HILLS WILL BE TALKING ABOUT CHET ROSCOW . . .
THE KID WHO SAID THERE WAS A SHARK IN THE CREEK.
I'LL BE A BIG JOKE, JUST LIKE THE CAPTAIN.
I WANT TO RUN.
ALL THE WAY TO CALIFORNIA.

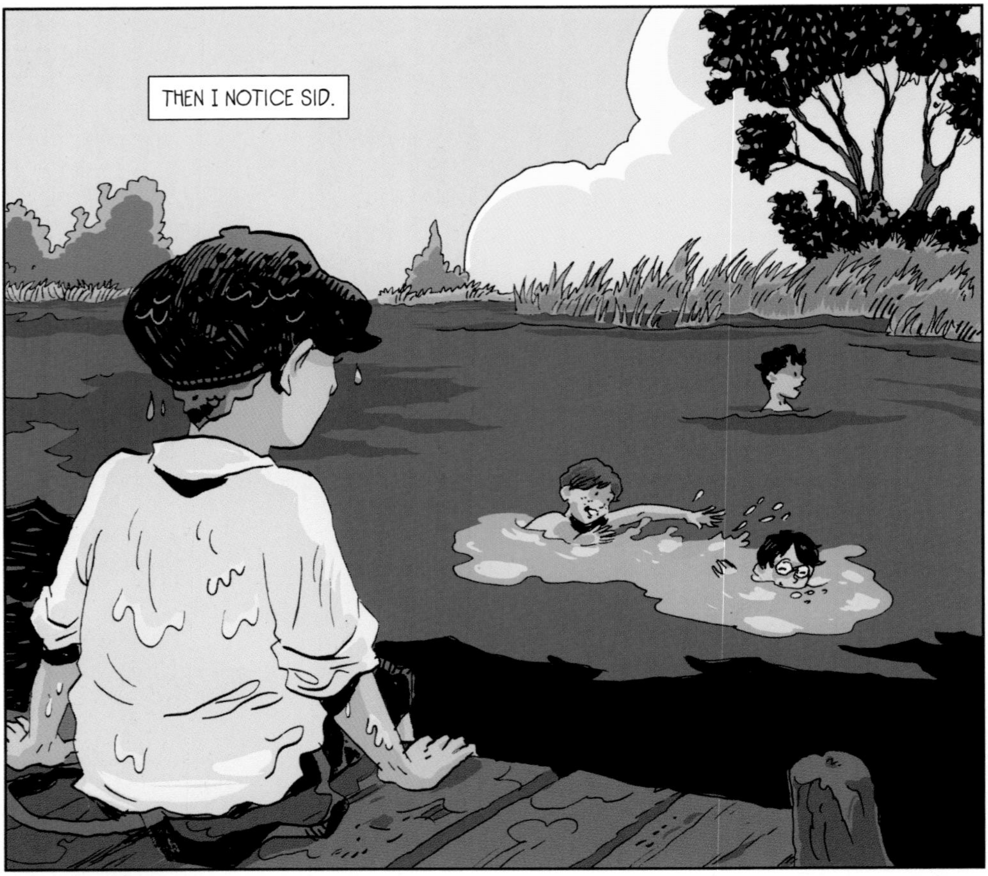
THEN I NOTICE SID.

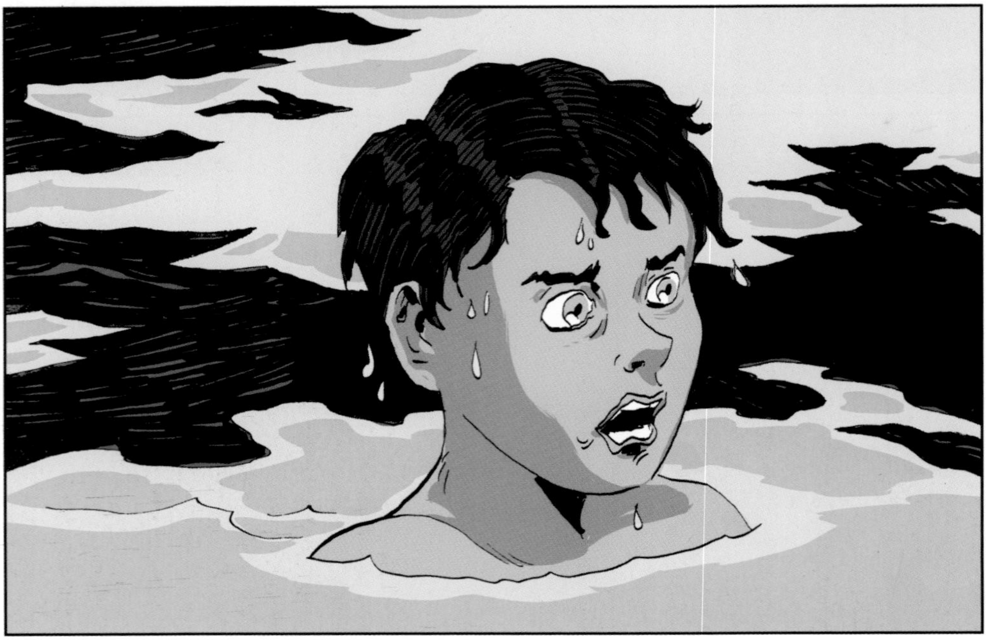

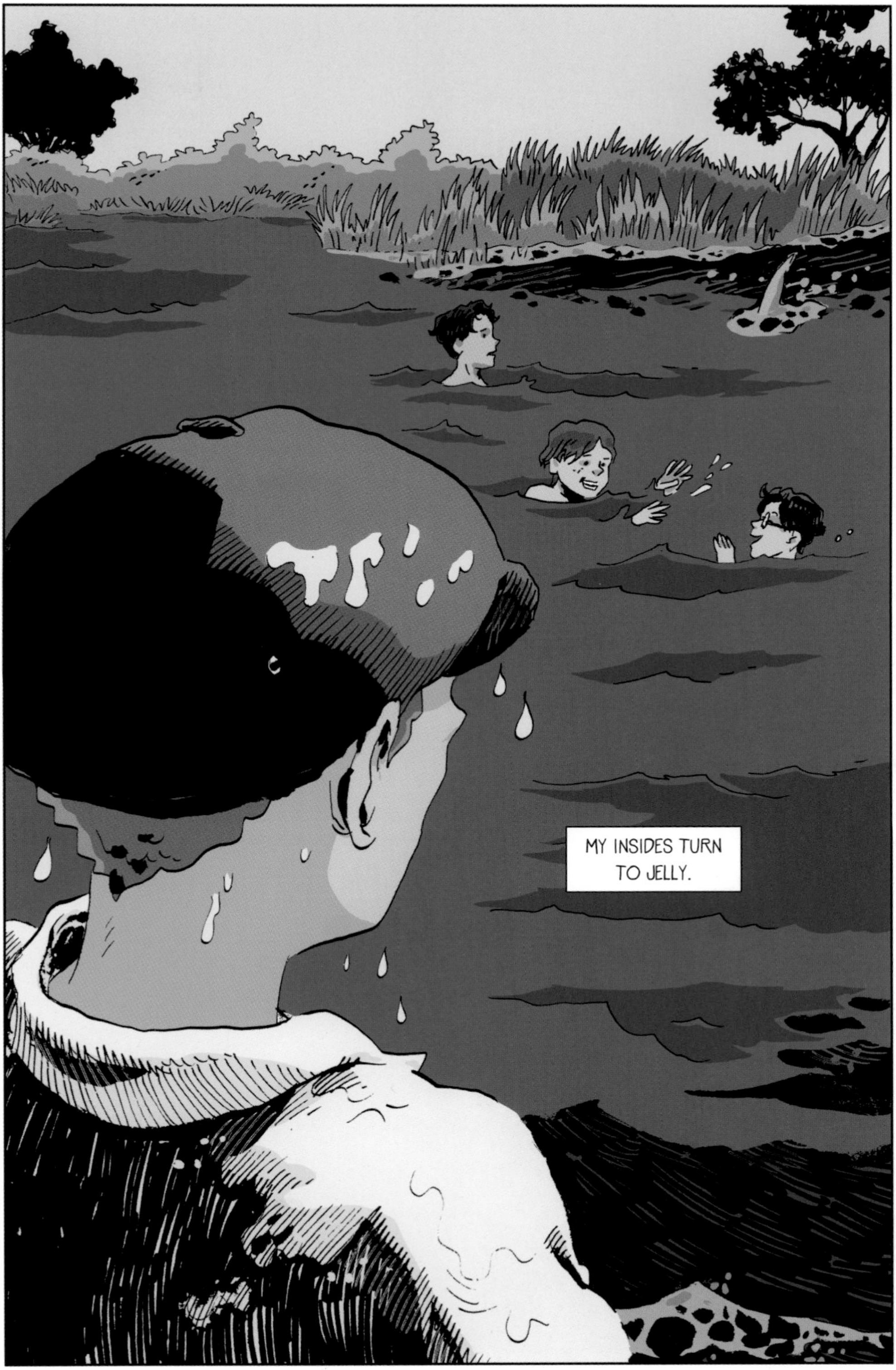
MY INSIDES TURN
TO JELLY.

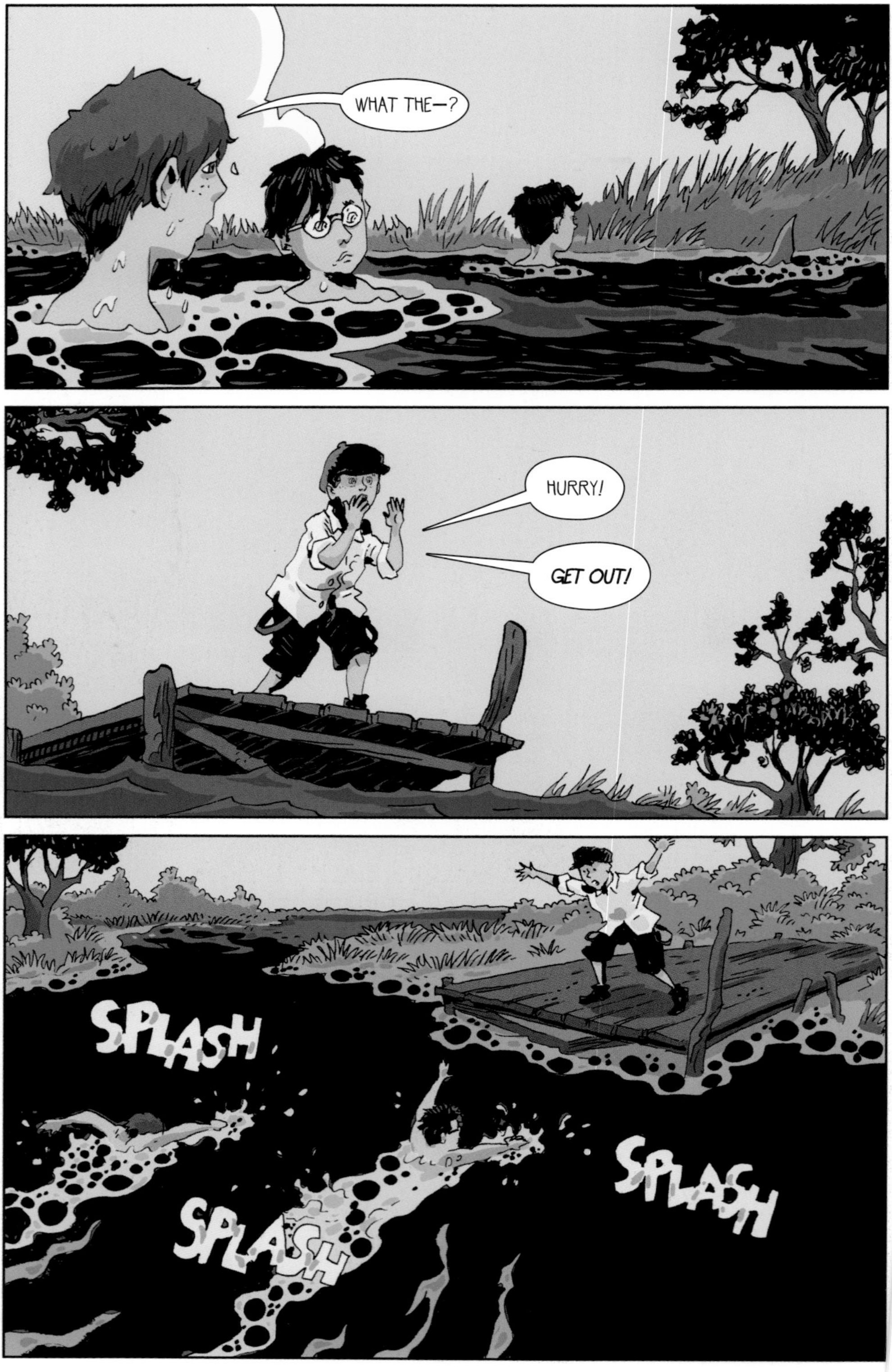
WHAT THE—?
HURRY!
GET OUT!
SPLASH
SPLASH
SPLASH

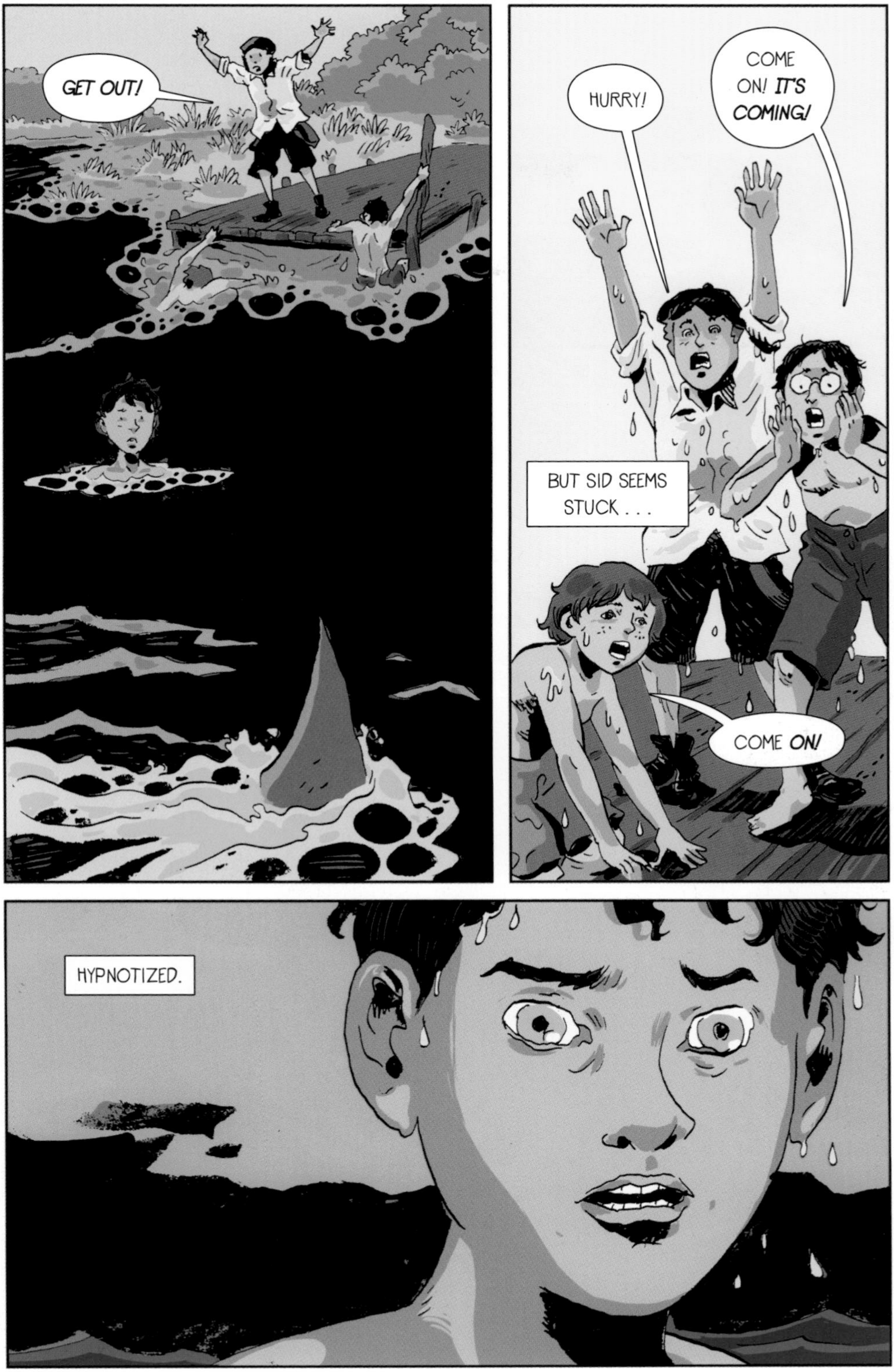
GET OUT!
HURRY!
COME ON! IT'S COMING!
BUT SID SEEMS STUCK . . .
COME ON!
HYPNOTIZED.

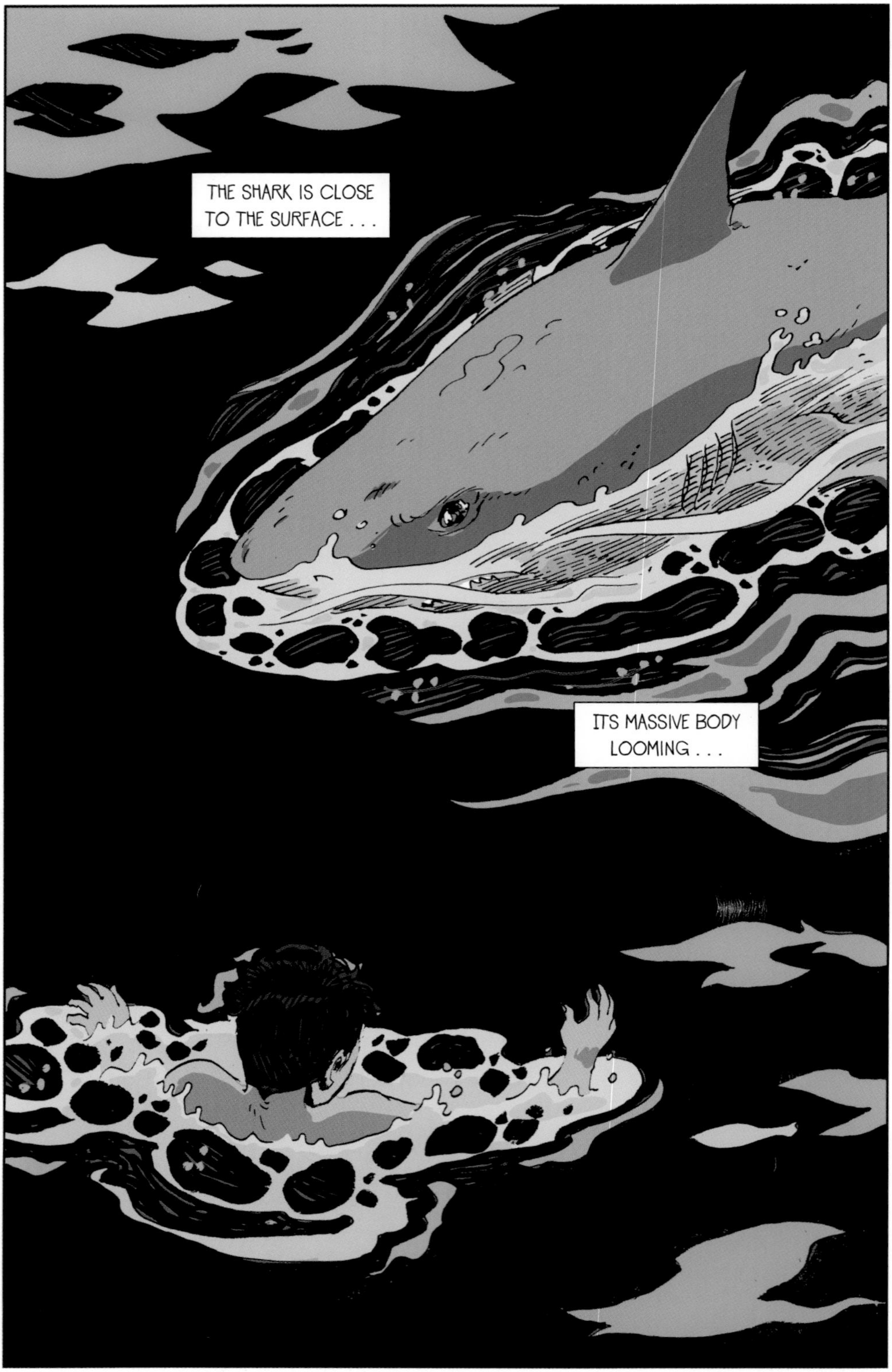
THE SHARK IS CLOSE TO THE SURFACE . . .
ITS MASSIVE BODY LOOMING . . .

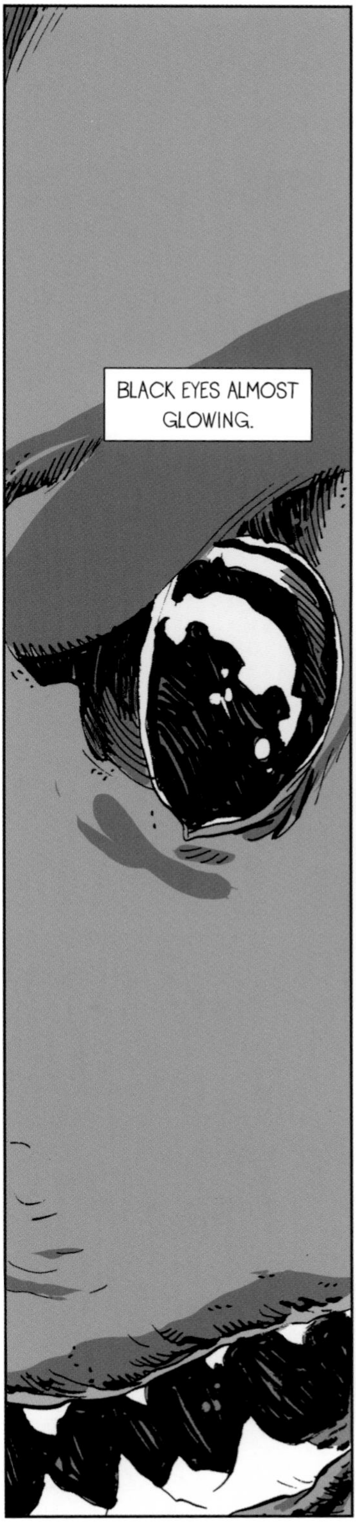
BLACK EYES ALMOST GLOWING.

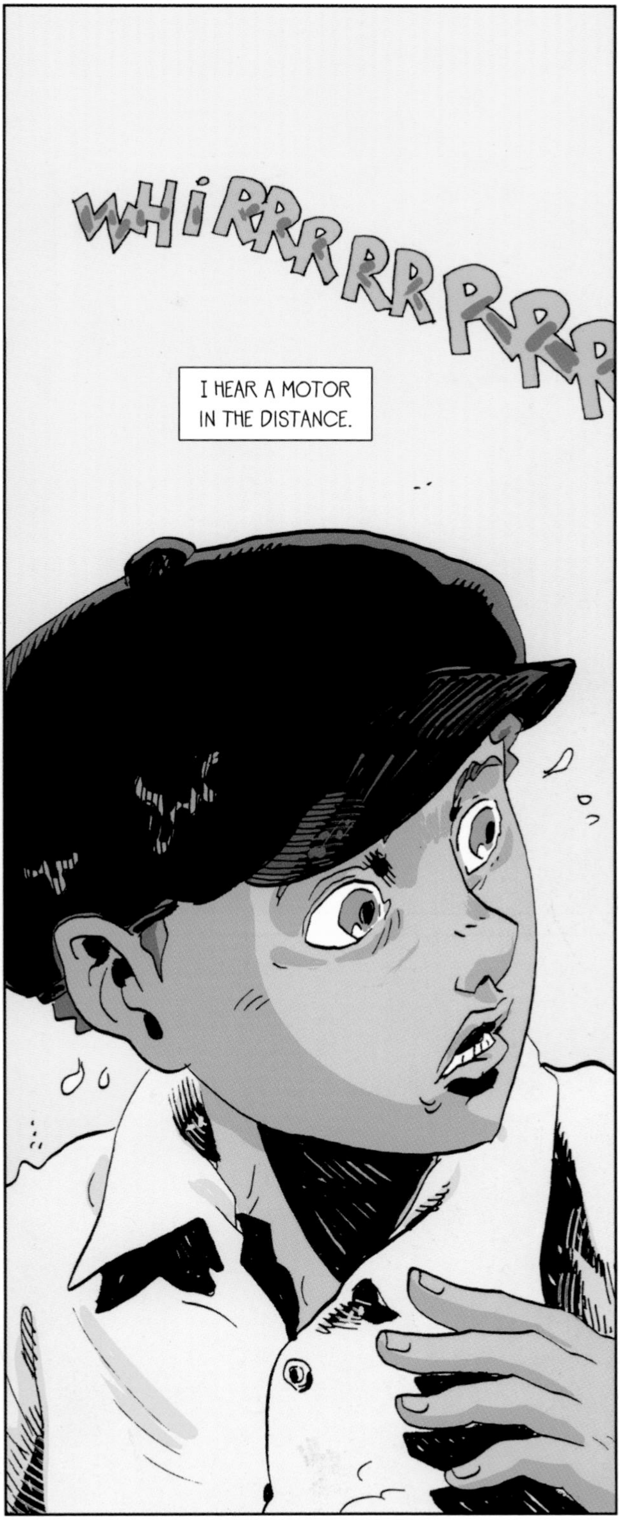
WHIRRRRRRRRRR
I HEAR A MOTOR IN THE DISTANCE.

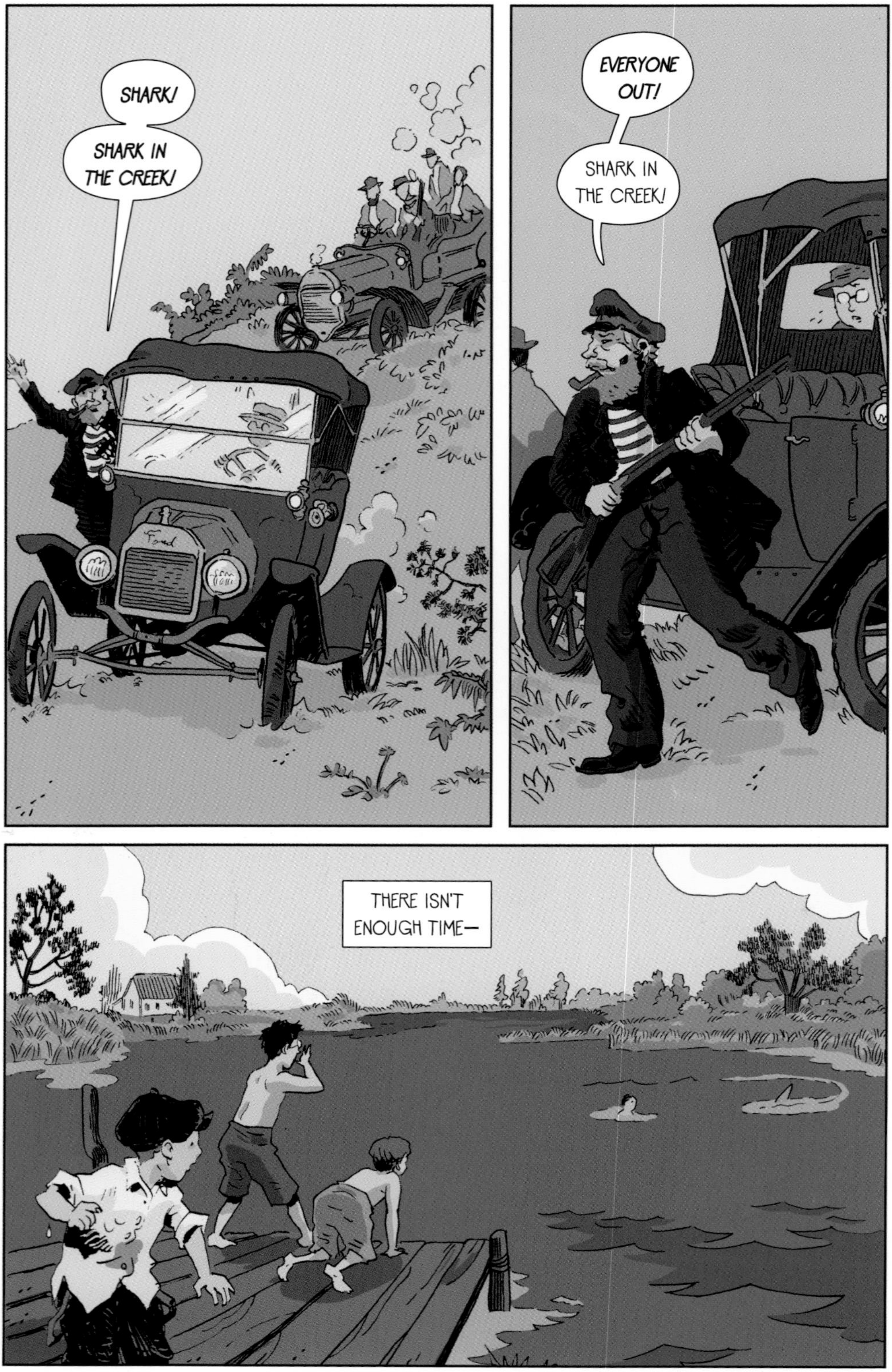

SHARK!
SHARK IN THE CREEK!
EVERYONE OUT!
SHARK IN THE CREEK!
THERE ISN'T ENOUGH TIME—

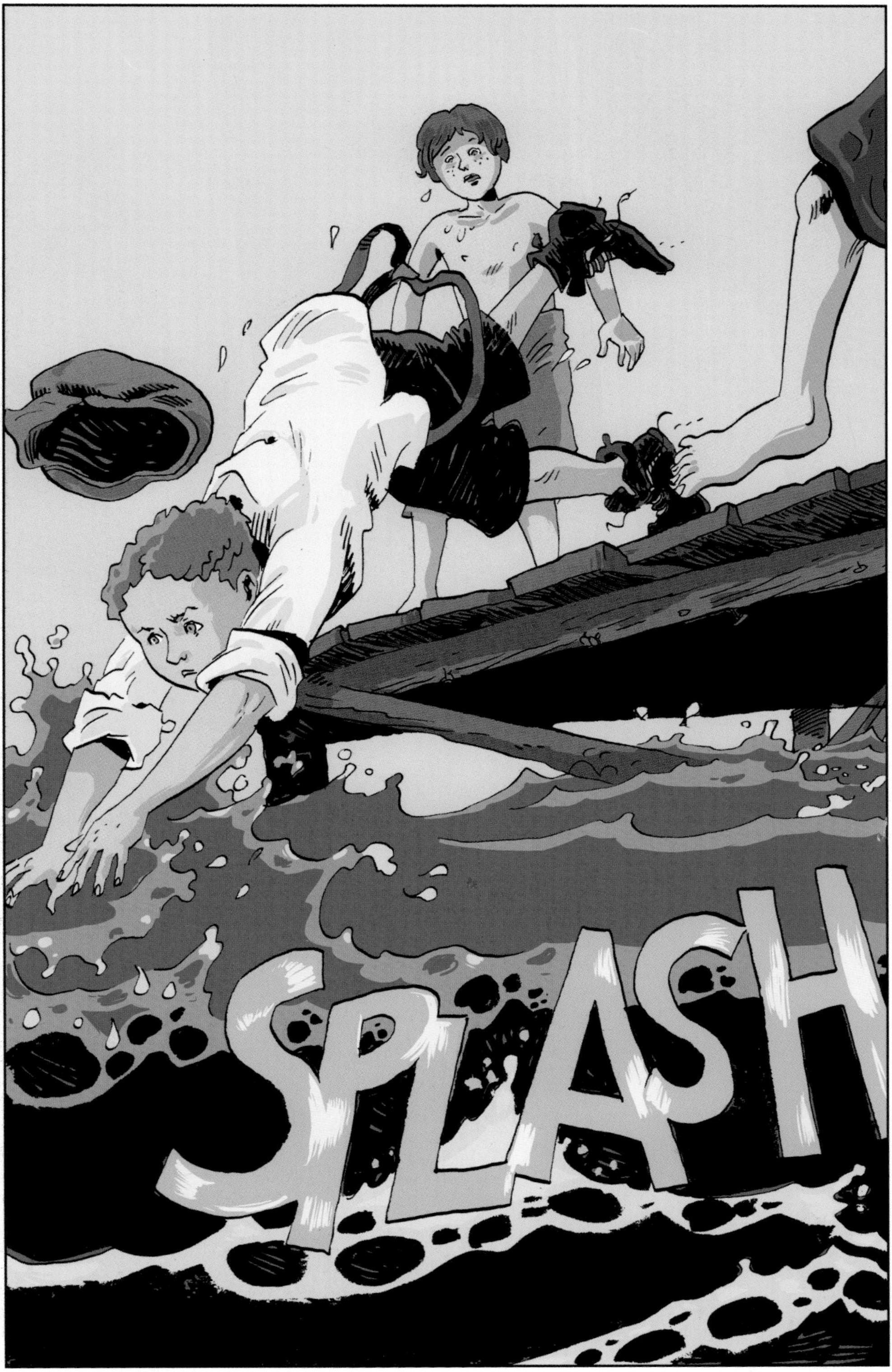
SPLASH

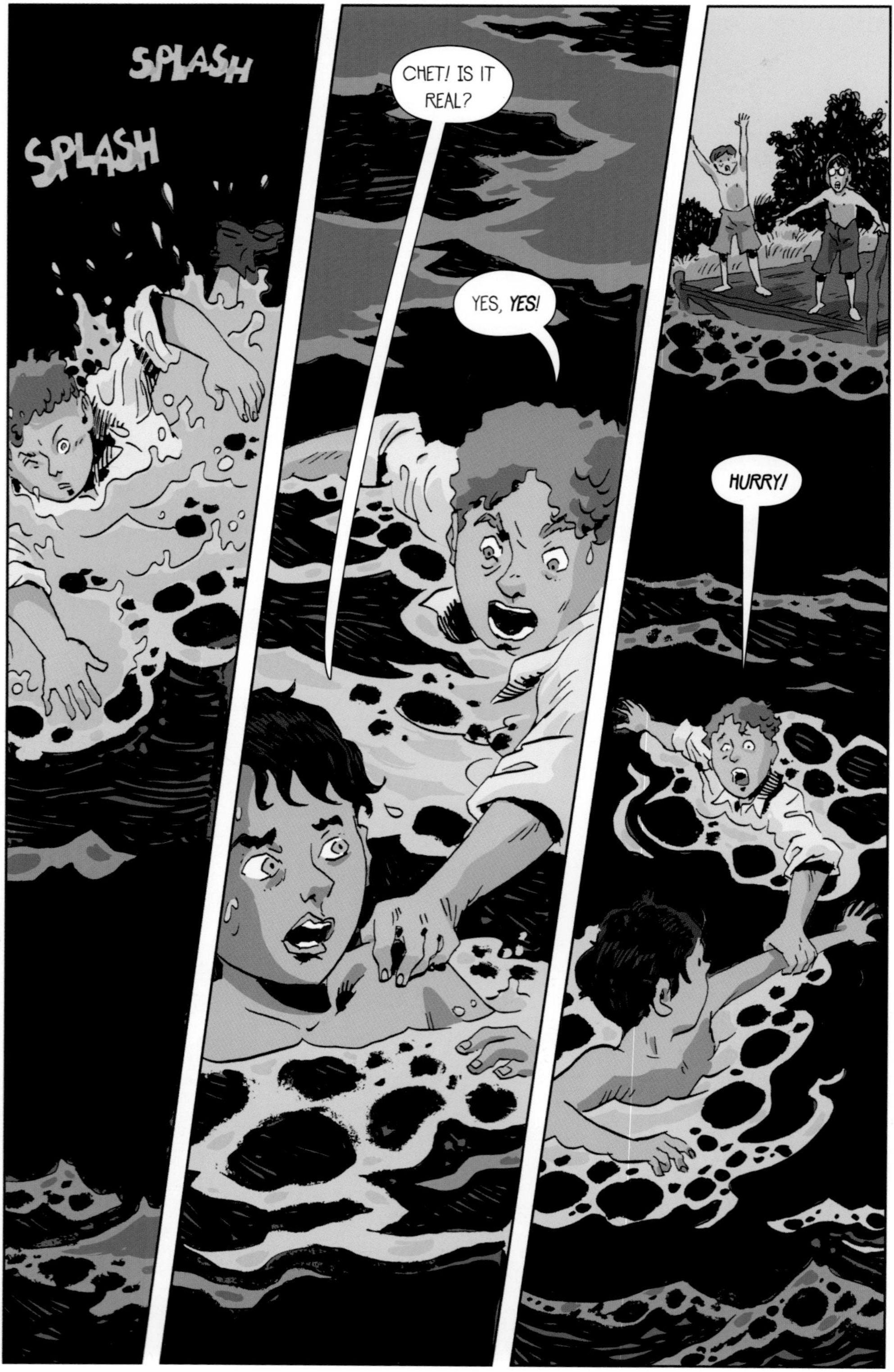
SPLASH
SPLASH
CHET! IS IT REAL?
YES, YES!
HURRY!

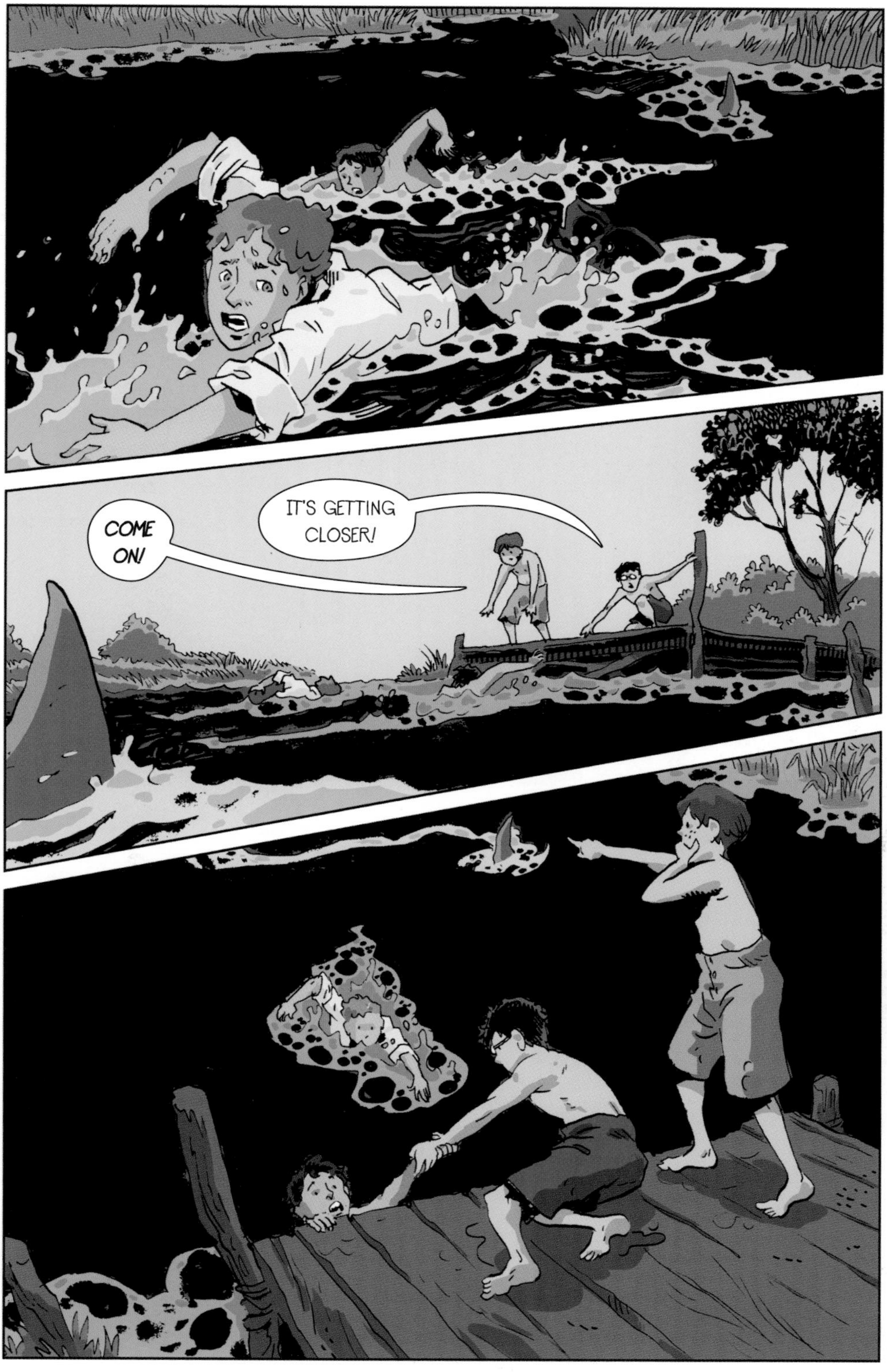
COME ON!
IT'S GETTING CLOSER!

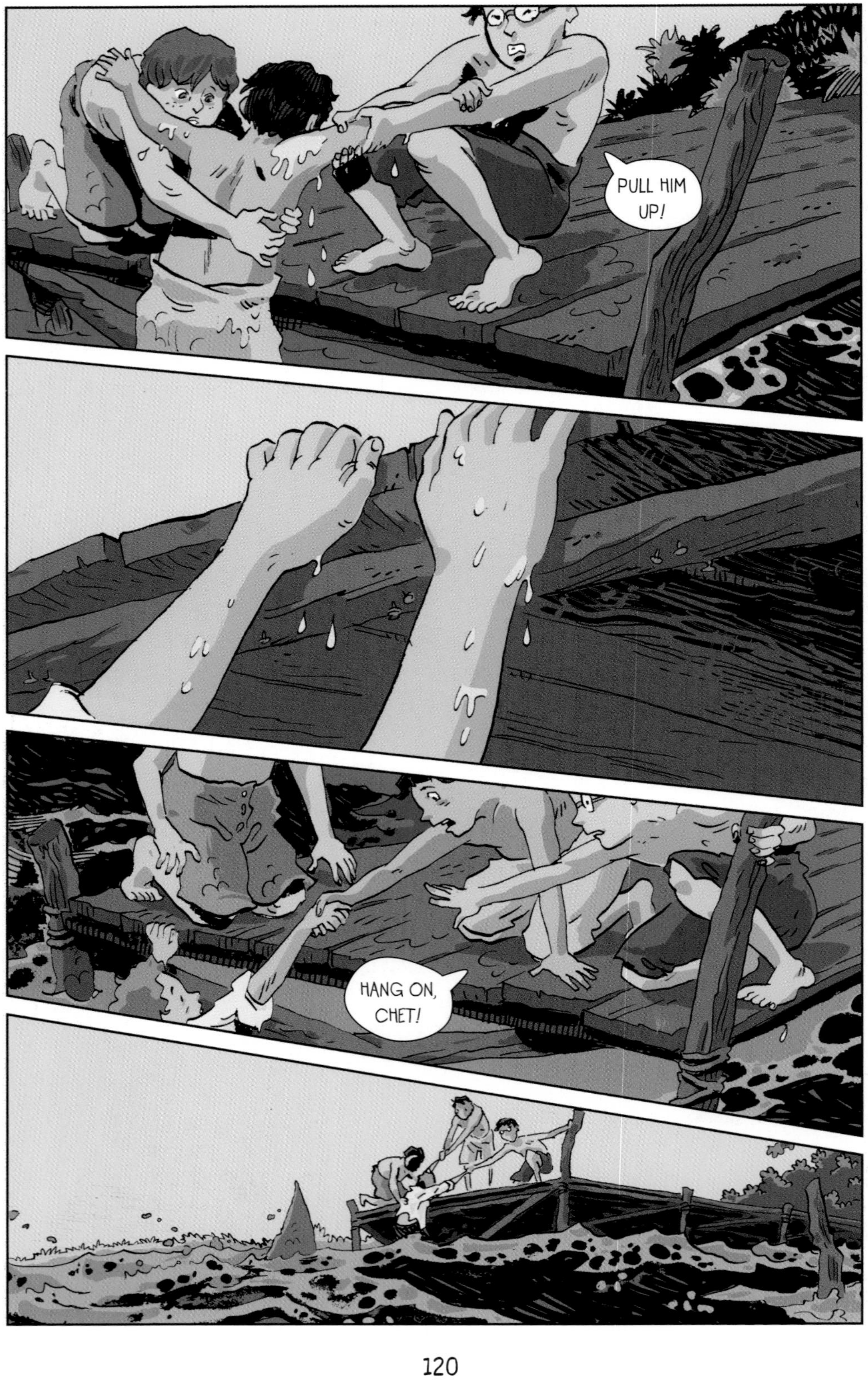
PULL HIM UP!
HANG ON, CHET!

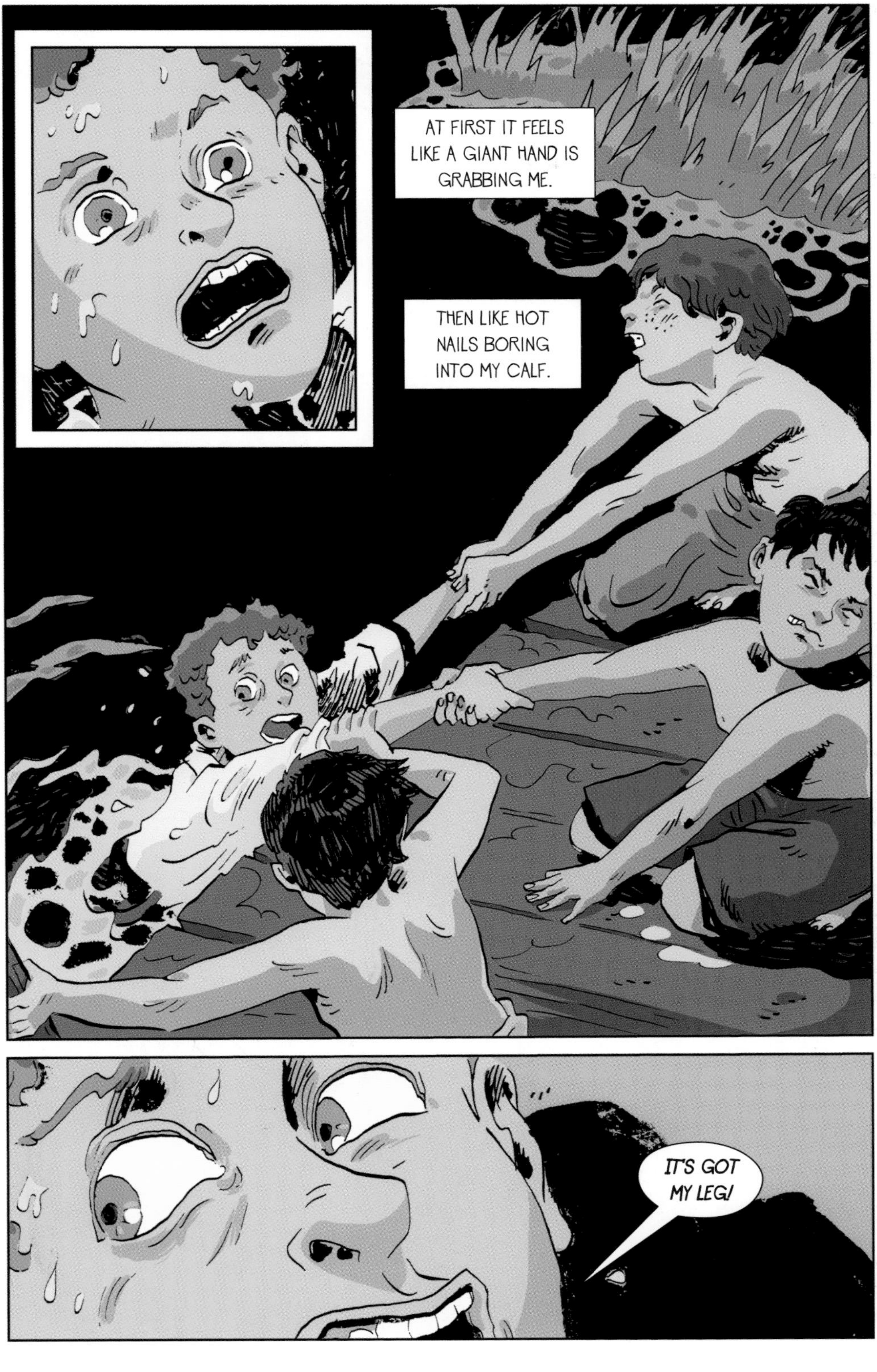
AT FIRST IT FEELS LIKE A GIANT HAND IS GRABBING ME.
THEN LIKE HOT NAILS BORING INTO MY CALF.
IT'S GOT MY LEG!

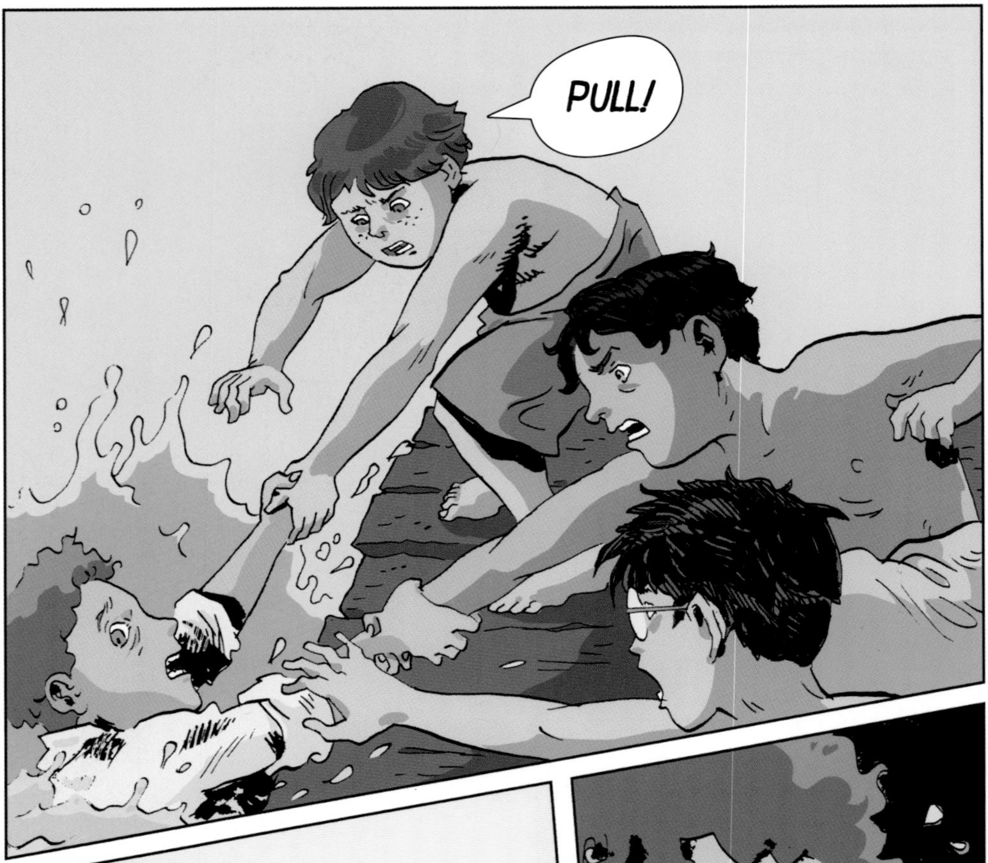
PULL!

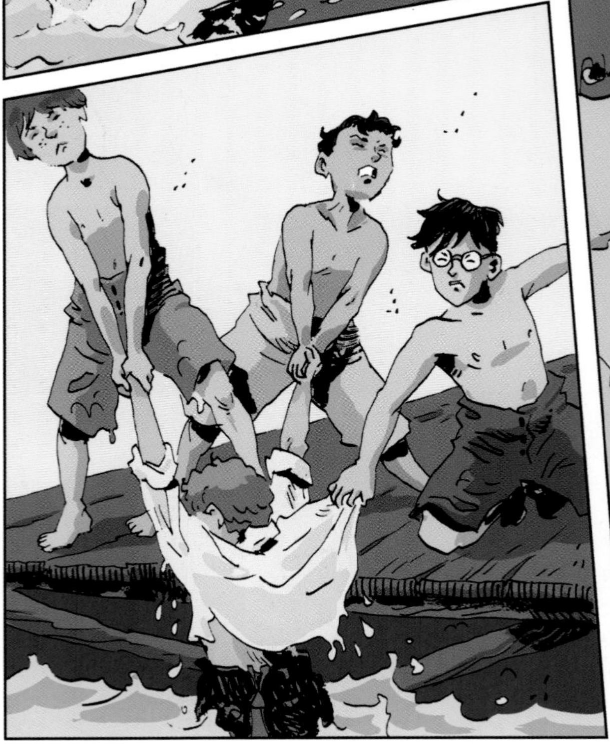

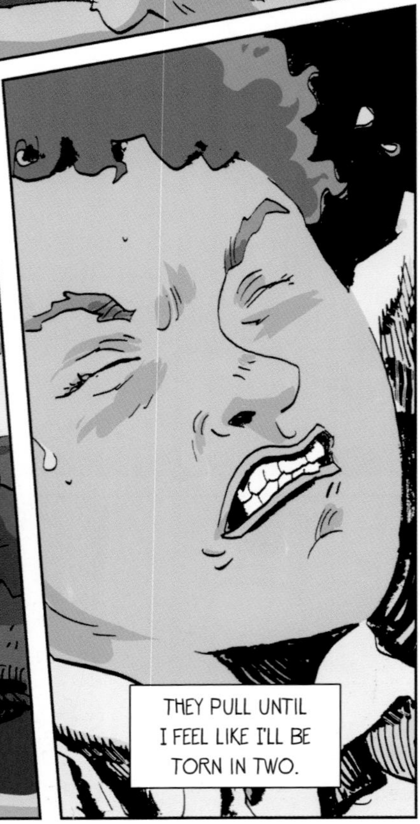
THEY PULL UNTIL
I FEEL LIKE I'LL BE
TORN IN TWO.

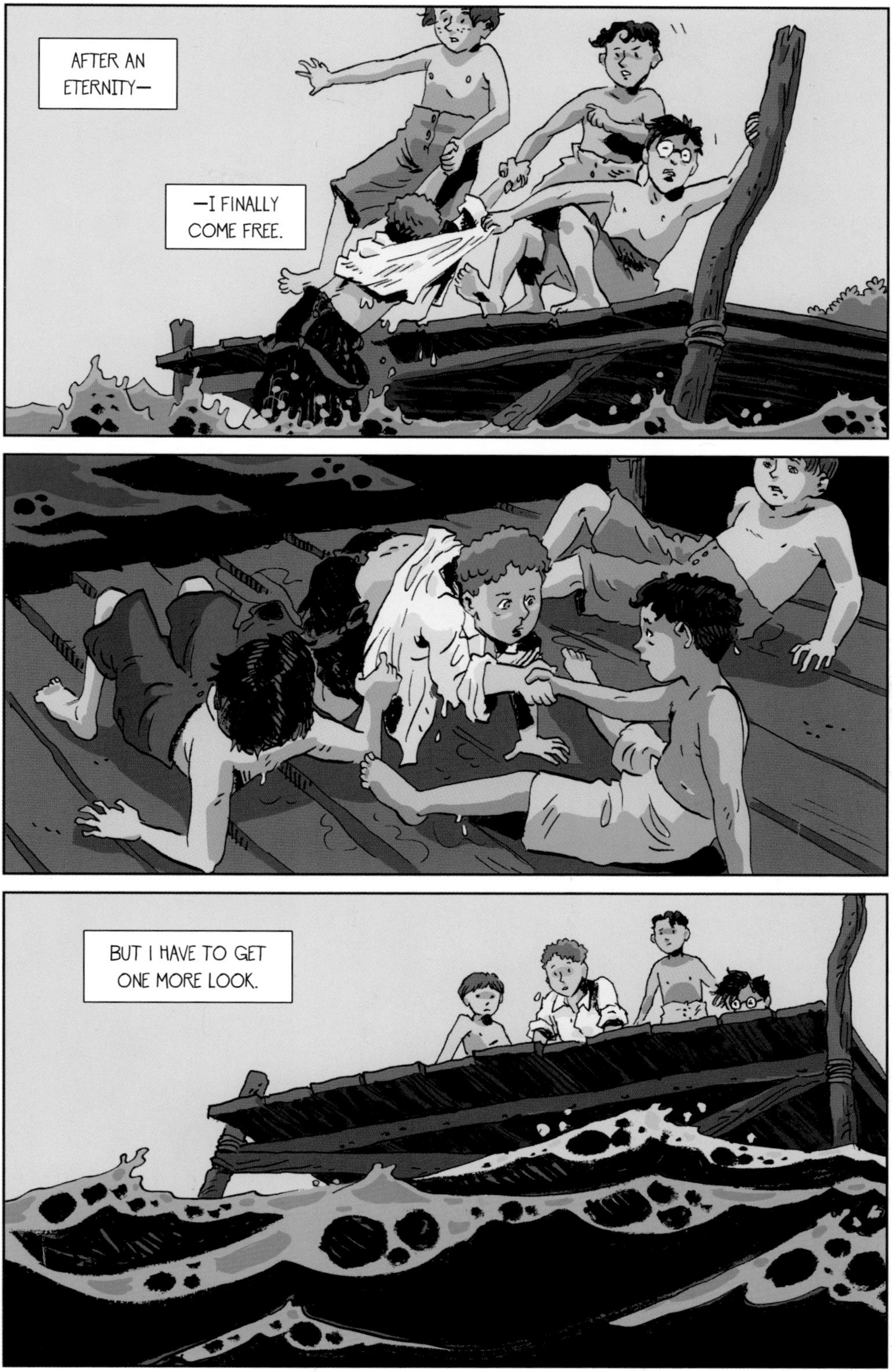
AFTER AN ETERNITY—
—I FINALLY COME FREE.
BUT I HAVE TO GET ONE MORE LOOK.

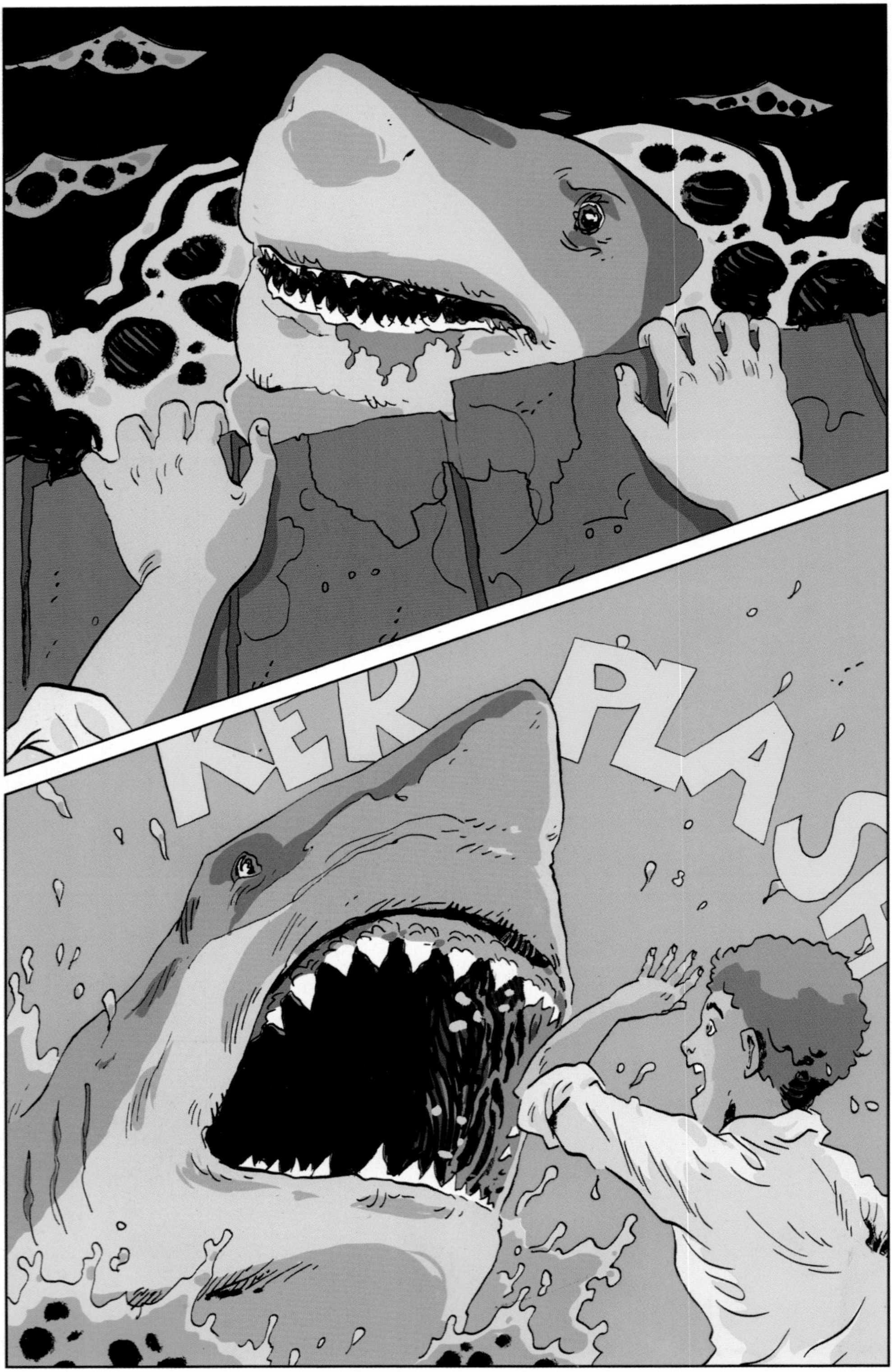
KER PLASH

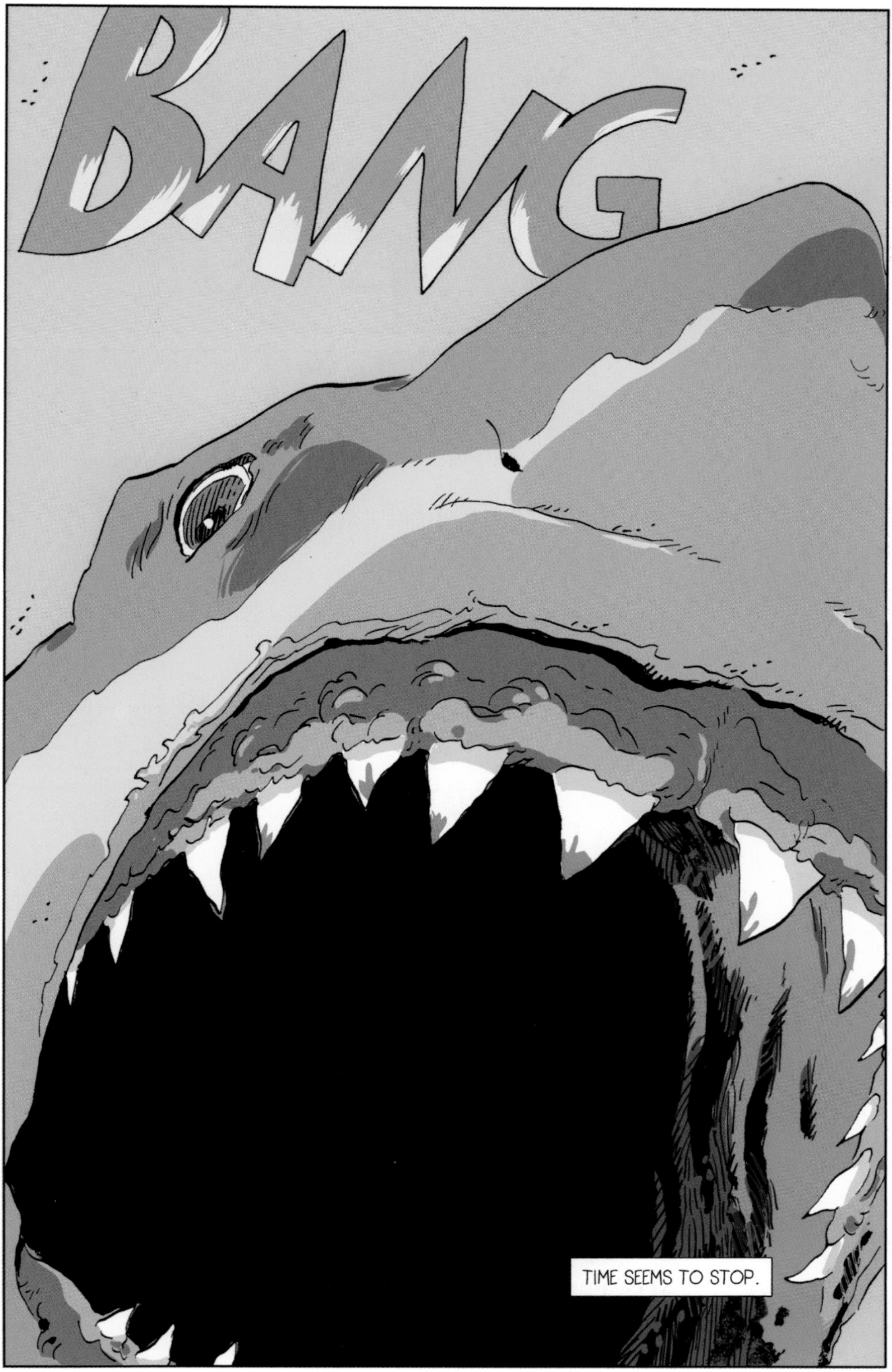
BANG
TIME SEEMS TO STOP.

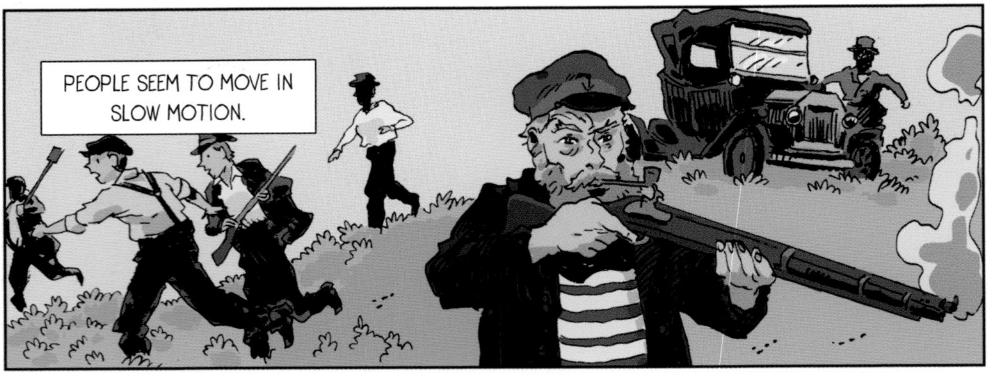
PEOPLE SEEM TO MOVE IN SLOW MOTION.

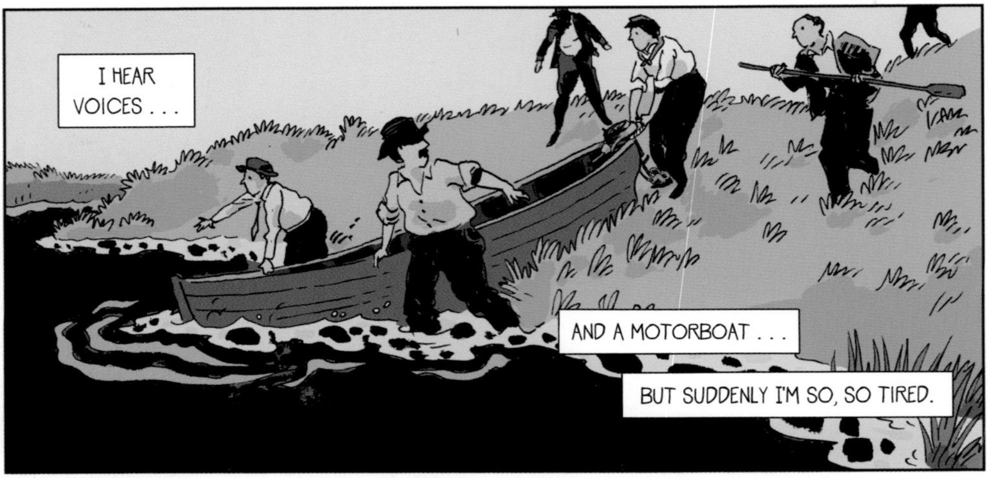
I HEAR VOICES . . .
AND A MOTORBOAT . . .
BUT SUDDENLY I'M SO, SO TIRED.

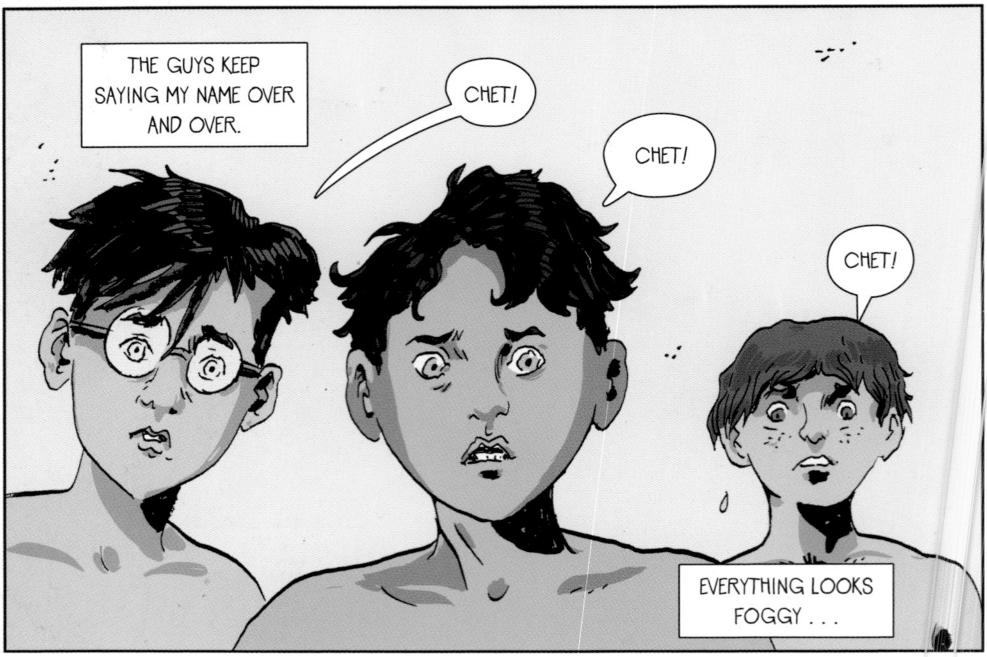
THE GUYS KEEP SAYING MY NAME OVER AND OVER.
CHET!
CHET!
CHET!
EVERYTHING LOOKS FOGGY . . .

WHAT AM I DOING IN A PILE OF KETCHUP?

DIDN'T I CLEAN THAT UP?

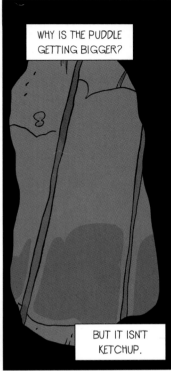

WHY IS THE PUDDLE GETTING BIGGER?

BUT IT ISN'T KETCHUP.

CHET CHET CHET CHET CHET

THE FOG GROWS THICKER . . .

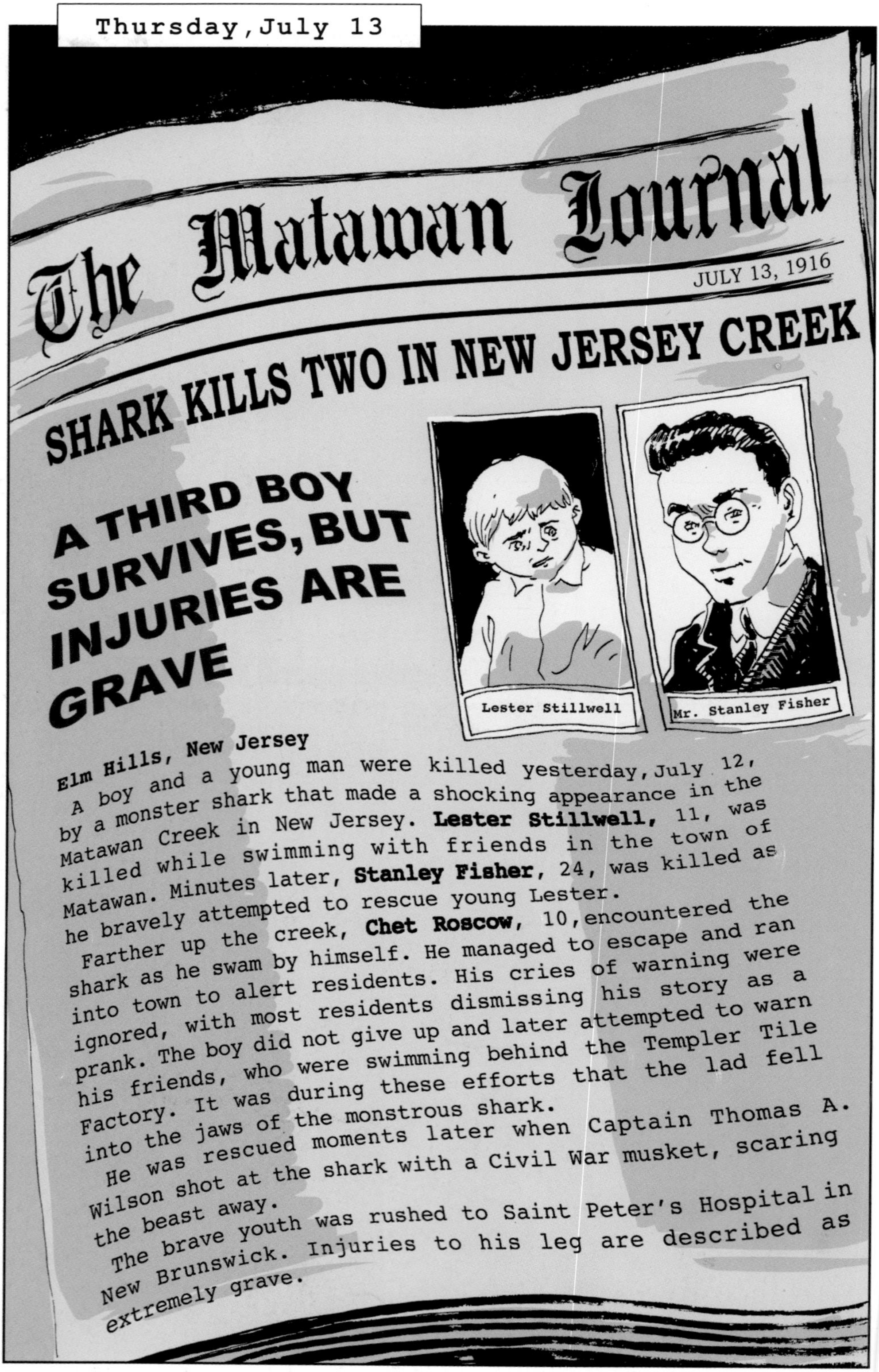
Thursday, July 13
Lester Stillwell
Mr. Stanley Fisher

The Matawan Journal

JULY 13, 1916

SHARK KILLS TWO IN NEW JERSEY CREEK

A THIRD BOY SURVIVES, BUT INJURIES ARE GRAVE

Elm Hills, New Jersey

A boy and a young man were killed yesterday, July 12, by a monster shark that made a shocking appearance in the Matawan Creek in New Jersey. **Lester Stillwell**, 11, was killed while swimming with friends in the town of Matawan. Minutes later, **Stanley Fisher**, 24, was killed as he bravely attempted to rescue young Lester.

Farther up the creek, **Chet Roscow**, 10, encountered the shark as he swam by himself. He managed to escape and ran into town to alert residents. His cries of warning were ignored, with most residents dismissing his story as a prank. The boy did not give up and later attempted to warn his friends, who were swimming behind the Templer Tile Factory. It was during these efforts that the lad fell into the jaws of the monstrous shark.

He was rescued moments later when Captain Thomas A. Wilson shot at the shark with a Civil War musket, scaring the beast away.

The brave youth was rushed to Saint Peter's Hospital in New Brunswick. Injuries to his leg are described as extremely grave.

AM I ASLEEP?

AM I AWAKE?

AM I ALIVE OR DEAD?

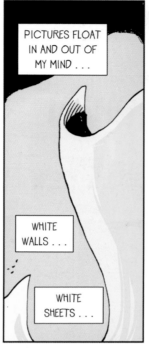

PICTURES FLOAT IN AND OUT OF MY MIND . . .

WHITE WALLS . . .

WHITE SHEETS . . .

DOCTORS . . .

A NURSE WITH A SOFT VOICE.

AND UNCLE JERRY, ALWAYS BY MY SIDE.

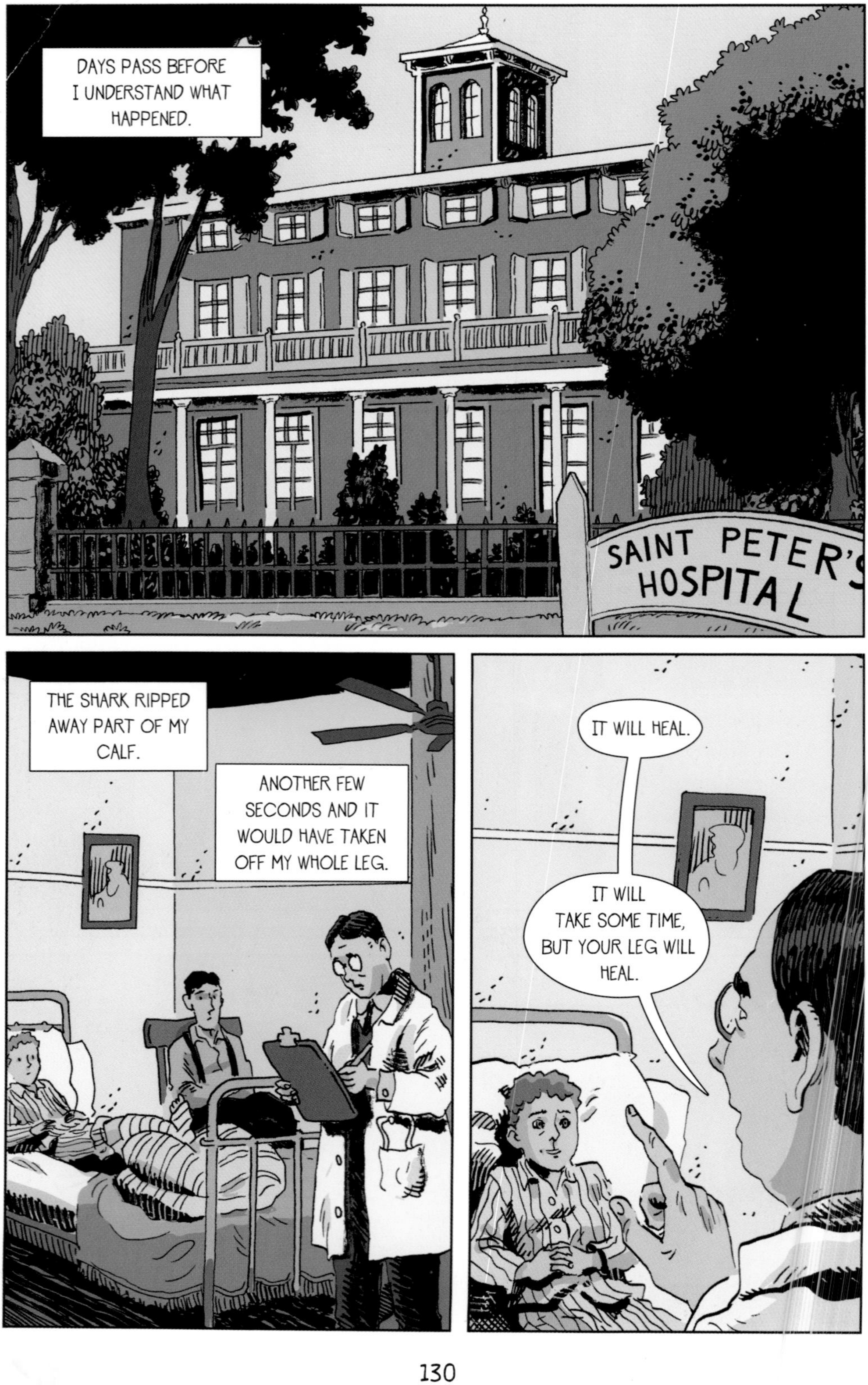
DAYS PASS BEFORE I UNDERSTAND WHAT HAPPENED.
SAINT PETER'S HOSPITAL
THE SHARK RIPPED AWAY PART OF MY CALF.
ANOTHER FEW SECONDS AND IT WOULD HAVE TAKEN OFF MY WHOLE LEG.
IT WILL HEAL.
IT WILL TAKE SOME TIME, BUT YOUR LEG WILL HEAL.

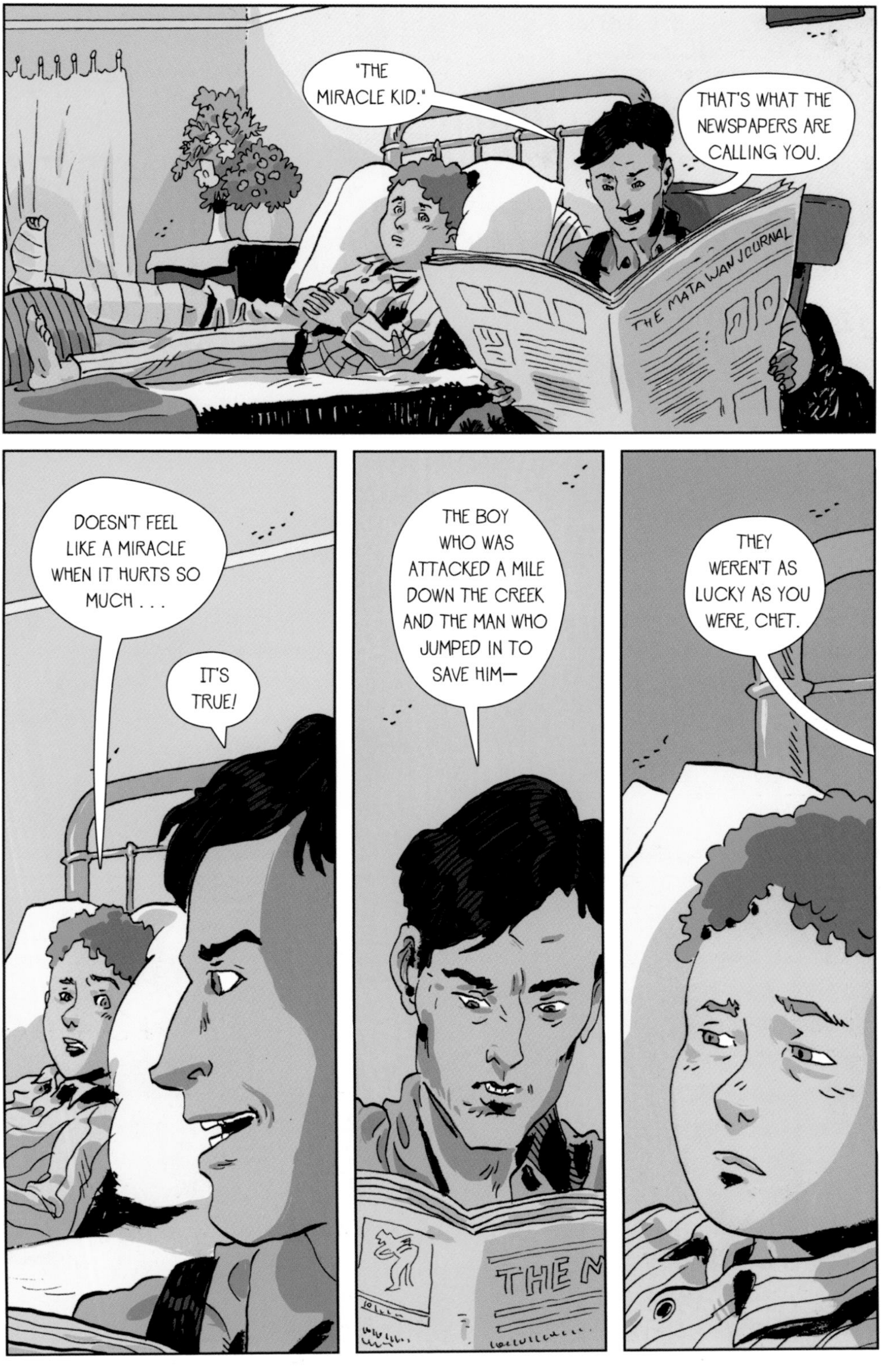
"THE MIRACLE KID."
THAT'S WHAT THE NEWSPAPERS ARE CALLING YOU.
THE MATAWAN JOURNAL
DOESN'T FEEL LIKE A MIRACLE WHEN IT HURTS SO MUCH . . .
IT'S TRUE!
THE BOY WHO WAS ATTACKED A MILE DOWN THE CREEK AND THE MAN WHO JUMPED IN TO SAVE HIM—
THE N
THEY WEREN'T AS LUCKY AS YOU WERE, CHET.

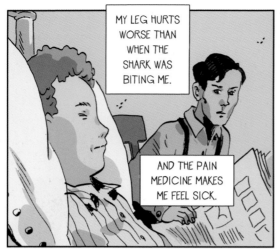

MY LEG HURTS WORSE THAN WHEN THE SHARK WAS BITING ME.

AND THE PAIN MEDICINE MAKES ME FEEL SICK.

I WISH MAMA AND PAPA WERE HERE.

THEY TOOK THE FIRST TRAIN AS SOON AS THEY HEARD.

THEY'LL BE HERE BEFORE YOU KNOW IT.

THE DOCTOR SAYS I'LL HAVE A LIMP.

THAT'S RIGHT—JUST LIKE MINE.

BUT I KNOW IT WON'T SLOW YOU DOWN A BIT.

SLEEP WELL, KIDDO.

I LIE THERE . . .

BUT I DON'T WANT TO SLEEP.

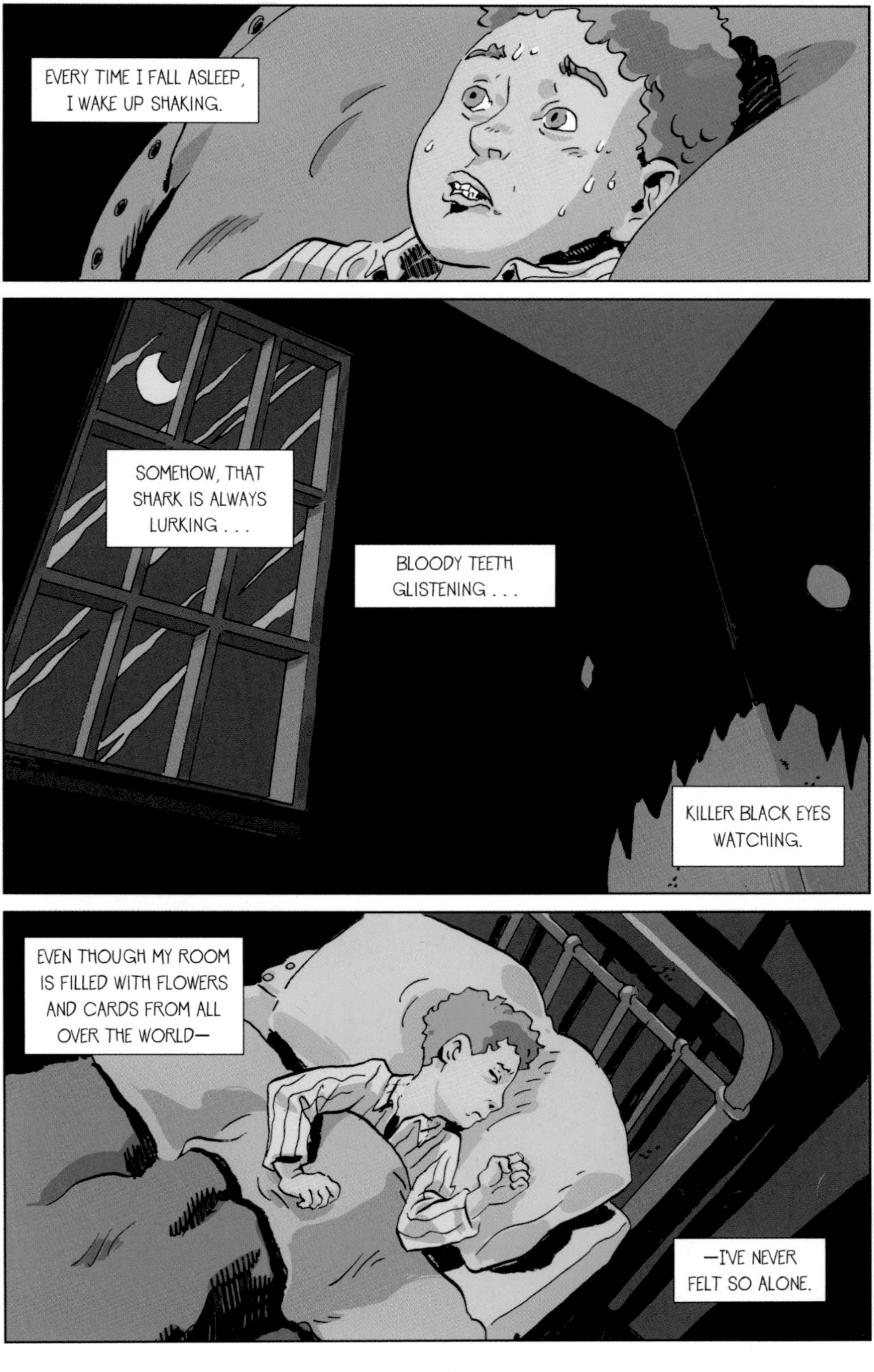
EVERY TIME I FALL ASLEEP, I WAKE UP SHAKING.
SOMEHOW, THAT SHARK IS ALWAYS LURKING . . .
BLOODY TEETH GLISTENING . . .
KILLER BLACK EYES WATCHING.
EVEN THOUGH MY ROOM IS FILLED WITH FLOWERS AND CARDS FROM ALL OVER THE WORLD—
—I'VE NEVER FELT SO ALONE.

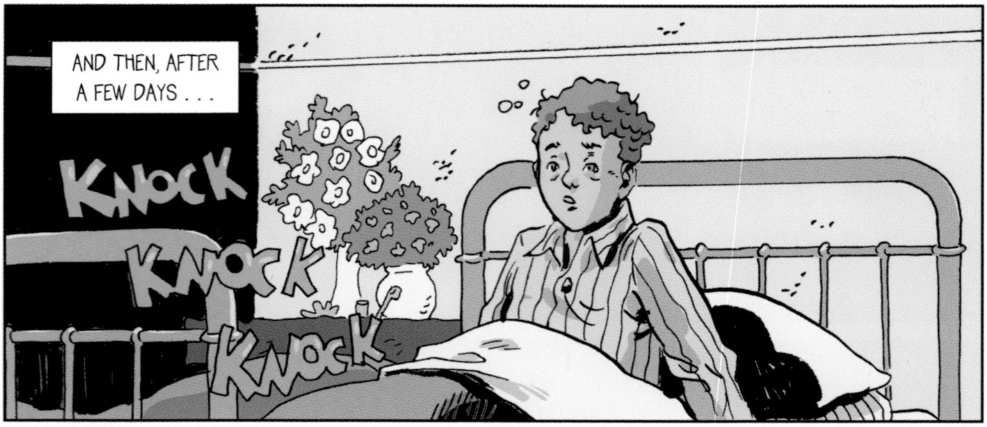
AND THEN, AFTER A FEW DAYS . . .
KNOCK
KNOCK
KNOCK

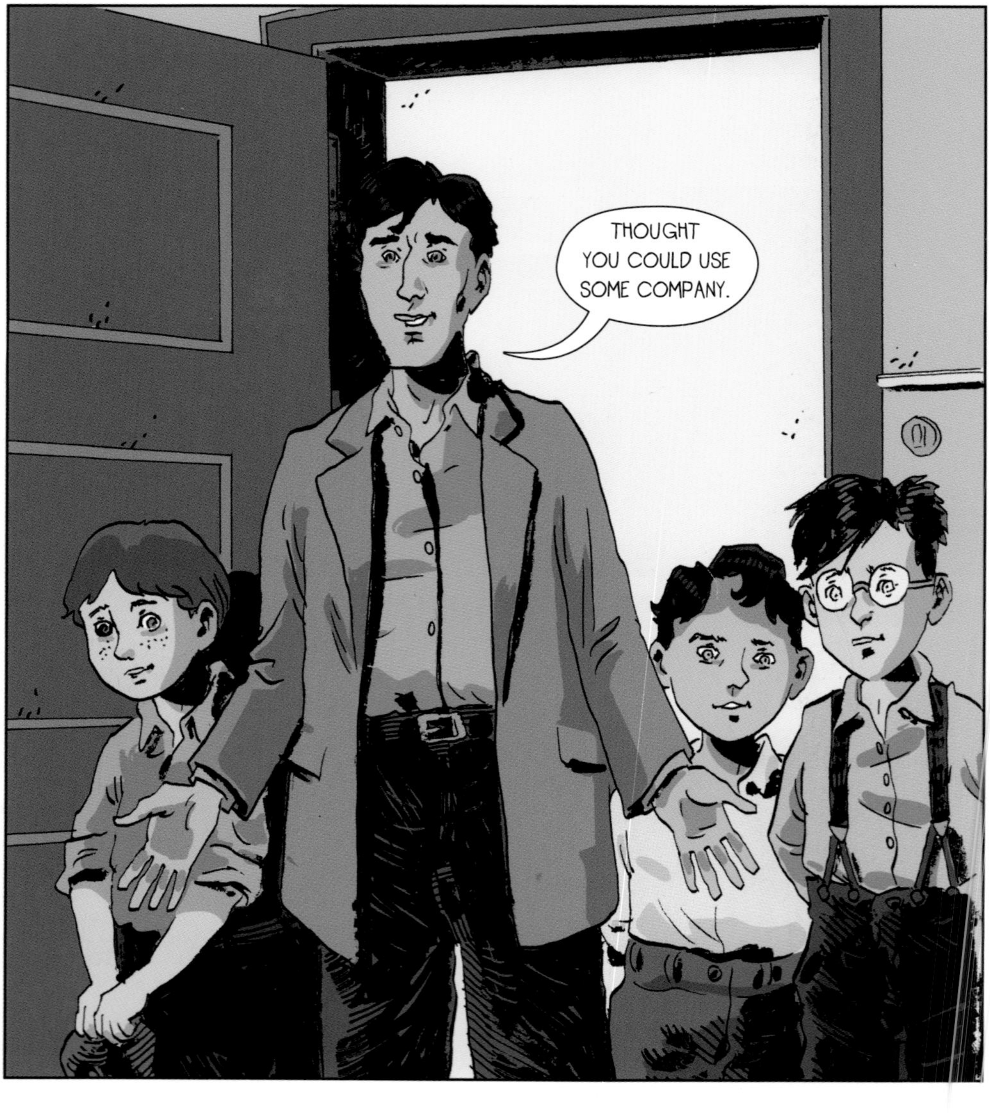
THOUGHT YOU COULD USE SOME COMPANY.

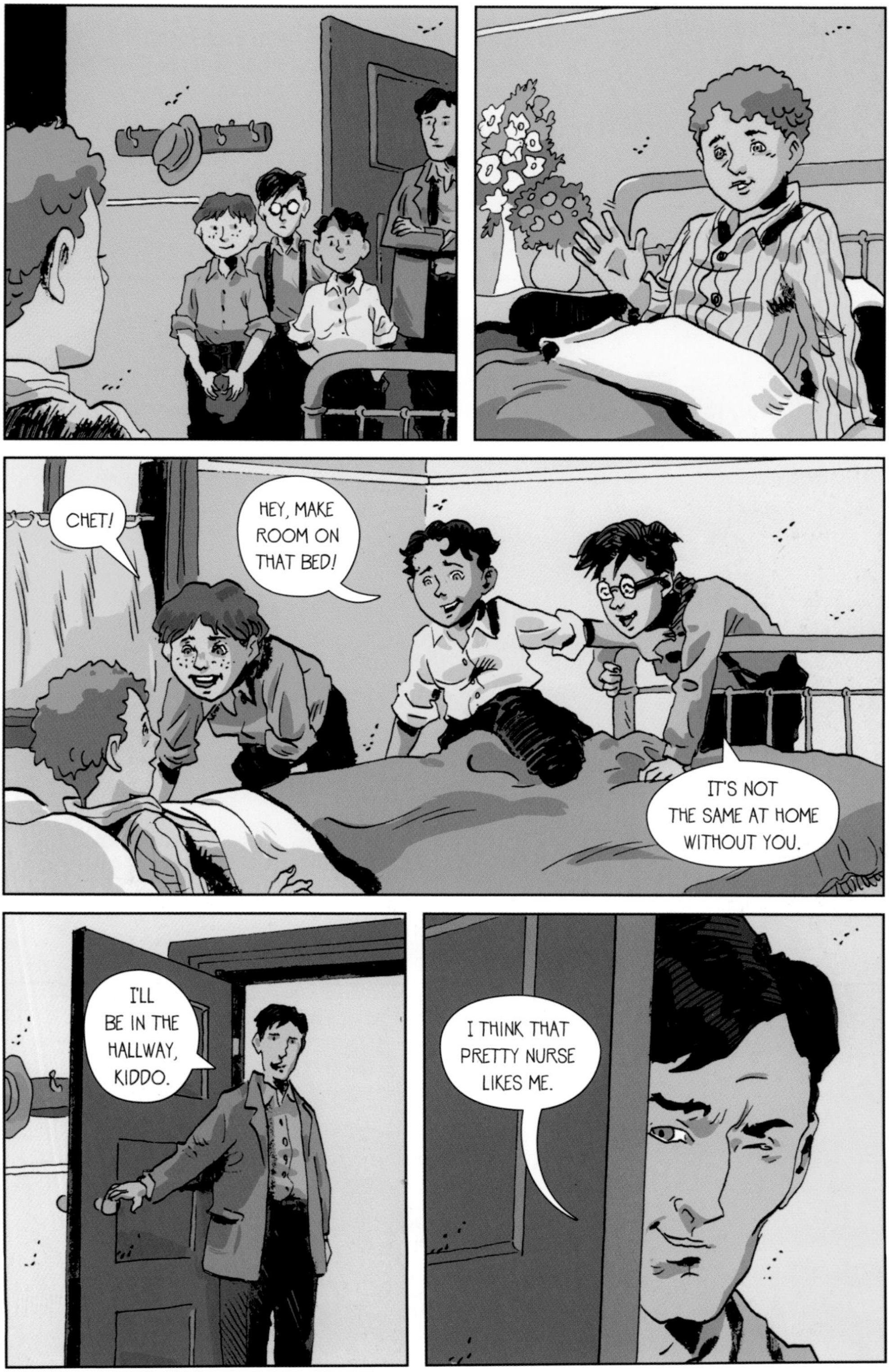
CHET!
HEY, MAKE ROOM ON THAT BED!
IT'S NOT THE SAME AT HOME WITHOUT YOU.
I'LL BE IN THE HALLWAY, KIDDO.
I THINK THAT PRETTY NURSE LIKES ME.

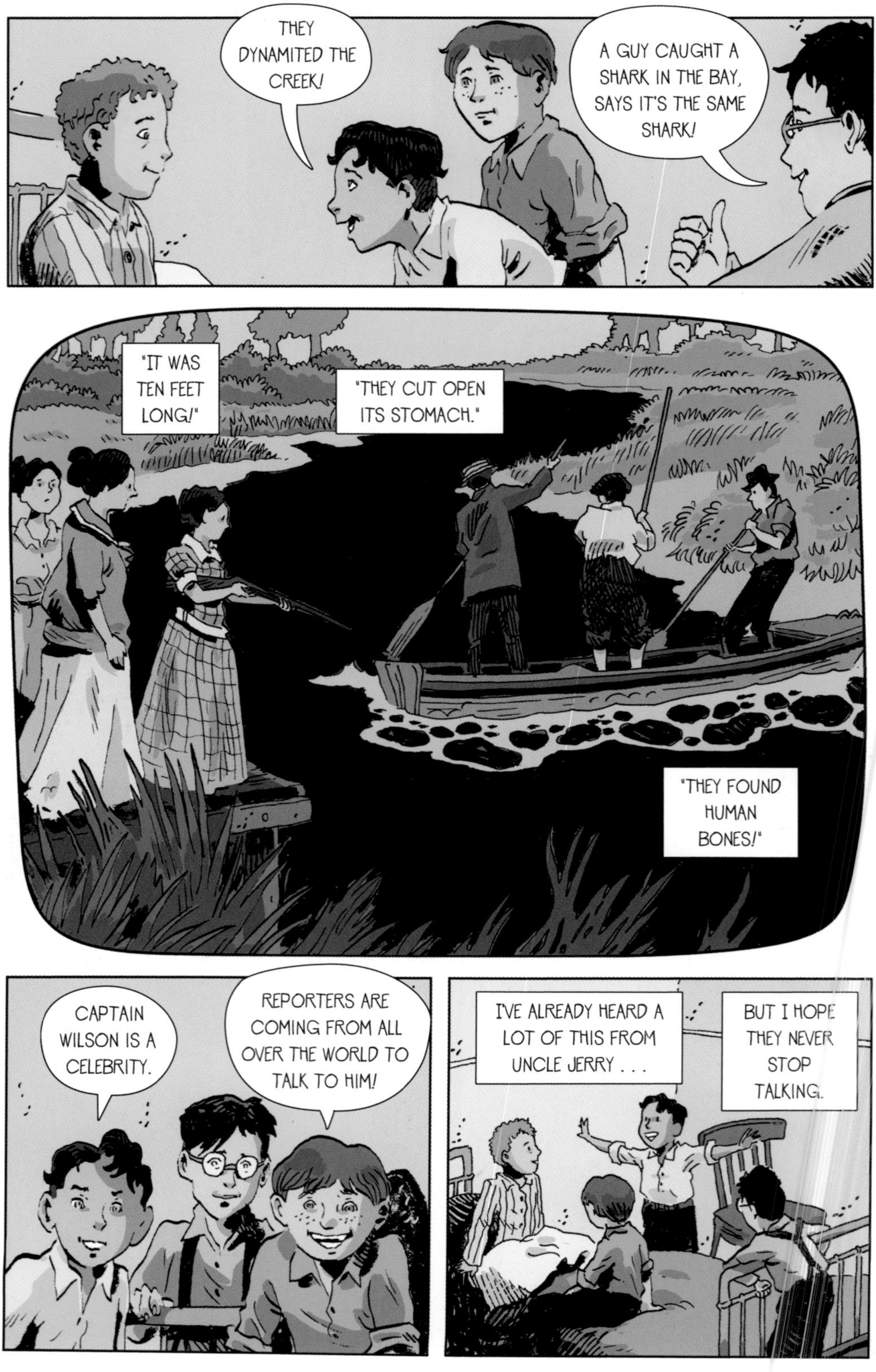
THEY DYNAMITED THE CREEK!
A GUY CAUGHT A SHARK IN THE BAY, SAYS IT'S THE SAME SHARK!
"IT WAS TEN FEET LONG!"
"THEY CUT OPEN ITS STOMACH."
"THEY FOUND HUMAN BONES!"
CAPTAIN WILSON IS A CELEBRITY.
REPORTERS ARE COMING FROM ALL OVER THE WORLD TO TALK TO HIM!
I'VE ALREADY HEARD A LOT OF THIS FROM UNCLE JERRY . . .
BUT I HOPE THEY NEVER STOP TALKING.

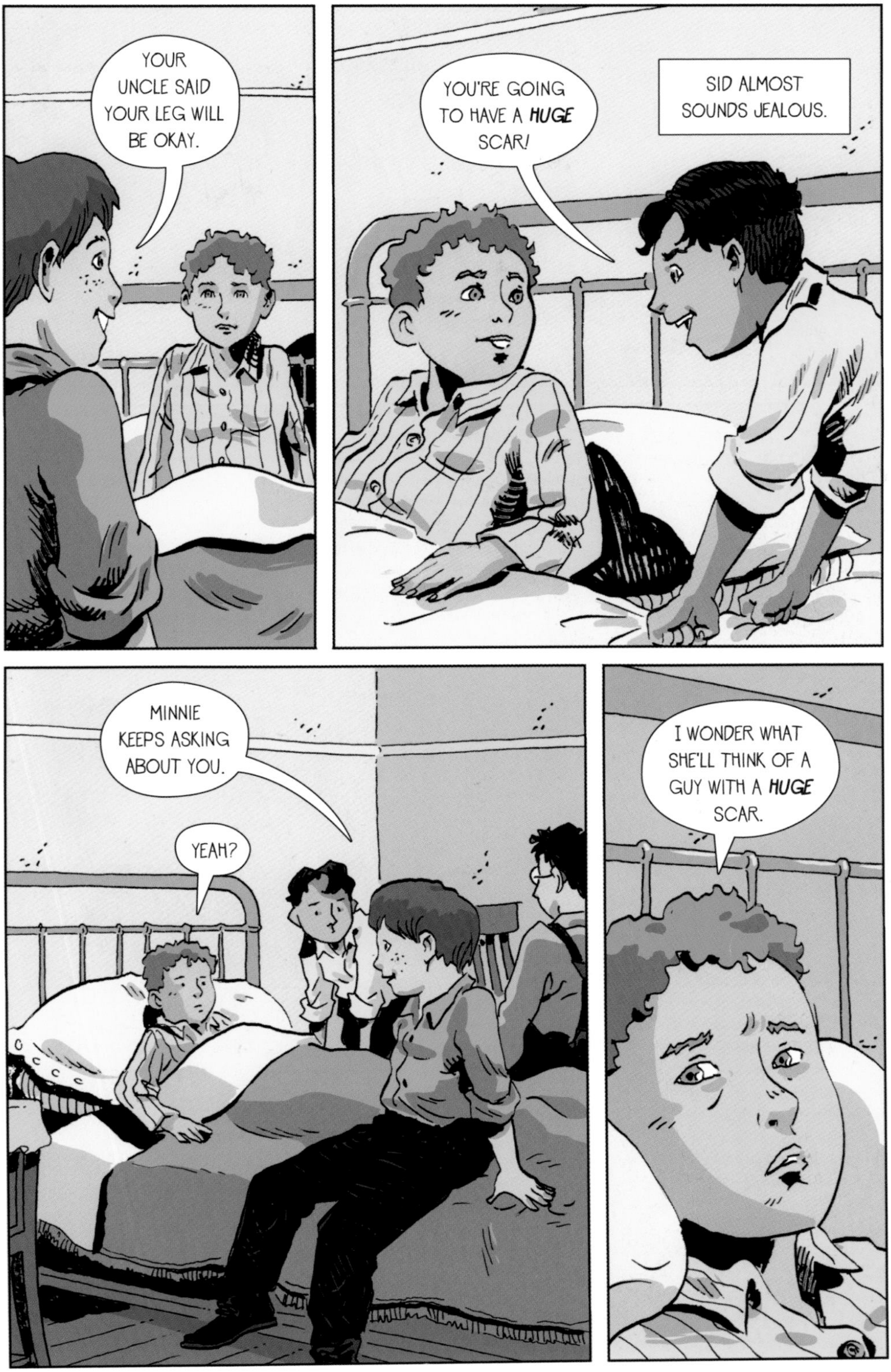
YOUR UNCLE SAID YOUR LEG WILL BE OKAY.
YOU'RE GOING TO HAVE A HUGE SCAR!
SID ALMOST SOUNDS JEALOUS.
MINNIE KEEPS ASKING ABOUT YOU.
YEAH?
I WONDER WHAT SHE'LL THINK OF A GUY WITH A HUGE SCAR.

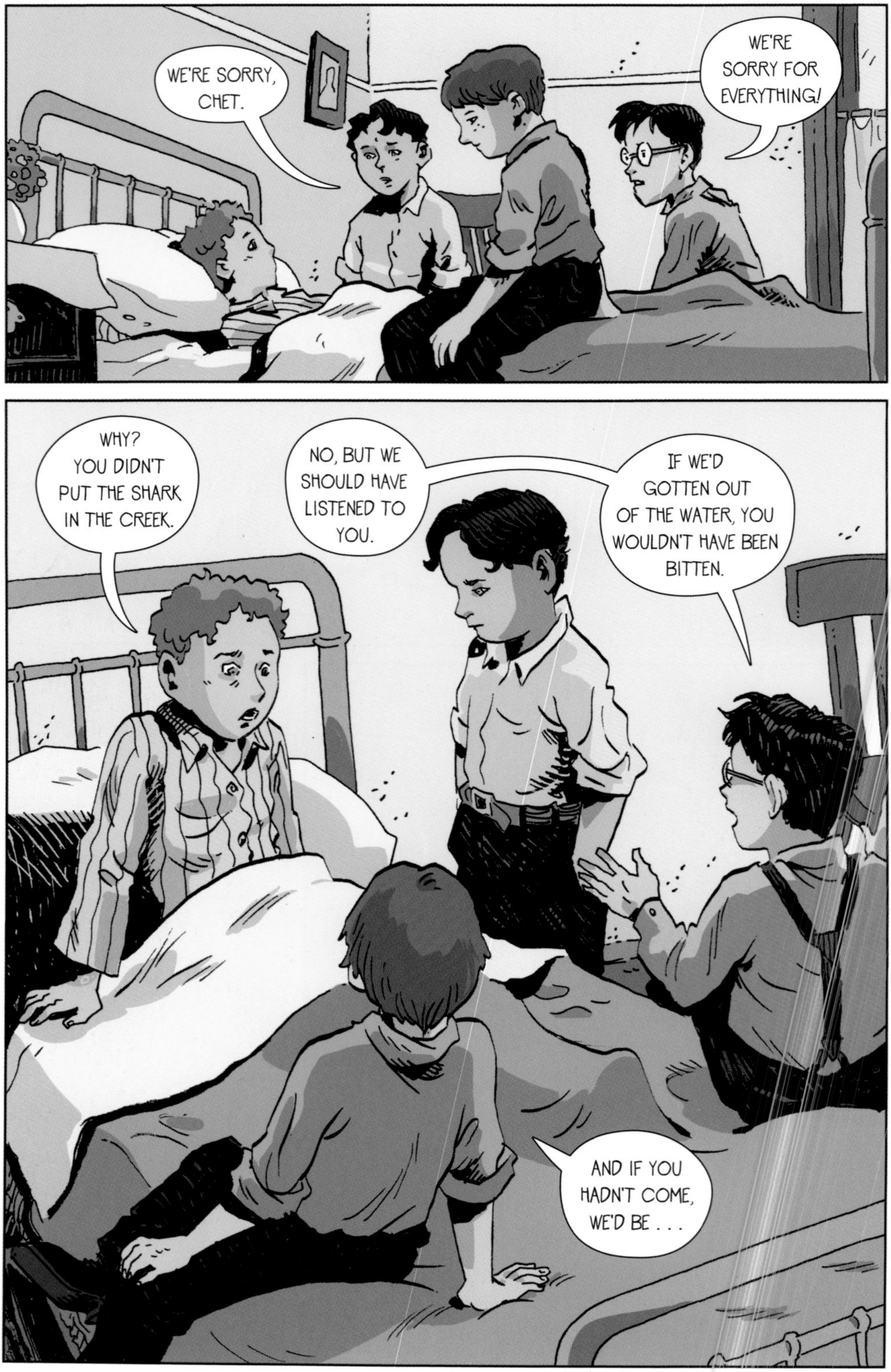
WE'RE SORRY, CHET.
WE'RE SORRY FOR EVERYTHING!
WHY? YOU DIDN'T PUT THE SHARK IN THE CREEK.
NO, BUT WE SHOULD HAVE LISTENED TO YOU.
IF WE'D GOTTEN OUT OF THE WATER, YOU WOULDN'T HAVE BEEN BITTEN.
AND IF YOU HADN'T COME, WE'D BE . . .

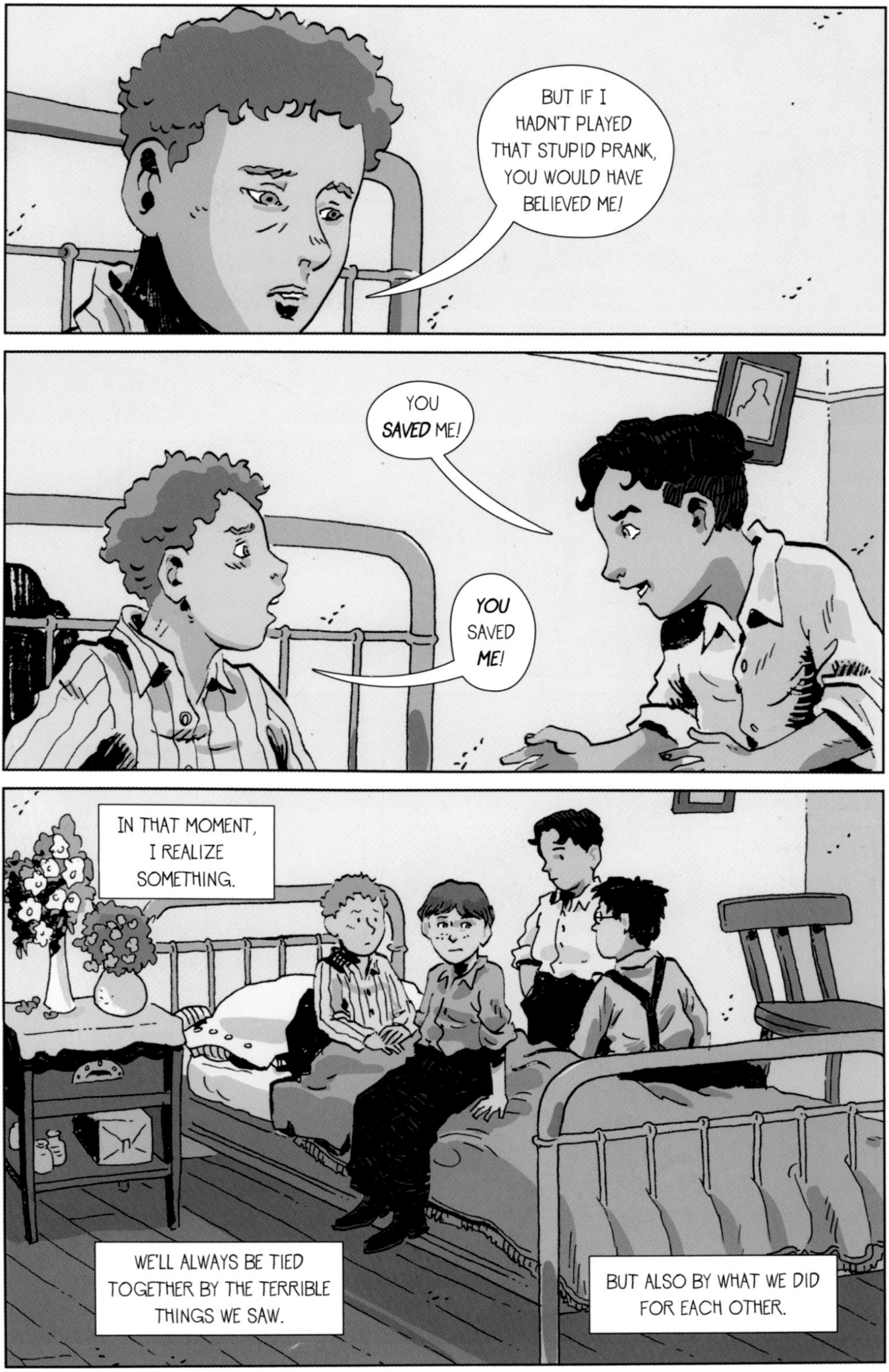
BUT IF I HADN'T PLAYED THAT STUPID PRANK, YOU WOULD HAVE BELIEVED ME!
YOU **SAVED** ME!
YOU SAVED **ME!**
IN THAT MOMENT, I REALIZE SOMETHING.
WE'LL ALWAYS BE TIED TOGETHER BY THE TERRIBLE THINGS WE SAW.
BUT ALSO BY WHAT WE DID FOR EACH OTHER.

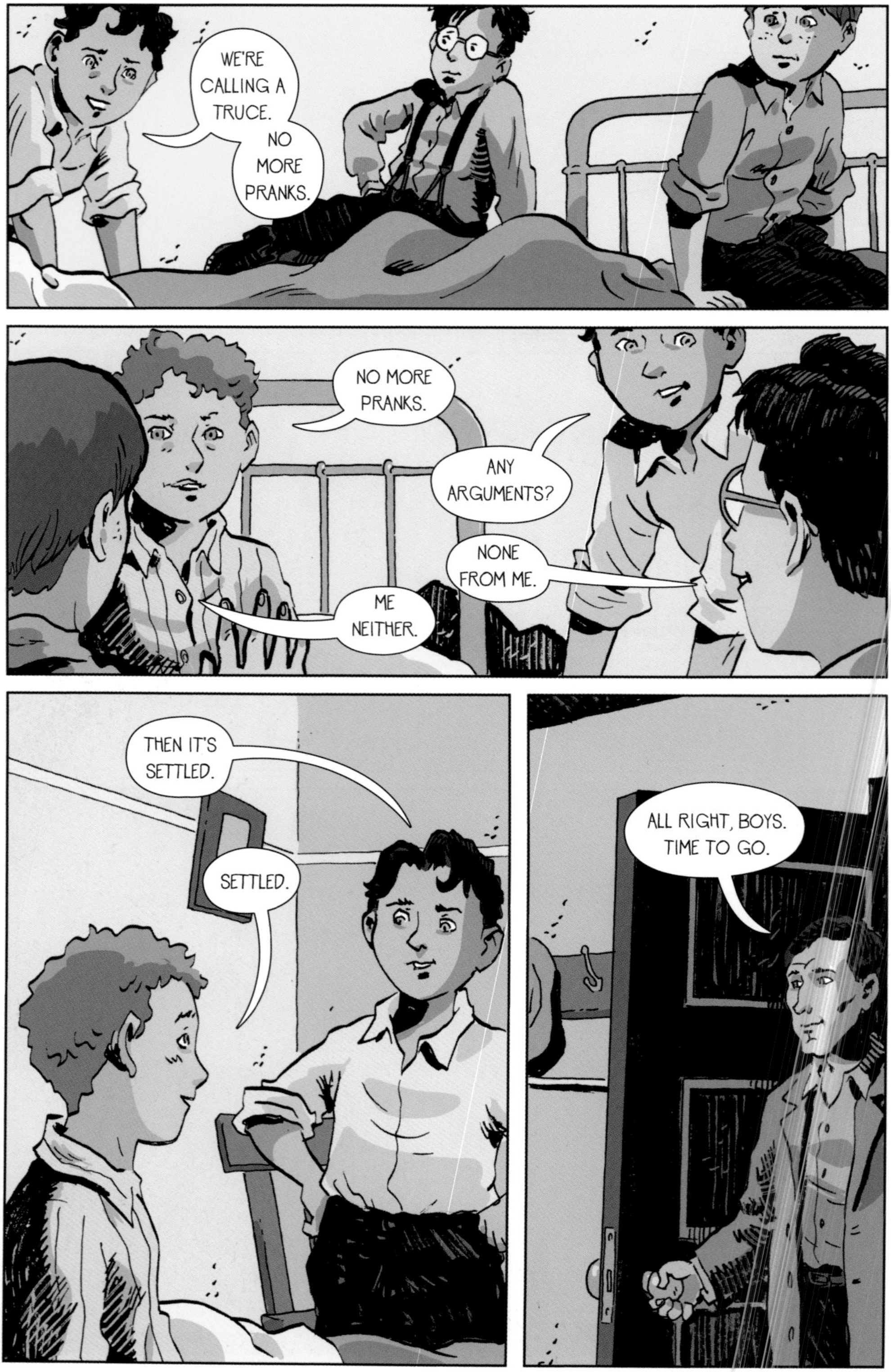
WE'RE CALLING A TRUCE.
NO MORE PRANKS.
NO MORE PRANKS.
ANY ARGUMENTS?
NONE FROM ME.
ME NEITHER.
THEN IT'S SETTLED.
SETTLED.
ALL RIGHT, BOYS. TIME TO GO.

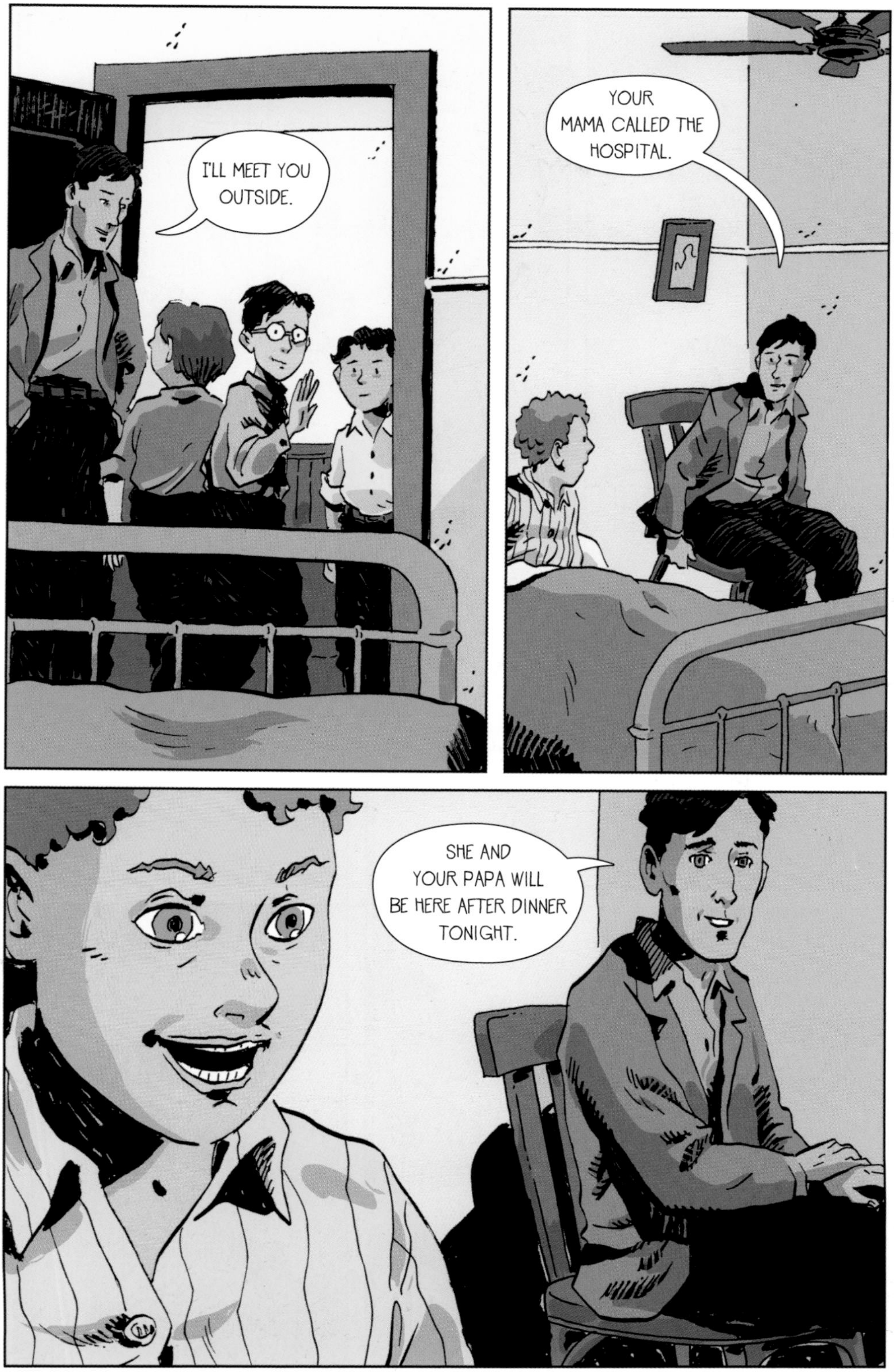
I'LL MEET YOU OUTSIDE.
YOUR MAMA CALLED THE HOSPITAL.
SHE AND YOUR PAPA WILL BE HERE AFTER DINNER TONIGHT.

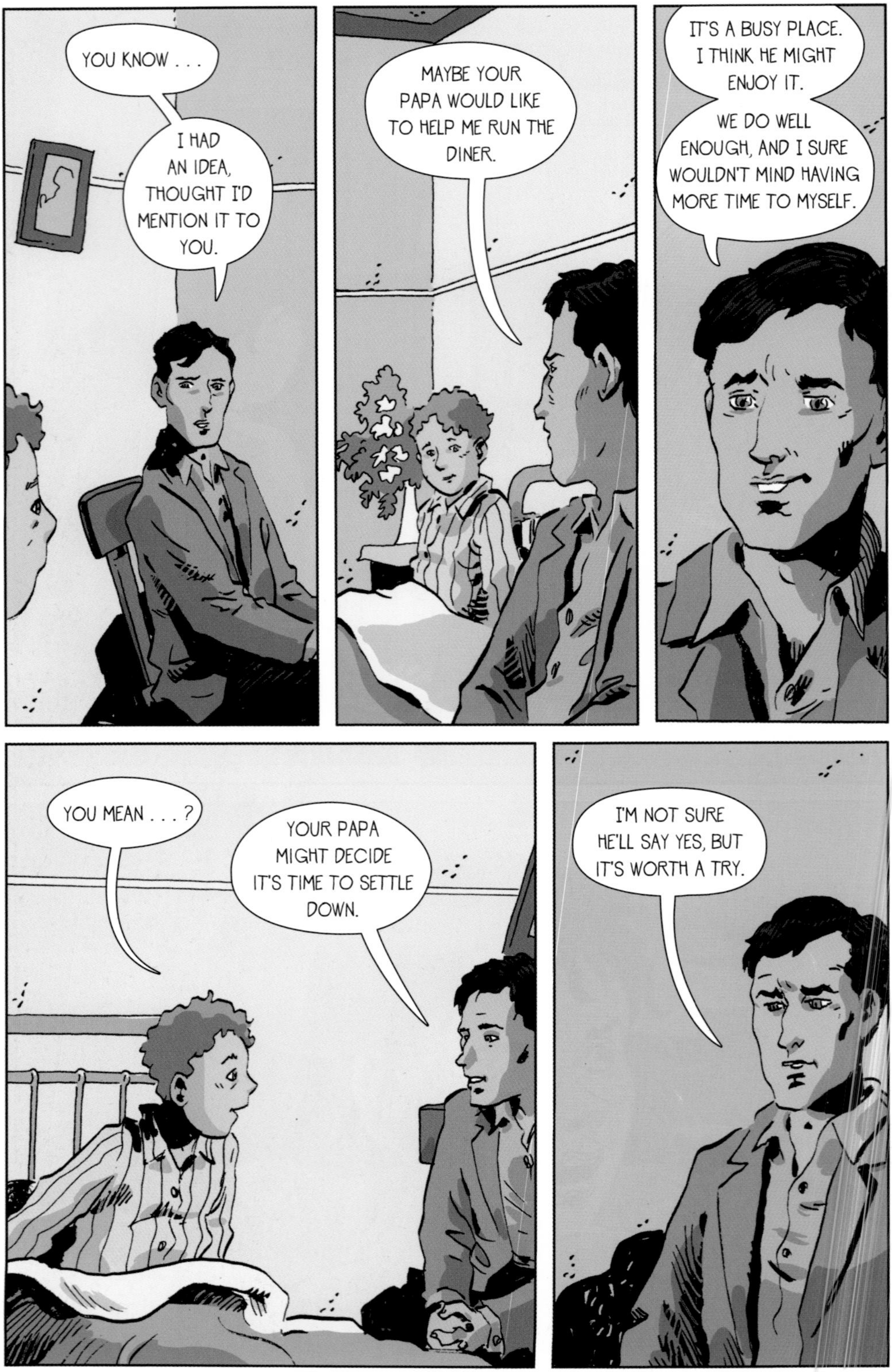
YOU KNOW . . .
I HAD AN IDEA, THOUGHT I'D MENTION IT TO YOU.
MAYBE YOUR PAPA WOULD LIKE TO HELP ME RUN THE DINER.
IT'S A BUSY PLACE. I THINK HE MIGHT ENJOY IT.
WE DO WELL ENOUGH, AND I SURE WOULDN'T MIND HAVING MORE TIME TO MYSELF.
YOU MEAN . . . ?
YOUR PAPA MIGHT DECIDE IT'S TIME TO SETTLE DOWN.
I'M NOT SURE HE'LL SAY YES, BUT IT'S WORTH A TRY.

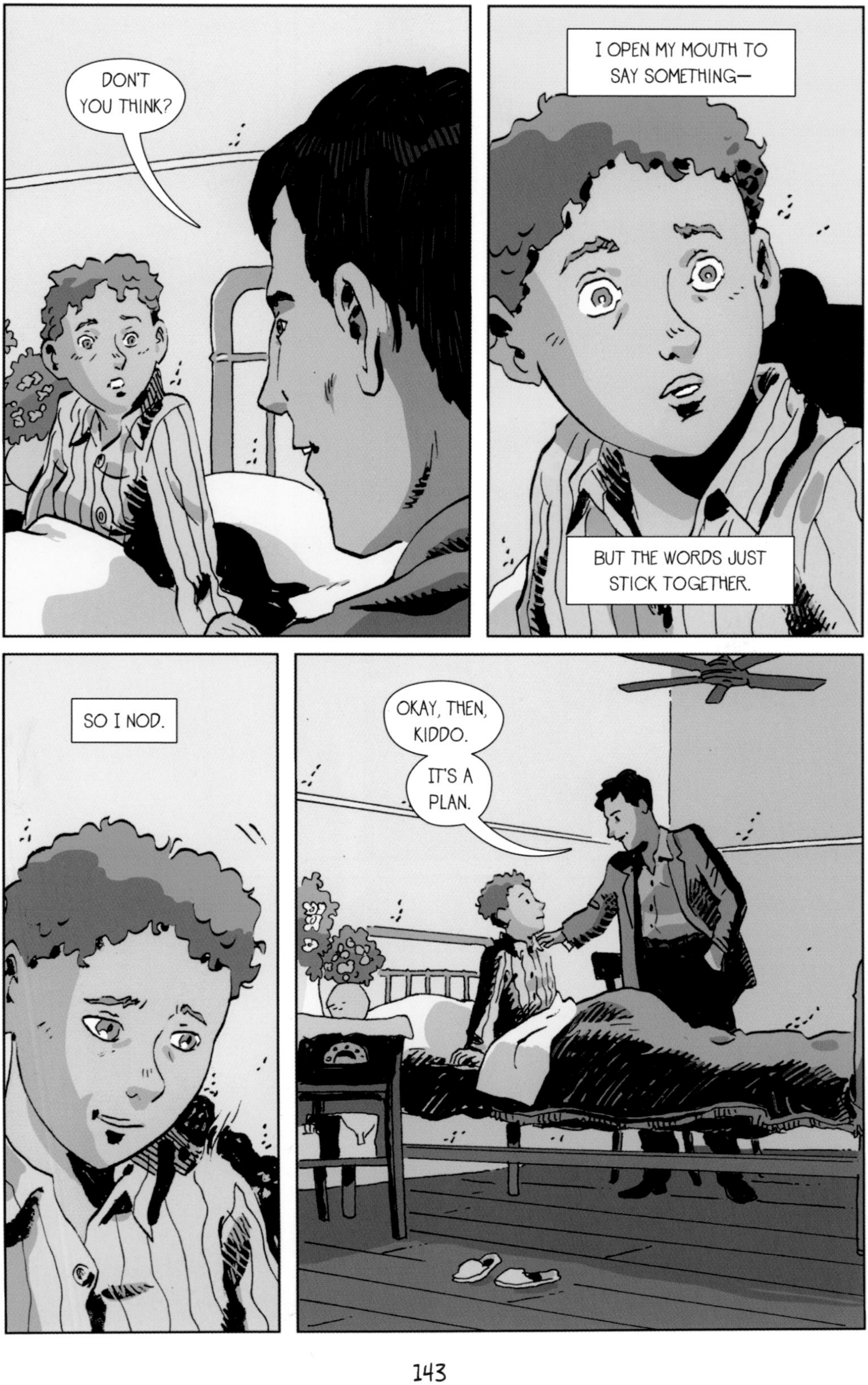
DON'T YOU THINK?
I OPEN MY MOUTH TO SAY SOMETHING—
BUT THE WORDS JUST STICK TOGETHER.
SO I NOD.
OKAY, THEN, KIDDO.
IT'S A PLAN.

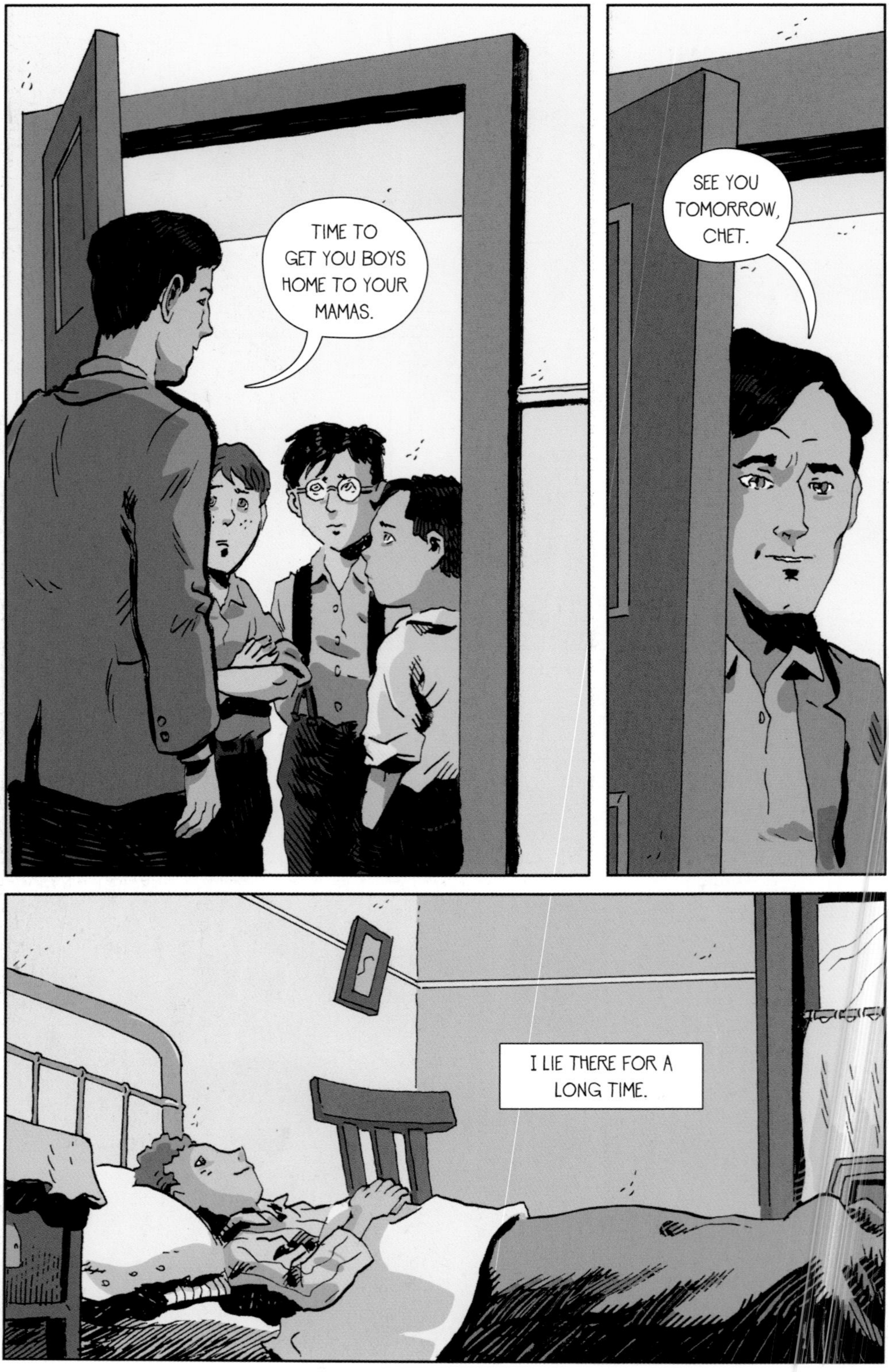
TIME TO GET YOU BOYS HOME TO YOUR MAMAS.
SEE YOU TOMORROW, CHET.
I LIE THERE FOR A LONG TIME.

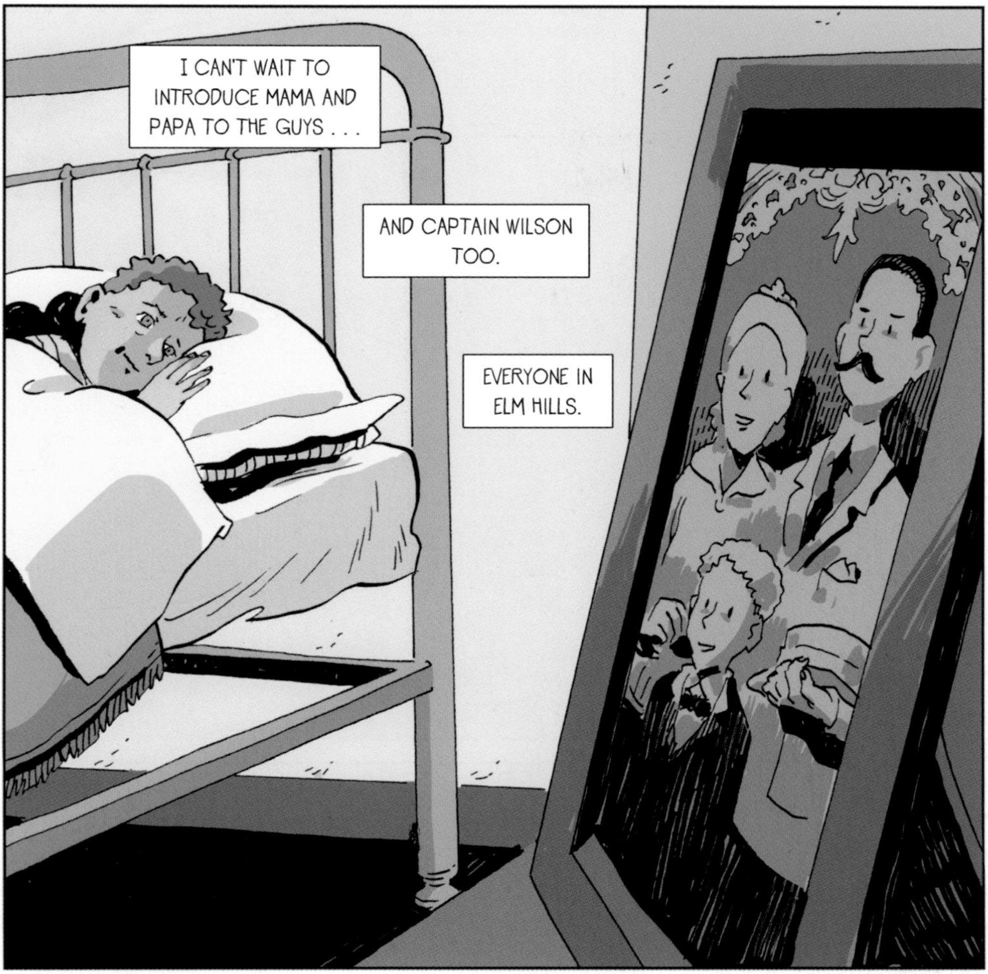
I CAN'T WAIT TO INTRODUCE MAMA AND PAPA TO THE GUYS . . .
AND CAPTAIN WILSON TOO.
EVERYONE IN ELM HILLS.

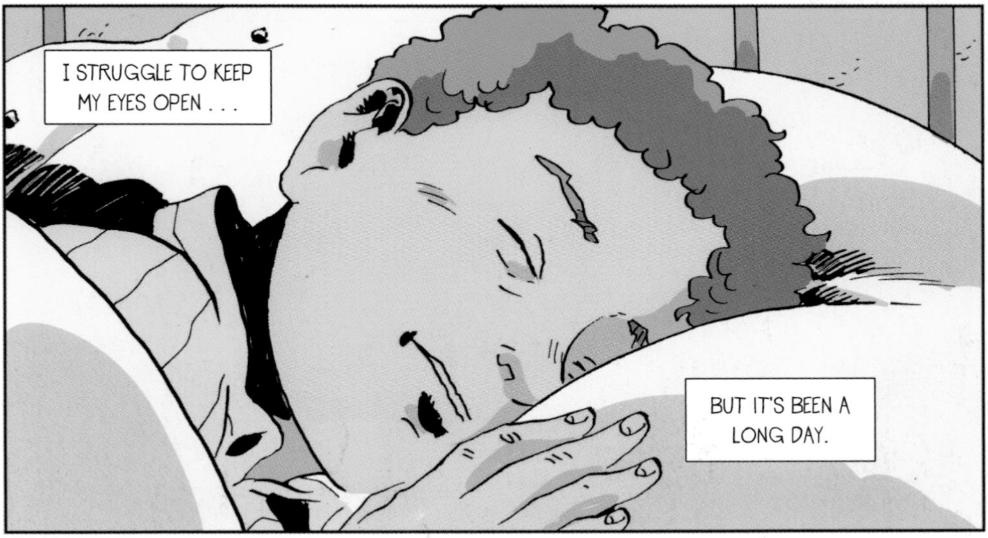
I STRUGGLE TO KEEP MY EYES OPEN . . .
BUT IT'S BEEN A LONG DAY.

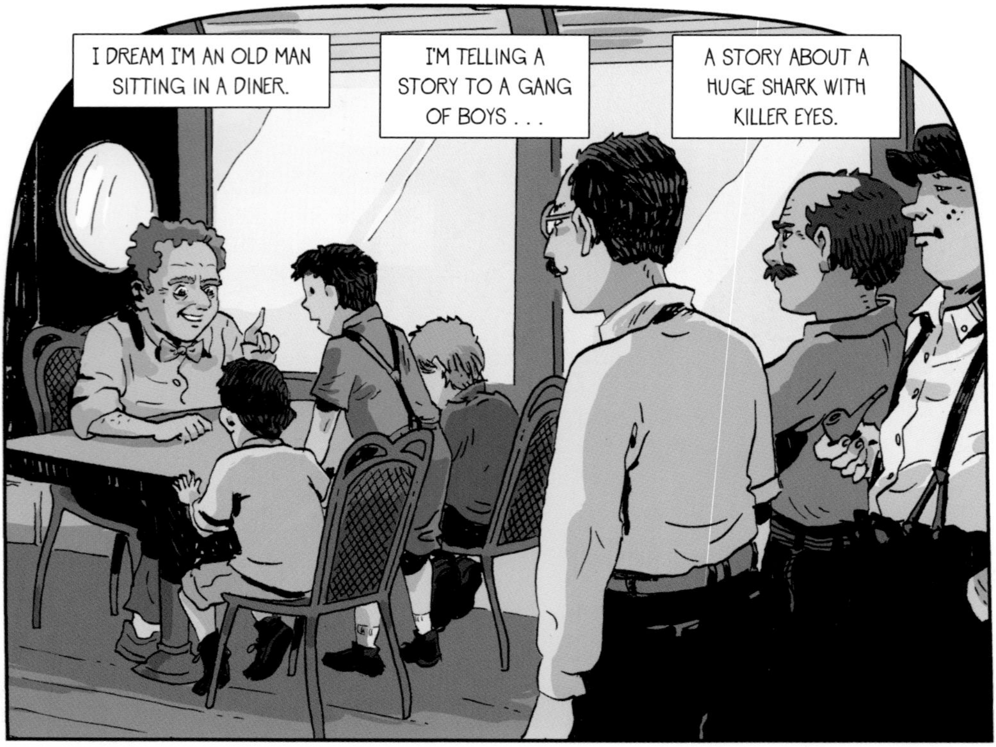

I DREAM I'M AN OLD MAN SITTING IN A DINER.
I'M TELLING A STORY TO A GANG OF BOYS . . .
A STORY ABOUT A HUGE SHARK WITH KILLER EYES.

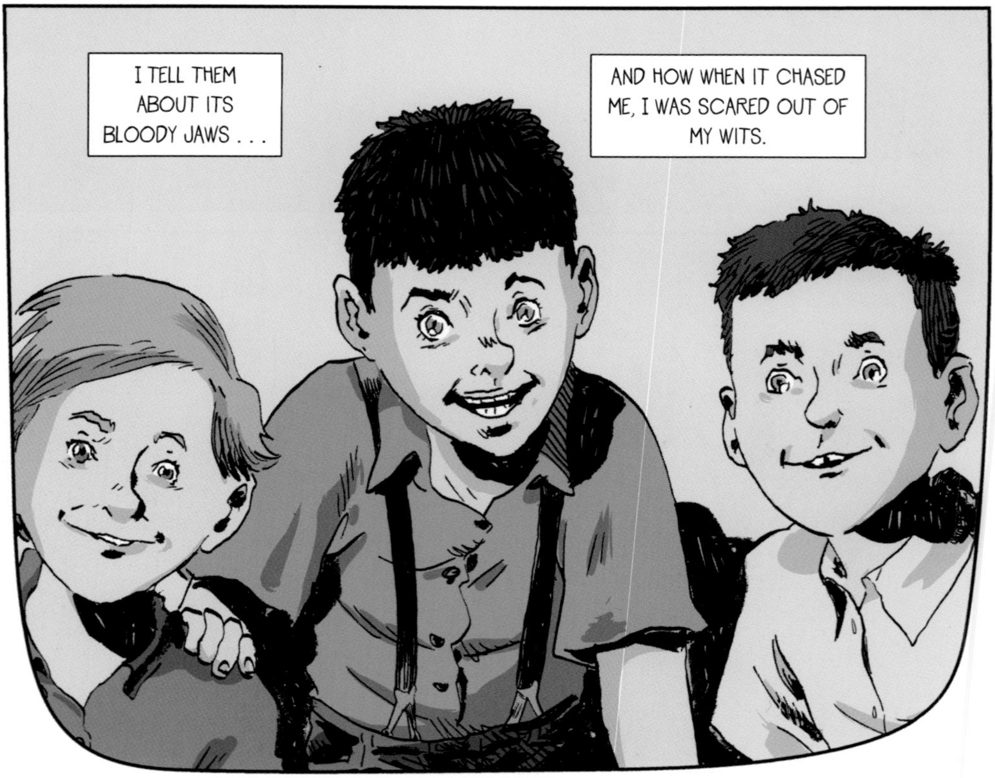

I TELL THEM ABOUT ITS BLOODY JAWS . . .
AND HOW WHEN IT CHASED ME, I WAS SCARED OUT OF MY WITS.

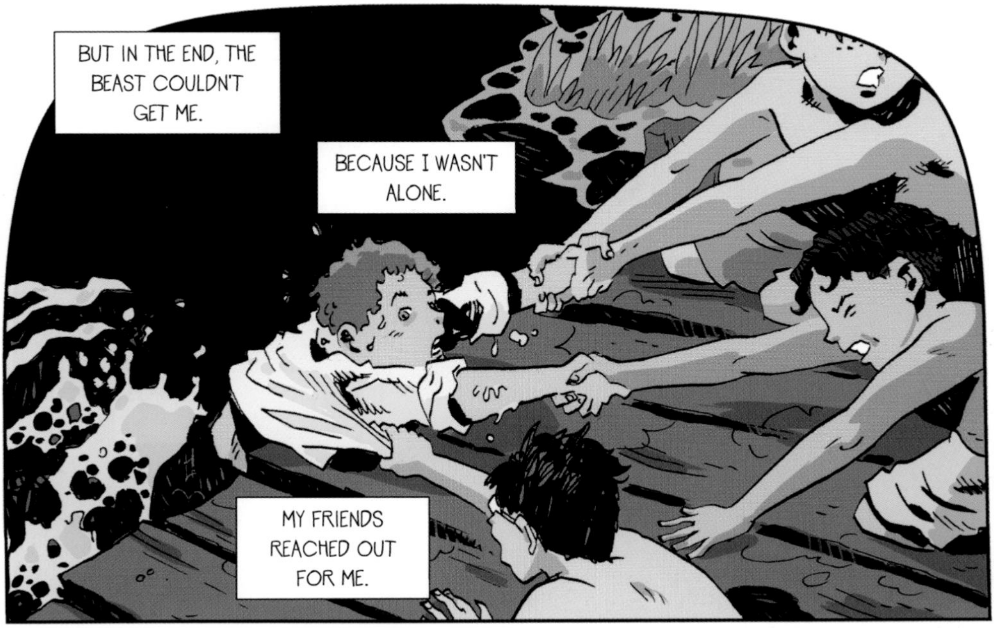
BUT IN THE END, THE BEAST COULDN'T GET ME.
BECAUSE I WASN'T ALONE.
MY FRIENDS REACHED OUT FOR ME.

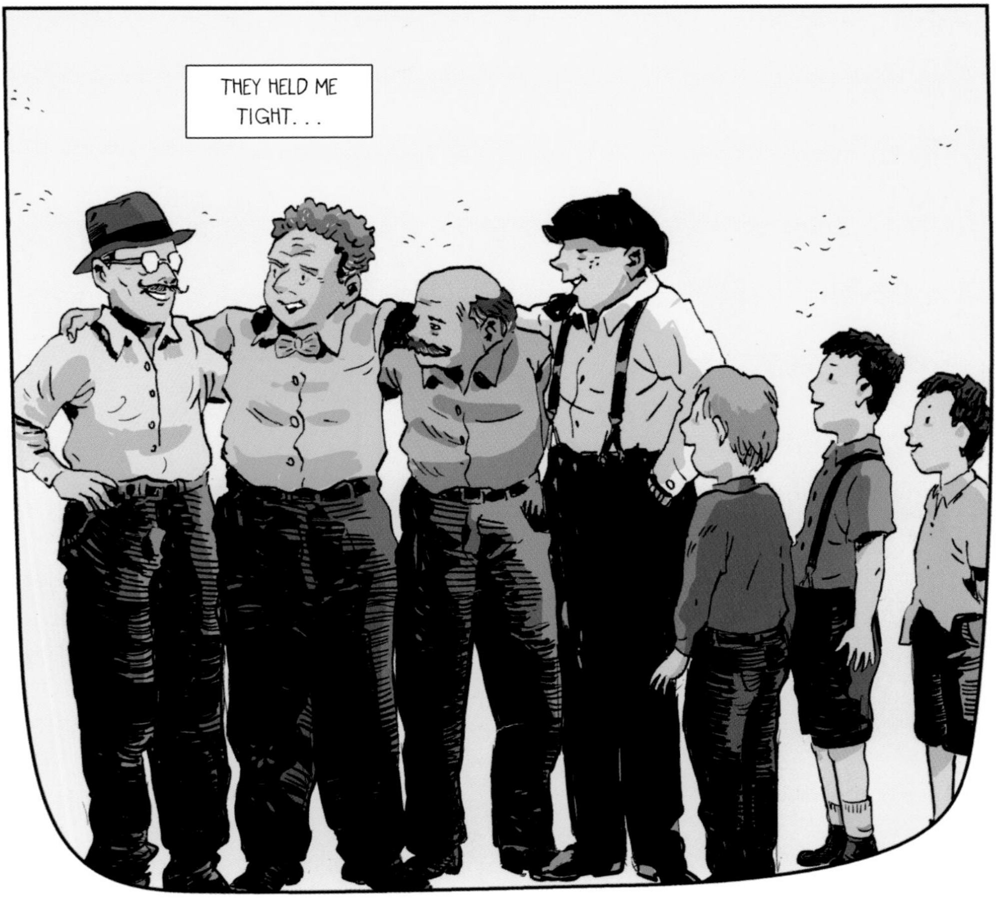
THEY HELD ME TIGHT. . .

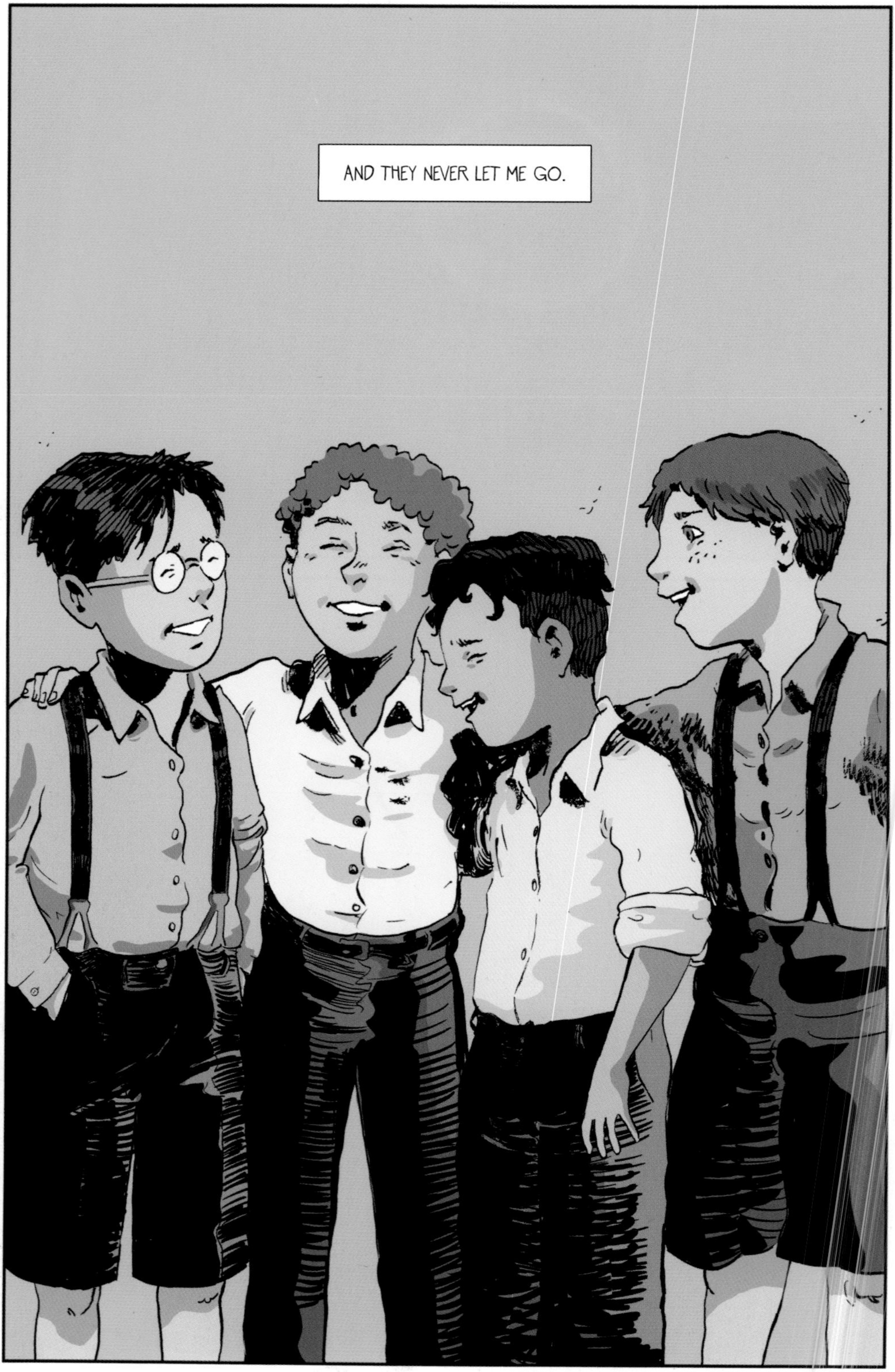
AND THEY NEVER LET ME GO.

TURN THE PAGE
TO READ MORE ABOUT
SHARKS AND THE DEADLY

SHARK ATTACKS
OF 1916

DEAR READERS,

IT'S BEEN MORE THAN 100 YEARS SINCE THE FAMOUS SHARK ATTACKS OF 1916 SHOCKED PEOPLE AROUND THE WORLD. THOSE EVENTS ALSO CHANGED OUR IDEAS ABOUT SHARKS. BEFORE 1916, EVEN RESPECTED SCIENTISTS WERE CERTAIN THAT SHARKS WERE SHY, WEAK-JAWED CREATURES THAT WOULD NEVER HARM A HUMAN BEING. LITTLE WAS KNOWN ABOUT THE OCEAN AND ITS CREATURES. THE SCIENCE OF STUDYING THE OCEAN—MARINE BIOLOGY—WAS JUST BEGINNING.

THE EVENTS OF JULY 1916 INSTANTLY TRANSFORMED SHARKS INTO THE MOST FEARED AND HATED CREATURES OF THE SEA, AND MAYBE THE MOST FEARED AND HATED CREATURES ON EARTH. MOVIES LIKE *JAWS* TURNED SHARKS INTO HORROR MOVIE MONSTERS, "MAN-EATERS" PROWLING THE OCEANS FOR A TASTE OF HUMAN FLESH.

IT'S CERTAINLY TRUE THAT SOME SPECIES OF SHARK—THE GREAT WHITE, THE TIGER, THE BULL, THE HAMMERHEAD—CAN BE VERY DANGEROUS TO HUMANS. BUT IT IS EXTREMELY RARE FOR A SHARK TO BITE A HUMAN. IN FACT, SOME PEOPLE SAY THAT A PERSON AT THE BEACH IS MORE LIKELY TO BE KILLED BY A FALLING COCONUT THAN BY A SHARK. (I AM NOW VERY SUSPICIOUS OF ALL COCONUTS.)

AS I HAVE LEARNED MORE AND MORE ABOUT SHARKS, MY FEAR HAS TURNED TO FASCINATION AND RESPECT. THESE ANIMALS ARE NOT MINDLESS KILLERS. THEY ARE COMPLICATED CREATURES WHO HAVE BEEN ON EARTH SINCE THE TIME OF THE DINOSAURS. THEY ARE ALSO VITALLY IMPORTANT TO THE HEALTH OF OUR OCEANS.

READ ON TO LEARN MORE ABOUT SHARKS, WITH SOME HELP FROM MY FRIENDS CHET, UNCLE JERRY, SID, DEWEY, AND MONTY.

Lauren Tarshis

THE REAL-LIFE SHARK ATTACKS OF 1916

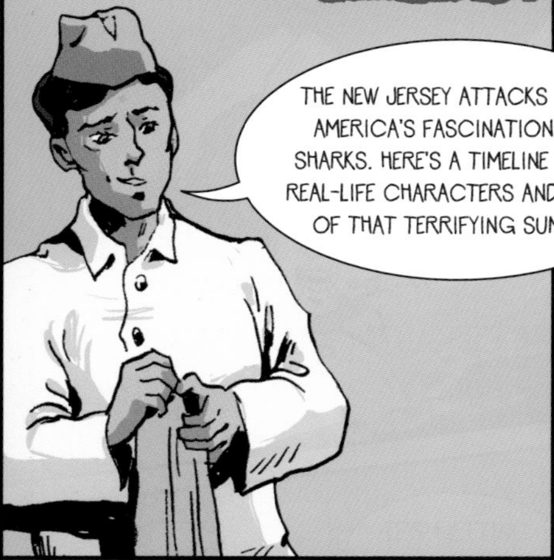
THE NEW JERSEY ATTACKS BEGAN AMERICA'S FASCINATION WITH SHARKS. HERE'S A TIMELINE OF THE REAL-LIFE CHARACTERS AND EVENTS OF THAT TERRIFYING SUMMER.

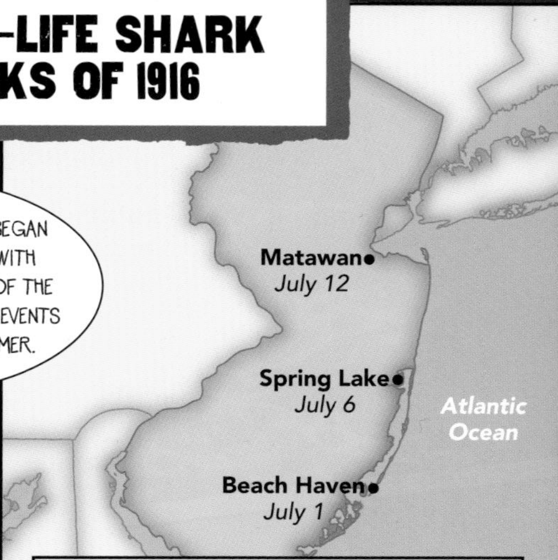
Matawan
July 12
Spring Lake
July 6
Atlantic Ocean
Beach Haven
July 1

SHARK ATTACKS ON THE JERSEY SHORE, 1916

JULY 1:
CHARLES E. VANSANT,
A 25-YEAR-OLD BUSINESSMAN, IS ATTACKED WHILE VACATIONING IN BEACH HAVEN WITH HIS FATHER AND SISTERS. A LIFEGUARD TRIES TO SAVE HIM, BUT MR. VANSANT DOES NOT SURVIVE.

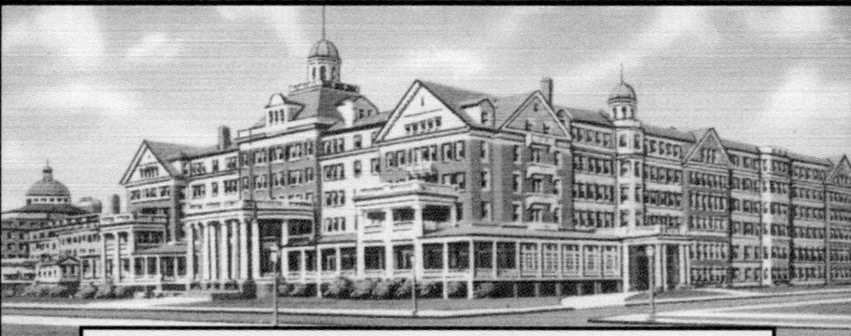

THE ESSEX & SUSSEX HOTEL, SPRING LAKE, NJ

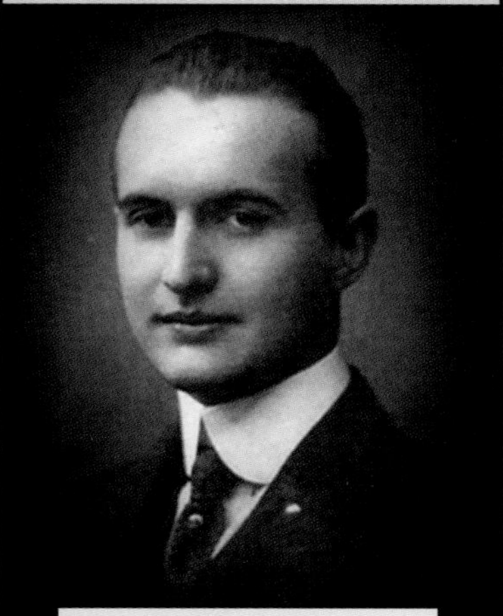

CHARLES E. VANSANT
AUGUST 22, 1892–JULY 1, 1916

JULY 6: FIVE DAYS LATER, ABOUT 50 MILES UP THE COAST IN ANOTHER POPULAR VACATION TOWN CALLED SPRING LAKE, 28-YEAR-OLD **CHARLES BRUDER** GOES FOR A SWIM ON HIS LUNCH BREAK. A SHARK ATTACKS HIM 130 YARDS FROM SHORE. LIFEGUARDS TRY TO SAVE HIM BUT HE DIES IN THE BOAT ON THE WAY BACK TO THE BEACH.

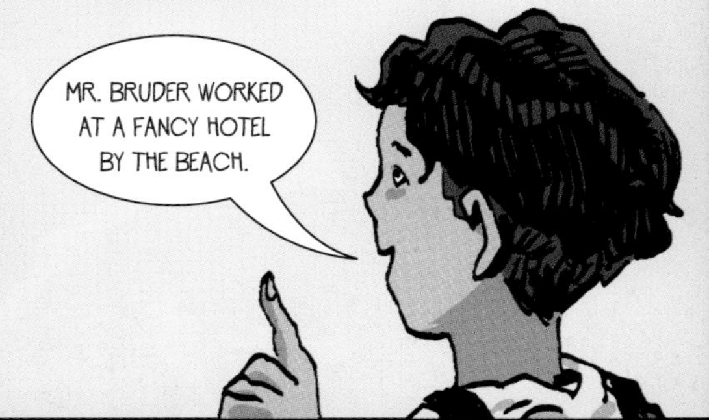
MR. BRUDER WORKED AT A FANCY HOTEL BY THE BEACH.

JULY 8: A SHARK IS SPOTTED A FEW MILES NORTH, IN ASBURY PARK. A LIFEGUARD GETS IN A BOAT AND BEATS THE SHARK WITH AN OAR TO SCARE IT AWAY.

THE MATAWAN ATTACKS

JULY 12: NOT EVEN A WEEK LATER, THE SHARK ATTACKS AFFECT A VERY DIFFERENT PLACE: MATAWAN, NEW JERSEY. UNLIKE BEACH HAVEN AND SPRING LAKE, MATAWAN IS NOT ON THE SHORE.

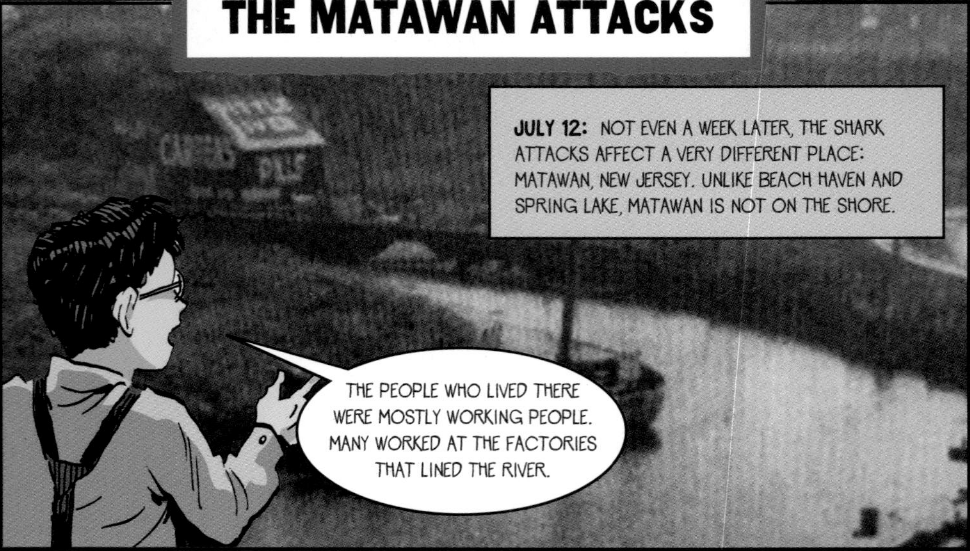
THE PEOPLE WHO LIVED THERE WERE MOSTLY WORKING PEOPLE. MANY WORKED AT THE FACTORIES THAT LINED THE RIVER.

ABOUT 1:30 P.M.: A RETIRED SEA CAPTAIN NAMED **THOMAS COTTRELL** SPOTS A SHARK WHILE CROSSING A BRIDGE OVER MATAWAN CREEK. HE RUNS INTO TOWN TO WARN OTHERS, BUT NO ONE BELIEVES HIM. THE IDEA THAT A SHARK COULD BE IN THE CREEK SEEMS IMPOSSIBLE.

ABOUT 2 P.M.: HAVING LEFT EARLY FROM HIS JOB AT THE BASKET FACTORY, ELEVEN-YEAR-OLD **LESTER STILLWELL** IS SWIMMING IN THE CREEK WITH SOME FRIENDS WHEN A SHARK PULLS HIM UNDER. HIS FRIENDS RUSH UP MAIN STREET. A SHOP OWNER NAMED **STANLEY FISHER** DOUBTS THERE IS A SHARK, BUT FEARS LESTER IS DROWNING. HE GRABS TWO OTHER MEN AND THEY DASH TO THE CREEK. A CROWD FOLLOWS.

ABOUT 2:30 P.M.: HALF A MILE DOWN THE CREEK, FOURTEEN-YEAR-OLD **JOSEPH DUNN** IS SWIMMING WITH HIS BROTHER AND SOME FRIENDS WHEN THEY HEAR SHOUTING ABOUT A SHARK. THE BOYS RUSH TO GET OUT OF THE WATER, BUT THE SHARK GRABS JOSEPH'S LOWER LEFT LEG. BYSTANDERS PULL JOSEPH TO SAFETY AND RUSH HIM TO THE HOSPITAL. HE SPENDS TWO MONTHS RECOVERING, BUT SURVIVES.

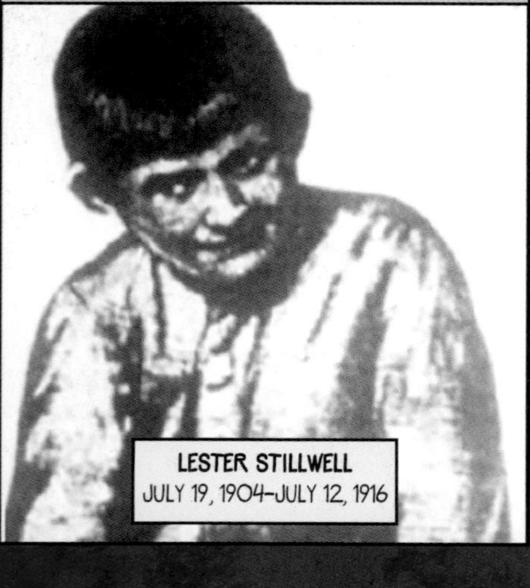

LESTER STILLWELL
JULY 19, 1904–JULY 12, 1916

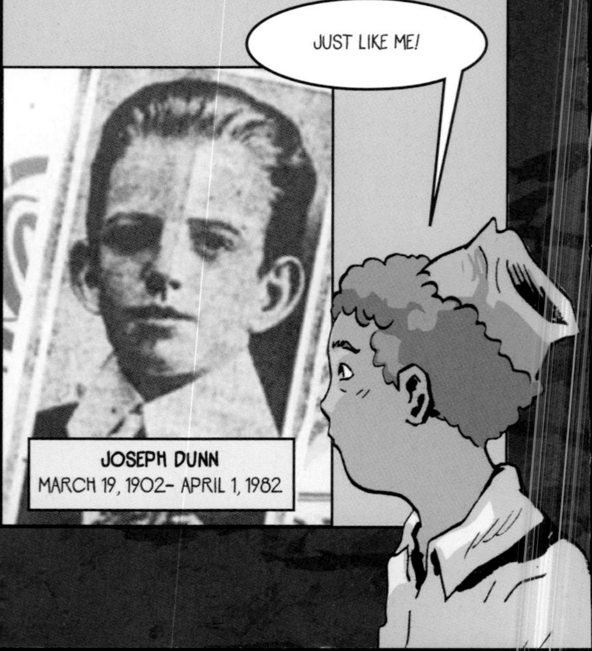
JUST LIKE ME!

JOSEPH DUNN
MARCH 19, 1902– APRIL 1, 1982

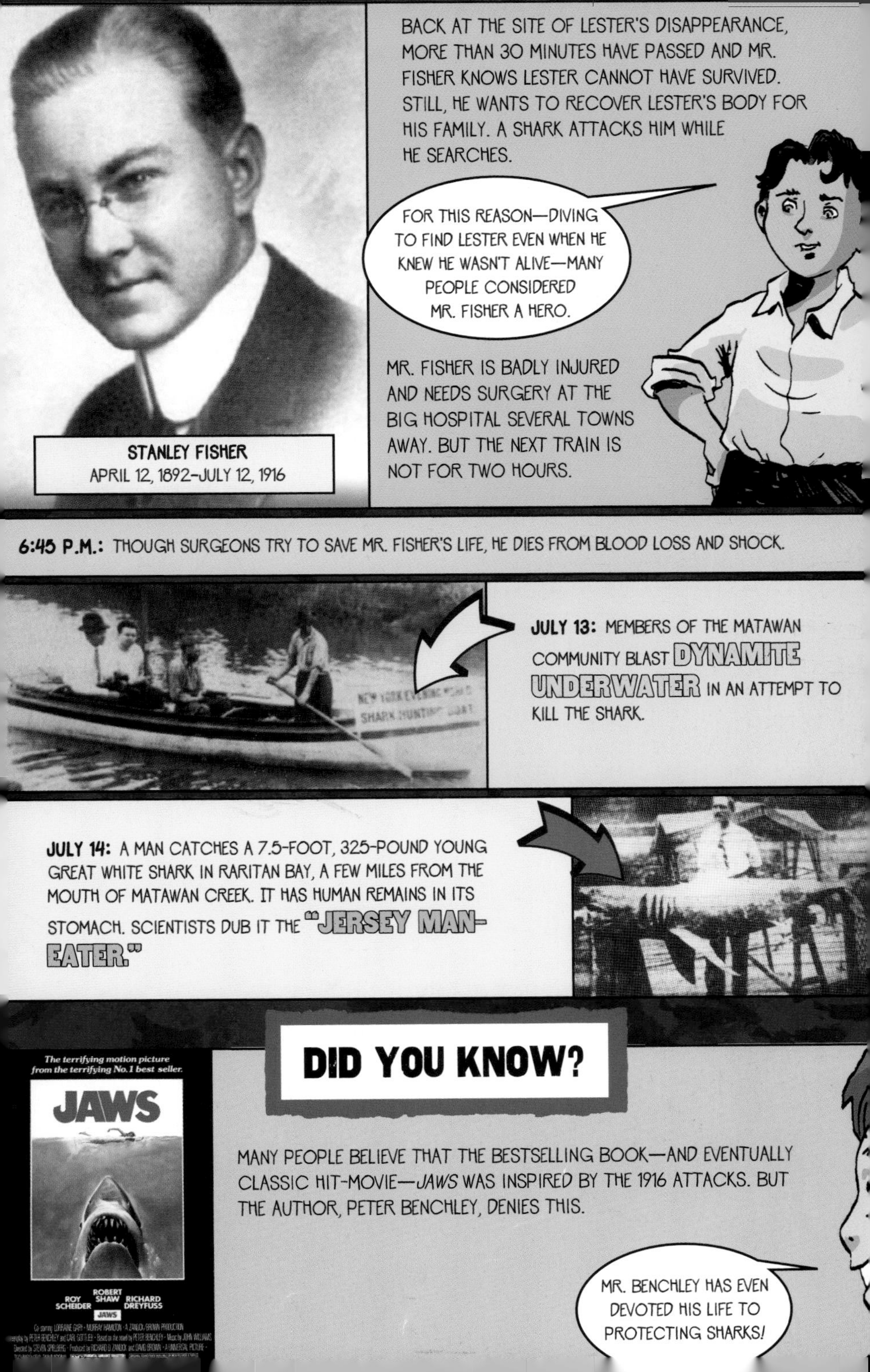

STANLEY FISHER
APRIL 12, 1892–JULY 12, 1916
BACK AT THE SITE OF LESTER'S DISAPPEARANCE, MORE THAN 30 MINUTES HAVE PASSED AND MR. FISHER KNOWS LESTER CANNOT HAVE SURVIVED. STILL, HE WANTS TO RECOVER LESTER'S BODY FOR HIS FAMILY. A SHARK ATTACKS HIM WHILE HE SEARCHES.
FOR THIS REASON—DIVING TO FIND LESTER EVEN WHEN HE KNEW HE WASN'T ALIVE—MANY PEOPLE CONSIDERED MR. FISHER A HERO.
MR. FISHER IS BADLY INJURED AND NEEDS SURGERY AT THE BIG HOSPITAL SEVERAL TOWNS AWAY. BUT THE NEXT TRAIN IS NOT FOR TWO HOURS.
6:45 P.M.: THOUGH SURGEONS TRY TO SAVE MR. FISHER'S LIFE, HE DIES FROM BLOOD LOSS AND SHOCK.
JULY 13: MEMBERS OF THE MATAWAN COMMUNITY BLAST DYNAMITE UNDERWATER IN AN ATTEMPT TO KILL THE SHARK.
JULY 14: A MAN CATCHES A 7.5-FOOT, 325-POUND YOUNG GREAT WHITE SHARK IN RARITAN BAY, A FEW MILES FROM THE MOUTH OF MATAWAN CREEK. IT HAS HUMAN REMAINS IN ITS STOMACH. SCIENTISTS DUB IT THE "JERSEY MAN-EATER."
DID YOU KNOW?
The terrifying motion picture from the terrifying No. 1 best seller.
JAWS
ROY SCHEIDER
ROBERT SHAW
RICHARD DREYFUSS
MANY PEOPLE BELIEVE THAT THE BESTSELLING BOOK—AND EVENTUALLY CLASSIC HIT-MOVIE—*JAWS* WAS INSPIRED BY THE 1916 ATTACKS. BUT THE AUTHOR, PETER BENCHLEY, DENIES THIS.
MR. BENCHLEY HAS EVEN DEVOTED HIS LIFE TO PROTECTING SHARKS!

MORE SHARK ATTACK FACTS

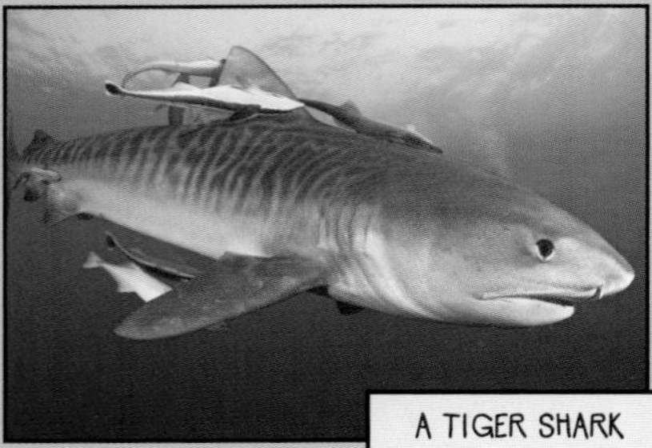

A TIGER SHARK

OF THE MORE THAN 350 KNOWN SPECIES OF SHARKS, **ONLY FOUR SPECIES** ARE PARTICULARLY PRONE TO ATTACK A HUMAN: THE BULL SHARK, THE GREAT WHITE, THE TIGER SHARK, AND THE HAMMERHEAD.

SHARK ATTACKS ARE VERY RARE! EACH YEAR, **ONLY ABOUT FIVE PEOPLE** DIE IN ENCOUNTERS WITH SHARKS.

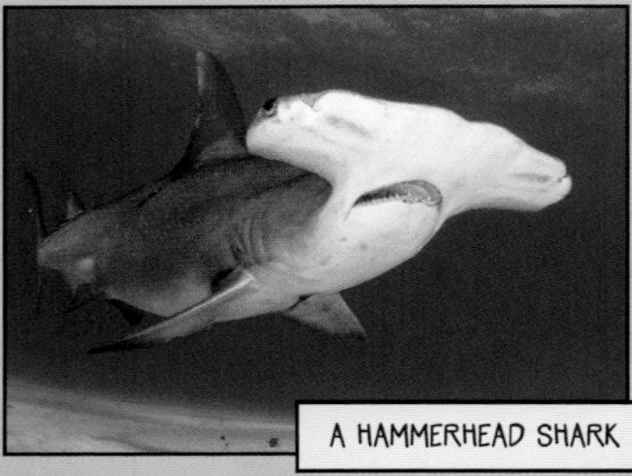

A HAMMERHEAD SHARK

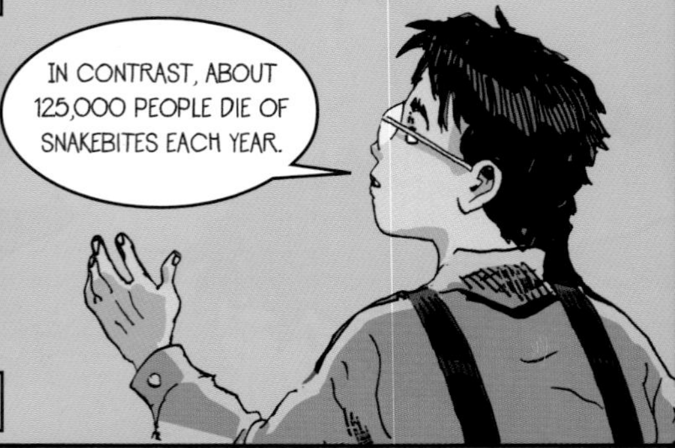
IN CONTRAST, ABOUT 125,000 PEOPLE DIE OF SNAKEBITES EACH YEAR.

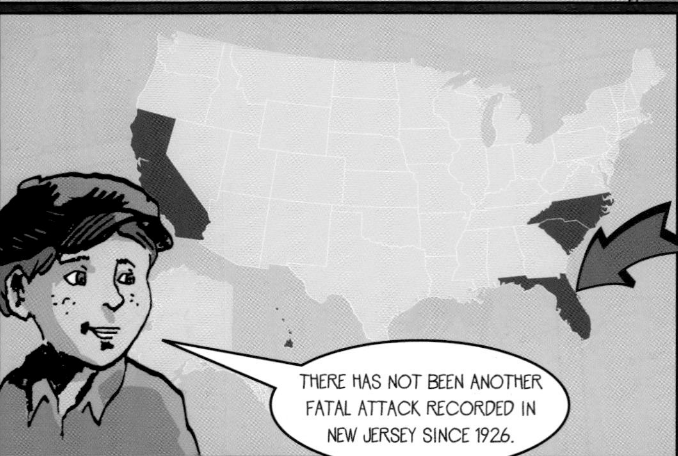
THERE HAS NOT BEEN ANOTHER FATAL ATTACK RECORDED IN NEW JERSEY SINCE 1926.

FLORIDA IS THE NUMBER-ONE SHARK ATTACK STATE IN THE U.S., WITH AN AVERAGE OF THIRTY ATTACKS A YEAR. CALIFORNIA, HAWAII, NORTH CAROLINA, AND SOUTH CAROLINA HAVE ALL HAD A FEW ATTACKS TOO.

SOME SCIENTISTS BELIEVE THAT MOST SHARKS **DON'T MEAN TO ATTACK HUMANS** BUT MISTAKE SURFERS OR SWIMMERS FOR LARGE SEA MAMMALS, LIKE SEALS.

THIS COULD EXPLAIN WHY MOST SHARK ATTACKS ON HUMANS **ARE NOT FATAL**—A SHARK TAKES ONE BITE, REALIZES ITS MISTAKE, AND SWIMS AWAY.

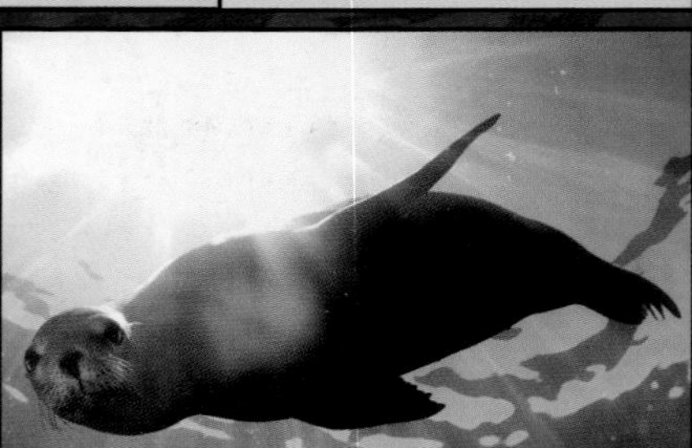

SHARK SAFETY

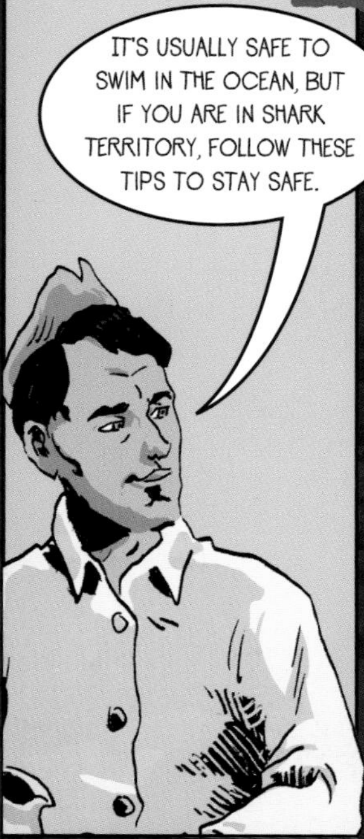
IT'S USUALLY SAFE TO SWIM IN THE OCEAN, BUT IF YOU ARE IN SHARK TERRITORY, FOLLOW THESE TIPS TO STAY SAFE.

SWIM ONLY ON BEACHES WHERE THERE IS A LIFEGUARD. AND IF SHARKS HAVE BEEN SEEN IN THE AREA, STAY OUT OF THE WATER.

SWIM IN GROUPS. MOST SHARK ATTACKS HAPPEN TO PEOPLE SWIMMING ALONE IN THE OCEAN.

IF YOU ARE BLEEDING, STAY OUT OF THE WATER. SHARKS CAN DETECT ONE DROP OF BLOOD IN AN OLYMPIC-SIZE POOL.

LEAVE YOUR JEWELRY ON LAND. FLASHING METAL CAN ALSO ATTRACT SHARKS.

AVOID SWIMMING AT NIGHT OR AT DUSK. THIS IS WHEN SHARKS FEED.

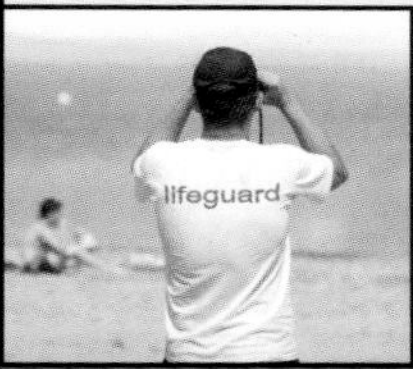
lifeguard

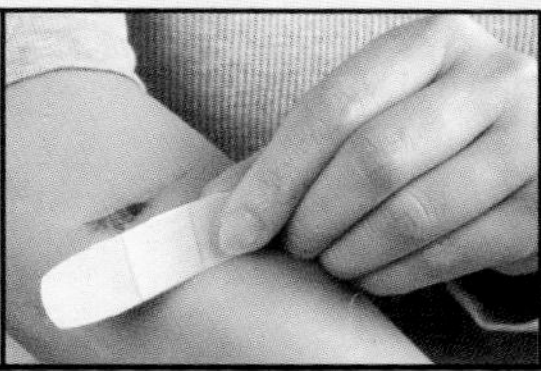

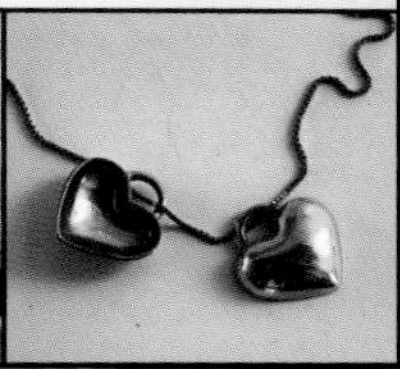

WHO IS MORE DANGEROUS?

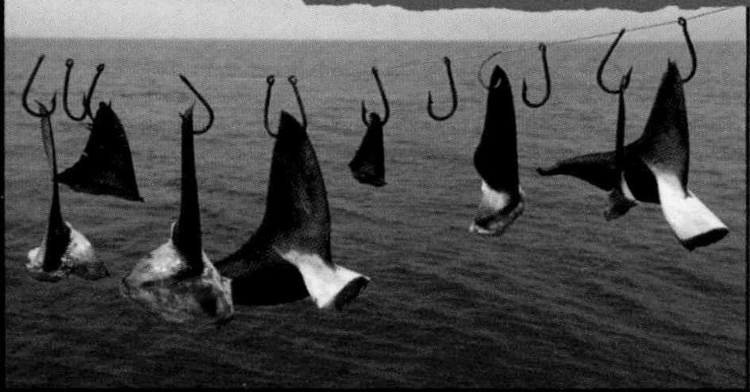

EVERY YEAR **HUMANS KILL NEARLY 100 MILLION SHARKS,** MAINLY FOR THEIR FINS, WHICH ARE A PRIZED INGREDIENT IN SHARK FIN SOUP. MANY SHARK SPECIES ARE IN DANGER OF DISAPPEARING FROM OUR OCEANS FOREVER.

SHARKS ARE IMPORTANT TO THE **HEALTH OF OUR OCEANS.** IF BIG SHARKS DISAPPEAR, THE BALANCE OF LIFE IN OUR OCEANS WILL BE DAMAGED. RATHER THAN FEAR SHARKS, HUMANS NEED TO WORK TO PROTECT THEM FROM OVERFISHING AND OCEAN POLLUTION.

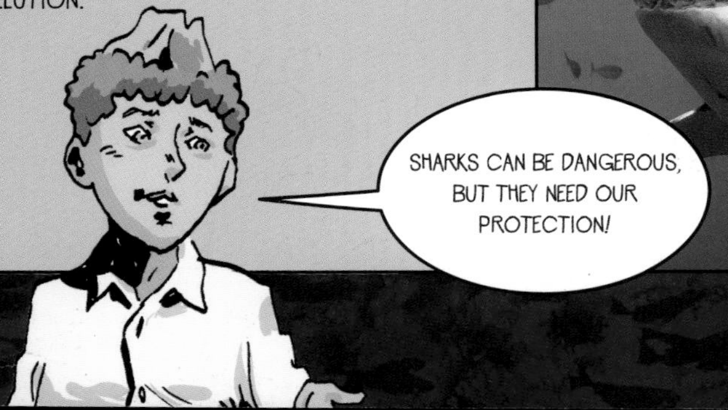
SHARKS CAN BE DANGEROUS, BUT THEY NEED OUR PROTECTION!

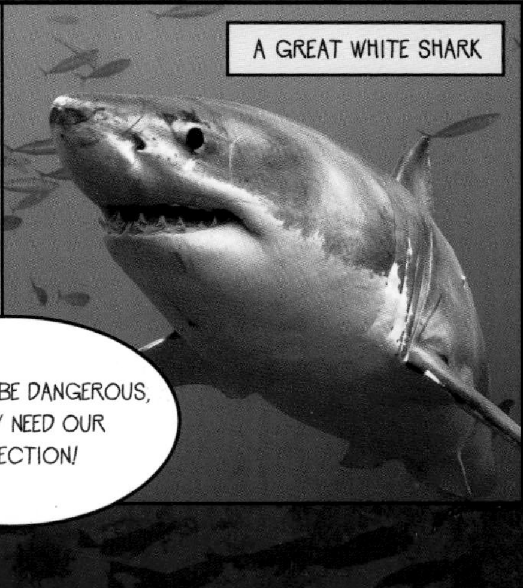

A GREAT WHITE SHARK

SELECTED BIBLIOGRAPHY

Capuzzo, Michael, *Close to Shore: The Terrifying Shark Attacks of 1916*, New York: Crown Books, 2003.

Fernicola, Richard G., and Guilford, M. D., *Twelve Days of Terror: A Definitive Investigation of the 1916 New Jersey Shark Attacks*, Connecticut: The Lyons Press, 2001.

Peschak, Thomas, *Sharks and People: Exploring Our Relationship with the Most Feared Fish in the Sea*, Chicago: The University of Chicago Press, 2013.

Savolaine, John Allan, *Stanley Fisher: Shark Attack Hero of a Bygone Age: How Brave Men Faced a Relentless Killer Shark in a Small New Jersey Town the Summer of 1916*, Middletown, NJ: Riverside Prints, 2016.

Gambion, Megan, "The Shark Attacks That Were the Inspiration for Jaws," *Smithsonian*, 2012.

Wilkinson, Alec, "Cape Fear," *The New Yorker*, September 9, 2013.

MORE SHARK BOOKS YOU MIGHT LIKE

Capuzzo, Michael, *Close to Shore: The Terrifying Shark Attacks of 1916*, New York: Crown Books, 2003.

Tarshis, Lauren, *I Survived the Shark Attacks of 1916*, New York: Scholastic, 2010.

Tarshis, Lauren, *I Survived True Stories: Nature Attacks!*, New York: Scholastic, 2015.

OTHER I SURVIVED GRAPHIC NOVELS

Tarshis, Lauren, *I Survived the Sinking of the Titanic, 1912: The Graphic Novel*, New York: Scholastic, 2020.

FEATURING ME, GEORGE!

AND ME, PHOEBE!

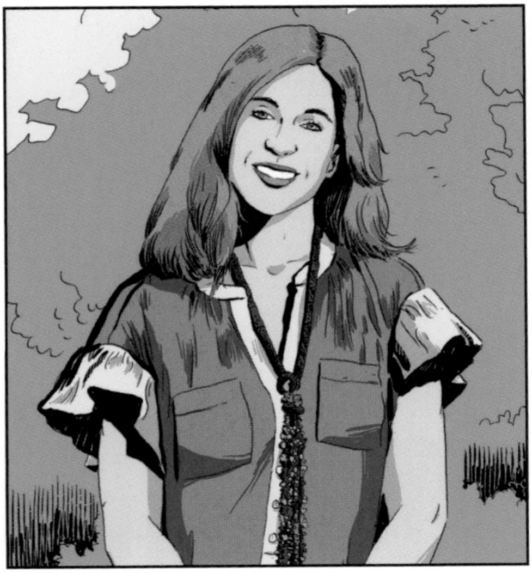

LAUREN TARSHIS'S

NEW YORK TIMES BESTSELLING I SURVIVED SERIES TELLS STORIES OF YOUNG PEOPLE AND THEIR RESILIENCE AND STRENGTH IN THE MIDST OF UNIMAGINABLE DISASTERS AND TIMES OF TURMOIL. LAUREN HAS BROUGHT HER SIGNATURE WARMTH, INTEGRITY, AND EXHAUSTIVE RESEARCH TO TOPICS SUCH AS THE BATTLE OF D-DAY, THE AMERICAN REVOLUTION, HURRICANE KATRINA, THE BOMBING OF PEARL HARBOR, AND OTHER WORLD EVENTS. LAUREN LIVES IN CONNECTICUT WITH HER FAMILY, AND CAN BE FOUND ONLINE AT LAURENTARSHIS.COM.

GEORGIA BALL

HAS WRITTEN COMICS FOR MANY OF HER FAVORITE CHILDHOOD CHARACTERS, INCLUDING STRAWBERRY SHORTCAKE, TRANSFORMERS, LITTLEST PET SHOP, MY LITTLE PONY, AND THE DISNEY PRINCESSES. IN ADDITION TO ADAPTING LAUREN TARSHIS'S I SURVIVED SERIES TO GRAPHIC NOVELS, GEORGIA WRITES ABOUT HISTORICAL EVENTS SUCH AS THE WORLD WAR II BATTLES OF KURSK AND GUADALCANAL. GEORGIA LIVES WITH HER HUSBAND, DAUGHTER, AND RAMBUNCTIOUS PETS IN NORTHERN WASHINGTON STATE. VISIT HER ONLINE AT GEORGIABALLAUTHOR.COM.

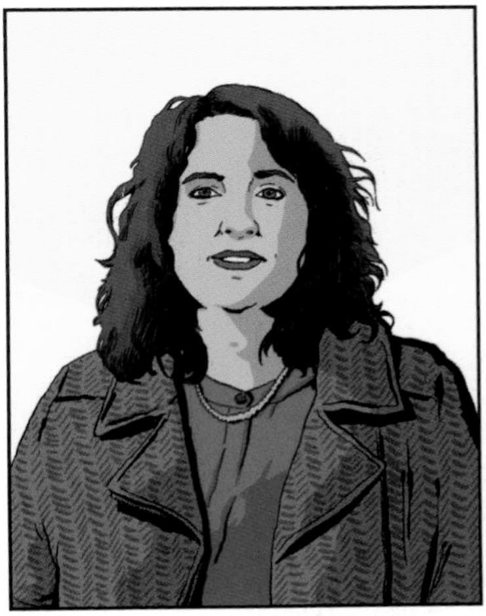

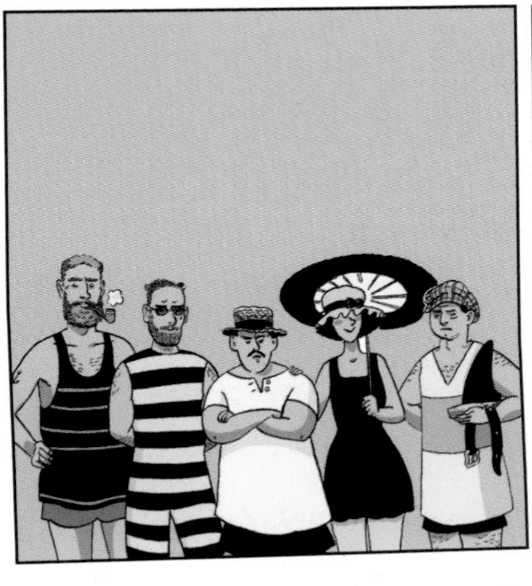

HAUS STUDIO

WAS FOUNDED IN 1997 BY A GROUP OF FRIENDS WHO SELF-PUBLISHED THEIR OWN COMICS. THEY ARE LOCATED IN BUENOS AIRES, ARGENTINA, BUT COLLABORATE WITH WRITERS AND PUBLISHERS AROUND THE WORLD. IN ADDITION TO THEIR ILLUSTRATION WORK, THE TEAM RUNS AN ART SCHOOL AND HAS ORGANIZED COMIC BOOK CONVENTIONS AND OTHER EXHIBITIONS IN LATIN AMERICA. HAUS STUDIO ARTISTS CONSIDER THEMSELVES STORYTELLERS MORE THAN ARTISTS, AND THEREFORE LOVE WORKING ON PROJECTS WITH RICH STORIES TO TELL.

DISCOVER THE SERIES THAT STARTED IT ALL!

I SURVIVED

WHEN DISASTER STRIKES, HEROES ARE MADE!

I SURVIVED
TRUE STORIES

REAL KIDS. REAL DISASTERS.